Taming a King

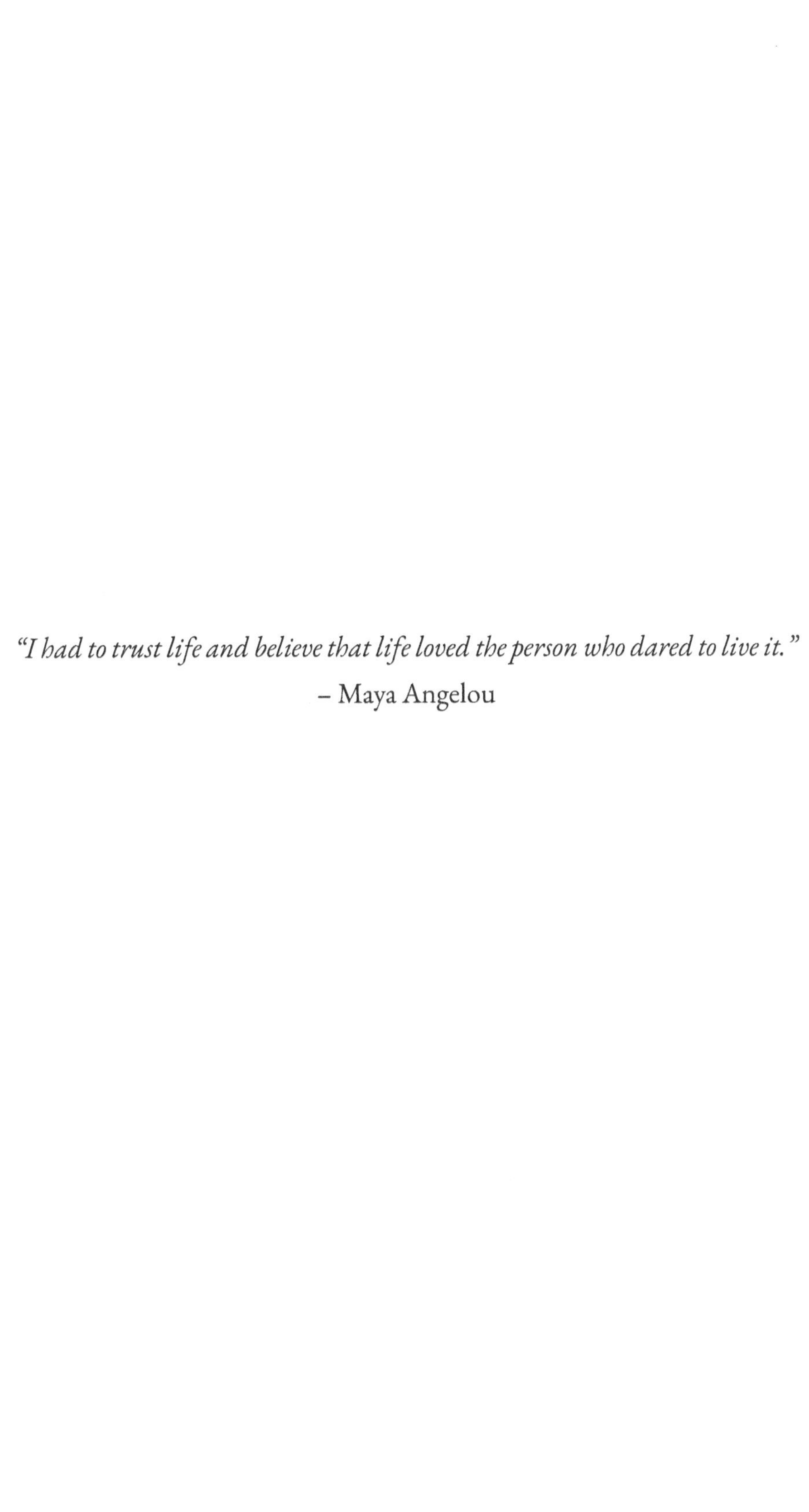

"I had to trust life and believe that life loved the person who dared to live it."

– Maya Angelou

Taming a King

A Novel

Rita A. Gordon

12:56 a.m.
California

Contents

Dedication 1

Author's Note 3

Prologue 5

1. B. S. 13

2. Basic Needs 21

3. Feels Like the First Time 31

4. Seize the Day 45

5. Meeting of the Minds 67

6. Strawberry Letter 23 73

7. Mess 79

8. Misunderstood 88

9. Over Some Wine 93

10. Reset 109

11. Space and Time 113

12. If Only 124

13. Sunshine 137

14. London 148

15. We Could Be Better 158

16. Between Brothers 173

17. Love of My Life 179

18. Only in the Moment 190

19. Falling or Flying 199

20. Moan 206

21. When I'm in Your Arms 214

22. The Business at Hand 219

23. Pretend 228

24. The Great Equalizer 237

25. Conversation 240

26. The Look of Love 245

27. Find Him 254

28. Rain 262

29. Happy Birthday 268

30. To Have and to Hold 277

31. Kiss of Life 284

32. The Reveal 290

33. Peace 296

34. Talk to Me 301

35. I Would Die For You 305

36. The Note   309

37. We Are One   314

38. Running   318

39. Love Will Lead You Back   328

40. We'll Be All Right   335

41. An Act of Congress   341

42. Loose Ends   344

43. The Final Straw   348

44. Fate   350

45. Tell Me   355

Epilogue   360

Blurb   368

Excerpts   369

Acknowledgments   377

About The Author   379

Connect With Rita   380

Also by Rita A. Gordon   381

Dedication

To the brave ones.

Author's Note

Taming a King follows the saga of Aedan King and June Ross as they navigate business, family, and romantic relationships while discovering that love is stronger than any wall we build to protect ourselves and our hearts. Those who have read *30 Days in Belfast* have received glimpses of the main character, Aedan King. This is the conclusion to his story.

Some passages in this work describe difficulties, including trauma due to the loss of a parent and sleep terrors. Additionally, some passages allude to and describe gun and other violence both on and off the page. With that in mind, I advise you to consider your health and well-being before diving into June and Aedan's story.

Prologue

Fairy Tales

"We delight in the beauty of the butterfly, but rarely admit the changes it has gone through to achieve that beauty."
– Maya Angelou

June

I STOPPED BELIEVING IN fairytales years ago. Long before my first kiss, I learned there is no such thing as a knight in shining armor. Before my first sexual encounter, I realized real princes don't exist. Years before my first heartbreak, I concluded that I'd never sit beside a king. Staring down the barrel of a gun, I learned that the only person coming to my rescue...was me.

Exhausted, I close my eyes.

The sun streams brightly through the shop windows, warming my face. I'm seduced by the soft lull of diners' voices surrounding me. Briefly, I glance at my watch and then turn to observe the patrons. Smiling faces, chopsticks in hand, conversations between bites—it all feels surreal. Though I'm in a restaurant, there is no scent hovering in the air hinting at the deliciousness awaiting me. That's how it is in Japanese restaurants—clean, calm, aesthetically pleasing, unsurprisingly good.

The warmth from the sun is suddenly gone, replaced by a shadow suspended above me. I turn, expecting familiar faces, but find the devil cloaked in a black hoodie instead. Before I can scream, a heavily tattooed hand clasps my neck and the touch of a cold steel blade converges with my cheek.

"Don't say a word," the deep raspy voice says.

I don't know if he actually says the words or whether they are a figment of my mind, forged from fear. Just as quickly as he appears, he's gone. The sound of a pop followed by the clunk of something collapsing captures my attention. I turn toward the sound; the walls are splattered with what I pray is sauce and the sound of a siren in my head overtakes me. *What's happening?* I can't stop the noise that sounds like the scream of electricity cutting through the silence when you're trying to sleep, only louder.

"No," I scream.

Mom?

***

Could've Been

"If you love somebody, let them go, for if they return, they were always yours. If they don't, they never were."
– Kahlil Gibran, A Tear and a Smile

Aedan

Golden rays of light stream through the walls of windows of my penthouse apartment, warming the polished concrete floors and illuminating the kitchen. Standing at the counter, I reflect on the past thirty days with Rose as I prepare coffee. Dating is new to me. I've rarely had anything more than a one-night stand, and on those rare occasions when I saw a woman more than twice, it was just for the sex. No feelings. No friendship. No chance of forever. Then I met Rose.

It was the first time I'd considered something more with a woman. My sister teased me that I didn't remember the names of the women I was with. I didn't. Well, that's partially true—I recalled their nicknames, like Miss Wednesday. Then Rose came to Belfast. I'll never forget her name. She left a lasting impression that still lingers like lust.

The first week of our relationship went smoother than I had expected. That turned quickly. A few weeks ago, I made a mistake in siding with a family member on something. Last night, I apologized, hoping she would forgive me. She said she did. I hope so. When I kissed her at the art exhibition, then again following my lame attempt at an apology, and later in the library that evening before I left, I was convinced what I felt was real. Rose had awakened feelings I forgot were possible. I wanted her. I wanted…more.

The sound of my house alarm pulls me out of my head and back to the moment. It signifies that Niall is about to exit the elevator and enter my foyer. My brother is the only one with full access to come and go from any of my private residences.

"Great job managing security last night. Man, that exhibition was great. Rose crushed it." I call from the kitchen before Niall enters the room.

"Yeah, even your Taoiseach agrees. Did you see his statement come through the news feed?" The voice of a woman I'm all too familiar with responds. *Rose?*

I set my coffee cup on the counter and round it just as Rose comes into view along with my brother Niall. I rush to her side, snake my arm around her, and hug her. I'm about to dip my head to brush my lips against hers, but her back stiffens. I kiss her cheek instead. Something is off. I release her, take a step back, and stare at her. My eyes shift from hers to Niall's, then back to Rose. Her expression is flat. I realize Rose is not here to be with me.

Damn it. I fucked up and I have no one to blame but myself. Even though I saw this coming, it still stings. I take a deep breath and use my tactical training to calm me. I need to keep my shit together. Schooling my expression, I pat my brother on his back and then return to the counter.

"Rose, it's great to see you. I wasn't expecting you to be with Niall, but I recall you saying you planned to see Brianna before you left this morning. I could have taken you. Can I make you a cup of coffee? Are you hungry?"

"Thanks, but no. I had breakfast earlier." Rose smiles like she does when meeting someone new for the first time. It's pleasant but unfamiliar.

I lock eyes with my brother. He's wearing a look I've seen right before he gives me bad news. "Niall, talk to me," I urge him, wanting to get whatever it is out in the open. I gesture for Rose and Niall to sit at the counter. Niall pulls out a chair for Rose. I observe every telling move they make. "It's okay, mate. Say what you came to say," I press—my heart races.

Rose nods to Niall, and I know what's coming before the words leave his lips.

"Aedan, we talked about this a few weeks ago."

"You mean this as in Rose." Niall nods.

"I can't let go of what I feel for Rose. God knows I tried. I went as far as to push her toward you at every opportunity I could. Ultimately, I was resigned to the idea that she would return to you. That was until...." Niall pauses, looks at Rose, and smiles before turning to me. He checks his expression. "That was until Rose expressed her true feelings for me. We came here to talk to you. To lay all the cards on the table, together...as a couple." I sense relief in my brother as he finishes.

I pinch my chin between my thumb and forefinger a few times, turning over his words in my head. The woman I want wants Niall. I turn away and take a deep breath. This is not what I want to hear.

I tried to make it work with Rose. To build on what we started. Now, Niall and Rose are declaring the start of their relationship. I hate that heat from anger rises within me—not directed at Rose or my brother. I only have myself to blame. He admitted his feelings for Rose on her second day in Belfast. When Niall asked me about planning our stay with Brianna that day in the kitchen, I realized my brother was taken with Rose. I'd been monitoring him hovering over Rose on her first day, but she openly rejected him. I took it as a sign...my opening. To what? Was it a competition? *No.* I was bored with my random hookup behavior. Rose was the first relationship I had tried to make work. Still, even I can't deny the connection I witnessed between them. I own my behavior. I could have tried harder...if I really wanted her. I turn around.

"I'm sorry, Rose. I was careless while also learning how to do something new. You deserve to be with someone who feels as deeply for you as my brother." I lock eyes with Niall.

Rose gets up, rounds the counter, and hugs me. I give my brother a reassuring smile as he watches. *We'll be all right.* I think to myself.

"Aedan, you're a wonderful man. I never doubted how safe I was with you. You've repeatedly proven that, but my heart beats for someone else. I can't pretend I don't feel what I do for Niall." She pauses and looks at me. "I'm heading back to the States tonight, but I promise I'll return to Belfast. I hope we can remain friends and talk more when I return." She smiles, seeking reassurance from me.

I brush the long curls from her face and tuck them behind her ear. Lowering my hands, I untangle Rose from around me and hold her at arm's length. "Come get your woman, Niall, before I steal her back." I smile tentatively down at Rose. I wish I could kiss her one last time, but I don't have a death wish.

Niall extends his hand, and Rose rounds the counter, placing her hand in his. He pulls her to his side.

"Aedan, I need to get Rose back to her hotel. She has a few things to finalize before flying out. I'll drop by later, and we can talk more." Niall stands, puts his hand on the small of Rose's back, and leads her to the elevator. I watch, devastated, as the elevator doors open; they get in and it closes.

Damn.

I exhale, releasing the tension I've held since Rose and my brother first arrived. To say I was disappointed when Rose didn't come to my house last night is an understatement. Having her show up in my brother's arms on her thirtieth day in Belfast is devastating. She made her choice, and I respect her for that. But I believe she came into my life to teach me a lesson. The right one's out there...somewhere.

San Francisco

Chapter 1

B. S.

"Every sunset is an opportunity to reset. Every sunrise begins with new eyes."
– Richie Norton

June

Nina Simone once said, "You've got to learn to leave the table when love's no longer being served." These words resonate with many people, including me. Because, even at the age of twenty-eight, newly minted as one of *Forbes* thirty under thirty female tech titans and as the newly appointed COO of Ross Enterprises, the largest technology company in the country, all is not coming up rosy for me.

It's a sunny September day in San Francisco. The sound of the blood pounding in my head blocks out the bustling street noises. I focus on the click clacking of my black stilettos while I power walk towards Steak Restaurant.

"June." My name comes in a command, not a question. This is not some random person recognizing me on the street, but the Barry White base-laden voice of Troy, my chief of security, coming from behind me, demanding my attention. It's one of my least favorite things he does. I'm not used to people asserting authority and addressing me like a misbehaving child.

I take a breath and check myself—he has no mal intent. No, Troy is reining the wild version of me in, and his tone is a subtle reminder of the importance of security protocol. He's just doing his job, and despite my instinct to resist, I need to assimilate to his way of doing things. With my history, that's going to take a lot of effort.

"June," he repeats. I slow my steps slightly, allowing Troy to take his place beside me.

Having a bodyguard after years of caring for yourself takes getting used to. Usually, I only have a security escort when I do political rallies in large public crowds, on rare occasions when I plan to party late, or when I travel to countries with severe travel advisories. But that changed the day I became COO of Ross Enterprises, the company founded by my uncle, the wealthiest man in the country, Rick Ross. And despite feeling uneasy with the constant monitoring, I understand that my new position comes with heightened security measures. After all, I'm now working for the newly appointed CEO and my cousin, Rose Ross.

Like Rose, I'm no stranger to running operations at a publicly-traded high-tech firm, but this is my first foray as an executive in a Standard and Poor's Five Hundred company. I formerly led operations for Saola Technology, an AI company founded by Alexandros Adler, a friendly competitor to Ross Enterprises. It took several weeks to convince me to join Ross Enterprises, which included intense negotiations with my former CEO. But I am officially about to begin my new role in January. And Troy, Rose's chief of security, is training me and my newly assigned personal security detail on the protocols for Ross Enterprises' top executives.

"No disrespect, Troy. I want to get this done and over with." I continue walking and stop when I reach the restaurant entrance to allow Troy to do his job. On the ride over, he ran through the protocol for handling unscheduled stops during the day. It was simple. Under all circumstances, Troy takes the lead. In the future, my lead security associate, Mack, who is a few steps behind us, will take over my security in the U.S. When I travel abroad, there are assigned teams in the countries where we have company operations centers.

"One minute," Troys says while I take in the view.

The restaurant is on the ground level of a concrete and steel office building in downtown San Francisco. The black sign with prominent white lettering spelling the restaurant name "Steak" punctuates our arrival. Several people sit on the outside patio, enjoying the warm weather. The tinted exterior windows obscure my view from the street of restaurant patrons seated in the window. Pop music coming through the outdoor speakers emphasizes the vibe. A member of the restaurant staff opens the door as we approach. Troy steps ahead, conducts a visual sweep, and holds the door open for me to enter. Mack stays outside, stationed in front of the building.

Not your typical jeans-and-corporate logo hoody-wearing tech executive, my outfit stands out from the crowd. Taking a page from my mom, I consider myself an impeccably dressed hipster flaunting my brand of style. I'm wearing a black pencil skirt with thin mustard yellow silk tuxedo stripes down the sides, complementing the black short-sleeved T-shirt with the yellow Erykah Badu Live butterfly album cover under my black blazer.

When I enter the restaurant, Troy stands beside me with his six-foot-five imposing figure. The large restaurant is buzzing with people chit-chatting but is not overly crowded. As a frequent patron and one who is particular about where I sit, I know the restaurant well. A member of the wait staff immediately comes to assist me.

"Miss Ross. It's lovely to see you again. We weren't expecting to see you until Thursday. Let me get you seated."

"That won't be necessary. I'm here to meet one of your guests. Thanks." I turn to Troy. He nods and steps closer to me. I turn and walk through the maze of tables. I scan the room before my eyes land on a table near the back of the restaurant where an attractive couple is sitting. My target. The handsome mocha-colored gentleman flashing a flirty smile at his guest could double for a younger version of Philip Michael Thomas—the woman sitting directly across the table from him is a petite version of a black Barbie. When I reach the table, in one fluid motion, Troy grabs a chair from a nearby table and positions it for me to sit on. I sense all eyes are on me and Troy as I take off my blazer, hand it to Troy, then sit down. Not one to sit with my back to other patrons, having him behind me provides relief.

"June?" The man's eyes open wide with surprise. Of course, he's not expecting to see me. He quickly schools his expression, which is soon replaced with defiance.

"Leon," I say calmly.

Underneath the table, I rest one hand over the other and pull at the 'L' on the gold love ring on my right hand. A habit I developed when I was feeling anxious. The tap of a glass being put on the table catches my attention, and I turn toward the noise. It's Leon's lunch guest.

"What's your name?" I ask the woman.

"Mari."

"Hi Mari, I'm June Ross. I have somewhere to be, so this will only take a minute," I assure her, then turn back to Leon.

Mari's eyes widen like saucers. "June Ross of Ross Enterprises. Oh my god," she squeals. "I'm such an admirer of yours. I saw you on Tech Talk Today. The way you shut down that CEO trying to say why women don't make good CEOs was priceless. It's a pleasure to watch you work." Mari turns to Leon. "Babe, you didn't tell me you knew Ms. Ross. She and her cousin Rose are badass tech titans."

The slight tick in Leon's jaw when Mari says "babe" is more than telling. *Busted*.

"Like I said, Mari. Give me a minute. You can watch me work. Afterward, you can do what you want with the information you learn today." I address Mari, but I continue to lock eyes with Leon.

I look over my shoulder and nod to Troy. He reaches into his suit pocket, takes out his phone, and taps the screen, deactivating Leon's tracker. The loud thud of the hammered pattern platinum bracelet on Leon's wrist hitting the table makes Mari gasp and Leon wince. I lock eyes with Leon, reach across the table, pick up the bracelet, and then hand it over my shoulder to Troy without breaking my stare.

"I wasn't joking when I told you every aspect of my life is under a constant microscope, Leon. And up until one second ago, that included you. *Babe*," I say, mimicking Mari. "I believe I'm using the correct nickname. After today, please don't attempt to contact me. We're done." I pause. Then, I curve my lips into a half-smirk. "Unless you think you can get through my man of steel." I flick my thumb over my shoulder toward Troy.

Leon narrows his eyes. It's a look I've seen him use when he's not happy with someone on the other end of a business call. It's a look he has never used on me until now. He's an influential businessman who enjoys running his company and never seemed intimidated by my success. He also didn't seem the type to have a string of women at his beck and call, so I took a chance dating him. Now, watching Leon, the look of irritation from being caught tells me everything I need to know. I was wrong.

Fortunately for me, unfortunately for him, Troy tracks my every move and those closest to me. So, when Troy said he wanted to discuss Leon before I left the office to head to my offsite meeting, I knew something was amiss. Troy proceeded to detail the two rendezvous Leon had with Mari. They hadn't stayed overnight with each other, but they were trending in that direction. If I had anything to do with it, that wouldn't happen.

"Take me to him." The words left my lips before I realized it. "Is he close?" I inquired, remembering I had thirty minutes before my next meeting.

"Five minutes out, on First Street."

I did the quick math in my head. I had time. And I wasn't about to let this situation continue any longer than necessary. I had Troy take me directly to Leon so that I could deal with him face-to-face. As head of operations, I'm not the type to let an issue linger when I have a solution. I execute it. This leads me to my current situation as I sit across the table from Leon, telling him it's over.

"Troy. Let's go." My voice is unfazed, as if talking about the weather.

Before Leon can pull himself together to speak, I stand, turn my back to him, and walk toward the exit with Troy in tow. I hear a slight "humph" come from behind me, which signals that someone at the table understands the message printed in bright yellow lettering against my black T-shirt which reads, "You need to call Tyrone." I had no idea how apropos the phrase would be when I left the house this morning. I was trying to coordinate with an impulse-buy skirt and had no intention of taking my jacket off until Troy debriefed me on what he found out about Leon.

In the background, I hear Mari exclaim, "What the ever-loving fuck? Boy, bye," followed by the scraping of a chair and clicking of heels behind us.

I slide into the back seat of the SUV. Troy is in the front passenger seat. He positions the mirror so he can see me.

"Damn. That two-timing jerk. I should have known it. I should have slapped that stupid smug smile off Leon's face when I first met him. But no," I say, extending the o in no. "I had to date the idiot. What a colossal waste of my time." I take out my phone and scroll through it. "Is this it, Troy?" I turn my screen toward the rear-view mirror and Troy's gaze. "It says there were two prior meetups in total. Am I missing something?"

"That's it. This was the third, and one more was on the books," Troy says.

"That stupid jerk seriously thought he'd get to sleep with someone behind my back. Well, I guess the tables turned. It sounded like Mari isn't taking that b.s., either. Next time, Troy, don't wait until someone I'm dating kisses someone else to alert me. I trust you. I want to know at first meet cute. Skip that. I'm officially done with relationships. I have my hands full with my new job."

"Don't let one jerk spoil it for you."

"That's one too many. I'm done. How close are we cutting it to my next meeting?"

"We have time."

Belfast

Chapter 2

Basic Needs

"Some people feel the rain. Others just get wet."
– Bob Marley

Aedan

"Mr. King. Your next meeting is in five minutes. You have an hour between your last meeting and your dinner reservations. Carl is on standby with the car. Should you need it tonight, I've also secured the Penthouse at the Fitzwilliam," Lorn, my executive assistant, instructs. He is as efficient as they come.

"Thanks, Lorn." I stand, retrieve my suit jacket from the coat rack, and put it on.

It's been a while since my last date, if a date is what you call drinks and dinner with a woman who ends up on her knees at the end of the night. Rose breaking it off with me to be with Niall was a turning point in my life. Whereas I used to have an equal mix of work hard and play hard, I now pour myself deeper into the work portion of that equation. Did I attempt to return to my ways of one-night stands to satisfy my basic needs? Briefly, but that only lasted so long. I haven't had one since my last disaster of a date.

I remember her clearly. I met her at a bar. I was initially drawn to the green dress she was wearing. It reminded me of the one Rose wore on our first date in Dublin and how it complimented her honey-colored skin. *Rose.* That night with Rose changed me forever.

I was standing in the lobby, leaning against a wall with my hand in my pocket, awaiting her arrival. All eyes were on Rose—including mine—as she stepped out of the elevator and glided across the room in a green ombre silk slip dress. The beautiful, bronze-colored woman was impossible to miss amongst the sea of homogenous guests.

Rose walked directly up to me with her hand open in a low-five position to her side, not wanting to draw more attention than she already had. I interlocked my fingers with hers, then kissed her cheek.

"Rose, you look spectacular. Touring suits you."

"A bit of an improvement from my jeans. You think?"

I cleared my throat. "That's an understatement. Look around—everyone stopped what they're doing to stare."

"Is the dress too much?" she asked.

I leaned in, inhaling her essence, and whispered in her ear. "It's not the dress that has their attention. It's the beautiful woman working the dress."

She was adorable when she looked down to hide her blushing.

No. Ms. Green Dress was nothing like Rose. Yet, after a few drinks and flirty exchanges, I took Ms. Green Dress to my hotel room. I never take one-night stands to my house. That's not the vibe I bring into my personal space—I don't want clingy women wanting more than I have to offer. I'm always up front in setting expectations. Ms. Green Dress was there to satisfy my basic needs. One night. Just sex. That's it—then we're done.

That night was a turning point for me. Shortly after reaching the room, the woman I was with was all too eager to please me. After weeks of going without sex, I was going to take what I wanted.

"On your knees," I told her. She quickly obliged. When I think back, something in her eyes left me feeling cold as I watched her carefully unzip my slacks and free my shaft. Although my brain told me to push her away and leave, my body betrayed me. The warmth of her hands locked onto my length and her lush lips opened to take me in. A wave of guilt washed over me, along with my release. Later, I would reciprocate using my hands only, but I didn't want anything more. We never entirely took our clothes off. I never kissed her. When I was done, I washed my hands and left.

The experience left me confused and frustrated. I hated to admit that my sister was right when she teased me relentlessly about being with women whose names I couldn't remember. I couldn't remember Ms. Green Dress's name. All I could recall was that it sounded like Karen, Kayla, or Kristen. Something with a K sound that didn't keep me interested. That was over a month ago. Now, I'm on my way home to prepare for another attempt at sex with someone I don't feel anything for. Fingers crossed.

The walk home doesn't take long. Belfast is a small city, and I own quite a bit of real estate between our office buildings and residential loft buildings.

The sound of the alarm slices through the silence, followed by my brother calling my name. I run my hand through my inky black hair, glance in the mirror one last time, and walk into the living room. I only came home to drop off my equipment. There is no need for a smart tablet on a date, but I check my firearm and slide it into my side holster. It's Friday night. I'm off duty, ready to chill, and if the date goes well, I might get some much-needed relief that doesn't involve soap, shower, and my hand.

"Niall. Don't you have somewhere to be?"

"Not at the moment."

"It's Friday night, man. What's happening? When are you seeing your lady again?"

"Don't worry. I'll see Rose soon enough. I came by because I'm worried about you. You've been hitting work hard. Delegate. Ben's doing a great job stepping into the new role we gave him. Why don't you offload additional assignments onto him?"

"I like getting my hands dirty occasionally. You know, the thrill of being in the field."

"Aedan, you're the chairman of the board, for Christ's sake. Get out of the field. We have plenty of work to do to ensure our shareholders are happy that won't put your life at risk."

My brother has a point. As the CEO of King Enterprise, a multibillion-dollar security and logistics conglomerate we run together, I have several team members worldwide who could do the work. We provide protection services for some of the most prestigious individuals in Europe.

"You know I'm not one to sit behind a desk," I counter.

"Then focus on the most high-profile assignments. I have something brewing in London if you want to take over. It's low-risk but a high priority. I planned to spend time with our new team there to bring them up to speed on one of our new clients, June Ross. She's Rose's cousin, and replaced her as COO. I'll send you the file."

"I got it."

"She'll take over the operation in Belfast soon. You'll get to meet her then." Niall walks over and puts his hand on my shoulder. "Consider it. That way, I can book more time with *my* lady."

"The only reason I'll agree is so that you get time with Rose. I know how important she is to you. And to our family, for that matter," I tell him, because she is. Rose stepped in on behalf of my sister to curate a flawless art exhibition for our foundation and returned in the fall to train Brianna's students. She's been a godsend in more ways than one.

"Thanks, man."

"Now that that's out of the way, you'll be happy to know I'm headed out for the night."

"Come on. You can do better than She's So Good For One Night," Niall says, his voice dripping with sarcasm. "I thought you were on the path to settling down."

"I'm not there yet."

"Man, I know the thing with Rose didn't go down the way you wanted, but the right one is out there for you."

"It's not like that, Niall. I'm good." My phone buzzes on the counter. I pick it up, but not before my brother catches a glimpse of the screen.

Ms. Fredag: Looking forward to tonight.

"You're shitting me, Aedan. Miss Friday? I understand we all have our basic needs, but seriously. After what happened this past summer, I thought you were over this." Niall closes his eyes and shakes his head.

I reply to the text.

Me: See you soon.

"Don't worry about it. I need to head out." I hold Niall's gaze. "I heard what you said. We can grab lunch tomorrow." I grab my jacket off the chair, put it on, and signal for the elevator. When it arrives, I step in and hold the door open. "Stella prepared dinner. It's in the fridge if you're hungry. Although I'm sure you have something completely different waiting for you at your place. I'll catch you later." Stella, our chef, alternates between my and Niall's house. Although we're both vegetarians, she usually makes us different meals for occasions like this when one of us pops by the other's house.

"I gave her the day off. I'm about to raid your fridge. Enjoy your date." Niall salutes me, and then the elevator door shuts.

***

Walking into the crowded restaurant takes a second, but I spot my date sitting at the bar, conversing with a gentleman beside her. Had this been Rose when we were dating, I'd feel a certain way about this scenario, but it's not Rose, so I don't. Her back is toward the entrance, so she doesn't notice me as I approach. Her auburn hair flows over her bare back and pops against her skin, compliments of her turquoise halter top. I walk up behind her.

"Leslie." I touch the small of her back, and she slowly swings her chair around to face me. "Apologies for being late."

Leslie, also known as Ms. Fredag, owns The Beauty Bag, a women's salon and spa next door to the tie shop I frequent. I'm not sure whether Leslie orchestrated the meeting, but she conveniently came out of the salon to head to a nearby coffee shop as I passed the door to her salon. Her looks caught my attention, but the connection I hoped to feel when she extended her hand and shook mine was nonexistent. Still, I reached out, and she took my offer. That was a few weeks ago, and I recently made plans to make it an ongoing Friday event.

"It's fine. I was just having a drink."

"Our table is ready." My voice is firm and curt. I offer my hand to Leslie as she slides off the bar stool. I'm not here to make friends. I plan to eat, drink, and return to her place to relieve some of the tension from the week.

Leslie turns toward the gentleman she was conversing with at the bar. "Nice to meet you. Have a good evening." He nods and she stands next to me.

"Did I interrupt something?" My voice is noticeably clipped. I don't mask my annoyance. Niall may have been right about me harboring something, but it's not a feeling for Rose I'm harboring; it's the thought of knowing the woman I was with wanted someone else. And Leslie is giving those vibes.

Leslie flips her hair. "He was just asking about—"

"I'm sure he'll figure whatever it is out," I interject. "I'll order you another one of whatever you were drinking."

I escort Leslie to the table, help her to her chair, and sit on the opposite side.

"It was a French seventy-five. Thank you."

The waiter comes over and I order drinks. Even though Leslie is not a vegetarian, I order a starter of roasted Brussels sprouts because they're a hit with everyone.

"How was work?" Leslie asks.

Staring at her, I press my lips together. Leslie doesn't know it, but there isn't much we can discuss regarding my work because I sign non-disclosure agreements with my clients.

"As you can imagine, Leslie, my day is full. How was your day?" I deflect.

I half-listen as she talks about her day running The Beauty Bag, a topic that doesn't hold my interest. Not that there is anything wrong with facial care and makeup. I prefer women with natural beauty like Rose who don't have to create an illusion. Rose is a stunning woman with honey-colored skin, naturally luscious full lips, and long curly hair. She's the last woman I found who could hold a stimulating conversation besides my sister, Brianna. I enjoy how Rose seamlessly slips in and out of a discussion about various topics. She's well-traveled, cultured, educated, and speaks multiple languages like my brother and I. One minute, we'd be discussing literature and art—the next moment, we were comparing stories about international travel or martial arts techniques. I miss our engaging conversations, and although we're no longer together, I ensure my calendar is open to her when she comes to Belfast for work and visits Niall.

The first few months following my breakup with Rose were difficult, and I had to take a different approach to navigating our relationship. She was no longer my Rose. She's now Rose Ross, the newly appointed CEO of Ross Enterprises and my brother's woman. I took my shot, but it misfired. But I'm not bitter; Rose and Niall were destined for each other. This is why I'm sitting across the table from Leslie, who has no clue I haven't heard a word she's said.

"But if we.... Don't you think, Aedan?" The sound of my name slices my still-fresh wounds, bringing me back to the table.

Improvising, I say, "I'm not sure I understand the question."

"I was asking if you thought we might get more rain. We have time to eat and make it to the Fitzwilliam before the storm starts."

I can't do this. There is no way I can sit through idle chit-chat with this woman and then get in the mood to have sex with her. It doesn't matter how long it's been since I was with a woman. I'm not feeling her. *This was a bad idea.*

My phone buzzes. I flip it over, slide my finger across the screen, and put it to my ear.

"Listen, Leslie. I need to take this. Do you mind? I'll just be a minute." I stand.

"That's fine," Leslie says. I head toward the hallway to the restrooms to take the call in private.

"Perfect timing, man," I tell Niall, who's laughing on the other end of the phone.

"You didn't have to pick up," Niall says. "Although I purposely called instead of texting just in case you needed a lifeline."

"Thanks for the save, man. I owe you." I release a breath.

"Then my spidey senses were correct. Make your exit and I see you soon," Niall urges me.

"So, you didn't actually need anything."

"Nah, man. I'm just here eating your food and drinking your wine."

"See you in a bit. Save me some." I end the call.

The heartiness of Niall's laughter before the call ends relieves some of my angst. For now, I have a reprieve from repeating my experience with Green Dress Woman. I need to get my shit together. Being with a woman with whom I had no connection feels suddenly foreign. I want something more.

I *need* more.

San Francisco

CHAPTER 3

Feels Like the First Time

"The direction you choose to face determines whether you're standing at the end or the beginning of a road."
– Richelle E. Goodrich

June

"PEACE," I MOUTH TO my best friend Nicole while holding up two fingers, signifying the same. I wave goodbye and step into the back of the black luxury SUV. Before heading to the airport, I stopped by Nicole's house to borrow one of her swanky Italian designer umbrellas. Multitasking is my typical modus operandi as I simultaneously listen to my dad over the phone.

"Dad, you have a wife who can handle that stuff. I don't understand why you need me to schmooze it up with your friends. Honestly, I don't know half the people on your guest list," I say, talking into my multicolored wired earphones.

Since Troy became my chief of security, he has urged me not to use commercially bought wireless earphones because they can be hacked. He says he has an alternative solution, but I'm set on doing this my way. This five-dollar pair works great and can easily be replaced if I lose them. It's also obvious to others through my big hair that I'm wearing them. Years ago,

I learned to put them in while running errands. People were less likely to ask questions if they didn't think you could hear them, although I never listened to music while wearing them in public.

"Princess, I'd like you to celebrate with us."

"Ugh. I'm a grown woman, Dad. Call me June."

"You'll always be my princess."

"Jasmine is the youngest. I'm officially passing the princess baton to her."

"Princess," he warns. I get it. I want to say something flippant, but I don't. It's not the point. But that's my dad, always focused, staying on point—moving on. It's the "moving on" part that bothers me the most.

"You know I'm traveling out of the country for my new job. It's a big role, and I want to start on the right foot. You sure you need me there?"

"This is a milestone birthday for me. I love you and want you there to celebrate with me. If you're concerned about work, I'll call Rick to ensure it's not an issue. Besides, he'll be here too, with your aunt."

"No, oh my god, no, Dad. Don't call him," I plead. The last thing I want is for my dad to call his brother, Rick, who happens to be my chairman of the board. "Dad, you can't intercede like that on my behalf. This is my job we're talking about, not grade school." I pull at the L on the love ring on my right hand.

"He has to listen to me. I'm the oldest."

"Wow, by one year. Dad, you're pushing this."

"Listen, princess, having you there is important to me. Jeannette would also love to have you there. It's a milestone for her, too, you know. She mentioned sending you a note."

"I responded, letting her know that I was traveling."

"Which is the reason for my call. I know she's not your mom, but—"

He's right, Jeannette is not my mom—never will be. Can't he see he may have moved on, but I haven't?

"No one can replace Mom. You seem to keep forgetting that."

I close my eyes briefly. My mom could do it all, from taking her children to the beach to taking a stand on the front lines of a protest. She was that kind of woman: beautiful, strong, caring, yet defiant. I open my eyes.

"I haven't forgotten, baby. I was going to say Jeannette really cares for you."

"Dad. I have to go. I'm on my way to the airport. I'll let you know if I can make the schedule work. I love you." If my uncle Rick, the person who founded the company I work for, was going to attend, I had to be there, too.

"I love you too, princess. I'll see you at the party." I feel the finality in his statement before he ends the call.

I sigh and then turn my attention to Troy, seated in his usual spot in the front passenger side of the vehicle.

"Troy." I catch his gaze in the rearview mirror.

"I can't help you with your dad," he says.

I shake my head. People are afraid of my six-foot-five man-of-steel, and rightfully so, but not me. He has a subtle sense of humor, which he only reveals to certain people. It seems I'm one of the chosen few.

"Funny. But that's not what I wanted to talk to you about."

"How can I help you?"

"I don't get it. We've been farming out all this security work to King Enterprise. Why haven't I seen a request for a proposal for your company?"

King Enterprise was founded by Aedan King in Belfast and consisted of multiple subsidiaries, many of which were run by his younger brother, Niall King. I'm heading to Belfast to execute the agreement with King Enterprise to provide physical security for Ross Enterprises' executive team's newly formed European operations. After getting familiar with Troy and his work over the years for Ross Enterprises, I expected his company to be a contender for the contract.

"Not my endgame." In typical fashion, Troy's response is brief.

I like it when people get straight to the point, but I need more information from Troy. He has proven himself an asset to my uncle numerous times. Rose and I work for the country's most powerful man, and having Troy as head of security has ensured he is in a situation to build a level of generational wealth that most would die for.

"I'm just looking out for you," I confess.

"Understood."

"It will take more than a one-word answer to pull me off this topic, Troy," I press.

"You can get the full story from your uncle Rick or Rose if you want to know more. But long story short, my company has been capturing market share in advanced technological devices used by security companies. Look at your wrist." He pauses, allowing me time to see what he's talking about. I look down and twist the platinum bangle on my wrist, similar to the one he took from Leon a few months ago. My eyes shift back to the rear-view mirror and Troy's eyes, willing him to continue. "You're wearing my product. I'm building my company around innovative technological devices that interplay with physical security and logistics components."

"Why am I not surprised? You're a man of few words and remarkable strength, but now I see a strategic businessman behind the mask. I suppose if I want to know something about you, I should stop wondering and ask," I say, surprised that he disclosed as much as he did about himself.

"You don't need to worry about me."

"For the record, I despise these things." I twist the bracelet on my wrist.

"Get used to it."

I blow out a breath and roll my eyes. "You sent a brief for me to review during our flight. Care to give me the cliff notes version before we board?"

"You sound just like your cousin."

"It's in our genes. Rose and I think alike. It's precisely why she wanted me to backfill her in operations. So, what should I expect across the pond?"

Traffic is unusually light, so it doesn't take long for us to reach the airport. Our vehicle undergoes security checks before entering the tarmac area near the terminal building. Troy exits the vehicle and then opens my door. I exit the car and stand a few inches from Troy, holding his hand to steady myself. Even in four-inch heels adding to my five-foot-five frame, I have to step back to look at Troy. I've learned firsthand why my cousin always joked about Troy being her six-foot-five man-of-steel. He is a fine, fierce dark chocolate man covered in muscles neatly packaged in a black suit and white shirt. Like my cousin, who opposed having a security detail, I'm learning how to navigate having Troy around and doing my best to get used to protocol. But, unlike my cousin, I have no experience in self-defense. Rose is trained in several martial arts techniques. However, I know from a traumatic experience I had at the age of eight that if something is going to happen, there is nothing I can do to stop it. Life is short. I spend mine living carefree. Even so, I value Troy and the work he and his team perform.

"We have over ten hours to cover the file. I'll brief you on the plane." He gestures, guiding me to walk toward the metal airplane stairs. I look up at the private jet illuminated against the dark sky to see the staff waiting at the top for me to board.

As soon as I enter the plane, I settle in one of the leather chairs with a table and retrieve my laptop from my bag. Troy is in the front, giving instructions to the staff. When he's done, he sits opposite me.

"Once we reach cruising altitude, I can walk you through the brief. I suggest you pull up the files for a point of reference," he instructs. My phone buzzes. I unlock the screen and take the call.

"Hi, Rose. I didn't expect a call from you this late," I say, leaning back in my seat.

"It's your first official trip since joining. I've said it before, but welcome to Ross Enterprises. I'm so happy to have you on the team and diving in head first on our expansion efforts."

The opportunity to work for Rose is exciting. Although I have a biological sister, Rose and I have grown so close that I consider her a sister. We became almost inseparable while growing up together.

"Thank you for the opportunity."

"Are you kidding me? You were born to do this. Adding you to the c-suite is the last piece of the puzzle to help propel the company even further than my dad expected."

"The time you spent transitioning with me has given me a great start. Is there anything else I should know before I fly out?"

"I hired you for your expertise. You got it from here."

"Thanks."

"Listen, I wanted to connect with you on two things before I head on stage."

"That's right, madam CEO, you're in hot demand now."

"Yeah, right." Rose chuckles.

"What do I need to know?"

"Someone at the RTÉ reached out and wants to conduct an interview to discuss our expansion in the region. Since you're in the area, I've asked the PR team to divert that interview to you. They'll give you the talk track and help you with any pointers."

"Nothing I can't handle."

"I know this is your sweet spot. God, I'm so glad I hired you." My cousin sighs and I sense her genuine relief.

"You said you had two things. What's the other?"

"Right. I know you'll partner with Aedan on the expansion. Don't let him—" Rose is interrupted. I wait with bated breath for her to continue. "Listen, June. They need me on stage. I have to go. Kick butt in Belfast. Talk soon," she says and ends the call.

Aedan? What did Rose want to tell me about Aedan that she hadn't already shared? Although I'm intimately familiar with the contract between King Enterprise and Ross Enterprises, I'll re-read the brief to see if I catch anything odd.

I run through scenarios in my head. Maybe this is about their relationship. She briefly dated Aedan during her first trip to Belfast. Ultimately, Rose ended up falling in love with his brother, Niall. Per Rose, Aedan is the typical handsome bad boy billionaire, not the type of guy to settle with one woman, and certainly not husband material. At least, that was the situation when he and Rose first met. She said she was the first woman with whom he had something that resembled a real relationship. Perhaps Rose wanted to warn me about getting distracted by Aedan. If that's the case, she doesn't have to worry—Leon ensured that won't happen. Aedan, in all his billionaire book boyfriend beauty, as she describes him, is off-limits.

Attempting to put it out of my mind, I distract myself by scrolling through the documents Troy sent me. When the cabin attendant approaches, I look up.

"We're all set for take-off, Ms. Ross. Our flight time today is ten hours and twenty-five minutes. We expect a temperature of sixty-two degrees upon arrival. I have the meal plan you requested. Would you like anything now? Perhaps your tea?"

"I'll just have water for now. Thank you."

"And anything for you, Mr. Troy?"

"I'm good. Thanks," he responds.

It's not long before the plane reaches cruising altitude. I recline in my seat with my hands stretched toward the laptop. Troy typically sends one file folder per trip with several folders contained within. Unlike Rose, who didn't want to know all the security-related details, I prefer to be apprised of everything. I want to know what requires immediate attention and the plan to handle any obstacles. I went into operations because of my deep-felt need to control my surroundings. I developed the need to control everything in my life once I turned nine.

"Are we good to go, Troy? I've previously read through the contracts for Belfast and London."

"Good," Troy confirms. "I'd like you to focus on the additional background on the people we're doing business with since you'll be spending quite a bit of time with them in the various countries."

"Is there something I should be concerned about?"

"No. But I know you like to know everyone's eccentricities."

"Eccentricities?"

"Just like you, others have them, too."

"I don't have..." Troy raises an eyebrow, giving me pause. "What?"

"Are you saying you don't have quirks?"

"Not one."

"Will you wear the earpiece I gave you?"

A sardonic laugh escapes, but I quickly rein it in. Troy doesn't find this funny, and rightfully so—he's here to protect me. "No. Troy, too much is going on in my head to listen to other people's secret conversations in my ear."

"Will you use a security handle?"

"No. But that won't stop me from responding should I be called by one."

"Will you allow security to drive your Aston Martin DBS?"

"Absolutely not. I conceded to let them drive me in the company car." What did he think I'd do? You can't drive and be cool with security at the wheel.

"On that note. I suggest you review the file. I'll notify the team that your preference is for them to contact you via text rather than phone. You'll have one main point of contact. Once I fully transition the team, you can work with them directly. Until then, I'm your point person."

"Is there a number I should program for the team?"

"You'll receive a message from the King Enterprise security team as soon as we hit the tarmac in Ireland."

"Got it."

As I review the files, I notice three files in the security folder—one for Belfast, Ireland, one for London, England, and one for the United States. I click on the one for the U.S. After extensive research, Seattle is the new city we chose to open operations in. I need to meet with the attorneys and developers there in a few months to plan a Seattle build-out. I pull up my calendar and notice that the appointment has been pushed out to accommodate the travel schedule of the two parties who will also be in attendance. One of whom is my good friend and colleague, Raven. I make a mental note to call Raven a few days before my arrival. I scroll through to the final file. It's labeled Saola, which is my former company. I'm familiar with most of the information, but a former colleague at Saola Technology in London is highlighted. I recognize the name.

"What's up with this guy, James, at Saola? You flagged this one for us to discuss."

"How well do you know James?"

"As well as I know any employee. He's a good performer, not stellar, but I remember he was ambitious. He needed to learn patience. Why did you flag him?" James wasn't someone I'd given a second thought to before or since leaving my job. Typically, I interacted with Alexandros and Aaron, the brothers whom I worked more closely with during my tenure. The younger brother, Andrew, did most of the hiring. I spent most of my time with Aaron.

"Digital records show he's been researching you since your move to Ross Enterprises. He reviewed your online business profile and searched articles about you."

"That's strange. Is he stalking me?"

"It's unclear. James viewed a few pieces about you online, like the recent press release announcing your move to Ross Enterprises."

"People do that all the time. Headhunters are notorious for that. Maybe he has a crush. Or maybe he's looking to make a move to a new company. He might be pumping himself up to ask me for a job. I doubt it's anything to worry about." I frown, unsure of the real reason Troy flagged James.

"I'll be monitoring him."

I click through a few more files, turn the computer toward Troy, point to the screen, and say, "Why is this file labeled *Queen of the Night*?"

"Queen of the Night is your security designation. Queen for short. The people listed there are the security team, along with their handles. They are assigned to you and your exec team in various countries."

I roll my eyes and am unable to stifle the laugh that barks from me. "Come on, Troy. You have to admit, it's a bit much. Queen of the Night? What the hell? Who came up with this handle?"

"A member of the team."

"Right. I'm not answering to that name. They can call me Ms. Ross." I shake my head and continue reading through the files.

"It's the name they'll use when they need to be discreet. Otherwise, they'll use your given name," he clarifies.

It doesn't take me long to digest the information. Most of the items I had previously reviewed during my company orientation. It's rare for me to forget anything, but I have learned that trauma makes you suppress memories, like some things I can't recall from when I was eight. But there were more pressing things on my mind that I wanted more details about.

"Troy," I say, waiting for him to look at me before I continue. He turns and locks eyes with me. "I know you didn't end your research on Leon after

I confronted him last year. Tell me. What else did you dig up on him?" I want to know but don't want to know.

"There's nothing for you to concern yourself with. It's over."

I bunch my eyebrows. "I don't understand. It was over when I shut it down. But your curt response leads me to believe there's more." After only a few dates, I was surprised that Mari felt comfortable calling Leon her babe. There has to be more to the story.

"Thought all my responses were curt," he says flatly.

"True, but—"

"There's nothing more. Leon hasn't been with Mari since the day you saw him at the restaurant. She ended whatever they had that day. He hasn't contacted her or made any attempts to reach you. Leon's going about his life like nothing happened."

There it is. Same as always…moving on like nothing mattered. The story of my life.

"You mean he's being cautious because he knows he's still being tracked."

"As well he should be. I'll monitor him until I'm satisfied."

The corners of my lips instinctively curl into a slight grin at his declaration. "I knew I liked you," I confess. Staring at Troy, I detect what appears to be a smug look of satisfaction, which briefly crosses his face.

The rest of the flight is uneventful. Troy and I either work or sleep during the remainder of the flight. Before long, the plane buzzes with activity again as we near our destination.

"Would you like anything else before we land, Ms. Ross?" the attendant asks.

"No, I'm good," I confirm. The attendant returns to their station and secures everything for landing.

Closing my eyes, I take a deep breath to settle the nerves I feel at the newness of all this—my role, the country, all of it. I wonder if this was how Rose felt on her first trip to Belfast. The pressure that comes along with helping her run one of the largest companies in the world is huge. I blow out a breath. *I can do this.*

I reflect on the circumstances that brought me to this point. Never would my eight-year-old self, paralyzed by trauma, have envisioned my current life: to be a black woman who's COO of one of the most renowned companies in the world. I'm following in the footsteps of my brilliant cousin, knowing that from this point forward, my life will never be the same. Knowing that nothing ever feels quite like the first time.

Belfast

Chapter 4

Seize the Day

"The purpose of life is to live it, to taste experience to the utmost, to reach out eagerly and without fear for newer and richer experience."
– Eleanor Roosevelt

June

Nine hours later, my phone buzzes. As Troy predicted, my new security team contacts me when the plane hits the tarmac. I stare at the text from the unknown number.

Unknown: Ms. Ross, this is your King Enterprise security point of contact. Please lock this number in your phone accordingly.

I save the number to my contacts as "My Man" since Troy is adamant about using security handles instead of real names. I chose something to remind me that I've sworn off men even though I didn't know whether my contact was a man or woman. For now, the unknown person on the other end of the text will be my man. I text back.

Me: Done.

My Man: Great. I'm here for you 24x7.

Troy unfastens his seatbelt as he talks to someone through his earphones. I observe in silence as he peers out the window and then goes to the front of the plane. When it is time to exit, he nods.

"Ready?" he asks.

I unbuckle my seat belt, grab my belongings, and head toward the front of the plane. A crew member takes my things.

"I'll bring these down for you," the crew member says.

"Ready," I tell Troy.

Troy walks ahead of me as I carefully descend the metal stairs.

Two black cars are waiting on the tarmac. Troy escorts me to the last car, where a tall, handsome man with a black suit, white shirt, and black tie awaits near the open door. I head toward him, nod, and smile.

"Hi, Miss Ross. I'm Ben," the clean-shaven, chiseled-faced gentleman with a flat expression tells me. I recall seeing his picture in the security brief Troy sent, but the picture didn't do him justice. *Are all the King staff this good-looking?* No wonder Rose always talked about being distracted when she was in Ireland.

"Nice to finally meet you, Ben," I acknowledge him.

Ben. His name is also familiar to me because he's part of the security team that saved Rose's life during her trip to curate the exhibition. Unbeknownst to Rose, some unsavory characters were plotting to kidnap her. The report indicated that Ben kept an entire vehicle full of nefarious characters from exiting to carry out their activity. He also acted as her proxy to secure precious art worldwide for her exhibition. Subsequently, Ross Enterprises signed King Enterprise to provide security for our European operations, and they are the only teams allowed to provide protection services to the Ross family besides Troy.

"You and Troy will ride in this vehicle." Ben gestures toward the vehicle. "I'll ride ahead of you. You should have received a message on your phone upon arrival. If you need anything twenty-four hours a day, use that number."

"I received it. Thanks, Ben." I slide into the back seat and Troy sits in front. Ben goes to the lead car and gets in.

Belfast, like most coastal cities in Ireland, is small yet beautiful. During the short drive, I take in the lush green scenery rushing past the window like silent film strips on a movie projector. This is my first trip to Ireland. Although I learned much about Ireland from Rose and the debriefs she provided me on the work she did during her first and subsequent visits, I still want to absorb all I can.

My role in taking over the business operations portion is to continue Ross Enterprises' expansion in Europe and the US. Ireland is the first leg of my multi-country journey for the company. I'm excited that my career is continuing on a fast-paced trajectory. I also realize it's unusual for someone my age to be responsible for a well-established multitrillion-dollar global operation. Still, I have my former CEO, Alexandros, and new boss, Rose, as mentors if I need advice.

The ride to the apartment complex is short and the SUV soon stops in front of a ten-story, steely grey building. Troy immediately opens my door and helps me out. I stand beside the car for a moment. I inhale and take in my surroundings. The ten-story building in front of me will serve as my home away from home for the next week. Ross Enterprises' executives typically stay in corporate suites near their business entity, but the Belfast units are not done yet. Completing work on remodeling Ross Enterprises' luxury corporate suites will take another few months. Instead of staying at a hotel, Aedan suggested the most secure location outside Ross' corporate suites is one of his residential buildings, specifically where he resides.

"After you." Troy gestures for me to walk toward the side of the building to a private entrance leading to the penthouse residences.

When we reach the building, Troy positions his eyes in front of the iris scanner at the entrance, which opens the door to a small corridor housing an elevator. Per the security brief I reviewed, my biosignatures were pre-programmed ahead of my travels to provide me secure access to the buildings I will frequent during my stay.

"Everything is set for you. Try it." Troy gestures toward a black glass panel to the right of the elevator door. This time, I lean in and allow the tool to scan my iris. The elevator doors open immediately.

"The only ones with access to this elevator are you, me, Niall, Aedan, and Ben."

"Can I provide others biometric access?"

"Only the people listed as tier one family members."

"Like Jake," I say, knowing that King Enterprise's security team is also looking after my brother, our company's CFO.

"Yes."

"So, no random hookups," I tease. Amongst my two siblings, I'm known to be the wild child in the family, wearing outlandish graphic tees, at times leaving the house with uncombed hair, the mostly likely to try something new, and occasionally, I have one drink too many, but only with people I feel safe around. However, random hookups are not my thing.

"No. You have to let anyone else in manually." Troy's lips press together and his eyebrows furrow.

"Don't look at me that way."

"Were you planning something?"

"No. I'm just QCing your work." I tip my head and give Troy a wry grin.

Troy's tightly pressed lips reinforce that he's not amused. The elevator dings, alerting us that we've reached the penthouse floor.

"You're in penthouse B. I'll be staying one floor down. This floor consists of only two private units. Yours is slightly smaller, but it's about six thousand square feet, so you should be very comfortable. Mr. King occupies the rest of this floor." Troy walks me to the apartment door. "You can do the honors." He gestures toward the panel.

Again, I position myself in front of the eye scanner, and when the door clicks, Troy enters. After he completes his security sweep of the apartment, he waves me in.

"Wow. This is a lovely home away from home." I walk across the hand-scraped black-stained mahogany floors toward a wall of windows overlooking Belfast.

"Everything is controlled from here," Troy says.

Turning, I find him standing near a white electronic device with a screen on the marble counter surrounded by various floral arrangements. Next to the arrangements are candy containers full of Pixy Stix and Pop Rocks packs. I go to where he is, lift one of the lids, remove a green straw, and open it. Sticking out my tongue, I pour the powdered contents into my mouth. Oh, my god, it's been a while since I had one of these. They were my mom's favorite. One of many things I hold onto to remember her. Pixy Stix, Pop Rocks, and pink popcorn. I know exactly who sent these. I look around the space. The open kitchen area is near the wooden dining room table, which can easily seat twenty people.

I turn to Troy. He tips his head to the device on the counter. "It works similar to the one you have at home."

"Voice commands, music and all?" I ask, looking around the room.

"Same."

"Lenni, play *Baby Come To Me* by Oliver Wolfe," I call out. The song plays through the sound system. I groove to the beat for a moment, popping my fingers. When they sing "Come to Me," I gesture my hands toward Troy, curling my fingers.

Troy's face is expressionless. I laugh and dance over to the dining table to a vase of lavender-colored carnations. Gently cupping one of the delicate blooms, I lean in and smell it.

"Lenni, volume down," I say, turning toward Troy. "Someone researched me. There is no way that hypnosis carnations were anyone's first choice of flowers. And certainly, not a man with money." People consider them cheap, but they're hearty, beautiful, and last long. But I don't bother articulating that. "Look, the petals are perfection."

I walk over to the couch, which is backed against a long wall filled with contemporary art. "How thoughtful. Even the décor is catered to my style." I pick up a paisley-patterned pillow from the couch and hold it up to emphasize my point. A professed modern hippie, I love flowers, pastel rainbow colors, and paisley prints.

"I expect this is all to ensure you feel welcome during your stay," Troy reassures me.

"What are you not telling me, Troy? I don't imagine there's one item here that you haven't approved. Spill the tea on who arranged this. I run operations for the company and certainly didn't request any of this," I clarify.

"You have generous people in your life who think fondly of you."

"Gee, thanks. Your response is so revealing—not."

Aedan may have insight into my preferred aesthetics, but he wouldn't know what type of carnations or treats I like, leaving only two other people I'm aware of. It doesn't matter. Soon, I'll be in the corporate suite. The start of construction directly results from Rose's goal of establishing their entity in Ireland by the time she formally became CEO. The fact that Aedan and his brother own so much real estate in Ireland is handy. One of their newly acquired buildings, named The Falcon Building, has enough space to house Ross Enterprises' operations. Once the final floors are built out, I can live and work in the Falcon building.

"Take your time getting settled. I'll be waiting at the elevator when you're ready to leave," Troy tells me and then exits the suite.

I call Jake. The phone rings once before he picks up.

"Hey, sis, if you're calling me, you must have reached your destination. How's the Emerald Isle treating you so far?" Jake asks in his typical laid-back, self-assured voice. My older brother is so smooth yet commanding; I'll admit, he's attractive. When he walks into a room, women's eyes immediately follow him. It's been that way since we were in school together. All my friends had crushes on him. What they didn't know back then, which remains true today, is that the ultra-suave man behind the suit is a total geek. He's one of the highest-paid chief financial officers in the country for a reason—his brain has had a lifelong love affair with numbers.

"Just arrived, so not much is happening yet. Are you heading out this way?"

"Of course. You sound like you miss me or something?"

"Always, but don't let that go to your big head."

"Right. You're the new big-time COO, not me. Anyway, I'll be there in a few hours."

"Quick question before you go."

"Shoot."

"Are you going to Dad's sixtieth birthday bash?"

"I rearranged my travel schedule to attend. Why?"

"He wants me there."

"But you don't want to be."

"No."

"We can discuss this when I arrive."

"Jake, I need to wrap my head around this now. If I go, I need to adjust my travel plans. This job is a big deal. I can't just put my life on hold because he asked. I don't see him doing that for us."

"Whoa, wait. Hold on, sis. Where is this coming from? Is this about Jeanette?"

"He didn't even allow us time to properly grieve before he moved on. Why do I have to appease him? I'm just so tired—"

"June. Stop. Take a breath. Two separate issues are going on here. Regarding the schedule, you can make it work. We were both scheduled to fly out on the day of his birthday. I'll have the EA update your itinerary so we can fly together the following day. Nothing else has to change with the schedule. This thing you have with Dad has gone on too long. I think you need to talk it out with him. Tell him how his behavior made you feel. But I suggest you go into it without the emotions, sis. We all grieve in our own way."

"He was supposed to be the rock of our family, not you."

"You see me as the rock. I was trying to be the big brother bearing your grief along with mine so you could be the happy, healthy kid you needed to be able to thrive. Dad handled himself the best way he knew how. Listen,

I don't want to see you upset like this. If you want to talk about it when I get there, we can."

"It's okay. Talking to Dad triggered me. I didn't mean to dump on you. I'm good."

"You didn't dump on me. But I do think you should attend the party. I suggest talking to him before then. But that's up to you."

"You're right." I blow out a breath.

"I don't want to be right. I want to help. You good?"

"Yeah. I'm good. I love you, Jake. See you soon."

"See you soon, love you."

I use the time to shower, change, and prepare for a partial workday. Once I'm ready, I step into the foyer, where Troy is waiting for me at the elevator. We leave the building on foot, heading to the office a few blocks away.

"I'm glad the rain held off. It's nice to get out and walk." I say, looking around. "Where's Ben?"

"Not far."

"I suppose he knows my exact location."

"Don't worry. We all have eyes on you. Ben will be waiting to take you up to your floor."

When we round the corner and the modern eight-story glass-clad, steel-framed Falcon building comes into view, I spot Ben standing in front, waiting.

Rose hired several staff members before I joined Ross Enterprises full-time. She held back on hiring a few critical leadership roles so I could select the rest of my team. This is the first trip where I'm meeting with my local team face-to-face.

It's eleven o'clock. Standing at the far side of the conference room on the seventh floor, I watch team members file into the room. The large video screen on the wall above an eight-foot-long credenza displays a Brady Bunch-type matrix of squares with people watching from their computers. The conference room is modern, but I can tell by the rich, dark color palette that a man designed it. A wall of windows borders one side, while the remaining three walls are clad in slate grey striated textured wallpaper. I make a mental note to talk with facilities about adding a pop of color to the otherwise monochromatic room.

Despite the aesthetics, I'm excited to meet the new team and anxious to get going in my new role. Leaving Saola Technology was bittersweet. I was on a fast track working for the CEO, Alexandros Adler, a firm but brilliant technologist. He recognized how efficient, innovative, and driven I was and made a point of mentoring me. *"I recognize a bit of me in you. You'll go far in your career,"* he had told me. He and his brothers are great that way—always encouraging me.

After accepting a role with them straight out of college, I was determined to succeed. Graduating a year early gave me a head start in my career compared to my peers. Head down, highly driven is a trait I thought I picked up from my father. Early on, I recognized things were fueling my motivation that had nothing to do with him or money. Experience taught me at a young age that tomorrow is not promised. I'm driven by my desire to seize the day and take the world by the reins. Horace said, *"Carpe diem, quam minimum credula postero."* "Seize the day, put very little trust in tomorrow."

When everyone is settled in the conference room, I lead the team through goal setting and establish short- and long-term strategies to support achieving our goals. As they work through their planning, I am pleasantly surprised by how well the new team gels, reinforcing that I made good hiring decisions.

The purpose of this first trip is to close the resource gaps strategically, so knowing I'm on the right track with the talent I hired gives me comfort. Still, I need to finish building my team across the new entities in Europe and the United States.

As with any planning meeting, mine runs late into the day. I glance at my watch as people file out of the conference room—four o'clock. Good, I have time to wind down before heading out for the day. I return to my corner office overlooking downtown Belfast. My phone vibrates with a text from Troy.

MOS: Aedan King is on his way up.

Me: Let me guess. He's not here to fill in for Ben.

Before Troy can respond, there's a knock at my office door. One of the assistants peeks in to announce Aedan's arrival. I hold up my index finger and then send a text message.

Me: Remember, I have early dinner plans. He has five minutes and then we're out.

Aedan and I aren't scheduled to do contract reviews until later in the week. I'm unsure as to why he wants to meet sooner. Rose warned me about him. Aedan is a hardcore, no-nonsense businessman who is used to getting what he wants when he wants it.

I stand and walk to the wall of windows and look out over the city skyline.

"Show him in, thanks," I say while taking in the view. The door clicks as it closes behind the assistant. I raise my phone and type a text message to my security point of contact.

Me: I understand Mr. King runs the company, but can you suspend future surprise visits from the enterprise? My calendar is tight. Thanks.

My Man: Noted.

The click of the door handle signals Aedan's arrival.

"June, it's nice to meet you finally. Welcome to Belfast." Aedan's deep, melodic, Irish-accented voice fills the room, tempting me to turn around. "I hope you found your apartment accommodating. Apologies, I wasn't available upon your arrival."

I turn with my hand outstretched and take a few steps toward Aedan. He slides his phone into his pocket, swallows, and his lips curl into a slight grin. *What's that about?*

I lock eyes with him and say, "I prefer Ms. Ross, Mr. King." My fingers feel small in Aedan's hand. The warmth radiating from him thaws my usually cold fingers, surprising me. After a second, I withdraw my hand.

"You can call me Aedan."

Standing before me, Aedan is every bit of the six-foot-three billionaire book-boyfriend male model my cousin had described. Like my brother, he exudes confidence, but something about him is different. Standing beside me with one hand casually placed in his pocket is giving more "King Aedan" vibes than the other way around. His broad shoulders and muscles in his black suit, white shirt, and blue tie highlight the impressive packaging. The photos I'd seen of him don't do him justice.

I'm mesmerized as he stares at me with eyes the color of the Mediterranean Sea, making it difficult for me to look away. It almost feels as if he can see through me to my soul, and I'm having mixed emotions about his effect on me. I want to run my fingers through the waves of his inky black hair and caress his sun-kissed skin. A smile teases my lips as I feel compelled to run my fingers over the three-day stubble on his face. Despite his undeniable good looks, the recent conversation with Leon at the restaurant replays like an Instagram reel, reminding me that I've sworn off men. I quickly shake off the spell, reminding myself that Aedan King is off-limits. He's my cousin's former fling, her fiancé's brother, and as far as I'm concerned—forbidden.

"Mr. King." I turn away from Aedan and look out the wall of windows at the city, forcing my brain to focus on business. I take a deep breath. When I pull myself together, I turn back to face him. "I wasn't expecting you today."

"Understandably. However, I'd be remiss if I didn't, at a minimum, stop by to welcome you on your first day in Belfast. Also, if you're free this evening, I'd love to show you some Irish hospitality and take you to dinner."

It's a simple request. Have dinner with a drop-dead gorgeous guy who is completely off-limits for more reasons than I want to admit. No. I'm not falling into the same den of distractions my cousin entered. I've sworn off men and have a business to build.

"Unfortunately, Mr. King, I'm already committed tonight. You and I have plenty of time scheduled to talk during my visit. Let me know, and I can have my assistant move our meeting if needed."

Staring at Aedan, I wait for a reaction to my rejection. There is none. The only hint he feels a certain way is that his eyes grow a shade darker. *What is that? Disappointment? Irritation?*

"Understood. You can always call if you need me for anything."

"I'll contact your assistant if I need to reach you."

"Are you good with the security team I've assembled?"

"Yes. They've been great."

"Like I said, just a call away. Have a good evening, Miss Ross." Aedan turns and leaves.

***

The car pulls up alongside the narrow cobblestone sidewalk in front of the matte black painted building lined with windows. A large hand-painted sign that reads Máire's Café Bar hangs just above the entrance. A line of people about twenty deep waiting outside to get in provides evidence that this is a popular choice. Troy clears a path for me to enter the restaurant. Inside, the place is lively, with people laughing and chatting over pop music playing through speakers strategically placed around the room. The hostess at the reservation desk looks up and smiles. Her eyes shift past me, and I'm certain they land on the striking man of steel behind me. They always do. That's the effect Troy has on people.

"May I take your name?"

"June." A deep, familiar voice rings out, capturing my attention.

"Jake." I barely get his name out before my tall, honey-colored brother, sporting short hair in small natural waves, wraps me in a bear hug and picks me up.

"I've missed you," he says like he didn't talk to me a few hours ago. I see him in weekly executive staffing meetings either via video calls or in person. However, this is how it has always been between us, ever since that day years ago. He always ensures I feel seen, safe, and loved. I force faded memories from my head and focus on my brother's loving embrace. He puts me back down and kisses my cheek. "Come on. We've got great seats," he says.

He bumps fists with Troy—their signal that I'm in good hands with Troy and my brother's security team close by. My brother puts his arm around my shoulders and leads me to our table, which I know will be perfectly positioned near the back.

"You couldn't come into the office today?" I ask, tightening my hold around Jake's waist as we walk.

My brother is two years my senior. After completing his master's in financial economics at Oxford University, he returned to the States to work for our uncle, Rick Ross. Through his brilliance and demonstrated leadership skills, he rose through the ranks and secured the prestigious CFO position. Leadership is inherent to him. Always has been.

"I had business in London. But I'm here now. I've been worried about you since our call earlier. You good?"

At age ten, he rose above our family trauma, taking me and my younger sister Jasmine under his wing and guiding us to make good decisions. He's been both father and brother to me, ensuring my sister and I knew he was there for us while my father struggled to field the needs of three youths in his care.

"Yeah. I'm okay."

When I completed my undergraduate studies, I opted out of pursuing a master's to begin employment with Saola, a small competitor to Ross Enterprises. Eventually, I gave in to family pressure and joined my uncle's company. Despite my close relationship with Jake, I never could have predicted how well we would work together on Ross Enterprises' executive team. The ease with which Jake, Rose, and I collaborate feels right.

We reach our table, and I'm greeted by another gorgeous gentleman, one whom I know well but didn't expect to see this evening. *Aaron Adler.* The man I nicknamed "London" because once, when he couldn't get a hold of my brother and called me, my brother asked who would call me looking for him. I said, "It's London calling." The name just stuck. It suits him. Smooth. Sexy. As always, I'm mesmerized by his handsome looks: his dark blond wavy hair and captivating grey eyes. He's sporting a three-day beard highlighting his chiseled features, which makes me want to reach out and stroke his face. Jake is the first to speak.

"I told you, man—like clockwork. You can set your watch by my sister just like our cousin Rose," Jake says.

London stands to greet me.

"London? What are you doing here?" Even in stilettos, he towers above me in his six-foot-four muscular frame, which causes me to step back to meet his gaze. London hugs me, kissing one cheek and then the other. He gestures for me to sit.

"I came to have dinner with my two favorite people." He sits beside me. "There was no way I'd let you be a few hours away and not come see you." His bright white smile against his naturally tanned skin makes him look like the Greek god he is. At least half of him is—his mother is Greek. His father is British. He's staring intently at me. He always does. I try unsuccessfully not to blush under his gaze. I suppose a fine man like him should be used to it.

"I told him you wouldn't mind, June. Although, it's not like I had any choice in the matter. You know this guy." Jake flicks his thumb toward

London. "When he found out you arrived in Belfast, he didn't hesitate to rearrange his schedule and hop in his plane."

"You make me sound like a stalker."

"If the shoe fits."

London shakes his head.

"Pay no attention to Jake. It's always good to see you, London. How long are you here?"

"Just a few days. I hate to admit it, but JR's right. I'm here to see you. It's been a while...." The look on his face tells me something else is on his mind. "Since the going away party we held for you, Alex constantly reminds me how sorry he was to see you go to Ross Enterprises, but I get it; taking over Rose's former role as COO is a wonderful opportunity."

I have fond memories of my tenure working at Saola Technology. I first learned about Saola when they participated in a campus tour to recruit students for internships and full-time opportunities. I had previously interned two separate summers at other San Francisco Bay Area high-tech firms. I could have taken the easy route and followed in my brother and cousin's footsteps by joining Rick Ross Enterprises, as it was called before Rose took over as CEO. But in my usual modus operandi, I opted to forge my own path. It paid off. I was able to help Saola Technology become one of the leading technology companies during my tenure there. Now, they're Ross Enterprises' top competitor.

"Man, my sister is in the number two spot in the industry. Her next stop is CEO," Jake gushes.

He's always been great at building me up. Still, I find it strange to hear him talk about my success with his best friend. Jake and London are the same age. They met while attending Oxford University together. Although

Saola Technology is headquartered in the States, they have a European entity based in London run by Aaron. I didn't know when I interviewed years ago with Saola that my brother's best friend was the CEO's brother. I didn't tell my brother about the job until I received my offer. That's when I learned of the connection. Sometimes life is fortuitous.

"I just stepped into my new role. Let's see how I do before you start succession planning. Besides, I'm excited to be working for Rose."

A wait staff member comes to the table to take our order.

"Are you okay with me ordering a round of sharable dishes, June?" Jake directs his question to me.

"Sure. You good with that, London?"

"Yeah."

Jake rattles off a list of menu items and drinks. The server suggests a few items before double-checking the list. "We'll be sharing, so bring us each an extra plate," he instructs before the server disappears into the kitchen.

London turns to me and says, "So, tell me, how are you getting settled in the new role?"

"Good so far. As I said, I'm still getting acclimated, but the team is strong. I have a few more key roles to hire. I'm excited about what's ahead."

"You'll be brilliant, just like Aaron and Alex tell me you were at Saola," Jake says, beaming.

"JR's right, you'll be great. But let me know if there's ever anything I can do to help you."

"Thanks. You have your hands full already."

"Never too full for you. Remember, I'm only a flight away. I can swing by next week to check in on you if that's okay, since my mate here is heading back to the States soon." London tips his chin in Jake's direction.

"It's called work, man. I'll return to Belfast with my sister in a few months. You know I'm holding the purse for this enterprise. I don't intend to spend the company's money globe-trotting," Jake says. He's right. As CFO, he runs a tight ship when it comes to finances. Numbers are his thing; he has a photographic memory, so there is no hiding so much as a penny from him.

"We all know you're a tightwad," London teases.

"Selective spending," I add.

"Fiscally responsible is what I call it. Trying to set an example, unlike your jet-setting image, Aaron," Jake retorts.

"As I recall, I wasn't jet-setting alone today."

"Just hitching a ride." Jake smirks.

"Anyway. June, I have a question for you," London continues.

Jake rolls his eyes knowingly at London, which piques my curiosity. "Seriously, man, I'm right here. You do remember what we discussed."

The waiter comes back with our drinks. "Your food should be up shortly. Is there anything else I can get for you?" the waiter asks.

"Thank you. Nothing at the moment," I say. The waiter leaves, and I turn toward my brother. "Let him finish, Jake. I want to hear whatever's got you on edge."

"Handle this when I'm not around, man. Better yet, table it until next year," Jake presses.

London shakes his head, undeterred. "This is January. It's a new year. I'm not waiting. Anyway, I've been nothing but transparent with you." This back-and-forth between them makes me slightly nervous about what's happening.

"What are we talking about? Jake? What's London been transparent about?"

"Man, I'm telling you, now is not a good time."

"Jake? What am I missing?" I press.

"June, I'm here for a few days. Would you like to have dinner with me tomorrow?" London asks, seemingly relieved to have spoken the words.

I give London a half smile while I digest his what he said, attempting to understand the undertone of his request. "Are you asking me on a date? Because you and I have had dinner numerous times over the past ten years. However, the look on your face tells me this is different," I say, cutting to the chase. I've spent many years hanging out with Jake and London.

We met during my brother's first year at university. Before flying to Paris to meet up with friends, I flew out to visit Jake during a break. I flew in early, so I joined him for dinner and drinks with his friends. When he and I walked in together, it surprised his friends since it was a guys' night out.

London was the first to speak. "Whoa, mate. I didn't know we were bringing dates."

"This is my sister, June. She flew in a day early."

London pulled out a chair, allowing me to sit near him.

There's not much we don't know about each other. That's the type of relationship we have—friends.

"Aaron, shut this down," Jake warns.

"It's okay, Jake. Let him finish."

"Yes. What do you say, June? I know the whole working together thing was a barrier before, but—"

Jake cuts him off. "Can you two please do this when I'm not around? I love you both. Really, I do, but I don't want to think about you two *that* way." Jake over-dramatizes the last sentence.

I can't help but laugh at my brother. He has a point; this might get a little strange. All the time we've spent around each other as young adults and working together has afforded us a level of openness I haven't experienced with others. Mainly because Jake has been like a proxy parent, and London—well, he has been around a lot due to my brother and the fact that we worked together until recently. Still, it's a compliment that London sees me that way. Usually, when I'm with them, they talk about other women—not me, and certainly not about me hooking up with London.

"Are you saying your sister is off-limits?" London asks.

"Jake, I'm a grown-ass woman—get over it. London, it's okay. We can table it for now. Let's talk when Jake's not around." I concede and touch London's hand briefly. He smiles and nods.

Jake lets out a heavy sigh of relief. I turn my nose up at him. "Anyway. Sis, how are you handling Troy's team? It looks like a presidential visit outside with all those black suits standing around."

"Hey, don't blame me for that. Some of those people are here for you and London."

"Point taken."

"Honestly, it feels overindulgent. You know how I am when it comes to authority."

"This is not the time to be rebellious. They're there for a reason."

"I'm doing my best not to give them a hard time. So far, the team is great."

"You'll get used to it, June," London assures me. "In your new role, having a security team is a necessity. Like it or not, you, your brother, and your cousin work for Rick Ross. That's a big deal."

He's right. My uncle is chairman of the board, the wealthiest black man in the country, and the founder of a company creating some of the most groundbreaking technology foreign governments would love to get their hands on—case in point: the attempt on Rose last year when the exhibition was put on in Belfast.

Like the rest of my family, working for him in a highly visible role will change my life forever. If secrets of my past were to come to light, it could put me in a vulnerable position. I twist my ring as a twinge of nerves snakes up my spine at the thought. Quickly, I tuck that away.

I should be celebrating another first. That's what it feels like taking over as COO for a company leading the Standard and Poor's five hundred. This is a milestone, like my first job, first kiss, first house, my first...time. Oddly enough, despite the significance, I still feel like myself. Like the carefree modern hipster that I've always been. *Am I ready for my first foray into the big league?* I look at my dinner companions as I ponder the thought.

Time will tell.

Chapter 5

Meeting of the Minds

"The meeting of two personalities is like the contact of two chemical substances: if there is any reaction, both are transformed."
– Carl Gustav Jung

Aedan

Looking down at my phone, I re-read the message, leveraging all my tactical training to calm myself down and keep from smashing it against the wall.

Queen of the Night: I understand Mr. King runs the company, but can you suspend future surprise visits from the enterprise? My calendar is tight. Thanks.

Suspend future visits from the enterprise. Has she lost her mind? I take a deep breath. It's my job to stay calm under pressure, no matter how infuriating the drop-dead gorgeous person delivering the pressure is.

I slide my phone into my pocket. The door to my office opens. Lorn says, "Miss Ross is here to see you." He doesn't have to tell me. The second he opened the door, hints of honey and amberwood caressed my senses, signaling her presence.

"Show her in."

Lorn steps aside. June walks past him and stands to the side of the doorway. She is stunning in her black pumps, accentuating her long, lean legs that disappear into her grey pencil skirt just above her knees. Her crisp white button-down shirt has puffy sleeves that taper into oversized French cuffs hanging over her delicate hands. The top two buttons are undone, and the diamond peace sign necklace kissing her neck catches my eye. *Beautiful.*

I stand and walk across the room. Within a few strides, I'm standing in front of June.

I extend my hand to her, saying, "Miss Ross, good to see you." She gives me a firm shake and then quickly withdraws her hand. I gesture for her to sit in one of two black leather club chairs near a small table where two walls of windows meet. I sit adjacent to her.

"Mr. King," June starts. "Thank you for hosting me."

"It's the least we could do since we'll lead security for your executive team. I trust your accommodations are suitable."

"The apartment is impressive. It seems you've uncovered quite a lot about me. The added aesthetics and flowers are a lovely touch. Thank you."

"Glad you approve."

"Mr. King, I appreciate the conversation, but I'd like to delve into our agenda. The email I sent outlined areas of concern. If you're okay, let's start with the executive staff."

"Sounds good."

"Great. All new employee security access approvals formerly reviewed by Troy will now fall under your enterprise. I'm interviewing VP level candidates to fill positions in Belfast and London. As soon as I've identified the final candidates, a member of my team will forward the names to you. Once I reach the final stage and narrow the list to those individuals I'm considering offering jobs, we'll cue you to begin background checks."

"Beyond the extensive background checks and providing secure access, will you require personal protection for the employees at the VP level?"

"No. Only C-suite staff will require personal security traveling to these locations. The company has no openings at that level. So, for now, your team can expect frequent visits from me, our CFO, and our CEO."

"Rose," I interject. A hint of a smile tugs at the corner of my lips when I say her name. My ex and soon-to-be sister-in-law is the woman who got under my skin and changed how I think about women. I remember the day of the art exhibition when Rose received the news that she had been hired for the CEO role. That was the day I lost her. Since then, I've been longing to recapture the feeling of having someone who is mine.

"Right. Outside of that, your team will be kept apprised of our visits and highly publicized meetings off-premises. We can schedule a fifteen-minute weekly brief to cover updates and new items. Consequently, please include me in meetings involving new tools or protocols."

"I have the agreements ready to be executed." I slide a document across the table to her. She flips through it and signs alongside my signature.

"Great. Any exceptions and redlines to documents given to staff should be escalated to me."

"Including those originating from my team as they pertain to the C-suite?" I raise an eyebrow, tossing the question to her.

"Yes. Is there a problem?"

"To avoid any confusion or misunderstandings, I suggest you add the security protocol to the executive agreements."

"For what purpose?"

"To capture your employees' acknowledgment of what they're agreeing to. Currently, they only receive a copy as part of a broader package. We have no confirmation they've read or understand its implications. Including it as part of the agreement ensures a signature is on file confirming they've read and agree."

"Do you have something you want to say to me specifically, Mr. King?"

"Two things. First, in your situation, having a security handle is a must. Second, there are conditions where texting isn't the most efficient way to reach your team. I understand you have a slight opposition to this."

"Of course. You have a solution?"

"Concerning communication between you and my team, I suggest using a one-tap-to-speak device like an earpiece, digital watch, or other device. I can provide you with a list to consider."

"I'll take it under advisement. You said two things."

"Your handle is Queen of the Night. Queen for short," I state.

"I prefer Miss Ross."

"That won't work."

"It'll have to," she counters.

"I'll give you more time to think about it—then we'll revisit this."

"We'll see. I have another pressing topic if you don't have additional items to discuss."

"I'm good for now. What did you want to discuss?"

"A producer at the local RTÉ requested an interview with a representative of Ross Enterprises. I'll take the interview. However, our PR team is concerned that there are residual rumblings from the situation with Carol from last year. I've been briefed on the talk track, but—"

"Leadership is concerned about your safety," I say.

When my cousin, Carol, made the news due to her arrest for participating in a scheme against Rose, it also highlighted Carol's biased views and disdain for Rose showcasing underrepresented artists at last year's exhibition. People with similar views naturally began confusing the name Ms. Ross, who they knew as the woman who curated the art exhibition. Subsequently, public awareness is heightened surrounding the news their company is establishing an entity in Ireland. People, mainly those on the side with my cousin, want to know Ross Enterprises' intention in the UK.

"We've received emails suggesting a contingent doesn't want Ross Enterprises here. The RTÉ will begin promoting the segment the day before the program airs."

"I suggest you let someone from your PR team take the interview—that's their job. They have all the information to address questions accumulated over the past few months, which should satisfy any extremists. The risk drops exponentially if they take the interview."

"No. I'm doing the interview. I'm not afraid of extremists. If you're concerned about risk, I can do this alone. I've had worse things happen than the threat of pissed-off extremist throwing crap at me. If your team can't handle that—."

"This is not about them. This can get ugly. My concern is for your safety. If you insist on doing the interview yourself, I'll take the lead in protecting you. But Miss Ross, you will follow my lead."

"You work for me. I'll do my job. You do yours."

"We both work for Rose." I tip my chin. "The agreement you're holding says as much." She narrows her eyes at me. "Have you set a date for the interview?"

"Not yet. The RTÉ is still awaiting word from my PR team on who will represent Ross Enterprises and when."

"Good. Since you're only here for a few days on this trip, we should consider arranging the interview to coincide with your next visit. That'll allow some of the press to die down and give us the time to arrange logistics for the interview."

"You have a good point. However, I'm not afraid of tackling this head-on this week if needed."

"I suggest we push out the timeline for your safety." My eyes shift from hers to the document beneath her fingers. She takes a deep breath. Good, she gets it.

"We can schedule it for my return in March. That'll give my PR team time to map out a staged approach to feeding the media information over the next few weeks. You know, strategically placed articles, etc."

"Great. Then let's focus our next meeting on logistics. This is not something we want to tackle at the last minute. Belfast may be small, but the publicity might garner attention from neighboring towns. My team and I need to be prepared for the unexpected."

CHAPTER 6

Strawberry Letter 23

"In the sweetness of friendship let there be laughter, and sharing of pleasures. For in the dew of little things the heart finds its morning and is refreshed."
– Khalil Gibran

June

ELBOW PROPPED ON THE couch, cheek pressed against my knuckles, listening to *Love Hangover* playing through the sound system, I stare at London as he dips his unagi into a mixture of soy sauce and wasabi, then pops it into his mouth. He's lovely to look at. Still, I can't believe he confided in my brother about his desire to date me. Sensing me staring, he turns, wipes his thumb across the corner of my lip, then licks his thumb. I should feel a certain way about the not-so-subtle gesture, but I smile in response, unaffected.

"I have a napkin, but thanks," I tell him, slightly annoyed to unknowingly be staring at his fine self with something other than makeup on my face. But then again, over the years, he's seen most sides of me.

"That's what friends are for."

"To fill in where siblings fail. My little sis would let me go for a whole meal and walk out in public with food in my hair. When I got home and my dad saw me, he would say, 'You need to pull yourself together.' Then he would pull whatever it was out of my hair."

"Siblings can be that way."

"I suppose."

"Thanks for accepting my dinner invitation."

"I was surprised you asked."

"Are you really? I didn't think I was being subtle around you."

"You were, or perhaps I wasn't picking up what you were putting down." He raises an eyebrow. "You know what I mean. Over the years, we shared a lot of fun moments, but—"

"But you didn't suspect I thought about you as anything other than a former colleague or my friend's cute sister."

"Something like that. Or rather, we've developed a good friendship over the years, and I'm comfortable with that."

"You never suspected there could be anything more?"

"Did I picture you as my man?"

"Yes, June. I know you well enough to say that openly. Having something deeper with you has been on my mind. That's why I talked with your brother first."

"I realize that now. That's why I agreed to have dinner with you, to talk as friends. London, I can't commit to anything more. Jumping into another relationship is not where my head is at. Besides that, I also don't want our relationship to unravel because I can't be more to you."

He nods in agreement. I take the last sip of my wine. London pours me another glass and then taps my glass with his.

"To the woman I want but can't have."

"To the man who has become my closest friend."

"Is that what I am to you now?" I nod. "Not that it's a bad position to be in. Who else gets rejected for a date but can still spend the evening sitting shoulder to shoulder on the floor in front of the coffee table eating sushi with the woman he wants?"

I was unsure what I expected when I told him we could have dinner here at my suite. He surprised me with my favorite meal. It's one I rarely get to enjoy since most of my meals are eaten outside of the home. Due to a past event, eating out in certain restaurants is triggering, so having Asian food is a rare treat. London is thoughtful that way.

He's one of the few who know my secret, which he learned when I visited Jake while he was attending university. London was tasked with planning an evening out; he informed us he had reservations at a popular eatery near St. Paul. Jake and I didn't know where we were heading until we arrived at the front door. I froze the second I saw the design aesthetic and the restaurant's name painted on the outside glass panes. I couldn't go in. My brother put his arm around my shoulder and escorted me to the corner. In the cab on the way back to Jake's place, he explained the situation to London, who had already made several calls before we were out of the cab. Twenty minutes after we arrived back at the apartment, we received a food delivery containing what seemed like half the restaurant menu items. Another delivery service showed up with a beautiful traditional Asian four-piece dinnerware set, including Hashi.

When London showed up tonight, he did not disappoint me. Like before, he came prepared with food and traditional dinnerware. I took a few pillows from the couch and tossed them on the floor in front of the coffee table, creating my version of a Zashiki.

Content, I eat my sushi and watch him watching me. It could work if I were in the right headspace and felt something for him. At the moment, my spirit doesn't sense he's designed for me. I wish he were. Do I want to run my hands through his curly waves? Of course. Do I want to straddle him and have him kiss away all my cares and ravish me? Abso-funking-lutely. But it's just a feeling. The comfort of having his friendship, trusting him, and knowing I'm safe in the hands of a man who has demonstrated over the years…he's got me. It's not enough. He's not mine. He sips his drink.

"Wow, that was a mouthful," I tell him, freeing my thoughts from the past.

"I have a lot to say when it comes to you, June. But I promised I wouldn't press you about dating if you gave me the evening with you."

"You haven't so far."

"I don't intend to. Getting to experience you this way—with you knowing my intent and not being turned off, is a good place to be. Thank you."

"For what?"

"Trusting me. For allowing us the time to figure it out. After my confession, it could have changed our dynamic for the worse. Instead, it's brought us closer."

"The truth has a way of doing that. It's the uncertainty of the unspoken words between people that drive wedges. That's where misunderstandings develop."

"When we write narratives in our heads about others instead of clearing the air."

"That's right. At the restaurant, I knew something was on your mind. I could have guessed. I could have made up something like you're upset with me for leaving Saola, or that I spend too much time with my brother when he's your best friend, or any number of false assumptions."

"You didn't do that."

"No, I didn't."

"Instead, you listened as I confessed that I want you as my woman." He reaches out, cups my face in his hand, and caresses my cheek with his thumb. "If only you were." He exhales. "And just note that your brother will always be exactly what he is to you—I'd never take offense to the time you spend with him. I'm just glad I finally had the chance to tell you what I thought about you."

"Yeah, and here we are, drinking, eating, listening to soul music, and establishing a new normal for ourselves."

"It feels good...being here with you gives me peace."

"Same," I tell him.

The song changes to *All for You* by Amerie. London stands and holds his hand out to me. I take his hand and he helps me to my feet. "Dance with me," he says, leading me away from the table to a clearing in the center of the living room.

It's not the first time I've danced with London; I doubt it will be the last. He doesn't pull me close, but he also doesn't let go of my hand as we begin dancing in time with the music. Unsurprisingly, he has good rhythm. I've known that for a while. We danced at many company parties and charity events that he and my brother convinced me to attend. I dance around him, hands still joined, while London tracks my movements with his eyes.

"I've always liked this version of you," I tell him.

"Which version is that?"

"The private, fun, non-corporate president side."

"Not many get to see this side of me. I like that I can be this way around you."

Lifting on my toes, I lean against London, kiss his cheek, and say, "Same." Then I push away, grab my glass from the coffee table, and guzzle down the rest of my wine.

"Little lady, you're going to be tipsy."

"I am. And I have you to watch over me. Lenni," I call out. "Play 'Strawberry Letter 23.'" I pour myself more wine and take a sip, waiting for the lyrics to begin. When they do, I set the glass down and go to London. He's shaking his head and watching me with a wry grin. He's always been amused by my antics. I dance to the music like I'm alone in the room. London snakes an arm around my waist.

"You're going to fall if you're not careful."

"No, I won't, handsome, because you're here. You got me." And he does.

Closing my eyes, I dance in his arms, vibing to the music, not thinking about anything. Not my life as a child and how it changed in an instant. Not about my cheating ex. Not about my father, my siblings...my job. I'm just vibing to Earth, Wind, and Fire, feeling the warmth of my friend holding me safe in his arms. At this moment, I have no fears. I'm floating.

CHAPTER 7

Mess

"In all chaos there is a cosmos, in all disorder a secret order."
– Carl Jung

Aedan

SCREECHING TIRES SNATCH MY attention, followed by a large crash, metal crunching and glass shattering. Seconds later, the deafening sound of my building security alarms blaring bounces off the walls. I go to the wall of windows in my penthouse apartment overlooking the street. Long black tire marks lead from the street across the sidewalk and disappear into the front of my building below. I reach into my pocket for my phone to call my team. *They're on it.* I say to myself.

"Please tell me this is not what I think it is," I prompt a team member on the other end of the call.

"Sir, someone's car just jumped the curb and careened into the front of the building."

"Is anyone hurt? Is the driver all right? Have you called for help?"

"I'm with the driver now. NIAS is on the way. We're securing the area."

"Just make sure everyone is safe."

"We got this. I'll divert your tenants to use the side emergency exits for now. Beware, from the looks of things that won't be a long-term solution. Once you survey the damage, you'll understand."

"I'm headed down now."

I take the private elevator to the lobby. When I reach the main floor, I go to the main entrance. *Fuck.* It's in shambles. Glaze panels lie shattered in sheets across the floor. One panel is partially draped over the hood of a car. A portly man holding his head is sitting on the brown leather Barcelona bench to the far right of the building. Emergency vehicle sirens echo off the concrete walls, which are now exposed to the elements sans glaze. I kneel beside the man whose car is lodged in my lobby on metal beams.

"Sir, I'm Aedan King. You just had an accident. What's your name?"

"Don," the man says, hunching over.

"Don. Do you feel any pain?"

Don rubs the back of his neck. "I...I'm not sure. I don't think so."

"You'll be all right. The emergency services are on their way to check you out. Do you recall what happened to cause the accident?"

Don rattles off his version of how the accident occurred. I reassure him he's in good hands with the NIAS team. Now, I need to assess the damage and decide what to do about my building and the safety of my tenants. I call my general contractor.

"Basil. Aedan here. I'm not sure what you're doing, but I'll need you at my building on Sutton Way immediately. Thanks."

"Ben called. I'm on my way," Basil assures me. I end the call.

The emergency service team quickly determines that the driver is under the influence of prescription medication, which he took on an empty stomach. Basil assesses the building structure and the extent of the damage and informs me that the entire first floor facing the street will need replacement because the glaze panels and beams were ripped from the building facade, damaging the frame. The repairs are estimated to take several months due to the glaze needing to be custom-made.

The news is disappointing. Not only will I need to temporarily relocate my executive residents while the building is under construction, but my tenants pay a premium to live in my building with the added security provided by King Enterprise. Dividing my residential security team among various locations is not ideal but necessary.

Over a few hours, I inform each resident of the situation at hand, outline where they'll be living, and estimate their timeline to return. My team has assigned movers to help them pack the things they want to take. As for me, I'll stay in one of the newly completed corporate suites in the Falcon building, which will provide me with easy access to my office and Ross Enterprises.

I tap my phone screen. "Ben. When the flight arrives, secure the queen and take her and her crew to the Falcon Building."

"Confirmed, Mr. King," Ben tells me.

"And Ben, let's sync following your shift to review the agenda for this week."

"It may be late."

"Understood," I confirm.

***

The sun is barely peeking over the horizon as I get ready to leave my penthouse. I spent yesterday briefing my security team, reviewing plans with my construction crews, and ensuring temporary accommodations for the tenants are secured. My tenants are primarily high-visibility young corporate millionaires. I want to provide consistency in temporary housing that mirrors the same standards they were used to in my building. Some tenants took the last available corporate executive suites at the King Enterprise building, while the remainder are set up in the Fitzwilliam Hotel luxury suites.

"Mr. King." My assistant, Lorn, is walking fast to catch up on my way to the office.

"Lorn."

"Mr. Adler is flying in this week."

"You typically handle all the arrangements. What do you need from me?" I ask, trying to extract whatever he's hesitating to tell me. Stepping into my office, I remove my jacket and place it on the coat hanger beside the door.

"Mr. Adler usually likes to stay in the corporate suite. The King Enterprise suites have all been booked since the incident, and the Falcon building suites are all occupied."

"Lorn, put him in the penthouse at the Fitzwilliam Hotel. Assign his usual security details to be available twenty-four hours a day. That should take care of any inconvenience caused by commuting to our headquarters."

"Consider it done."

"For the future, he may seem hard-set in his requirements, but I assure you—he's flexible. You got this." I watch as the look of anxiety falls from Lorn's face. The Adlers are Greek-British-American brothers. As tech titans with global operations, they are powerful in their own right. Although Aaron and I have a business to conduct, I expect his visit to coincide with

June's due to the close nature of their relationship. My jaw ticks thinking about them together. *What is this I'm feeling?*

My phone buzzes. "Ben. What do you have for me?"

"The queen will be ready in an hour." I smile, hearing Ben's deep voice relay June's security handle while maintaining his composure. He warned me June wouldn't go for it. It doesn't matter—she's beautiful and carries herself like a queen.

"Keep me posted if there are any delays. Also, I want an active feed on the building sweep," I tell him.

"Patching you through now," Ben confirms.

I open the browser on my computer, which shows me a live video feed of my eight-member team walking through each room and every floor of the eight-story Falcon building. All employees have been previously checked. There are only a handful onsite since operations have been running for less than a year.

Thirty minutes later, my phone buzzes. "All clear," Ben says.

"On my way over before the queen arrives," I say. I can visualize June's face when she hears someone refer to her as the queen. It's then I realize that June is consuming my mind. *This woman will be the death of me.*

It doesn't take long to wrap up office activities. I exit the building and go to the eighth floor of the Falcon Building, where I've also temporarily relocated while my building is under renovation.

Ben's voice comes across my earphones. "The queen is heading your way,"

I look in the mirror near the front door and check my holster before entering the foyer.

I exit my suite just in time to see June in a discreet conversation with the security team. "I'm heading back down now, Troy. You know this place could use a technical upgrade." The covert tap on her ear causes me to smile inside, knowing she took my advice.

"What would you suggest?" I ask.

June quickly turns to face me. The book she's holding falls to the floor. She's stunning. *Beautiful as a rare flower,* I tell myself. June's long, unruly curls rest on her shoulders, framing her tiny face in a lush afro. Her bluish-green paisley shirt reveals bare skin from her neck and between her tiny breasts, showing signs she is not wearing a bra. The cream pencil skirt accentuates her figure in a look that can only be pulled off by her petite frame, baring curves in all the right places. We lock eyes. In a few steps, I close the distance, standing beside her. I'm captivated by her beauty and the hint of honey and amberwood surrounding her.

I bending and retrieve her book. I turn it over and take note of the cover, scanning her slender legs as I rise. "Gratitude," I say, punctuating the title. "Your journal, Ms. Ross. Don't forget to mention your thanks for the man who helped you in the hallway today."

I'm met with pursed lips that reflect she's not amused.

"Thank you," she says, taking the book. I note her reining in her urge to snatch it from my hand. "Remember, you're the cause of me dropping it. Oh, and I was referring to auto-closing doors."

"I'll take that into consideration."

"Is this your thing? Sneaking up on women in hallways?"

"Should I have announced I was about to use the elevator with you? That's not usually how things like this work."

"No. Don't change on my behalf. I'll make sure Troy escorts me in the future," she says with a clipped tone.

"Have you forgotten my job is to protect you, June? We happen to be neighbors, and there's that little technicality that I own the building."

"You can call me Miss Ross. Only my family and friends call me June. But you know that already from our previous conversation."

This woman.

"Or can I use your security handle?" I press my lips together, fighting a grin. She's cute when she's annoyed. But June needs to learn, despite my urge to pull her across my knee and spank her for acting like a brat, that I'm not the enemy. I have her back.

June expressed her dislike to my team about the handle I gave her. Queen of the Night is a rare flower in the cactus family that can survive in harsh environments and grows best attached to another plant. Its spectacular bloom is rare—it only appears at night once a year. It's rare, like June.

Troy briefed me on June's various stipulations surrounding how she preferred that our security team work with her. He didn't explain why. As good as my resources are, I can't uncover any document Rick Ross doesn't want to be discovered.

Troy clarified that June is still coming to terms with having to be constantly monitored. Rebelling is a means to express her free spirit. She's not fighting me. I train my team to recognize these signs in their clients. It's a defense mechanism. She's struggling to retain hold of the notion that she can defend herself. I've seen this before...in Rose. The difference is that Rose can defend herself from some physical threats. Years of tactical training under Troy and her former chief of security have provided her with the skills necessary. Yet, Rose learned the extent to which she needed our services. June has no tactical training; without it, her petite frame makes her even more vulnerable. But as long as I'm around, she'll be safe.

"Another discussion we previously had, but of course, if you want to be ignored, go ahead," June says, pulling me out of my head.

We proceed to the elevator and I press the button. When the door opens, I gesture for June to enter. "Ms. Ross." I follow her into the elevator, taking her in as she stands facing the door.

When Troy briefed me about June, he told me it was rare for her to allow people close enough to see the real her. She has a reputation in the corporate world—high performing, highly efficient, get shit done way of working. But the brief said there's another side to June—the person who sometimes drinks too much and loves seventies music, art, flowers, and dancing. Thus, the handle I gave her—Queen of the Night. The name serves as a symbol of ephemeral beauty. It's short-lived, reveals itself at night, and only a privileged few are blessed to witness its beauty—that's June. The person she is when she feels free to let go and be herself. Other than a few women in her circle, there are only two men besides Troy that I am aware have seen the rare flower in full bloom. Jake and my friend...Aaron.

"Well, this doesn't feel awkward at all."

I raise an eyebrow. "Standing in the presence of such a beautiful woman *isn't* supposed to be awkward," I say.

"That's not what I mean. You're the CEO of a five-billion-dollar company, Mr. King. Don't you have people to do this stuff for you? Where's Ben?"

"You're Rick Ross's niece and the COO of a trillion-dollar company. Currently, my job is to get you from point A to point B."

She narrows her eyes at me and counters, "Operative word being niece, not daughter. So, you don't need to play guard dog."

"I promise—I don't bite...unless specifically requested. And don't underestimate yourself. You're second in command of one of the world's greatest companies, and a significant part of its success hinges on your contribution. That's a big deal. You're certainly worthy of my time."

June's not wrong. Ben or my team members could have been assigned to watch her, but I promised Niall I'd be on point for his future in-laws. Additionally, I've committed to pulling back from field work once June finishes staffing and training her teams in Ireland, London, and Seattle. This is the only life I've known since our father passed. We'll see how it goes.

The elevator door dings, alerting us that we've arrived on our floor. "You're stuck with me once Troy returns to the States. We can discuss what's next for your entourage when we've completed training and hiring the staff for Ross Enterprises. After you, Ms. Ross." I gesture for her to exit the elevator.

Chapter 8

Misunderstood

"You cannot shake hands with a clenched fist."
– Indira Gandhi

June

It's eight in the morning here, which means the Senate hearings in Washington, D.C. are over. I'm sure there's a video of the proceedings in my email. I trust Rose's testimony on the need for policies to ensure stricter protocols using artificial intelligence will land well with the committee. Plenty of people with nefarious intent want free rein with AI technology, and even more want access to the brain behind RE's technology—Rose.

The tight security on Capitol Hill made it feasible for Troy to travel with me without risk to Rose, but he'll be heading back to California tonight to meet up with my cousin. In his type of job, it was inevitable. My trial run with Aedan yesterday was brutal. We kept butting heads. But I need to embrace King Enterprise's team, not for my sake, but for the company. If Rose can do it, I can.

Purse, coffee, book, I tell myself, peering over my shades as I look around the suite to ensure I didn't forget anything. It feels good to be back in Belfast. I've got a great team and we're building a nice book of business, so I'm heading off to meet with my newest clients.

"All clear down here. Just waiting for you," the deep voice says in my earpiece. God, I love a good, strong-sounding man. I could listen to Troy all day. He should rethink his career and maybe do voiceovers for romance audiobooks. I shake my head, abandoning the thought, and try to close the door as I exit the suite with my hands full.

"I'm just heading down now, Troy. You know this place could use a technical upgrade."

"What would you suggest?" a deep Irish-accented voice says from behind me. My back stiffens. Stunned, I quickly turn, trying to collect myself, and my journal slips out of my hand onto the floor. *Aedan*. Just a few strides with his long legs, and he is standing next to me. *And here we go.*

In my brief interactions with Aedan, one thing is clear: he has some aversion to me. Every conversation seems more like a dispute than a discussion. Throughout the elevator ride, I listen to him talk about security. With everything going on in my life, I feel like I'm drowning, yet oddly enough, his presence, although unnerving, serves as a distraction. If he didn't act so cranky, he could have a calming effect with that deep, melodic voice and those dreamy eyes.

The elevator dings and I turn to him. "I'll ensure Troy retrieves me from my suite from now on."

"June." His eyebrows furrow in offense.

I place my hand against the retracted door, holding it open. "That's Miss Ross to you."

"Ms. Ross. I assure you there will be no need for that. You're perfectly safe with me."

"As I recall, you said those exact words to my cousin Rose. It's not my safety I'm concerned about." I want to say *you were on a collision path to crush her heart,* but refrain. "Besides, Troy has me covered."

"Sounds like you two have been discussing me. I hope Rose had good things to say about me." Aedan gestures for me to step out of the elevator. "After you. If you have time this morning, I can take you on a building tour."

"Let's just leave it at: we talked. Oh, and my day doesn't start on this floor. But you go ahead since you selected it."

"You're not working in this building today?"

"Not this morning. Ground floor, please." Looking up, I notice one of his eyebrows is arched as he tries to figure me out.

Staring at him, I want to generalize him with other men, making assumptions about what they think they know about me, but there is nothing typical about him. Only a few men can orchestrate a maneuver that saves your cousin's life in seconds. Aedan could do that because Rose was intentional about checking in with him and Niall. Through his astuteness, he uncovered an elaborate ploy to attack her that, had he not, could have cost her life.

"As I mentioned, I'll take over security for you when Troy returns to the States. I need to know your complete schedule."

Despite my desire to resist, the more he knows about me and my movements, the better he can do his job and the safer I am. Allowing someone else to fend for me after all these years of doing it myself makes me feel like a fraud.

"You're right," I concede. "However, Ben is my point of contact. I'll sync with him," I say. But my goading Aedan doesn't elicit the response

I expected. Instead, he gives me a sexy, knowing smile. I turn and face the elevator doors to avoid his gaze.

The elevator ride to the ground floor is quick. When the doors open, I'm relieved to find Troy waiting for me.

"Are you okay?" Troy asks in his typical Barry White voice. I wonder if he knows how swoon-worthy he sounds. I imagine my cousin pointed it out to him by now. His gaze shifts between me and Aedan as he awaits my response.

I look at Aedan but respond to Troy. "A misunderstanding. I'm fine."

"Good to see you, Aedan," Troy greets.

"Same," he says.

Troy gestures to me to continue walking.

"June…," Aedan starts. "Ms. Ross. If you don't have any plans, I can make dinner arrangements for tonight since this is your first week back here. Plus, it will be nice for us to talk since we'll be working together."

"I appreciate the offer, but I do have plans. Good day, Mr. King." I walk out of the building and toward the car. My driver stands near the vehicle with the car door open, waiting. Troy helps me into the car. He closes my door and then gets into the front with the driver. When I look out the window, Aedan is walking down the sidewalk, one hand in his pocket, as if our conversation had never transpired. And just like that, he's moved on like he did with Rose. Like my dad did after my mom passed. Like every man I've ever dated.

Unaffected.

Uninterested.

Upward and onward.

"I heard your discussion with Aedan. Are you serious about me waiting in the upstairs lobby?"

"Absolutely."

He stares disapprovingly at me through the rear-view mirror. "He has a point—I'm returning to the States. It's important you cooperate with him. In the interim, I'll have a conversation with Aedan," Troy assures me.

Whether he knows it or not, Troy not only provides physical protection, he also provides me with a sense of mental safety. The fact that he understands my history and can also keep me safe provides me with a sense of relief. But it also frightens me because, for so long, my only protection has been me. Logically, I realize Aedan isn't a threat to me, but the niggling feeling of someone walking up on me, in general, is unnerving. I could have told Aedan about my trauma response, but he should have known better.

"Thank you, Troy."

Overall, today was a good day. Meeting my new clients in Belfast was what I needed to feel grounded as I stepped into my new role with Ross Enterprises. So far, I've locked down two new clients. I have three more scheduled throughout the next two weeks, including a call with Knight Development Corporation, which can help me accelerate Ross' growth trajectory if I play my cards right.

My challenge is to get the rest of my life in order. I need to figure out this thing with my dad and navigate my new relationship with London, and then there's this fixation with protocol. At the end of the day, Troy transitions security to King Enterprise's team, leaving me with my newest challenge...Aedan.

CHAPTER 9

Over Some Wine

"Friendship is the inexpressible comfort of feeling safe with a person, having neither to weigh thoughts nor measure words."
– George Eliot

June

ALL THIS BUSINESS HAS worked up my appetite, and I need to head back to prepare for dinner. Getting ready is cathartic as I slip on my lavender microfiber cosmetic headband so my hair doesn't get messed up. I wash my face before applying moisturizer. I look at myself in the mirror.

I look like my mother did when I was young. I remember standing beside her, watching her in the mirror as she applied lipstick and mascara. Like me, she didn't wear much makeup. Her skin was flawless as glass. Mesmerized, I used to reach out and touch it.

"What are you doing, sweetie?" she asked.

"Seeing if it's real."

She laughed. "I'm real, sweetie." Then she would cup my cheek, smile, and apply her makeup.

I take a deep breath and apply my color-tinted moisturizer to avoid covering my freckles. Then, I apply mascara and a honey-colored gloss as a finishing touch. Once I remove the headband, I finger-comb my puffy afro into large curls, twisting them around my finger to tame my look. Voilà, I'm ready for an evening alone in Belfast. Well, as alone as a woman with an entourage can be. Let's see how this goes.

This should be interesting. Since Troy has returned to his security detail for my cousin, I need to rely on my new security team. I take out my phone and text my point of contact.

Me: I am heading to the restaurant to drink at the bar and eat dinner.

My Man: Did your assistant reserve a spot?

Me: I don't need to reserve a bar seat.

My Man: I'd advise reserving a table. I'll contact the restaurant.

Me: Is sitting at the bar against the rules or something?

My Man: We're here to protect and advise you.

Me: Advice received. I'll be sitting at the bar.

I'm about to put my phone away when it buzzes again. This better not be Ben and his team. They're doing too much.

I smile when I read the screen.

AA2: Hey, beautiful! I'm calling, so please pick up.

Before I can respond, my phone buzzes.

"Hey London, don't you have work to do? You and your brother run a tight ship at Saola." I hate to admit that after his confession and our commitment to our newfound friendship, I feel more comfortable with him than ever.

He was right that night—I had too much to drink. But as I suspected—it didn't matter. As usual, I let loose like I didn't have a care in the world. London held me while I danced, and I was in my personal slice of heaven for a while. When I grew tired and fell asleep on the couch in his arms, he put me to bed. He slept in the guestroom closest to mine to ensure I was okay. Later, I awoke from a nightmare at some late hour and tried to get out of bed to go into the kitchen to get water. He was at my side before I took the covers off, tucked me in, and brought the water. He sat beside me until I fell back to sleep.

The next morning, I awoke to a note on my dresser saying, *"Good morning, beautiful. There's nothing more satisfying than watching you be happy and carefree. Thank you for allowing me to be there for you. Safe travels. See you soon. Aaron."*

There's a subtle seduction in his tone when he says, "Hi, June. I take breaks to eat sometimes. That's why I'm calling. Have you had dinner yet?" The sound of his voice makes me feel giddy.

"I was just wrangling the entourage. You know it takes a village for me to step outside."

"I'll handle dinner arrangements. You handle your entourage."

"Thanks. Wait. What? Are you here?"

"Yes, I flew in to have dinner with you. What restaurant did you have in mind? You usually enjoy a cocktail first. We can stop at a bar and then head to dinner or do whatever you like. Just let me know."

I shake my head. *This man is too much.* If I hadn't witnessed the interaction between him and Jake when London announced he wanted to take me on a date, I would have thought my brother put him up to it so I'd end up with a good man. Despite my resistance to him—London *is* a good guy. When I first met him, I thought he was one of those "love them and leave them" types. I even teased him about it one night during summer break when I visited Jake while he was living in London. They were heading out to a party.

"How do I look?" he asked me.

"Like the heartbreaker you are." I didn't understand the perplexed look he gave me at the time.

I do now. Even then, deep down, I knew better. I watched how he clarified his intentions with the women he was with. If only Leon had been honest with me and allowed me to walk away before I got seriously involved with him.

"Okay, give a girl a second to process." Despite my best attempt to mask it, a laugh escapes. "You caught me battling with security to sit at the bar, but I'll make a reservation."

"I got it. I'll pick you up."

"No, that's okay. Just meet me there. Remember—the entourage thing."

"Right."

Over the past decade, knowing London and his brothers has taught me one thing: when they want something, they stop at nothing to get it. London wants me. As much as I love him as a friend, I hate to be the one to break his record of getting what he wants. After all, we are friends. *These aren't dates, right?*

"London—."

"Yes, beautiful."

"See you in a few," I say. I end the call and text my security team.

Me: Change of plans. Same place, table for two.

My Man: Two? I'll need a name.

Me: AA2.

Three dots pulse on my screen before disappearing. Note to self: talk to Troy later to see if it is typical for the security team to question my instructions. One last look at myself in the mirror near the door, and I feel good about my fitted black ankle pants, black ankle boots, and a custom off-the-shoulder black t-shirt with embellished red lips. I top it off with my leather moto jacket, and I'm ready to go. Initially, I considered not changing and simply going in my work clothes, which are stylish enough, but I'm feeling edgy tonight. Besides, it's raining.

Grabbing my umbrella, I exit the apartment and step into the hallway. Instead of Ben, I find Aedan waiting for me. His usually bright Mediterranean eyes are now dark and cloudy.

"Ms. Ross," Aedan's usual formal voice is noticeably absent, replaced by a clipped tone lacking the hint of familiarity I would have gotten from Ben. I school my expression to mask my surprise at seeing him.

"Mr. King. I'm sure my point of contact updated you on my plans."

Aedan doesn't respond. He gestures for me to enter the elevator. The ride down to the lobby is quiet. Aedan executes his duties like any other member of the security team I've recently experienced. Yet there's a hint of something I don't understand hovering between us. Outside, he opens the car door for me. I slide into the back seat. He takes his place in the front seat on the passenger side.

The ride to the restaurant is short. There's a small line forming near the front door. When the car stops, I instinctively reach for the door handle, but Aedan opens it before I can. He extends a hand to me. I take it and step onto the sidewalk. He's standing so close that his scent surrounds me. I linger a second longer than I should, taking it all in.

I step ahead of him, then turn back and say, "Thank you." Aedan nods in response and escorts me to the restaurant door.

When I walk through the restaurant entrance, London is waiting for me. He closes the distance between us, pulls me into an embrace, and kisses my cheek. From the corner of my eye, I glimpse Aedan approaching. I hold my hand up, keeping him at a distance. His approach surprises me because he knows I'm meeting someone. Aedan steps to the side.

"You look beautiful as always," London says, untangling himself from me and looking me up and down. "Simply stunning," he adds.

"Thank you."

I step forward and turn to my side. Aedan continues watching me. His eyes shift between me and London, who's holding my hand. I notice a slight tick in his jaw. *What's his problem?*

"Our table is ready if you're ready. Are you okay?" London tracks my gaze to where Aedan is standing. "King. Good to see you, mate." He tips his chin up. "JR mentioned your team was taking over for Troy. I didn't expect to see you walking in to escort June personally."

I look at London. "Just how well do you know, Mr. King? Hopefully, well enough to convince him I'll be fine without his services tonight?"

"I'd say I know him well enough."

"Hey, mate. Ms. Ross, much to her dislike, is stuck with me this evening." Watching Aedan, I detect a slight twitch at the corner of his mouth. He's enjoying this.

"Aren't Kent and his team here?" I press, pleading with my eyes.

London tips his chin to a dark corner. I follow his eyes and see Kent in one corner and another man strategically standing adjacent to him. "You know I always got you," he tells me. "She's safe with me, mate. I'll signal you before we head out," he tells Aedan. Surprisingly, Aedan nods, leaving me curious about their relationship.

"I think you promised me a drink, handsome. Shall we?" I say, wanting to get a break from the testosterone sandwich.

London places his hand on the small of my back and tips his head to Aedan before leading me to our table in a private booth.

"You've gone from following in your brothers' footsteps to being followed by the head of one of the largest security companies. I almost feel like I need to invite him over. Almost." He smirks. I roll my eyes.

"I'm baffled by the whole thing. Hopefully, he'll stick to his lane and I'll stay in mine. So, about that drink. I'll have a sidecar."

London lifts his chin and catches the waiter's attention. The waiter comes to our table, takes our drink order, and then leaves.

"Don't sweat it. King's a good guy. My brother and I have known him for years now. He was made for the role he's in. I think his environment and family situation have a lot to do with how he operates."

"I suppose so. He's so tense sometimes that it's scary. I imagine it will be useful for my TV interview tomorrow. One look at him and his guys and I doubt anyone will mess with me."

"What are you talking about? You said your PR team was able to quell some of the noise. Are you telling me there's an increased risk of trouble?"

"Don't worry. Whatever happens, I can handle it."

"That's the point. You're not handling this alone. I need to know you're safe. It's different here in the UK. I'll connect with Aedan."

"You don't have to involve yourself in this."

London rubs his thumb across my cheek and says, "You seem to be under the impression that I don't care about you."

"I know you care. I'll ask the team to brief you," I concede. Troy always emphasized ensuring that people close to me know when the security level is heightened at an event to give them a chance not to participate. That won't deter London from spending time with me, not just because he has his security team, but because of his feelings for me.

The waiter returns with our drinks. "May I take your order?"

"Would you like me to order you pasta?" London asks.

"I'll have stew and champs tonight. The rain has me in my feelings and my hair is a mess."

He relays our order. "We'll both have lamb stew and champs. Please bring the lady extra butter. Thank you." As long as I've known him, he's always paid attention to small details about me. The server notes our order and then disappears to the kitchen.

I sip my drink and smile to myself. I love a good sidecar. I angle myself to experience his reaction to what I'm about to say. "You didn't bring my brother this trip. I should video call Jake so he knows what you're up to."

"JR knows exactly where I am. You know we don't keep secrets. He'll be back on this side of the pond soon enough."

"What exactly did you two talk about anyway? Are you putting our business out there?

"Our?" He reaches out and touches the necklace he gave me, and then his eyes shift to mine. The sexy smile he flashes makes me blush inside. "Does that mean we're a 'we' now?"

"You know what I mean. I'm referring to your not-so-subtle attempt to ask me out on a date. Then our subsequent night in, and now this."

"I've never been subtle."

"We talked about this. We're not dating. This is two good friends having dinner."

"And I accept that, but I admit I wish we were more to each other. We've always run in the same circle of friends. Previously, there was the issue of long-distance, working together, or you were dating someone else, so I held off saying something. Now, you'll likely spend two-thirds of your time in Europe. You're so close, June. The timing feels right."

For you, but not for me, I want to tell him, but instead, I say, "You're saying there are no more visible obstacles to keep us apart."

"You tell me. I can only be to you what you want."

"Did Jake tell you what happened with the last guy I was dating?"

"I didn't press him. It's not his story to tell. You don't have to go into details if you don't want to."

"You need to know what happened so that you'll understand what you're up against and why my answer, so far, has been no."

"Then tell me."

"Shall I cut to the end or start at the beginning?"

"Tell me whatever you're comfortable with. I'm listening to see whose face I need to smash."

"This is not Rory from winter break. That won't be necessary." It's strange how memories are triggered. I hadn't thought about Rory in years. Not since that night in December at my twenty-first birthday celebration thrown for me by Jake.

The celebration was twofold: I was turning twenty-one and was about to begin my first real job at Saola Technology after graduating a year ahead of my age group. It was the perfect time to host a party. All my friends were on winter break and didn't have to worry about studies. The guest list was invite-only. However, someone decided to use their plus one to invite a guy who I'd only dated for a total of thirty days before breaking up with him for being a lying, cheating asshole. Rory. I didn't see him right away. I suppose he must have come late. It didn't take long for him to find me.

London flew out for the occasion; he said it was to personally deliver his gift: a platinum diamond-encrusted peace sign necklace. My mom used to wear a gold one. After she passed, I never saw it again. I told him how I admired it. His thoughtfulness and generosity moved me so much that I spent most of my time with him: first dance, first slice of cake. With close to one hundred attendees, as usual, my brother kept a watchful eye on me. He didn't need to. Not with London around. I was dancing with London when Rory came in. He must have been out drinking before arriving because he walked over to me, catcalling my name like a bum off the street, brash, belligerent.

"I'm here for my dance, sweetcakes," Rory announced.

"Do you know this guy, June?" London had heard about Rory but had never seen him before that moment.

"It's Rory. He shouldn't be here."

Rory, who was about five inches shorter than London, looked him up and down. "Who the fuck are you?" Rory exclaimed.

"I'm the one taking out the trash."

Before I realized what was happening, London gripped Rory's throat and fast-walked him backward toward the entrance, with my brother following close behind. I never asked him where he learned that technique or why, but the panicked look in Rory's eyes spoke volumes.

When London returned, he apologized for me having to see that. Then, with my brother standing beside me and London on the other side, I celebrated another first with him and had my first drink.

"To my beautiful, brilliant sister. May all your wildest dreams come true. Cheers."

"The world is your oyster. Cheers," London chimed in.

That's when I had my first drink, a Harvey Wallbanger. Nicole had a Tequila Sunrise, London had a Tom Collins, and Jake had an Old Fashioned. Of course, it was a seventies-themed party because that's my thing.

Looking back, I realize that London has always been there for me. He's always shown a soft spot for me in some form or another. Following that night, I never saw or heard from Rory again.

"I'll be the judge of that. And Rory got what he deserved. Now, talk to me," London insists.

The server returns with our order and re-arranges the table to accommodate the plates. I sip my drink while London watches me patiently, waiting for the server to finish.

"Will there be anything else?"

"Not at the moment, thank you," London says, and the server leaves.

While I add butter to my champs, London sips his drink. He won't touch his food until I'm done prepping. I eat a forkful of potatoes and moan.

"Oh my god. So good."

London reaches across and wipes my lips with his napkin and says, "Bon appétit, beautiful."

"Thanks. You know Troy has to track anyone I'm with."

"I'm aware."

"Troy alerted me that Leon—"

"The guy you were seeing."

"Yeah. Troy informed me Leon was meeting another woman—not just that he was meeting her, but it had become a pattern and was not business-related."

"He was cheating on you."

"In the process."

"Call it what it is, cheating."

"He hadn't slept with her—."

"Yet. He was dating you and seeing her. That's cheating."

"Right."

"How did you handle it? Because I know you. You're a beautiful wild card when you want to be. What did you do?"

"Interrupted their lunch meeting. Made his newfound girlfriend aware of who he *used* to be to me."

"I don't like the sound of this. I'll follow up with Troy to get the details on this guy so I can talk with him."

"Don't you dare." London angles his body toward me and puts his arm on the table, indicating he's agitated. "I dealt with him. It turns out his date recognized me from the media. If she's a true admirer of mine, she'll steer permanently clear of him."

When his date referenced a TV interview where she saw me put a CEO in his place, I secretly smiled. I've been known to be a rebel—I have been since an early age. I'm no stranger to tackling tough issues in public. Whether I'm battling dirty executives harming society, drafting policy around AI, or fighting public battles to impose stricter gun laws, I don't back down from a challenge. Dealing with Leon was a piece of cake compared to what I've been through.

"The guy's an idiot. I would never do that to you."

I place my hand palm up on the table. London places his hand in mine. I hold his hand, staring into stormy grey eyes until his temper comes under control. After a few moments, he sighs, brings my fingers to his lips, and kisses them.

"I know you wouldn't." I squeeze his hand, then pull away.

"Thank you for sharing, but I sense that's not the underlying reason for your telling me no."

"Because I love you too much to risk ruining what we have."

London smiles wide. "I didn't expect that."

"Let me clarify. I love you like—"

"Christ, woman. Please don't say you love me like JR."

"No, yuck."

"Why yuck?"

"Because I never wanted to kiss my brother."

His eyebrows raise in response to the bombshell I've dropped on him.

"You want to kiss me? I can make that happen."

"Hold your horses. *Wanted* is the operative word."

"Still, you wanted to. Now that I know the desire exists, let me show you what you've been missing." I laugh, but London's smirk shows no cut to his confidence. "You're getting a kick out of this."

"I wasn't trying to."

He puts his index finger under my chin and tips my face toward him. He's so close I could lick him if I wanted. "You know I can kiss that laugh right out of you," he says, and his sexy, deep British accent sends a shiver straight to my lady parts.

I take a deep breath to control myself. Because if there is one thing I'm sure of, a kiss from a fine, confident man like Aaron Adler will most certainly silence me. I swallow. "I don't doubt you. But I feel differently about you." I remove his finger from my chin and lean back to give myself space from the man whose face I'm seconds away from sucking.

I shove a scoop of champs in my mouth. Once again, he wipes my face, but instead of his napkin, he uses the pad of his thumb.

He licks the potatoes from his thumb and says, "But still, you wanted me."

"I did. And stop looking at me like you're hungry for more than potatoes."

"Stop telling me things like you've been lusting after me."

"I didn't put it like that." I close my eyes and shake my head. London is on a roll and is too hot to handle now that I've revealed my secret.

"Let's make a deal."

"God, I'm afraid to ask, but here goes. What am I getting myself into, London?"

"You don't see yourself dating me because you don't want to ruin our relationship. Correct?"

"Right."

"But eventually, you will date again."

"When I'm ready, yes."

"You're not sure whether you still have feelings for me, are willing to take a chance on a new relationship, or are waiting for the right person because the recent breakup is clouding your judgment. Yet—here you are...with me. Something in you wants to try again."

"True. You should have been a therapist." My lame attempt at a joke earns me a small smile.

"June, when that moment strikes you...when your mind is open to exploring something new—in that moment when you want to lean in and kiss someone, or—"

"Or do something like run my fingers through their hair or nibble their ear," I say, finishing his thought.

He smiles. "I'd like that—but at the point when you're ready for that again—come to me."

"Wait. I don't understand. What are you asking? What if I'm not with you when that moment strikes?"

"I can only hope I'm the one that fueled that moment for you."

"But if what if you're not...."

"June, can't you see? At that point, you've opened up to the possibility of more. Come to me. Let me hold you. Tell me everything you're feeling at that moment."

"That feels like cheating. Are you asking me not to commit myself to anyone until I've explored my feelings for you?"

"I'm asking you to give me a chance to know that the things you felt for me years ago are either still there or gone. Let me give you the kiss you denied yourself. If we aren't meant to be, you'll know at that moment. I'll accept that."

"I swear you're persistent. And confident. It's cute, but all that is beside the point. I can't commit to anything more with you than what we are."

"I'm not asking you to. Although technically, this is a date."

I think about my life with London. The times we've shared, either working alongside each other or hanging out with my brother. He's a good guy. He's caring and confident, and I know if he were my man, he'd take wonderful care of me. But the thing I've felt the most all these years was a crush on the cute guy who's my brother's best friend—admiration for a smart man who was my superior at Saola. I feel a closeness cloaked in the comfort of being with him, and I'm afraid to let go of it. In my heart, I know he's in my life for a reason, but as what?

On the surface, what London's asking me seems simple. He wants to be there when I come out of my self-prescribed singleness. I've never been the type to divide myself between men. So, spending time with a man other than him isn't ideal. I don't want to take chances with anyone else. If we are meant to be, then the time we spend together will reveal whatever truth lies between us.

I sigh. "Okay, I can commit to that. The first step, the first kiss, on my journey to find my forever begins with you. You get one shot, handsome, but it has to be organic. If it doesn't feel right, I'll tell you."

"I have no doubt you'll tell me. Are you still up for a nightcap?"

"Of course. Why you book hotels when you're in town is a mystery to me. You typically end up at my place."

"Even though I've known you most of your adult life, I don't want to be presumptuous. Besides, you haven't agreed to be my woman, and I'm not interested in becoming a permanent fixture in your guest room."

"Good point."

"Although, I love nightcaps with you."

"I think you're only interested in the dance party portion." I laugh.

"I promise not to let you fall."

"You never have."

Chapter 10

Reset

"I can do things you cannot, you can do things I cannot; together we can do great things."
– Mother Teresa

Aedan

When protecting my clients, I take every precaution necessary to ensure their safety. Sometimes, that includes doing things they don't want to do, like following protocol. I don't know if June's adversity is to protocol, authority, or me—perhaps all of the above. Despite her resistance, I know she will do what I ask her to keep her safe.

June enters my office for our security briefing. She walks over to the credenza, where family photos in various-sized frames line the surface. She zooms in on one with Rose and me, picks it up, and examines it.

I remember the day we took that picture as if it were yesterday. Last year, I convinced Rose to take a break from working on the art exhibition and go on a mini holiday with me. I promised to take her on a tour around Northern Ireland.

"That photo was taken at Clochán an Aifir," I tell June.

"The Causeway."

"That's right."

Rose is wearing the blue and grey scarf I gave her. It was so cold that day that I had to warm her hands with mine. Afterward, we returned to the car, and she scrolled through the photos.

"Look. This picture of us is beautiful, Aedan. It is one of those pictures you see in the movie when the guy and girl break up, and then they look back at some old photo during a flashback to happier times and the music queues, and they go searching for each other years later."

"You got all that from that picture? It sounds so tragic."

"Rewrite. It's one of those pictures which a mother shows her daughter and says, 'I hope you find what your father I had the day we took this picture.' Then they hug and cry together before the Hallmark Channel credits roll."

"Em, much better. But I am hoping it goes something like this. 'This picture was the first of many to document the lives of two people who spent a lifetime loving hard, playing hard, and working hard to save the planet and humanity together.'"

"That works, too. Although kind of mushy—I mean, lovely," she teased.

That was the first night I made love to Rose. It was the first time I felt I could have something more with a woman. I want to feel those things again...but with the right woman. It turns out we were both wrong about our predictions of that couple's future.

"Seems you still have a thing for my cousin," June says, pulling me out of my head.

"As you noticed, those are all family photos. You may have missed the one with my siblings, Rose, and me. Rose will be my sister-in-law soon. We've long since resolved what's between us. So no, I'm not carrying a torch for her. Have a seat, Miss Ross." I gesture toward the chair. June walks over to the table and sits in one of the chairs. I join her.

"I stand corrected."

"Listen, I think we got off on the wrong foot the last time we were together."

"On the contrary, we didn't get *off* on anything, Mr. King."

I chuckle, surprised by the sensual undercurrent of her comment. "Okay, let me put it another way. My tactics regarding getting to know you were…" I pause, considering my words. "Not as smooth as they could have been."

"So, you *were* trying to be smooth with me?"

"You're not going to make this easy on me, are you, Miss Ross?"

"I'm not easy."

I pinch the bridge of my nose. This woman is gorgeous and grating at the same time. If I didn't know Rose as well as I do, I would have thought she onboarded June to spite me. But like her cousin, June is brilliant and the perfect person to fill Rose's shoes as COO.

"We should discuss logistics surrounding your upcoming interview." She nods. "The team members are already on-site at the RTÉ, securing the location. When we arrive, I'll escort you from the car and into the building. Follow my lead, stay close to me, and don't stop walking unless I do."

"Do you anticipate the crowd getting out of hand?"

"I always anticipate the worst."

"You didn't answer my question. What do your sources tell you about this situation?"

"Despite your PR team's effort to calm the concerns of those interested, there are lingering sentiments against Ross Enterprises' expansion here. We expect the crowd to be loud but non-violent. I recommend we enter through the back of the building."

"No, I'm not hiding. Everyone knows this interview is taking place today."

"Then, under no circumstances should you deviate from protocol. If you do, you potentially put other lives at risk than your own."

"Don't worry. I understand."

CHAPTER 11

Space and Time

"A real friend is one who walks in when the rest of the world walks out."
– Walter Winchell

June

WHEN THE CAR ROUNDS the corner, I glimpse the enormous crowd in front of the RTÉ building. Now, I grasp the magnitude of what Aedan meant during the morning briefing when he mentioned that the security team intentionally prepared for the worst-case scenario. A news story about Carol pushing for tighter immigration policy, referencing Ross Enterprises' hiring practices as an example, broke just two hours before my interview.

Before I left the office to come here, Aedan informed me that a large crowd had gathered outside the studio. These were supporters of Carol, who had previously been arrested for her involvement in disrupting the Annual Patron of the Arts Exhibition and aiding the people trying to kidnap Rose Ross. I reviewed the briefing on the plane during my first visit to Belfast.

"Let them eat cake. Why direct provision works." The title of the original blog post written by Carol was about her campaign to keep direct provision alive and introduce her recommendation for further restric-

113

tions to impose on immigrants of African descent. The post was subsequently removed, and an apology was issued from the trade paper due to Aedan's intervention. The post, which referenced the direct provision system wherein thousands of Black immigrants to Ireland were placed upon arrival, was meant to garner support and incite hatred.

The air in the car is heavy, as if we're on the cusp of something. Twisting my ring, I stare ahead at the road partially obscured by the seatback and Aedan's body, as if it would provide me with answers. It doesn't.

Aedan breaks the silence. "When we arrive, do not exit the car until I open the door and help you out."

"Do you anticipate the crowd will be unruly?"

"With the recent stories posted online and all the news coverage, we can be sure there is a fairly large contingent who may be disruptive."

"Okay, I'll wait for your instructions." The car slows as we approach the building. The darkened sky has more to do with the weather than the tinted windows. The cobblestone streets are damp from a burst of rain making its way up the coast. A wall of people blocks the view of the front doors to the six-story pale brick building lined with windows.

"Seems I have quite the reception." I pull at the L on my gold "love" ring.

"Remember what I told you."

"I remember." The government issues on immigration and the influx of thousands of immigrants into the country are not my doing nor mine to solve. Aedan briefed me on several protests related to immigration that have taken place over the past few years and were unrelated to Ross Enterprises or the work Rose did last year. The catalyst for this crowd is his cousin Carol. Her contingents are here for the sole purpose of attracting media to her cause. Carol's agenda fuels them to want to take down a woman of African descent. Another foreigner in their eyes. In this case, we happen to represent the largest black-owned company in the world.

"Wait for me and follow my lead. My team will exit their cars first and secure a path. Do not respond to questions or leave my side until you have cleared lobby security inside the building."

"Got it."

The car stops, and I watch the team exit the front vehicle. The crowd scatters like leaves in the path of a leaf blower. When the team from the leading and rear cars reaches our vehicle, Aedan exits with a trench coat. He opens my door, extends his hand, and helps me out.

"Wait. Put this on."

"What is this for?"

He doesn't respond because he doesn't need to. I promised to follow his lead and stick to protocol. He holds a black trench coat out for me. I slip one arm in and then the other before facing Aedan. Hints of sandalwood and brown sugar envelop me. Standing before me, Aedan pulls the jacket closed and secures it with a belt. Looking up, I lean closer, allowing him to pull the hood over my head. His eyes never leave mine. The buzz from the crowd fades as I hold his gaze.

"Let's go, June," he says, then drapes his arm around me. "The queen has arrived," he calls to his team via earphones. He leads me through the crowd.

The crowd is peppered with anti-immigration protesters, bystanders, reporters from various networks, and vloggers. Some people chant, while others call out countless questions to me, waiting for a response.

"Miss Ross, tell us about your plans…" We continue pushing our way through the crowd. "Miss Ross, what do you think about the recent post by Ms. Murphy? Do you think the government should...." *Don't respond. Don't respond. Just keep walking.* I quietly repeat the mantra as more questions are tossed at me like grenades exploding above my head as I pass. "Miss Ross, what do you think about the recent article regarding direct provision?"

There's a muted pop and someone screams. It triggers a wave of panic, gasps, and coughing. Then, a crush of people rushes toward me, attempting to escape the source of disruption. *It's tear gas.* Somewhere deep in the crowd, someone either sprayed or tossed a tear gas container. There is a scuffle. I don't turn to see what's happening. We continue moving forward.

"Keep your head down." Aedan ushers me faster. A woman nearby screams when something hits her.

In unison, a wave of voices says, "Whoa." And then I sense the crowd fall away. Ben is on one side and Aedan is on the other. Aedan tightens his arm around my shoulders and continues ushering me toward the building. Ben clears a path to enter the building while the rest of the security team encircles us, keeping the crowd at bay.

Silence envelops me as I step into the building, the doors closing behind me, muting the chaos of the crowd. In the building, the team leads me through several layers of security until Aedan and I reach the elevator. The elevator doors close, and so do my eyes. I blow out a breath, inhale, and open my eyes.

Aedan stares at me while pushing the trench hood over my shoulders. "You did good."

"Because of you and your team."

The elevator door dings, alerting us that we've arrived at our floor. When the doors open, I am greeted by Ben, who'd preceded us. I follow him down a muted beige hallway with Aedan in tow. He stops in front of the door to my designated green room. The door opens. I step in and see London leaning against a wall. He pushes himself off and comes to greet me with open arms.

"Hey, beautiful." He wraps his arms around me and squeezes me tight. For a brief moment, I absorb the comfort his presence provides.

"What are you doing here?"

"I heard that the crowd was going to be rough. I wanted to be here for you." He puts his hands on my shoulders and steps back. "Are you okay?" He looks me up and down, then searches my eyes for answers.

"I—I'm good. The team…" I turn toward Aedan, who is silently watching the scene. He nods. "The team did great." Stepping back, I remove the trench coat and hand it to Aedan. "Thank you. I understand now why you gave it to me."

"We were lucky—this time. I'll be right here and take you to the studio when it's time," he says. He's right. We were lucky. There were no firebombs at this protest.

I turn to London. He steps closer to Aedan and me, removes an earphone from his ear, and hands it to Aedan.

"Thanks, mate," he tells Aedan. Aedan walk out the door, closing it behind him.

"You heard everything?" I ask.

"Yes."

London opens his hand to me. I take it and lean into him, trying to steady myself and not show the residual effects of fear. "I hate this."

"Talk to me, beautiful."

"Why can't people just be fucking normal? All the chaos outside is unnecessary. Can't these people see I'm not Rose?"

"You represent her. They're here to distract you. Don't let them. You have the lead. Don't allow anyone to take that from you."

"This is so hard."

London cups my cheek, dips his head, and kisses the corner of my lips. "I know," he whispers. "If it were easy, would it still be worth it?" I shake my head. "You have an interview to do. How can I help you?"

I pull away from him and walk toward a full-length mirror on the wall. "Exactly what you're doing. Be here for me." Be that friend who comes to find me just when I need him. Be my rock in a foreign country as I face foes who don't want people who look like me around. But I don't say that part aloud. Instead, I fluff my hair and fix my outfit.

I'm grateful for London. He didn't have to be here. He has his own business to run—a reputation to uphold. I laugh.

"What's so funny?"

"I'm being vulnerable when I tell you this."

"You're always safe with me."

"I spend a lot of time being scared because I insist on doing the difficult stuff alone, knowing that whatever it is, I can get through it even if it hurts. Even though sometimes I want to collapse on the floor in a ball when it's all over. Yet, when it's done, I feel an overwhelming sense of relief."

"Rightfully so."

"London, I should be afraid, but I'm not. When I stepped out of that car into a screaming crowd of people and someone tried to attack me, Aedan and his team had my back. I'm not used to that. When I walked down the hall, dreading facing the media, and the green room door opened, I saw you—the fear fell away." I walk to London and slide my arms around him. "I'm glad you're here."

He wraps an arm around me, and with his free hand, he dusts his thumb across my lips. "So am I. We'd be making out right now if this were the right space and time. I hope you know you mean the world to me." He smiles and I tap him on the bicep.

Untangling myself from him, I say, "You do a great job showing me just how much."

There's a knock at the door and Aedan steps in. "It's time," he says.

"Will you be here when it's over?" I ask London.

He purses his lips and shakes his head. "No. King and the team have a plan to exit you discreetly. If you're up for it, I'll pick you up for dinner later this evening."

I stand on my toes and kiss London on the cheek. "Okay, dinner," I say, then turn to leave.

"June."

"Yeah."

"I promise you'll be fine. Embrace the lead and don't look back."

I exit the room with Aedan. A production team member takes over, leading me to the studio where the interview will occur. Aedan watches as a team of people preps me for the interview. Someone touches up my makeup, and another reviews potential questions I'll be asked. Once they clear, I stay in the director's chair, quietly reviewing my notes. Aedan walks over and kneels beside me.

"I'll be inside the control room waiting for you to finish your interview. Once you're done, they'll remove your microphone, and I'll escort you out. As before, don't stop to answer any questions on the way out." I nod. Aedan leaves and disappears into the darkened room behind the cameras.

"Next up, we have June Ross from Ross Enterprises," a faceless voice says.

The television crew begins their production dance. Someone puts a microphone on me. Another person escorts me to the empty leather club chair on a small platform. A short, round vase filled with white flowers sits on a small table between the chairs. I sit in my designated spot. The show host, Sharon Collier, sits in a club chair across from me.

"Counting down. Five. Four. Three. Two. And we're back."

Sharon begins her introduction. "Welcome back to Belfast Today, where you get up-to-the-minute happenings nationwide. I want to introduce our next guest. June Ross is the chief operations officer for one of the world's largest companies, Ross Enterprises. Ross Enterprises recently established an entity in Ireland that provides businesses with an artificial intelligence platform that they say will transform how work gets done. Miss Ross, your company recently acquired space from King Enterprise. Can you tell us how the build-out is going?"

"First, thank you for inviting me here. Yes. We've situated the company in the eight-story Falcon building. Currently, operations are going as planned. We are betting big on building a large part of our technology in Ireland. We hope to attract the brightest and best talent in Belfast."

"Employment opportunities are always a plus. However, when we hear about artificial intelligence technology, one typically associates it with machines replacing jobs that humans previously did. Is that the case with Ross Enterprises?"

"On the contrary, our business provides companies with a means to operate more efficiently through AI technology, which in turn frees up funds to allow them to grow their company faster. Companies can leverage those dollars to reinvest in hiring talent to help expand their customer reach."

"When you put it like that, it sounds like a win-win situation."

"Facts tend to speak louder than speculation."

"I'd like to change the subject for a bit. Most recently, your newly appointed president, Rose Ross, was here for an extended trip."

"That's right. Last summer, Miss Ross hosted the Annual Patron of the Arts Exhibition on behalf of Brianna Morrison."

"Following Ms. Ross' visit, news circulated that an arrest was made of one of Mrs. Morrison's close family members. What are your thoughts about Carol Murphy getting out of jail?"

"Sharon, I have no comment regarding the circumstances surrounding Ms. Murphy's arrest last year. It's unrelated to Ross Enterprises' operations. Do you have any additional questions I can answer for you related to Ross Enterprises and its presence in Ireland?"

"Where do you stand on Ireland's immigration policy as it relates to opportunities at Ross Enterprises in Belfast?"

"At Ross Enterprises, we fully intend to abide by the local laws about hiring."

The interviewer tries several more times to get me to talk about Carol, but gives up once she understands that the only questions I'll answer relate to my company.

"Well, that's all the questions we have, Miss Ross. Thank you for taking the time to talk with us at Belfast Today." Sharon stares into the camera. "Next up. Cooking with Catherine."

"Cut, someone says off-camera. "Collect her microphone."

I stand, and a crew member begins unwiring my microphone. I walk toward the direction I last saw Aedan. He appears out of the darkness.

"I have the queen," Aedan says into his headphones. "Ready?" He waits for my response.

"Yes."

Aedan leads me out of the studio and down the hall to a different set of elevators than we previously used. The elevator ride is quiet. I study Aedan's stoic face, trying to understand his seemingly detached stance. It bothers me how men can easily disassociate themselves from everything. It was evident in Leon. I witnessed it firsthand with my dad. I waited years for him to show some outward emotion that signified that he cared for Mom as much as I did. Instead, I watched him move on with another woman, making me question his love for Mom. And, in turn, reflecting our importance, or lack of it, to him.

The elevator ride to the ground level is swift. When the doors open, Aedan's team encircles me as we walk toward the rear exit. He doesn't look at me but focuses on leading me from the building. He has the look of a man on a mission.

London

Chapter 12

If Only

"No human relation gives one possession in another—every two souls are absolutely different. In friendship or in love, the two side by side raise hands together to find what one cannot reach alone."
– Kahlil Gibran

June

One hour and twenty-five minutes. *I can handle that,* I tell myself as I ascend the metal stairs to the airplane. I do quick math in my head. That's about 25,500 words further along that I can get reading my book. I can listen to twenty songs on my *Feel You There* playlist. Not that I have a man to feel me anywhere. Or clear out one hundred and seventy work emails—all acceptable alternatives to an awkward, forced discussion with Aedan. *Where is Troy when I need him?* I sigh.

Instead of sitting across the aisle from me on the plane, Aedan sits in the seat facing me. *Damn it. Why does he have to be so fucking fine?* He looks at me in a way that feels as if he's penetrating my soul. Heat rises from my core. I open my tablet, attempting to avoid his gaze.

"You look regal. That style is very becoming," he says, lifting his chin.

"Are you complimenting my hairstyle, Mr. King?"

"I am."

Like most of his responses, it's terse. My cousin warned me about that. She said Aedan was like Troy in that sense, and so far, she's right.

"They're knotless fairy twists," I tell him, although that likely means nothing to him. Nor does he know how long it takes to accomplish a style that extends the length of my hair six inches. I wonder what he knows about black women beyond his experience with my cousin. Like me, Rose usually wears her hair naturally or sometimes pressed, depending upon the look we're trying to achieve. However, I've never seen her in braids. Aedan continues staring at me like he's about to devour me.

I need to break this spell he's casting over me. "Troy mentioned James in his initial security brief with me. Is there anything more on this guy? Should I be worried?"

"I'm tracking his activities. He's been quiet. There is nothing new to report."

"London would tell me if something came to his attention."

"Perhaps." His eyes shift from me to the cabin window and then back to me. "The lunch date with Aaron seems to be last minute. Are there any other outings my team and I need to be aware of that we don't have on schedule?"

"It's not a date. It's a luncheon."

"Okay, luncheon. As I told you before, Ms. Ross, my team needs to prepare in advance. It's for your safety."

"Have I told you I've managed just fine without security for years? Besides, it's awkward having you follow me when Kent and his team can easily handle me and London."

"I'm doing my job."

"I get that. But when I'm with London, two security teams feel like overkill."

"If something happens, Kent's priority is to protect Aaron."

"And London will protect me," I counter.

"No. I'll protect you because I go where you go. Now, Ms. Ross, is there anything else I need to know about your schedule?"

"I'm not done—"

"Discussing my role? Unless you have more information about your schedule, we are done." I narrow my eyes, glaring at him. He holds my gaze unflinching. "I'll accept your silence as affirmation," he adds.

Bastard.

***

Traffic in central London is a nightmare. Instead of taking London up on his offer to pick me up from my client meeting, I decided to meet him at the luncheon event location. The last thing I want to do is make him late for his presentation. When I arrive at the venue, he's outside waiting for me. I anticipate an awkward exchange between the two friends, but there is none. When London approaches, he pauses, allowing Aedan to open the car door for me. Aedan doesn't need to be here. He could have assigned any member of his team to my security detail. Yet, something holds him to me. I hate to admit that I feel it, too.

London lifts his chin to Aedan. "King," he greets him. Aedan nods and extends his hand to help me exit the car. As I step out of the car, I lock eyes with Aedan. A look of understanding passes between us. They may be mates, but this is not a casual visit between friends. Aedan has a job to do.

I go to London. He snakes an arm around my waist and pulls me into him. My jumbo hair twists are so long that they, along with me, get wrapped in his embrace. "What are you trying to do to me, June?" He tugs at my hair, tipping my head back so that I am staring up at him. He dips his head and presses his nose to mine. "If only," he whispers. The warmth of his breath caresses my face. The look of desire in his eyes makes my knees weak. He doesn't have to finish his sentence.

"If only you were mine, I'd give you the world." Those were the words he said to me the last night I saw him in Belfast. We were standing near the door to my apartment. I leaned against him, and he wrapped his arms around me. Between us, evidence of his desire pressed against my body. He's looking at me now with the same intensity as when he spoke those words before kissing my cheek. Then he left.

"Hey," I whisper. "You know you're not supposed to touch my hair."

"You're not supposed to look so edible." He kisses me on the forehead, releases me, and takes my hand, lacing his fingers in mine. "Come on."

I follow London into the building. The luncheon is being held at the rooftop restaurant.

"I appreciate you being my plus one."

"The way you flashed those sultry grey eyes when you asked…how could I say no?"

"Then this is a date?"

"No." I press my lips together and smile to keep from laughing out loud.

London and I are seated in front, to the left of the podium, at the guest speaker table, which is a mix of executives from various high-tech companies. Several round tables, each with table settings for eight, are strategically spaced in a room that could easily hold a hundred people.

Looking around the room, I notice familiar faces from Saola. I have fond memories of my time working for the Adler brothers.

The program begins, and speakers from our table go to the podium one by one, introduce themselves, and give a plug for their respective companies and their contributions to AI technology. During this time, the staff serves drinks, light appetizers, and salads. As the servers begin clearing the plates and preparing to serve lunch, the moderator announces London as the keynote speaker.

He wipes his mouth with a napkin, then whispers in my ear, "Hope I'm not as boring as this meal they're serving. I promise dinner tonight will be amazing."

I turn to him and smile. "You're oozing with charm and a brilliant businessman. You could never be boring. Now kick butt with your keynote."

He chuckles. "See, this is why you're here. You're just what I need. Thank you." He squeezes my hand and then goes to the podium.

As he takes the podium, I scan the room. All eyes are on him. Why wouldn't they be? He's handsome and charismatic. I spot Milly from the Saola marketing team looking toward the stage with a mile-wide smile. She always had a thing for London. Next to her is...James? In a room full of people focused on the stage, his eyes are locked on me. *Why?* I stare at him until his eyes shift from me to London on stage, then back to me. What's his problem? I look away and search the room, conscious that Aedan is somewhere watching me. Like a magnet, my eyes are immediately drawn to him standing in the corner. I see a hint of something briefly pass in his expression. He tips his head toward the stage. I comply and refocus my attention on the keynote.

"But there's a team of people that makes all this possible, which consists of current employees and alumni sitting in this room," London says. When he says alumni, I know he's referring to me. Our eyes lock. He nods and I smile. He continues, and I listen proudly as he delivers an inspirational and informative keynote.

When he's done, everyone applauds. Someone stands, and everyone in the room joins in, including me. He doesn't wait for the audience to sit before exiting the stage. He returns to the table and places a hand on the small of my back.

"You have them eating out of your hands," I tell him.

"That's the effect you have on me. Have a seat, beautiful." I sit, and he pushes my chair in for me. "Did you have the main course?"

"No. I was waiting for you."

He looks around at the plates on the table and the partially eaten meals. "It doesn't look very appetizing. There are forty minutes left in this program. My portion is complete. I'll take you for a proper lunch before the real estate tour. You okay with that?"

"Sure."

London stands, helps me up, and we head toward the nearest exit. I turn before the door closes and notice Aedan is no longer in the room. In the hallway, our security teams are waiting. I spot Aedan at the end of the hall. We walk in that direction. I don't know what to tell Aedan about where we're headed, but I discover I don't need to. London has a conversation with him before we exit the building.

Aedan is masterful at masking his feelings. Unlike our conversation on the flight this morning, he seems unfazed about the change in plans. Or maybe it has more to do with his relationship with London. It's not my business as long as there's no tension between the two.

For lunch, London takes me to one of his favorite restaurants, Circolo Popolare, where we have a nice Italian meal. The conversation is light and easy. We don't talk about relationships or work. We take time to catch up on our lives and be normal people. At this moment, he's not the president of Saola's European operations, and I'm not the chief operations officer for a trillion-dollar company. I listen intently as he gives me the scoop on some of my brother's crazy antics when they were in school together. And he laughs at my corny jokes. When my hair falls close to my fork, he sweeps it over my shoulders so I don't get food in it. There's an ease in the way we are with each other. He eats some of my pasta, and I taste his truffle pizza.

"I wish I could be here with you tomorrow," he says.

"Closing your client in Geneva is more important."

"Not more important than you. You know that."

"Still, you need to be there. Like I'll spend my time between here, Ireland, and the US. It's who we are."

"I'll be with you at the rally at city hall in San Francisco."

"You and I haven't traveled together this much since university."

"You're good company."

"Speaking of company, I'll get a reprieve from your mate for the few days I'm back in the city."

"He's not so bad. You two are a lot alike."

I bark out a laugh. "He wishes. I'm just happy for the break."

"I was concerned initially, but I contacted Troy, and he assured me Mack would meet us at the plane as soon as we land."

"Tell me you're not all in my business."

"I can't lie, I'm all in your business. And before you ask, your brother didn't put me up to it."

I stare at London for a few seconds, reading all the unspoken words in his eyes. "You don't have to say more. This won't be like the RTÉ thing, but thank you."

"Now, don't give my mate a hard time tomorrow, okay?"

"I'll try."

I'm tempted to ask about his relationship with Aedan but decide against it. Whatever is between them is theirs. My focus is protecting what I have with London—a friendship I never want to let go of.

***

My day so far has been busy yet beneficial. London wasn't kidding when he said we could fit in time to see all the office spaces his agent lined up.

I walk across the space, noting the modern parquet chevron floor design on my way to the wall of windows overlooking the busy streets. "This is a bright, airy space. Considering we're in London and it's overcast most days, the space still has a good vibe. The architecture is beautiful. The square footage supplies room for expansion. Accessibility is perfect. This is a contender." I turn towards London, leaning against the doorframe, hands in his pockets, watching me and looking content. He's been that way most of today.

"Brilliant, that's three out of three." He smiles smugly, pushing himself off the wall. He closes the distance between us in a few strides, surrounding me in his aura.

"You give good recommendations."

"I know a little something about this city."

"I suppose it works in your favor that most of the locations are within walking distance of Saola."

"There's that. So, have you considered my suggestion about bringing Raven Nichols onto your project team? Our plan was always to pair you two had you stayed with Saola."

"She's smart. I never met anyone like her. The information she holds in her head—wow, she's like a legal search engine."

"She doesn't forget a thing."

"I took your suggestion and reached out to her boss. Alejandro and I worked out an agreement. I added her to the team to help structure a deal with the real estate development firm I identified. Her expertise will come in handy. If she does well, I'll bring her on as lead counsel."

"She won't disappoint."

"I suspect she won't. We both learned from the best. You and your brothers have a reputation for developing powerhouse women. Does that bother you, after all your time and investment in growing talent, to see us leave and fly on our own?"

"Why would it? That was our goal—impart every bit of business learning we have and allow you to shine. I'm doing my part to pave the way for women to thrive. Isn't that how it should be?"

"Not everyone feels the same as you."

"I can't speak for everyone. But I am proud that you and Rose hold the number one and two spots at one of the largest companies in the world." He puts his arm around my waist. "Are you ready to head out, or do you want to see more spaces?"

"I've seen enough."

***

Spending the day with London has been lovely. He somehow got Aedan to back off, albeit slightly. I believe stealth mode is what they call it, although I miss catching glimpses of Aedan. *Do I miss him?*

Our dinner restaurant is lively. Of course, London would pick a hip spot swimming with people. Returning to his roots in his namesake, London, building Saola's European operations, he seems at home—this is his playground. Unlike me, he belongs here.

I look around to find quite a few eyes on us. I tip my head toward a group of female patrons checking us out. "You're drawing a lot of attention."

"Right? I can say the same for you. You are stunning. I haven't been able to keep my eyes off you all day. And the hairstyle you're wearing—those twists. My God, woman, if only you were mine, I'd show you how much you mean to me." He caresses my hair and brushes it over my shoulder.

"You make a point of telling me every time I see you. Now, calm down. If you pull my hair again, I'll smack you."

"I'd love that."

"You're too much. You know that?"

"You already know my intentions. Tell me who I need to talk to next to get a chance with you—you uncle, your dad, Rose?" he chuckles. "Talk to me, June."

"I've sworn off men."

"Because of Leon. Do you think I'd hurt you that way?"

"No, but..."

"June, we talked about this. Don't put me in that general all-men buck-et. You've gotten a glimpse of what life would be like with me." He knows me too well. And I've spent enough time around him to know how good it could be. The luxury, travel, and lifestyle would leave nothing to be desired. But is it enough? Would there be a deep burning love? There are moments like this when London is so close that I wish the air crackled between us. When I wish my eyes sparkled for him. When I wish I could give him what he wants—my heart.

I can't.

"You're right. There's not much I don't know about you. I made a promise to come to you when I'm ready. I'm not there."

"I understand."

"So, who are you backfilling my vacant role with?" I ask, changing the subject.

"I see what you did there." He smiles and brushes a thumb across my cheek. "We plan to promote someone. You did an awesome job of men-toring the team and creating a strong leadership bench for us to choose from."

"Alex should be happy."

"Although he's happy with your success, he's still secretly sad you left."

"I love that man to death. Do I need to call him or something? I'm surprised he gave my leaving a second thought."

"You're joking, right? Look at the lengths we were willing to go to keep you at Saola. And what's with the love you have for my brother? I feel slighted."

"Get over yourself." I laugh, but it's cut short by a weighted chair scrap-ing across the floor. My head instinctively snaps in the direction of the noise. I'm unable to see what's happening because London reaches his arm across my lap and positions his upper body in front of me. I lean forward, attempting to peek over his shoulder, but he won't let me.

"I don't give a fuck what you say. I'll hunt him down and kill the bastard." The heavily German-accented man's voice echoes through the restaurant. I'm stunned by the outburst. It's the kind of activity I'd expect in a local pub on the wrong side of town, not an established high-end London eatery. The room falls eerily silent as everyone focuses their attention on the source of the commotion.

I rest a hand on London's arm.

"Don't move." His voice is stern, showing a side of him I rarely see. "Let the team do their job."

I cannot move to verify, but I sense a familiar presence nearby, followed by a familiar scent I know all too well. I look to my side to confirm my suspicion. *Aedan.* His mere presence calms me.

"What are you doing? Let me go," the unruly man screams.

"It's under control, June. Seven seconds. It'll be over," Aedan's voice descends on me just above a whisper. I count the seconds in my head. Seven. Six. Five. Then, as if nothing had happened, the voices of the other patrons slowly fill the restaurant again. Aedan returns to his former post.

London removes his arm, giving me space, and turns to me. He cups my cheek and holds my gaze like he's searching for something to signal that I'm okay. He knows my life story. He senses my mood. I hate this part—there's always a constant reminder that there are bad people out there who won't hesitate to hurt someone. I nod. He pulls me into a hug. "They're gone," he reassures me.

I turn toward the original direction of the commotion. The wait staff swiftly clears the table that's no longer occupied. Near the front door, Aedan stands guard with Kent watching us.

"Is this my life now, London?"

"It'll never be like before." I don't want to admit he's right. As long as I stick to protocol, I have nothing to fear in public. Still, the memories linger.

"I need a drink."

"Sidecar?"

"Please."

He raises his hand and flags a server, but the manager comes over instead.

"I apologize for the commotion, Mister Adler, Miss Ross. Your meal is on the house."

"That's not necessary. The lady will have a sidecar, and I'll have Middleton 84 neat. Thank you."

"I'll bring that right away, sir." The manager says and walks away.

And just like that, life goes on.

CHAPTER 13

Sunshine

"You cannot protect yourself from sadness without protecting yourself from happiness."
– Jonathan Safran Foer

June

FOLLOWING THE COMMOTION AT the restaurant, when it's time to return to my hotel, I decline London's offer for a nightcap. At the hotel, we pause near the entrance to my suite while the King Enterprise team does their security sweep. Reflecting on the day's events has me lost in my feelings. He rubs his thumb across my hand, pulling me out of my head.

"You okay?"

I smile at him and nod. He returns my smile—it's warm, welcoming, seductive. I lean in, embracing him. He wraps his arms around me, and I'm seconds away from stealing the kiss I've long since denied myself. As I stand one leg on either side of his, the warmth of his body against mine makes my body buzz. How do I resist London when all I want is for him to pick me up, take me inside, and spread me on the bed? He senses it because he dusts his lips across mine instead of kissing my cheek.

We're locked in a moment of uncertainty, wavering about which direction to take our relationship. We want the same thing for different reasons.

I continue leaning against London in the doorway as we wait for Ben to complete his security checks.

"It's been a while since we've spent an entire day together," he whispers. His lips are so close to mine that claiming them is a heartbeat away.

Kiss me. Take me. Make all the pain from the past disappear. Make me forget that bad people exist. Make me feel alive, I say to myself, in a futile attempt to Jedi mind trick him into hearing me. But he doesn't. He won't touch me that way unless I say the words aloud. I want to say them solely to satiate the throbbing between my thighs. I don't dare. It's not fair...to him.

"I had a good time."

"Promise you'll call me if you need anything before I see you again."

"You're insane for flying to the States to attend a rally with me."

"I'd be insane not to. Promise me—if you need anything—."

"You got me." I finish his sentence.

"Always." He holds me a few moments more, stroking my hair while I rest my head on his chest and listen to his heartbeat. When Ben emerges from the room, London untangles himself from me. "I'll see you in San Francisco," he says, then touches my cheek and leaves.

That was an hour ago. Since then, I've had a glass and a half of wine while wading waist-deep in my thoughts. How do I make Dad see my way of thinking regarding Mom? Can I pull off this growth strategy for Ross Enterprises? How do I navigate this thing with London? He's so charming. I even changed into my body-con tank dress, contemplating whether to pay him a late-night visit, but I couldn't bring myself to drag him into my mess. *What's happening to me?*

I sip my wine and then check my phone. There are three missed messages, one from Jake, Jasmine, and the other from Nicole. I don't bother to open them. I place my phone on the counter and push it away. It accidentally collides with the wine glass, knocking it over and causing it to break. Red wine splashes across the white countertop. *Damn it.*

I round the counter, grab a handful of paper towels, and clean my mess. When I think I'm done cleaning, I notice drops of red liquid on the counter. *Shit.* It's my blood. Twisting my hand, I locate the open wound and use a paper towel to apply pressure to the cut. I get another glass and pour myself more wine. Trickles of blood track my movements. *Shoot, how deep is this thing?* I run my hand under the tap, allowing water to wash away the blood and flush my wound. The swirl of blood mixed with water triggers an old memory of blood pooled on the floor. *It wasn't a dream.* My mind races. I feel faint. Grabbing my phone, I head toward the door. I need to get out of here. I need air. I can have London get me. As I reach for the door, my phone buzzes. Maybe it's him. I check to find a calendar notification I'd previously set, marking the hour of my last moment with her. *Mom. Oh god, I miss you so much.*

I'm overcome with an onslaught of emotions. The room begins spinning. I press my back against the wall, using it to maintain my balance as I slide down. As I collapse, my shoulder collides with the side table, causing a flower vase to fall, crashing to the floor, splattering water, and sending shards of glass across the room. Scattered shards reflecting the pieces of my life I've had to pull together one by one since the day she died.

I bury my face in my hand, hiding the assault of angry tears streaming down my cheeks. My breath comes out in short, jagged bursts as I try to steady it.

"No," a deafening scream escapes me.

Bang. The door from the adjoining suite slams against the wall. A woosh of air swirling with sandalwood envelops me before strong arms surround me—one on my waist, the other beneath my bent knees. *Aedan*. I'm weightless as he lifts my body from the floor and carries me away.

"Are you okay? June, talk to me. What happened?" His voice is ripe with concern, attempting to extract me from my anguish.

"What? Where are we going?" I ask, confused, covering my face as hot tears stream from my eyes, soaking my hands.

"Ben, I need you up here. Now. Secure this room and get a clean-up crew in here." Aedan's voice is low yet commanding. My mind is reeling while memories of the day I'll never forget run on repeat. Surf-sized waves of grief wash over me and I struggle to breathe.

Aedan lowers me onto a chair. His arms' comfort is soon replaced by a blanket covering me. He wraps his hands around my wrists, gently coaxing my hands from my face.

"June. Please talk to me." His voice is steady and low. "What is this? You're hurt. Who did this?" Even with my eyes closed, I sense his absence when he walks away. Seconds later, he takes my hand and places it on his knee. "You'll feel a slight sting, but it won't last." He says right before something cold and wet touches the spot where I cut myself. The sting causes me to flinch, but I don't pull away. Cool air from his breath caresses my skin as he blows on my wound to dry it. Then he presses on the cut, and I know without looking he's done. I pull my hand away and bury my head in my hands.

Aedan takes my wrists and pulls my hands away again. "Whatever it is, it's okay. I got you. You'll be all right. Just talk to me, sunshine." It's as if a switch flips at the sound of the sentiment. My eyes fly open and land on Aedan kneeling before me. He reaches up and tucks a stray lock of hair over my shoulder, away from my face. Gone is the scowl that usually greets me, replaced with eyes that are soft yet searching. "There you are. Now, tell me what's going on."

I want to get up and return to my room, but I can't move. This is all too much. What do I tell him? How do I express that I feel everything all at once layered over my life? How do I convey that the lingering pain of losing my mom cuts me to the core as memories of that fatal day consume me? How do I dissolve the hardness in my heart, forged like hammered steel since the day I confronted Leon? Who will help me bear the weight of becoming the most recognizable COO in the world? I can't reveal that I live with the guilt of loving a friend who wants more than I can give, and I'm sinking.

"I...I'll be all right." I can get through this. I always do. I inhale to get my breathing under control. "Can I have some water?"

"Give me a second." Aedan rubs his fingers along my wrists before letting them go. He stands, goes to the kitchen, opens a water bottle, pours it into a glass, and brings it to me.

"Have a sip. You're safe here," he assures me.

"Thank you, but I should go." My words come out in a whisper. I move to stand, but Aedan places his hand on my shoulder.

"No. You need to talk to me. Tell me what's going on. How did you get this?" He touches my hand with the band-aid on it. "Why is there broken glass in your suite?"

"I have to go."

"June. I need to understand what's happening. Did Aaron do something?"

"What? Oh my god, no. He'd never.... Why would you think—?"

"Then you need to explain to me what happened. I'm not leaving you alone."

"It's okay. I can manage. I'll be fine."

"If you want, I can call Aaron and have him stay with you here. But under no circumstance will you be alone—not tonight. Even if I have to sit in a corner and watch you."

"Aedan." My voice is barely above a whisper.

"Your choice. It's Aaron or me. Either way, you won't be alone."

"Don't disturb him."

"Then you have to talk to me. I promise I won't bite." The corner of his mouth tips into a wry grin. "That is unless you request it."

I stare at Aedan; his devilish grin makes me smile, easing my angst.

"I won't ask you to bite me any time soon."

"Hmm. It sounds like there's still a chance. I'm a patient man." He winks. I don't know how he did it, but I feel lighter.

Aedan stands, walks to the credenza across the room, and grabs a few sheets of facial tissue from a box. My eyes follow his movements. He's a stunning specimen—strong, confident, and commanding. He often drives me crazy, but right now, he's managed to calm me down and capture my attention. He turns, holding my gaze as he heads toward me.

He hands me the tissue. "You may have noticed that you're in my suite." I nod. "Ben is looking after yours. Someone will come to clean up the glass and refresh your suite. I'll take you over to grab whatever you need. You'll be staying in the main bedroom here tonight. I'll take one of the spare rooms." He gestures his hand toward the hall. "First, you need to talk to me, June. I'm here to protect you but I need to know what I'm dealing with. What happened in there?"

With slow, deliberate movements, I clean my face. He's waiting for me to say something that'll help him help me. I want to tell him everything. I need to tell him. But can I trust him? If I open up and share the things that haunt me—memories I wish I could bury beside my mom, memories I can't seem to shake—how will he see me then?

Only a few people know about our family history. When the article about my mom made it to the San Francisco Chronicle, it put a target on my back and anyone at close range to me. My dad couldn't get them to retract the story, so my uncle leveraged his power to bury it—to remove all digital footprints that tie me to that fated day. People may have seen me that afternoon in the restaurant. Although no one knew my name or who I was with, they knew I locked eyes with the devil. He's still out there. He can never know who I am. It would be equivalent to handing a criminal the keys to the bank vault. Some people already want to find any weakness in order to gain access to the technology our family has developed. This man would likely do anything to keep me from placing him there that day.

I tilt my head to talk to Aedan, who towers above me. "Can you sit?' His six-foot-three muscle mass frame is not only intimidating, but also distracting. "You're easier to bear when you're sitting."

Aedan laughs, lightening the mood. "The lady wants me on the floor?"

"Well, I suppose you can kneel like before."

"Bringing a King to his knees?" He laughs harder this time, which also makes me laugh.

"I only meant you're less intimidating when you're not standing over me."

Aedan grabs a matching lounge chair, positions it across from me, and sits.

He leans forward with his arms resting on his thighs and his hands clasped. "Better?"

"Thanks. I don't know what came over me tonight. As you witnessed, the day was beautiful—it was extremely busy but good." I glance over Aedan's shoulder at a watercolor painting of Tower Bridge hanging above the credenza where he retrieved the tissue. His suite mirrors mine but in reverse and with slightly different decor.

"Nothing stood out as unusual for me. You stuck to the schedule. I assume something changed when you got back to your suite. I heard noises. You screamed. What happened?"

"I accidentally knocked over my wine glass. I didn't realize I'd cut my hand while cleaning it up."

"At that point, you should have alerted me. Your cut is not that deep, but it could have been worse. I can't protect you if you disregard protocol."

I didn't think it was that bad, but I don't tell him. Instead, I say, "I'll remember for next time. I thought I had stopped the bleeding but noticed a trail of blood on the counter and went to rinse my hand. The sight of all the blood swirling in the water triggered a memory. My phone buzzed. I'd set a re-occurring event years ago." I close my eyes, recalling the moment. I press my fingers to my eyes as a fresh wave of emotions threatens to overtake me again.

Aedan touches my knee. His gestures are subtle yet comforting. I take a deep breath, uncover my eyes, and look at him. He nods.

"When I was eight, my family and I went out for a day of shopping. We had a lot of stores to cover in a short time, so we split up. My dad and Jake went to men's stores and took my little sister Jasmine. She was daddy's girl—still is. I went with my mom. I loved shopping with her. Even at the age of eight, I tried to emulate her style. She was a wonderful dresser—so was my grandmother. I remember her watching an old movie—Mahagony. I was fascinated by the seventies clothing styles. I suppose that's why I dress the way I do now. Modern hippie is what I call it."

Aedan smiles. "I can see that. You have a great sense of style."

"We had a late start. By the time we got around to eating, it was around three o'clock. My father and Jake hadn't completed their shopping yet, so Mom and I got to pick the restaurant. They planned to join us once they finished shopping. We both love Japanese food—and went to our favorite restaurant. I secured a table while Mom went to the counter to place our order." I close my eyes, reliving that moment, thinking about the late afternoon sun shining through the window, the people, the sounds. I remember everything before the moment that ended it all.

When I open my eyes, Aedan extends his hand to me. Instinctively, I place mine in his. "A guy in a hoodie came rushing through the front door toward the register. He didn't see me. He didn't even know I was there until..." I take a deep breath. "Until he shot her. He shot her in the back. That fucking coward shot my mom in her back. I couldn't do anything about it. She turned. The look in her eyes revealed the moment she knew something was wrong. She was hit, but still, she was searching for me. She fell to the floor. I started to get up, but someone grabbed my shoulders. The gunman waved his hand over the counter and demanded the clerk give him money. The others behind the counter were hunched down with their hands up. After the clerk handed over the money, the gunman shoved it in his pocket and swung his gun around the room toward the rest of us. Everyone ducked. Not me. When I looked into his eyes, they were black as coal. I couldn't see the rest of his face because it was covered. Seconds later, sirens blared in the distance; he lowered his gun and left. I ran to the counter and pushed past several people who were huddled over my mom, who was lying in a pool of blood."

"June." He squeezes my hand.

"She's gone. I always thought my mother would die by the crack of a baton at the hands of police during a protest, not by a bullet from a gun of a fucking criminal looking for a fistful of cash. He's still out there. I'll never get her back and never forget that day." I can't control the flood of emotions that rush like a raging river carrying me out to sea. I cover my face as my body begins to shake. I feel myself being pulled to my feet and into Aedan's arms.

He holds me tight. "You're okay. I got you." I linger in his embrace, letting the strength in his voice and the stroke of his hand on my back soothe me. The memory of my mom lays fresh like an open wound between us. "Just breathe."

I should have seen this coming. Throughout the day, the upcoming anniversary of her death lay dormant in my mind. Now at the forefront, its hand on my neck, forcing me to remember. Convincing me that if I could solve her murder. That if I could find the monster and confront him, then I could free myself of the trauma of that day.

Focus, I tell myself. I inhale and allow his scent to envelop me. Count his breaths. Think about the good things she left behind. Her beauty my sister and I inherited. My sense of style. My love of flowers. My courage. I slide my hands up Aedan's chest and press against the wall of muscles. He stiffens and then releases me.

"I apologize," he says as he steps back from me. The storm brewing in his eyes transforms them from shades of aquamarine to sapphire.

"It's fine. I'm a mess. You were trying to help me. I shouldn't have unloaded all that on you. There's nothing that can be done. I should go." I rub my hands down the sides of my dress.

With his hands curled at his sides, he turns and walks away, possibly processing my words, his actions, or both. I remember when Rose described how passionate the King brothers were and how they responded when angry. It's a look I never thought I'd have a reason to see, but now I'm witnessing an angry King. *But what's bothering him?*

"June." He turns toward me and gestures for me to walk toward the door. "Let's go get your things for tonight. I meant it when I said you're not staying alone. Are you sure you don't want me to contact Aaron?"

I shake my head. "I'm sure. Are you angry with me?"

"No, June. I'm mad at the monster who did this to you. I promise you'll always be safe with me."

CHAPTER 14

London

"There is a charm about the forbidden that makes it unspeakably desirable."
– Mark Twain

Aedan

THE SUN STREAMS THROUGH the luxury suite high above the London skyline. Gone is any semblance of rain from yesterday, along with faded memories of last night.

"I'll be waiting at the door," I say into my earphones to Ben, who is escorting a room-service staff member to my suite. I don't want to risk anyone ringing the bell to the suite and waking June.

She had a rough night. I listened as she expressed her feelings about what happened to her mom until she was all talked out and tired. Then, she fell fast asleep, feet tucked under her, curled in a ball on my lounge chair until it was time to hold her in my arms again.

She never opened her eyes when I picked her up, carried her to the room, and put her to bed. Sitting in a chair nearby, I watched her for an hour as she slept. A sliver of light coming through the crack in the door cast a soft hue on her face. The beautiful brown eyes I love to stare into were hidden behind closed eyelids. Locks of hair splayed wildly across the pillow like a crown. Even sound asleep, she's captivating.

It was the right thing to do, putting myself on June's detail instead of Ben, which was my original plan. Ben is great with clients. I'd be lying to myself if I said I didn't think he could handle June's emotional crisis. He could handle her just fine—I watched how he managed with Rose in the past. My need to be near June goes deeper. Something in me gravitated to protect her. Reading her file before she arrived in Belfast gave me a sense of who she is. Talking to her last night helped fill in many of the blanks.

I know what it is like to lose a parent to an act of violence. I can relate to the feeling of helplessness but also the anguish in the inability to save a loved one. It's partially the reason I dedicate my career to personal protection services. I suspect it's also why Niall followed in my footsteps. Last night, June didn't need physical protection from some assailant. She needed an emotional connection to someone—space to be vulnerable—a place to free fall. And I was there to catch her.

"Do you need a break, Boss? I can take over for you," Ben says as he directs the staff to place the food on the table.

"No, I'm good, thanks," I observe as they rearrange the plates, one in front of each chair, and strategically lay hot food dishes with silver lids around the table. "That'll be all," I tell them, and then Ben and the hotel staff member leave the suite.

I stand at the threshold where the living space meets the hallway leading to the bedrooms. I lean, arms crossed, shoulder pressed against the wall, and stare, lost in thoughts of last night. It gives me comfort knowing that June is sleeping in the next room. She's safe. She's with me.

June is strong and beautiful. And I brace myself for when she wakes, anticipating the independent, feisty side will be on display. She's been combative with me since her arrival in Europe. Yet, last night, she surprised me with her vulnerability. I was even more amazed I could calm her down enough to tell her story. She drew me in as she chronicled her life. I wanted to pick her up, pull her into my lap, hold her tight, and kiss away her tears. But I can't.

My job is to protect her, not pamper her. The last thing I want to do is blur the lines. Had I done more last night, my behavior may have brought me dangerously close to doing just that. When I pulled her into my arms, I sensed a connection that shouldn't exist. I had to pull away, apologize, and provide her with space to punctuate the conversation her way. At times, that meant tears-soaked tissue or stretches of silence. My job was to listen unbiasedly, understand her concerns, and alleviate her fears.

I listened patiently as she intricately detailed the events of the day her mother was cut down in a random act of violence. Heat edged up my spine as an unexpected wave of searing rage washed over me. I didn't expect to thirst for blood. To feel the desire to hunt a monster down and kill him. Those feelings aren't foreign to me but rather ones I'd repressed since childhood. The way I felt back then, I feel now—compelled to help June eliminate the lingering fear by removing the threat. I'll need more information to do so, but now is not the time to press her on this matter.

"Hey," the soft lull of June's voice seduces me out of my moment of reflection. She emerges from the bedroom, her slim body draped in a set of blue silk paisley pajamas beneath a matching robe—her hair is scattered in messy twists that fall over her shoulders, framing her tiny face. She tips her head and leans her shoulder against the doorway, mimicking my stance.

"I hope you're hungry. There's quite a breakfast spread waiting for you." I tip my head in the direction behind me. I push off the wall and clear a path for her to pass. "We can eat, then I'll make sure you get resettled in your suite and…." I pause as June walks toward one of the chairs. I pull it out so she can sit. "Do you mind if I have breakfast with you?"

"After you've seen me crumpled into a ball on the floor, crying my eyes out? No. I don't mind. Have a seat."

"I'm sure I nailed ordering everything you like."

"There he is."

"Who would that be?"

"The confident King has returned." She smiles wryly.

"You got me. You know by now that I'm appraised of information you might not consider standard."

"Like what I eat, my décor preferences—things like that?"

"Amongst other things."

"Did you know about last night?" I give her a questioning look. "I mean, about the anniversary?" she clarifies.

"I'm aware of the date your mother passed but not the time. I'm only privy to what was on the police reports—the things that weren't redacted."

"My name and any identifiable information that could be traced back to me were removed."

"So, her killer wouldn't come after you."

She nods. "That's right."

"There were a lot of people who saw him and vice versa that day."

"None as close up as me, and no one else there was heir to one of the richest families in the US."

"You don't have to explain."

"I couldn't explain what came over me last night if I tried."

"Everyone handles grief differently. I wasn't aware of how you marked the anniversary. My father passed away, too, when I was young."

"How old were you?"

"Same as you. I was eight. But I wasn't with him at the time."

"My condolences."

I pour cream into my coffee and then take a sip before responding. "Thank you. I typically observe the day by having a shot of whiskey or two."

"I make no apologies for what you witnessed when you entered my suite." She opens her linen napkin and places it on her lap. One by one, she lifts the lids of the food dishes and chooses eggs, two slices of bacon, and a variety of fruit, mainly strawberries, as she plates her meal.

"I don't expect one. Never apologize for being yourself, no matter how raw or real."

"It's not usually like that." She holds up a piece of bacon. "You don't eat bacon. I'm surprised you ordered this."

"But you do. So, how is it usually?"

"Every once in a while, when I get stressed, I have nightmares."

"So, something triggered this episode. Was it what happened at the restaurant last night?"

"That had a lot to do with it. I have challenges in general eating out. I try not to let that deter me, but unexpected disturbances affect me."

"You don't eat at places that remind you of the last time you were with your mom."

"I can't."

"When you eat out, you sit with your back to the wall facing the entrance or eat furthest away from the entrance."

"It's the only way I can cope. I won't let fear completely consume me."

"But there's more causing your distress?"

"I suppose it was a culmination of things. You know, a new job and...." June considers whether to complete her thought.

"And?" I prompt.

"Things," she says, cutting our conversation short.

My lingering concern is whether any of what she's feeling has to do with Aaron. My knowledge of their relationship is limited to what I've witnessed when they're together. Having known each other for more than ten years, their level of closeness is to be expected. However, something shifted between them over the past few weeks. June is smart enough to handle whatever is happening between them. The question is, can I?

"You don't have to talk about it if you don't want to. We should eat," I tell her, then plate my breakfast.

This weekend is the first of many with June under my watch. She insisted on spending the weekend in London to get what she called "a feel" for what it would be like to live here. If this were another client, I would insist we confine business trips to the weekdays, which are less risky from a security standpoint. Because it's June, I conceded.

June picks up a strawberry and examines it before eating it. I watch, mesmerized, as she takes a bite, taking her time, savoring it like expensive wine. Her movements are deliberate but delicate. She has tiny wrists, which I imagine latching on to as I pull her toward me, like last night.

Clear your head, man. She's not your woman.

"Thank you again for this," she says, holding a berry. "I love fresh fruit in the morning, but you already know that."

I nod. "I've seen pictures of the gardens you've helped students plant in their neighborhood in San Francisco."

"Everyone should have access to fresh fruits and vegetables."

"Indeed."

"I find it strange that people like yourself who don't know me have so much personal information about me. It gives stocker vibes. Is that normal?"

"Which part of your statement are you referring to?"

"For you to know people's likes and dislikes. Like the flowers and the décor at the penthouse. This." She opens her palms and gestures toward the spread on the table.

"Not always. Your situation is different. I dug deeper into your background to make your visit more enjoyable."

"What if my man opposes all this?"

I raise an eyebrow at this news. "Your man. Aaron?"

"I didn't say he was my man."

"Then you'll have to forgive me. I wasn't aware of any other man in your life. I should know these things since I'm sworn to protect you."

"I think I should let him know about you, Mr. King. You might try to take advantage of me." She takes out her phone, taps her screen, and types a text to a contact labeled "my man." I watch her type but can't read the message. Then, she proceeds to eat her breakfast, without paying attention to me.

My phone buzzes. I slip it out of my pocket and read it.

Queen of the Night: What if I told you that a man named King kidnapped me and is now making me eat breakfast?

I respond.

Me: Thank him before he takes you over his knee and spanks you for being so smart. Now, eat your breakfast, Ms. Ross.

Her phone buzzes. She reads it, then looks at me. I smile smugly, then return my phone to my pocket. "I guess you do have a man after all."

She can't even hide how funny the situation is and laughs. "You're such a…"

"What? What am I besides *your man*, Ms. Ross?"

"Ugh. I can't believe you let me think it was someone else all this time."

"I did no such thing."

"Anyway. Why would you do all this?"

"Because of who you are—where you work. My need to provide customer service takes over and converges with my desire to control the situation, environment…"

"People."

"Your words, not mine."

"Unrefuted, but yes. I said what I said."

"Are you done?"

She shakes her head. "Confident. Commanding. Controlling."

"You make me sound bad."

"I'm stating facts. You're giving King Aedan vibes. I might start calling you that."

"Don't you dare."

"London calls you King."

It shouldn't bother me when she mentions my friend, but it does. Aaron is headed to Geneva this afternoon. Otherwise, she'd be spending the day with him. He doesn't know I'm monitoring James's activities, who works for Saola.

I school my expression and say, "He's a mate."

"In America, a mate is part of a couple."

"I thought we had previously established that I was your man. Are you saying you want to be called my mate?"

She laughs, appalled. "God no, but you did give me the handle Queen of the Night."

"Queen for short. It's a handle befitting you."

"Are you insinuating I act arrogant and aloof?"

"Not at all. It's a rare flower—like you. You wield power in your role as COO for one of the largest companies in the world. You're fiercely independent, courageous, and confident. Your beauty is unmatched." The words flow from a place within me I didn't intend to tap into.

Her expression softens. She tips her head and knits her brows, looking curiously at me. Perhaps she's plotting her next assault on my character.

"You think I'm beautiful."

"I call it the way I see it. The handle suits you."

"Okay, I didn't see that coming, Mr. King."

"The truth."

"I always want the truth, but I didn't expect something that..." She pauses. "Well, nice. At least not from you."

"I'm human."

"Yeah, from what I can see, you're definitely all man. I mean human." She smirks. "I just figured you were determined to be curt, commanding, and controlling—doing things to.... Let's say I assumed you wouldn't behave that way around me."

"Because you're special?"

"There you go again."

"You know what I mean."

"And here I thought we would get along, Mr. King."

"Eat your breakfast, Ms. Ross. We have a lot of territory to cover on your agenda today."

CHAPTER 15

We Could Be Better

"Study the past, if you would divine the future."
– Confucius

June

WHEN I APPROACHED BREAKFAST this morning, it was with nervous anticipation. I didn't know what to expect from Aedan after last night. It felt like we were dangerously close to breaking through the sacred barrier between bodyguards and their clients. I was slightly stunned that he called me sunshine. I started to address it, but thought it was better to let sleeping giants lie. A man like Aedan couldn't have meant anything by it. *Could he?* I've written it off as a sympathetic response to help the heap of mess he found on the floor. No. He performed his duties—calm me down and do whatever is necessary to keep me from crying my eyes out. His actions weren't about pity or comfort but protocol and containment—part of his playbook. Assess the situation, soothe the client, and secure the surroundings.

Still, when he greeted me in the hallway, he seemed different—more approachable. The lovely breakfast spread and warm reception were a welcome contrast to the usual actions of the controlling, commanding King I've come to know in the past month. I certainly didn't expect him to break protocol and dine with me. Rose mentioned that was something she'd often do with Troy, but Troy and I never shared a meal. Therefore, I never expected to share one with Aedan. Still, if there's one thing I learned in my time with Aedan: he thinks the name queen suits me. King Aedan suits him.

After breakfast, Aedan escorts me back to my suite, where I shower, change, and prepare for my day of touring around London. When I'm done, I don't bother texting Aedan that I'm leaving the suite because I learned during breakfast that the second my door opens, he receives an alert and a video of me or whoever is at the door.

He wasn't kidding. When I open the door, he emerges from his suite looking like the perfect Pinterest boyfriend, wearing a blue-grey-striate suit, crisp white shirt, and black tie.

"Ms. Ross."

"Mr. King."

"I take it there's no chance of you running into clients where we're going?" His eyes land on my tan T-shirt, which has brown puffy seventies-style lettering spelling out "shake your groove thing."

I look down and pull at my shirt beneath my blazer. "What's wrong with what I'm wearing?"

"Nothing. It speaks weekend wardrobe."

"Being it's Saturday, it should—in volumes. But don't worry, I won't embarrass you."

"There's nothing you can do that'll embarrass me."

Right. At that moment, his confidence is my catnip, and I'm committed to testing his tough-as-nails limit. "If you say so," I concede, secretly concocting a plan to get back at him later.

I curl my finger, gesturing for him to come to me. He looks at me curiously, one eyebrow raised and a hint of a smirk teasing at his lips. I step forward when he's standing within arm's reach, closing the distance. As usual, he smells amazing.

"What are you doing?" he asks as I tug at his tie.

"Mr. King, I never took you as a man who'd pretend not to know when a woman is undressing you." Holding his gaze, I remove his tie and undo the first two buttons of his shirt. When I'm done, I tap his chest. "There. Now, you match my style." I roll the tie into a ball, walk to the threshold of my suite, toss it in, and shut the door. I turn back to him and say, "Ready?"

The look of irritation soaked in seduction shadowing his face makes the few seconds of holding my breath worth it as I tried not to be captivated by his scent. He extends his hand, gesturing toward the elevator. He presses the button. When the doors open, I step inside and stand beside him, staring him down...daring him to do something—I don't know what.

To test me.

Tease me.

Tell me he feels the tantalizing tension between us.

But he doesn't. He watches me watching him, expressionless, until the elevator dings, signaling that we've arrived in the lobby. We exit the elevator and building in silence.

At the car, Aedan holds out his hand to help me. He locks eyes with me, then hesitates a moment before he says, "You look beautiful."

Well, damn. The man who's hell-bent on making my life miserable paid me another compliment. Recovering from my surprise, I say, "Thank you."

Our drive to the museum doesn't take long. When we arrive at Trafalgar Square, Aedan helps me exit the car. We walk through the square and up the steps to the Portico entrance of the National Museum.

Although the art museum is full of many historically significant works, my main focus for today's visit is seeing art pieces related to Black history.

"He should be inside," I tell Aedan as he holds the door open for me to enter the lobby.

The art historian serving as my guide will meet me inside the National Museum lobby. Stepping inside, I look to the right at the impressive staircase ascending to the museum's second floor. I turn in a one-eighty, observing the crowd and studying the building's architecture. I catch Aedan watching me as I take in my surroundings. I'm certain he senses my excitement at being there. I smile when our eyes meet. He's so handsome it's hard not to. He winks in response. My fingers instinctively flex with the urge to reach out and trace the chiseled contour of his jaw where it meets his beard, but I don't dare.

"He's here." Aedan lifts his chin. I'm not surprised he knows what the person I'm meeting looks like. I suppose it keeps him from tackling anyone to the ground who gets too close to me.

An older gentleman with grey sprinkled in his hair and around his sideburns approaches. He looks like he just left a university lecture, wearing an elbow-patched blazer over a sweater, brown corduroy slacks, and brown suede laced oxfords.

"Ms. Ross, it's nice to meet you. I'm Doctor Owusu." He extends a hand for me to shake.

"Good to meet you, Doctor Owusu. This is Aedan King." I hesitate to provide him with a label for who Aedan is to me.

"Mr. King, it's nice to meet you."

Aedan nods. "Doctor Owusu."

"Aedan, Dr. Owusu is a renowned art historian who focuses on Black British History and whose work has transformed our understanding of the topic. Dr. Owusu, I look forward to viewing the art you're prepared to show me today."

"By all means, let's begin." Dr. Owusu gestures toward the oversized bright white main stairs to the Sainsbury Wing of the National Gallery. Aedan follows behind as we ascend the stairs.

As we head up, I pause and turn slightly. Before I can completely turn around, Aedan steps beside me and places his hand on the small of my back. "Looking for me?" he says in a tone so smooth I'm briefly taken aback by how affected I am.

"We're going to see a real black queen today."

"Another one."

I roll my eyes. "Yeah."

We continue up the stairs, which take us into the Central Hall. Dr. Owusu gives me a brief overview of the paintings in the room as we bypass them and head straight to the portrait of Queen Charlotte.

"Queen Charlotte is said to have been of direct descent from Margarita de Castro y Sousa, a Black branch of the Portuguese royal house. Many scholars dispute this, saying the evidence tracing her lineage back to the house of Sousa is not compelling."

"When my cousin, Rose, curated the exhibition last year in Belfast, she experienced similar resistance when she showcased portraits of blacks who appeared white passing."

"In the case of the Queen, the Crown referenced the family's Black and Asian lineage years before Queen Elizabeth's coronation. I don't imagine these scholars will challenge the royal family."

Moving further into the museum, we explore another related topic—black kings. Once upon a time, I believed in tales of kings and queens. I clung to the idea that a knight in shining armor would ride up and rescue me right up to the moment a monster wielding a gun appeared. But I was mistaken. No one came to save my mom and me.

Not my dad.

Not the cops.

No one.

That was the day I stopped believing in fairytales.

"This is an early sixteenth-century piece," he says about Jean Gossart's painting, *Circle of Jan Gossaert: The Adoration of the Kings*. I zero in on Balthazar. The smooth, rich, ebony color of his skin, in contrast to the detailed gold crown and breastplate adorning him on top of his neatly pleated gown, is spectacular.

I lean in for a closer look. "Look at the detail in the gold breastplate and gold cuffs. It gives a lot of depth and texture to the painting. He's also wearing a large gold earring."

Aedan steps closer. "He's very prominent. I see why you wanted to see this one."

"The painting depicts what would have been real giant pearls hanging from the gold pieces," Dr. Owusu says.

I take out my phone and put it in Aedan's hand. "Take a picture of me in front of this." Dr. Owusu steps aside, and I position myself to the left of Balthazar. I put on my best stoic look. Aedan brushes a stray hair from my face and holds my gaze momentarily. He steps back and then winks at me. I smile in return. How can I not, with the look he's giving me?

"Perfect," he says, taking my picture. When he hands me back my phone, I pull up the picture. Aedan looks over my shoulder. "Just like a queen."

"We should keep moving. You have a few more pieces to see," Dr. Owusu indicates.

He's right. Another piece I'm interested in is a painting called *A Black Woman* by an unknown French painter. When we arrive at her picture, I stare, wondering what the circumstances were when the portrait was painted. Was she real? Is she someone the artist came upon during his travels? During the last leg of our tour, we explore paintings by Hilaire Germain, otherwise known as Edgar Degas. Dr. Owusu explains the significance of his contribution and the little-known fact regarding the artist's background as a Creole.

As we leave the National Gallery, we say our goodbyes to the professor before traveling to the British Museum across town.

"It feels strange heading to a place that possesses so much property belonging to Egypt, but again, the monarchy was built on the blood and backs of others."

"I don't disagree with you."

On the ground floor, we walk through a long hallway lined with stolen walls on either side of us, covered in paintings and hieroglyphics. We emerge from the stolen columns into a room filled with massive carved stone statues.

I inhale, pushing down my disgust at how these precious artifacts were acquired. "I don't know if I'm in the right frame of mind to do this," I tell Aedan.

"We can leave if you want."

"No." I bite the inside of my lip and look around. People from various cultures move between exhibits and each other like water flowing around stones. There's a constant hum of voices, but none stand out except Aedan's.

"June, tell me what you need. I promise I got you."

"Talk to me. Distract me, at least until we get through this section."

"You don't have to do this."

"I need to."

"If that's what you want." He places a hand on the small of my back, directing me to move forward. "The Irish have their issues with the British."

"The Protestant unionists and Catholic nationalists."

"That's right."

"Your father died when you were younger. Did that have something to do with it?"

"A by-product, yes, but someone on our side did it. It was a case of mistaken identity."

"Did they catch the person? Did they pay for their crime?"

As the crowd thickens, he places his hand around my waist, pulling me closer and moving me through the maze of massive stone figures. "Let's say the world has one less bad person."

Stopping, I look at him, searching his eyes for unspoken answers to my question. In return, I find steel blue and a smug look of satisfaction.

He begins moving, prompting me to walk. I touch his arm, and he stops. "Should I be afraid of you, Aedan?"

"Never. I can't say the same for others."

"Have you ever killed anyone?"

He looks over my shoulder and around the space, bustling with people. I glimpse members of his team strategically dispersed amongst the crowd. A museum guide and their small group stand beside a sculpture near us. Aedan puts a hand on my elbow. "That's a question for another time. Let's keep moving, Ms. Ross."

Aedan walks and talks with me as we navigate the remainder of the exhibits. Somehow, his presence calms my urge to run from the building, crying and searching for someone to curse for the atrocities bestowed upon my ancestors. This is the second day he's been able to do that. Very few people have been able to do what he has. My brother Jake has been my rock ever since my mom passed. London and Nicole also provide great support, but they've never seen this side of me—never witnessed my emotional breakdown. On the days when life becomes too much, I fend for myself or wallow in tears alone.

***

In the car on the way to lunch, I'm lost, swimming in the deep end of my mind. Recalling my days with Aedan, the weeks with London, the past year's transition from Saola to Ross Enterprises...my life sans Mom. I think about what it would be like to finally be free from living in fear of a man I don't even know. Who could I have been had he not existed?

"Please wait for me to open your door." The deep timbre of Aedan's voice brings me back to the present. The car slows. It comes to a stop as we arrive on an unassuming street bordered on one side by a steel and glass office building and juxtaposed on the other side by a tall limestone building.

"Sure." The door opens and he extends a hand to help me exit the vehicle. "I'm not a celebrity here. Very few people know or care about me here in London."

"Your perception doesn't preclude me from doing my job."

"Why do you do that?"

"What am I doing, Ms. Ross?"

Ugh. "Never mind." He can seem so detached. Why am I even allowing this man to get under my skin?

We enter the building and take the elevator to the eighth floor. It opens into a private club, of which London is a member. He acquired a membership for me when he heard I was establishing an office in the city. Because of my love of everything seventies, he thought it would be a cool spot for me to hang out when I'm in town. He was right. The aesthetics in the restaurant, bar, and lounge showcase an eclectic mix of rich colors and hues, giving Mod Squad vibes. Patterned burnt orange bar seats with brass finishings, yellow tufted curved lounge chairs, and black and white houndstooth patterned couches near gold side tables say "welcome to the seventies."

As part of the deal for me galivanting around London, Aedan joins me as my travel mate wherever I go. The one exception is when he clears the restrooms and stands guard at the entrance, barring anyone from entering until I emerge. It's probably one of the most bizarre aspects of having him around, besides his temperament, which wavers between comforting and commanding.

We take a seat inside. The server comes to the table.

"Ms. Ross. It's good to have you here. Would you like your usual?"

"My usual? How do you know my drink?"

"Mr. Adler called ahead."

"Yes. That's fine."

"And you, sir, what would you like?"

"Sparkling water is fine. Thank you."

"I'll give you two a chance to review the menu."

I nod, and he walks to the bar. I scan the menu. "They have a good selection. I'm hungry. I think I'll have the 180 Burger," I say, looking up at Aedan. "What? Why are you looking at me like that?"

"You don't seem bothered that my mate ordered for you."

"Yet you seem bothered by it."

"You like to control things. From my observation, you rebel against authority—it seems out of character."

"You have a short memory. Just this morning, I woke up to breakfast I hadn't ordered."

"I was doing my job. Providing options from your lists of preferences."

"That's the big difference between you and your...*mate*. He's seen every version of me. Just as I have with him. He knows my drink, favorite foods, music choice, favorite color, and all the important things, not because he researched me. He pays attention to everything I do when we're together and commits my habits to memory. It's the same with me—he loves expensive whiskey, prefers meat and potatoes, and is a good dancer. I suppose that's what happens when someone cares about you. So, no, it doesn't bother me that a man I've known most of my life orders my drink. I think it's cute. If you give me a second, I need to thank him."

I take out my phone and text London.

Me: Hey, handsome.

AA2: Hey, beautiful.

Me: Just wanted to say thanks for the drink. Cheers.

AA2: Wish I was there. Cheers. Tell King I said hi.

I hold my phone out and show Aedan the screen. "See? So, Mr. King, when the server returns, please tell him I'll have a burger. Medium rare." I smile wryly.

The server returns with our drinks. Aedan orders my burger and selects several veggie dishes for himself. The noise level rises as the space fills with people filing in after a morning of doing whatever Londoners do on the weekend.

I sip my drink. Aedan studies me momentarily before saying, "Something confuses me about yesterday."

"Is there a question in there, or am I supposed to read your mind?"

"Aaron loves you—"

"I love him, too."

"Yet you didn't want me to call him to be with you last night. Why?"

"We love each other. We're not in love."

"Still, why not have me call him?"

"He's my friend, not my man. There were several people I could have called to discuss what I was going through."

"But you didn't, and yet he was the closest amongst your network who could get to you. Why didn't you ask for him?"

This is not a conversation I want to have with Aedan. To pick at scars that have yet to heal. I sip my drink and then take a deep breath. "It wasn't necessary. I didn't want to burden him like that. I can take care of myself."

"But you let me help you."

"I didn't ask for your help. You took me from my suite. You should have left me where I was."

"You were hurt. You weren't in a position to be alone."

"I don't know what you want from me, Aedan."

"The truth."

"Why did you call me sunshine?"

The server returns with our dinner. I sip my drink while he arranges our plates on the table. Aedan orders me another drink. The server leaves. I hold Aedan's gaze.

"Why did you call me sunshine?" I enunciate the words.

"It felt right at the time. You were in distress."

"So, it wasn't meant as a sentiment. It was strategic."

"I didn't say that."

"You implied it."

"Why didn't you want my mate to return?"

"I'm not the kind of person who takes advantage of others. He would have come immediately. He would have taken me in his arms, held me, and done everything he could to make me feel better." He would have taken me to bed and made love to me until I forgot everything, including my name. He would have given me the world on a platinum platter. He would have made me fall in love with him. I want to say, but I can't say any of it. Because admitting it out loud won't change the fact that...I want something else...someone else.

"You don't want him that way." It's not a question.

"Let it rest, Mr. King."

"He's my friend. He's *your* friend."

"What is this, a pissing contest?"

"I'm trying to protect you. I need to know how."

"It's not your job to protect my heart."

"Fair enough."

"For the record. I don't want any man that way."

"I understand."

For the remainder of the meal, Aedan doesn't press me. I've shared with him more than I should have, more than I allowed myself to accept as true. I love London, and he loves me. But we're not in love. The truth is, I don't know if we ever will be.

Belfast

CHAPTER 16

Between Brothers

"No one can reveal to you nothing but that which already lies half-asleep in the dawning of your knowledge."
– Kahlil Gibran

Aedan

Keeping a former client safe as he traveled through a war-torn country ranks low on the level of difficulty compared to the past weeks with June. Since our weekend in London, I'm slowly beginning to understand her better. There's a soft, wild side that likes to walk barefoot, prefers carnations over roses, and wears graphic tees with her silk suits. Then there's the defiant side that pushes every button I have. Yet, I allow it because it's her. Because when she does, I want to pull her into my arms. Every. Single. Time. *What is this?*

The door alarm sounds. It can only be one person. Niall. I hear him before I see him.

"You better not have some woman in here."

I bark out a laugh. He knows better. "How's Rose?" I ask. I set my drink down and make him one. He plops down in an occasional chair, pulls out his phone, and sets it on the side table.

"Great. I'll be heading back to the States soon." I walk over, balancing two tumblers in one hand and a decanter in the other. I hand him a drink and sit on the chair opposite him.

"Another event?"

"Yeah, her uncle's birthday party. Her father will be there, and most of their family will be there. I'm surprised you're not escorting June. What's with that?"

"Troy trained a special team headed by Mack Jones to handle June's security stateside. He's with her now at a rally in city hall."

"And you're okay with that?"

No, I'm not, I want to say. "He's an expert—previously worked for the Secret Service. She's in good hands. Regarding the party, I expect it to be as secure as Fort Knox with the two elder Ross' in attendance. Not to mention you'll be there. Otherwise, I'd push the issue."

"You sure this has nothing to do with Rose? I realize the situation between you two is still fresh."

"Niall, I assure you I'm neither pining for your woman nor trying to avoid her. You two are perfect for each other." I laugh, hoping to ease my brother's bit of angst. We've talked about this several times. He believes I'm still harboring feelings for Rose after almost a year. I'm not. At this point in my life, I want something special—my person. Did I think at one time that it could be Rose? Sure. But I was fooling myself. She showed me I could have more. And I do want more—with the right woman. There are moments when I'm with June when she looks at me in a way that I sense she's my person. Putting it out of my mind, I pour myself more whiskey and top off Niall's glass. "Have you two settled on a date?"

"Not yet. Rose wants to get her bearings in the new role first. And we both need to figure out logistics around our living arrangements."

"You can split your time between countries. Maybe you should take your own advice and focus on key clients or remove yourself from fieldwork completely. Let's map out the team members who are ready for larger assignments. Then you can work from anywhere."

"We have time to work it out."

"Since we're talking about the Ross family, what can you tell me about Rick's brother, Reed Ross?"

"He's a good guy. Hard-driving like Rick. Why? What type of information are you looking for?"

"Has Rose shared any information that would shed light on his former wife's murder? It's still unsolved. I'm looking for something that could help identify the person."

"Technology was different then. There's not much information."

"Maybe June mentioned something to Rose that didn't make it into the police records."

"We haven't discussed it. All I have is the information obtained during our initial research. If anyone could shed more light, it would be those closest to her: Jake, Jasmine, or Troy. In case you haven't noticed, June is serious about her independence. There are very few people she trusts."

"She seems close to Aaron." I sip my drink.

Niall's eyebrows furrow. He swirls his drink. "There's a hint of irritation in your tone. What happened between you and Aaron?"

"Nothing. I'm making an observation."

"You think he has information you're looking for?"

"I doubt it." If there was the potential for her to be as open with him as she was with me, she might've shared details she thinks are insignificant, but that could lead to finding the person. But based on our conversation, she didn't want him to see her in a vulnerable state. I need to stay close to this.

"Then I suggest you talk to him about whatever's bothering you or check your feelings. He's been our mate for a long time. I haven't witnessed anything that gives me pause regarding him. Jake certainly would have cut him off if he'd seen anything, considering how protective he is with his sisters."

"It's nothing."

"Your demeanor says differently. What's going on? Are they dating now? Is that your hang-up?

"No."

"No, they're not dating, or that's not your issue?"

"They spend a lot of time together, but they're not a couple. Either way, it's not an issue."

"Bullshit."

"My concern is for her safety. There is a person out there who would likely harm her if given the opportunity. She's garnering a lot of publicity recently. At some point, he's going to put two and two together. And when he does, I want to find him before he finds her."

"It's been almost twenty years."

"This remains a point of failure when it comes to her security. I need to resolve this." I don't share the fact that I want to solve this for her sake. And I certainly can't admit to feeling something for her. Niall and Rose can't know. She already thinks I'm back to my old ways.

"Your best bet is to sit down and talk to June. See if she can share anything about that day to help you."

"She says sometimes she has nightmares about it."

"Then start there."

Niall's right. I need to talk to June.

San Francisco

Chapter 17

Love of My Life

*"I am no longer accepting the things I cannot change. I am changing the
things I cannot accept."*
– Angela Davis

June

It feels good to be back in San Francisco. Standing in front of City
Hall, the mayor and the governor on either side of me, and thousands of
people spilling into the streets. I'm home.

The crowd is highly energized as I continue my speech. "Enough is
enough when it comes to gun violence. In California, we have some of
the toughest gun safety laws in the country, but we can do better. Public
safety is an important part of our priorities, as outlined by the governor.
Those actions listed include tackling organized crime, strengthening law
enforcement response, holding perpetrators accountable for their behav-
iors, and getting guns and drugs off the street. I'm here to announce my
commitment to helping the state implement programs to remove illegal
guns from our streets."

I look over the sea of spectators, some waving signs that say "Save our
city," "Protect our children," and "House the homeless," while others are
whistling or clapping. I wave as I leave the podium, clearing the way for the

next speaker. My adrenaline is still pumping, and I feel euphoric as I step down from the platform. Photographers documenting the event surround me. *Smile, pause, turn, smile, pause, turn,* I repeat in my head, carefully positioning myself to ensure each photographer obtains their money shot. I look to my right and lock eyes with London, who winks in return. I smile for the last photographer, then hold my hand up, signaling *that's all,* before going to London.

"Let's get out of here," I tell him. The security team flanks us as we enter the building and pass through a side entrance to the car.

He helps me get into the vehicle and slides in beside me.

"You were great. Your speech resonated with the audience. I'm so proud of the work you're doing."

"Thank you. I realize it's too much to ask, but I want to create a world where no one has to go through what I did."

London reaches across the seat and takes my hand. I lace my fingers with his. "It's not too much to ask. How do you feel?"

"Good now that I'm out of the limelight, but it still freaks me out to be in public crowds like that."

"You appeared graceful and engaging. The city is lucky to have someone like you advocating on its behalf. I'm sure your family is proud."

"I'm sure my siblings are. Let's see how Dad responds once he has a chance to view the clips online."

"You think the work you're doing triggers him?"

"I have no way of knowing unless I ask. That's the challenge with him. He acts like nothing happened."

"You should talk to him about it. It could be a coping mechanism. We all have them, even you."

"You noticed?" I ask, even though I already know the answer.

"Everything. You want to take on the world all by yourself."

"That obvious?"

He lifts my fingers to his lips and kisses them. "Yes, beautiful. Don't forget you're not alone. And think about telling your dad how you feel."

"I'll consider it. Are you sure you don't want to see Dad with me?"

"I've already committed to meeting a few potential clients and have a call with our Chief Counsel. I won't be far from his office. How about I come up and get you afterward, or if you prefer, I can meet you back at your house before we head to dinner?"

"Let's meet back at my house so I can change before we head to dinner."

"Sounds like a plan."

Going from the Civic Center area to the Financial District takes little time. When the car pulls up to my father's office building, London helps me get out of the car and then pulls me into an embrace.

"You were spectacular today. Call me if you need me. I'll see you soon, okay?" I nod. He kisses me on the cheek and then returns to the car.

As I walk into the building with my chief of security, Mack, we're greeted by building lobby security. Although I don't visit my dad at the office often, the staff know me. Mack and I take the elevator straight to the executive floor. Upon arrival, I'm greeted by Dad's assistant, who takes me to his office.

"Mr. Ross is finishing another meeting. He'll be here shortly," she tells me, then leaves.

I walk over to the wall of windows and look out over the city. I wonder how different my life would be if my mother were here. Would I be as hard-driving at work? Would I have held on to everything my mom loved, or would I have made different choices? Am I who I want to be or who she was?

"Princess. How are you?" I turn around to find my dad walking toward me with open arms. I step into his embrace.

"I'm good, Dad. Just here, meeting with government officials."

He releases me and gestures for me to sit at the table. "I made a significant contribution to their upcoming campaigns."

I sit across from him, facing the window. "You did?"

"The strategies they've outlined to tackle city issues, if executed well, will improve the overall quality of living for everyone across the state. I support their work."

"I've been working with them to go tougher on crime and develop programs to keep guns off the streets."

"The statistics show the work you've been doing has a positive impact."

"I didn't realize you'd been tracking my work."

"Why wouldn't I be? You're my daughter."

"I just thought...." He raises an eyebrow, waiting for me to finish. "You seem to be unmoved by certain things."

"What are you talking about? I'm invested in everything about my children."

"And Mom?"

"Ah, princess. She's been gone a long time."

"She? She has a name. Josephine."

My dad gets up and stands at the window with his back to me. "I know."

"Then why can't you say her name?"

"Is this about Jeanette?"

"No.... Yes. How could you have moved on so quickly?"

"It wasn't quick. It just seems that way to you. You were so young."

"I'm a grown woman, Dad. I understand the concept of a year. Even now, I can say for certain it was too soon."

My dad turns around, walks over to his credenza, picks up a picture of me and my siblings, examines it, and then puts it down. "Stop, June. We have to let this go."

"This is the problem, Dad. You let everything go. Move on. What's next? Act like it never happened? Like we didn't need you? Instead of losing one parent, we lost two."

"Is that what you think? I wasn't there for you?"

"Look at me, Dad." He turns and leans back on the credenza. "The walls I've built surrounding my life since that day are so damn high that no one can break through. I was only eight. You had to have known how seeing my mother murdered would impact me. You couldn't save her, but you could have saved me."

"What do you want me to say? That I should have put you in therapy? That I should have been there with you? That's not how I was raised."

"It was up to you to break generational curses. To give your children a chance."

"We all make mistakes. I did my best. You have to know that not a day goes by when I don't think about her. She was the love of my life."

"That's hard for me to accept when I didn't see evidence of that following her death. It felt like you moved on and left us floundering."

"You've never floundered. You're tough as nails—the most resilient of my children."

"Don't you get it? I had to be, Dad. Because there's one lesson I've learned over the past twenty years: no one is coming to save me."

"That's not fair."

"It's life. Listen, I have to go."

"Will you return to SF for the party?"

"Sure."

***

I use the quiet time on the ride home to decompress from my discussion with Dad. The conversation didn't go as planned, but it's a start. When the car slows as it approaches my house, I push the last vestiges from my mind to focus on a fun night with the few people who get me.

I'm the first to return to my house. I head straight to my room to shower and change. By the time I'm done, London is back and in the shower down the hall. Dinner with Jake and Nicole isn't for another hour, so I go into the kitchen and make him a drink.

He walks up behind me and snakes an arm around my waist. "Is that for me?" He steps back, allowing me to turn around.

I hand him his drink. "Yeah, we have a little time before we meet the others." I take my drink and sit at the counter. London follows me.

"How'd it go with your dad?"

"Two steps forward. One back. I suppose it's progress."

"You'll get there. I imagine he's fighting his own demons in some form."

"He admitted Mom was the love of his life."

London extends his hand toward me. I place my hand in his. He lifts it and kisses my fingers. "I always thought you would be mine," he says, surprising me. I'm so overwhelmed with emotions that I can't hold back the tears. He stands and hugs me. "I'm sorry. I didn't mean to make you cry."

I put my hand between us and press his stomach. He steps back. "Don't make me get snot all over you." He hands me the closest thing, a paper towel. It's coarse, but I use it to blow my nose and then place it on the counter. "You caught me off guard."

"I caught myself off guard."

I stand, wrap my arms around him, and lean into him. "You know I love you."

"Yeah, we'll always have that between us. I loved you long before you walked in on my discussion with your brother wearing only cut-off jean shorts and a bra. But I believe someone else is out there waiting for you."

I remember that day. He had the same look in his eyes as he does now.

"Jake, can I borrow this?" I asked, walking into his living room.

"Hey, June," Aaron greeted, alerting me to his presence.

"Oh, didn't know you were here, Aaron," I said hastily, slipping my arm into the shirt and pulling it over my head.

That was the first time I felt like there was something more between us.

I hold his gaze. "Let's not talk about it. Let's just be us."

London dips his head, dusts his lips across my lips and cheek, and whispers in my ear. "Okay, beautiful."

We stand like this, taking in the moment that's us. I absorb the strength I need from his powerful arms, and he takes what he needs from me at this moment. For both of us, it's closeness and comfort in knowing we are loved even if we're not in love. We gather our things and get in the car when we're done. We hold hands the entire way to the restaurant. When we arrive, Jake and Nicole are already waiting in a private room reserved for us.

I smile as we approach the large, round, white marble table surrounded by cushy gold chairs. It's been a while since I've seen my best friend, and I already know what's in store for me. People think I'm wild. She's wilder.

"Girl, you and Aaron took your sweet time getting here," Nicole teases. I bend and hug her.

My brother stands and hugs me. "Hey, sis, your girlfriend has been hounding me about you two since she sat down." He releases me, then does a man-hug shoulder bump thing with London.

"Hey man, how's it going?"

"Good, mate. Hi Nicole, good to see you again." London helps me to my seat and sits beside me. "Brilliant, you ordered our drinks."

"That was me. June taught me well," Nicole pipes in.

"Don't make me sound like a lush," I tell her.

"You just want what you want when you want it, like my jeweled umbrella. It seems it was apparently raining men in Europe." She smiles smugly and sips her drink.

London and I exchange a secret look. We've resolved our unconditional love. "Okay, Nicole. I get where you're going with this. What London and I have is between us."

"Yes, please let it stay there," Jake presses.

"Although, he is fine as hell." I wink at London. He pulls me to his side and kisses my cheek.

"Thanks, beautiful."

Jake rolls his eyes. "Ugh, let's order already."

London and I laugh. "I already know what I want."

"What do you recommend, beautiful?"

"For you—the Wagyu ribeye. I'll have the petite filet."

"Let's order a round of truffle fries," Jake adds.

Nicole rubs her hands together. "Oh, that that sounds good. I'm having salmon as my main course."

The waiter comes to our table. Jake takes the lead and orders for us. "We'll start with the truffle fries. Then we'll have two salmons, one wagyu, and a filet."

The waiter takes our order and then leaves. Across the table, Jake gives me the same look he gives me whenever I have a conversation with Dad. "You good?" he asks aloud.

"I'm good." London grabs my hand beneath the table and squeezes it. My brother's eyes shift to London, seeking silent confirmation that I'm okay. He nods.

"So, Aaron, did you get to drive the DBS?" Nicole asks.

"Not yet. We had drinks before we left. The driver brought us here."

"Yet? Do you think my sister is going to let you behind the wheel? She won't let me touch the car."

"If you wear gloves, I might let you touch the door handle," I interject, laughing.

"Well, okay. What's your ticket to drive, Aaron?" Nicole asks, wearing a wry grin.

London turns to me and says, "I can be very compelling." He puts his index finger under my chin, turns my face toward him, holds my gaze, and, in a sultry voice, says, "What do you think, beautiful?"

Oh shit. *When you look at me like that, I'll do anything you ask,* I want to say. Instead, I smile and say, "I think it's your superpower."

"All right, enough of that," Jake says.

"Is it me, or is it hot in here?" Nicole asks, fanning herself. "Listen, Aaron, I'll pick one up tomorrow and you can drive mine." We all laugh in unison.

I revel in the moments of joy with my friends and family and think about London's words. *"I believe someone else is out there waiting for you."*

Who could it be? *Aedan.*

London

CHAPTER 18

Only in the Moment

"Words are the voice of the heart."
– Confucius

June

IT'S BEEN AN INTENSE past few months building out the proposal for Ross Enterprises' five-year expansion plans. My work meeting potential clients in the US and across Europe, the location strategy research on real estate, labor markets, and skills within the regions support a growth rate of over forty percent, and higher year over year, surpassing the standard rates. Now, it's up to the board to decide whether we move forward.

Sitting alone in the conference room high above the London streets, I stare at the monitor as the board challenges my proposal. An officer from PWC poses a question on financing to Jake. His brain is a machine regarding numbers and, without hesitation, he provides the needed information. To his left is Rose. To her left at the head of the table is her father and chairman of the board, Rick Ross.

The chairman speaks. "Members of the board. We had an opportunity to listen to Ms. Ross' proposal. It's time to vote. I move to accept the five-year expansion plan as submitted, allowing for an increase in spending subject to board approval as needed. Do I have a second?"

"I, Rose Ross, second the motion."

"Any discussion?" He pauses and I hold my breath. When no one speaks, he says, "Great. You have your devices. As usual, you can choose yes to proceed with expansion plans as stated, no, or abstain." My uncle restates the proposal. Then he says, "Please take a moment and vote. When you're done, slide your devices forward."

The room is dead silent. Again, I wait with bated breath, examining the faces that hold my fate in their hands. This is the biggest project of my career. If approved, it will make global headline news.

Seconds pass that feel more like hours. Hands slide tiny devices forward one by one until all eyes are on my uncle. I want to close my eyes and pray, but I don't. I don't move; I don't blink. I hold my breath. Because if I do anything more, I might just faint.

The chairman looks down and then toward the screen. "The motion passes. We have our expansion plan. Congratulations, Ms. Ross."

I release the breath I've been holding for the past six months. "Thank you for your vote of confidence." I scan the screen, monitoring expressions around the room. Rose winks at me. My brother tips his chin up and beams with pride. I did it. *Mom, I did it.*

"This meeting is adjourned," my uncle says, and the video disconnects.

I put away my device, gather my things, and check my watch. Four thirty. It's still early. I'm definitely celebrating tonight. My phone buzzes. It's Rose on video.

"Congratulations!" she says before I can greet her. My brother appears alongside her on screen.

"Congrats, sis. You did amazing."

"Thank you both. Now the hard work begins."

"You got this. We just wanted to congratulate you. Go celebrate. We'll have a drink with you when you return to the States," Rose says.

"See you then," I say, ending the call. I rush out the door.

When I get to the elevator, there is an out-of-order sign. *Ugh.* The contractors have come early to install the bio scanner. Undeterred, I run down the stairs in heels like an Olympian, silently screaming, "I did it" in my head as I swiftly descend six stories. I run and run. When I reach the ground floor, a guard holds the door open, and another stands to the side.

In the lobby is Aedan, waiting for me with a look I can't place. But I don't care. I don't stop. I don't think. I don't hesitate to jump into his arms. He catches me and holds me for a moment before lowering my feet to the floor.

He brushes the hair from my face and stares at me with a mix of duty and desire. "What are you doing?" His voice is deep yet tender.

"I did it. The board approved my plans."

He tips his head toward the door, and the guards leave the building, leaving us alone in the lobby. He stares down at me with questioning eyes. "Of course they did. Now, what are you doing? You didn't come looking for me; otherwise, you would have alerted me you were on your way."

"I—I was just excited, I didn't mean to...."

"I'm not complaining. You feel like you belong in my arms." Once again, I'm stunned by his admission.

I untangle myself from Aedan. "I didn't mean to attack you like that. I was just—"

"Excited. You told me." He smiles, and I'm seconds from melting. "I assure you, if this is considered an attack, I welcome it. Now, where are we headed, Ms. Ross?"

Oh. My. God. How embarrassing. I threw myself at this man and was seconds away from kissing him. *What is this?* "Back to the suite," I finally say, then walk with Aedan to the car.

The drive back is short and quiet. When the car pulls up alongside the curb, I ask, "How did you know I was in *that* stairwell? There are two, one on either side of the floor. I'm not wearing my tracker."

"You should be. I expect you to wear it moving forward. But to answer your question: your phone."

When the car stops, he opens the door and extends his hand to help me. I exit the car and stand before him. He holds my hand a little longer than he should. I hold his gaze longer than necessary. The tension hangs in the air between us, heavy and undeniable. For the first time, I'm unsure what to do.

I clear my throat. "I don't like wearing trackers."

"I don't like hunting you down. But I will. And wherever you are, I will find you."

"Is that a threat, Mr. King?"

"It's a promise."

On that note, I step into the empty elevator with a billionaire bodyguard on my heels, who I can't seem to get out of my head. I stand with my back to the elevator wall, facing him. The way he looks at me makes my heart race. I can't focus, one because he's freaking fine and the other because my feet are throbbing from my unplanned sprint earlier. I bend and remove one shoe and the other while Aedan watches me with wild, hungry eyes.

Holding his gaze, I ask, "What's with that look?"

"Miss Ross, please put your shoes back on. I don't want to have to throw you over my shoulder and carry you to your suite."

I laugh. "Businessman, bodyguard—"

"Whatever you're about to say, don't," he interrupts.

"What?" I smile wryly. "I was going to say comic."

"Put your shoes on."

My cousin warned me that Aedan was the ultimate dominant male. She was right when she said he liked to control every aspect of his environment. *"He does what he wants when he wants,"* she told me, which included adjusting her schedule to suit him or even randomly ravishing Rose when she least expected it. That was almost a year ago.

I've witnessed his need to control situations. On rare occasions, he suppresses that side of himself on my behalf. When I take a stance on something, he backs off. Sometimes. *Maybe he isn't so bad after all.* The question is, how far can I push him? Can I trust him? Rose entrusted him with her life, but not her heart. *Do I even want him that way?* I was seconds away from kissing him at the office. How would Rose respond if she found out? What would London say?

London.

"That's not happening, Mr. King." My shoes sway from side to side as they dangle from my fingertips.

"Which part? The shoes or me carrying you?" His words come in the form of a challenge.

I put one foot forward, open my arms, and lean forward slightly as if presenting myself to a real King and say, "Neither. This is who I am, Mr. King." I can't check the barefoot walking love child in my blood. There is no suppressing my free spirit. Aedan shakes his head. I tip my chin up. "You didn't answer my question."

"About?"

"That look you're giving me?"

"Look?"

"Yeah, look." I point my index finger and make a circular motion at him. "Like you're ready for dessert and I'm chocolate mousse with whipped cream."

"That's very specific."

"Specific or accurate?"

The elevator door dings, alerting us that we've arrived at our floor. Aedan gestures for me to exit ahead of him. I'm half surprised he doesn't follow through on his threat to carry me. Instead, he follows me to my suite. He opens the door, scans the space, and then steps back into the hallway. Before he closes the door, he turns back to me and says, "I may not look like it, but I have a sweet tooth. Have a good evening, Ms. Ross." He flashes a wry grin, then closes the door.

Bastard.

I press my back against the closed door and smile. Aedan is every bit the delicious late-night snack every woman craves. I just have one question: *is he worth the calories?*

***

I have to wash him off me. That is all I can think about in the shower as I wash his scent from me. I tried to have a drink when I got in, but sitting there surrounded by sandalwood, thinking about how it felt in Aedan's arms earlier and all the things I want him to do to me was too much.

After my shower, I put on my black cold-shoulder dress, some mascara, and a bit of gloss. I grab my purse and head to the door. I made a promise to London that I would come to him first if I felt a certain way, and I fully intend to honor it. I glance at my phone: five-thirty. He's still at the office. I place my phone on the counter alongside my tracker, exit the suite, and rush downstairs like the devil is on my tail.

The elevator doors open immediately. I press the button, and within seconds, I'm in the lobby and running out of the building. *Come on, come on,* I say to myself, willing a taxi to appear as I walk back and forth.

When I see the yellow "for hire" light lit on a black taxi, I flag it down, get in, and give him instructions on where to drop me. I pull at my ring and my knees bounce the entire ride. When I arrive at the glass and steel office building, I pay him cash and run inside, heading straight to the executive floor. When I reach my destination, I don't talk to the receptionist; I head straight down the hall. I stop when I see him sitting in a conference room full of people. *London.*

He smiles, and I try not to let his "happiness to see me" melt my soul, but it does. I can't help what we have between us. Instead of watching him wrap up his meeting, I go to his office and sit on his couch. Within minutes, he appears. He closes the door behind him and joins me on the sofa.

A moment passes between us as we stare at each other knowingly. He caresses my cheek, smiles, and says, "Talk to me, beautiful."

"The board approved my proposal."

He pulls me into a hug. "Congratuatlions." He leans back and looks at me. A tear escapes and runs down my cheek. "That's not what you came to tell me." He wipes the tears away. More take their place.

I shake my head. "I'm ready."

"But not for me."

"I promised you." I stand and go to the wall of windows, looking out over the cityscape as more tears stream down my face. He comes up behind me.

"You love him, don't you?"

I turn to face him and wrap my arms around him. He doesn't return the embrace. He looks down at me, searching my eyes.

"I don't know. I don't even think he likes me. All I know is that I don't want to lose you."

"You and I are tied at the hip—I doubt you could ever lose me. What do you need from me, beautiful?"

"To provide us the certainty we discussed."

"We both know that you're not mine to take."

"I'm giving myself to you."

"Where is Aedan? You should be with him." London untangles me from him, but I grab his hand and pull him back.

"I don't know where he is."

"What do you mean? How did you get here?"

"I left and took a taxi straight to you. My phone is in the suite. No one knows I'm here."

"What are you doing, June?"

"Following through on my promise. When you first asked me, it seemed strange at the time, but I get it now. You're right. We are linked, but I don't understand why. Maybe you're in my life to get me to this moment or perhaps to move past it. Whatever the reason, you're the only one who can put me on my path to forever."

"Come on, beautiful. I'll take you back to Aedan."

"No, Aaron." When I call him by his name, his eyes turn dark grey. "You told me I could come to you. I don't know what's going to happen between Aedan and me. What I do know is that I want this moment…with you. You have to give me that."

London snakes an arm around me. "I'm convinced you were once mine in another space and time."

"I feel the same. We can try."

"Are you sure you want to do this?"

I nod. "I do love you." I reach up and comb my fingers through his beard. He dips his head and presses his lips to mine. It's soft and loving, but he doesn't open my mouth to deepen the kiss. He pulls away and stares down at me as my eyes well with tears. "Kiss me like you want me."

"You're not mine to want."

"I need to know what it feels like to be yours. At least give me that." He puts his thumb on my chin, opens my mouth, covers it with his, and licks into me. When he does, when he sucks my tongue, when his body rises against me, and he lowers his hand to my hip, pressing my body to his until it molds around hard proof of his desire for me—I feel it. Closing my eyes, I cherish the moment, allowing him to consume me until I can't breathe.

He's right. I don't belong to him because at that moment—I want someone else deep inside me.

He releases me, adjusts himself, and says, "We have to stop. I'm five seconds away from stripping you naked. I'm taking you to someone who can finish this before I do. Because if I make love to you, I promise I'll never let you go."

I nod. He's right. There's only one man that can finish this. London takes my hand and leads me out.

Chapter 19

Falling or Flying

"Your task is not to seek love, but merely to seek and find all the barriers within yourself that you have built against it."
– Rumi

Aedan

"Find her right now," I bark into the phone, then hang up.

Staring at the monitors in my suite, I try to determine who will be the first to pinpoint June's exact location. *God damn it, woman. You'll be the death of me pulling a stunt like this.* I was showering when I heard the alarm signaling that she'd left. I went straight to her suite when her tracker and phone indicated she was there. But she wasn't. *What is she thinking? Why would she do this?*

My phone buzzes. "The Queen is on her way back," Ben assures me, but it doesn't quell my anger. I knew if anyone would find her—he would. He's like a freaking bloodhound.

"Where was she? I want to know the second she gets back to her suite." I hear the alarm signaling that the door is open.

"Is this fast enough?" I turn toward the only sound I want to hear—her voice. When I get sight of June, she's biting the side of her lip, standing at the entrance to my suite with Aaron. Anger, confusion, and relief wash over me, and I don't know whether to run and scoop her up or turn her over my knee.

"King, I heard you lost someone precious. I'm here to return her. Don't make the same mistake." I nod. An understanding passes between us. Aaron turns to June and strokes her hair, stoking my flames in the process. "You good?" he asks. She nods. "Don't run again, beautiful, but if you do, I'll be there when you need me."

"You always are. I love you," she says, wrapping her arms around his neck. My jaw ticks to see my friend with the woman I want. When she kisses his cheek, I think about how my brother must have felt whenever I touched Rose.

I think about the rage I should have felt that day in the library almost a year ago when he walked up behind her, dropped an arm around her, and whispered, "He'll come around soon enough." Rose turned, surprised to find Niall instead of me standing so close.

I watched from across the room as she squinted, searching his eyes for unspoken words of reassurance that everything would be okay—that she wasn't making a mistake taking a chance on me instead of him. The look Niall gave her was fire and desire. Then, she stepped back, handed Niall her drink, and angrily said, "Here. I'll need this more after dinner." She half smiled and took a seat on the couch.

Niall made use of the drink, tossing it back, and told her, "Give it time."

I'll never forget her pleading look, wanting me to come to her. I knew then she wasn't mine to take. My stomach turns at the thought.

"We'll always have that," Aaron says, pulling June's hands away before leaving.

She turns to me and stares. "I heard a king was looking for a queen."

"What were you thinking?" I cross the room and stand before her. "Why did you go out alone?" I cup her cheek and examine her, then drop my hand. "Are you all right? Talk to me, June."

"I don't know what you want me to say. I'm fine. I'm here. If you want me, I'm yours."

When June says, "I'm yours," she unlocks something within me. I want to pull her into my arms, press my lips to hers, and kiss her hard. I want to show her how much I've wanted her since meeting her. I want her to know she is mine. But I don't take her. I don't touch her. I don't do anything to quench my desire for her. I am sworn to protect June. My emotions could impede my judgment.

She steps closer, closing the distance, leaning into me, consuming me in amberwood and honey. Heat rises between us. She lifts a hand and traces invisible lines on my face, across my eyebrows, down my cheek, and through my beard. I want her so bad I can taste her, so I do. I grab her wrist and nibble her fingers.

"You have to stop, sunshine. We need to talk."

"I don't want to talk."

"Tell me why you left. What are you running from?"

"From a feeling. From forever. From anything and anyone who could break my heart."

"You went to Aaron. Why didn't you come to talk to me if you felt that way?"

"I trust him."

"You can trust me."

"Can I? Can you handle the truth of why I ran? Can you digest the reason London brought me here? Can you tell me you sent thirty men searching for me for more than a contractual obligation?"

Yes.

I want to tell her I'd send a thousand men to find her. That if she'd let me, I would give her the world. Instead, I say, "We can't do this. My job is to protect you." Grabbing her wrist, I walk her out of the room and across the hall to her suite. "Wait here," I command, then enter her suite and conduct my security check, meticulously going through each room. When I enter the main family area, June is at the counter pouring herself a glass of wine. "You were supposed to wait at the door."

"Why? I've proven I can take care of myself. Who's going to care if anything happens? Who are you protecting me from anyway? The one man who cares enough about me just left and entrusted me to you. He would have kept me for himself if he knew you were like the rest. Unmoved. Unfazed. I should have let him love me."

"You don't understand."

"Yeah, and you're doing a great job of being crystal clear. Goodnight, Mr. King."

I take a step toward June. It's hard to look at her, staring at me with eyes welling with tears fueled by anger interspersed with desire and whatever else she's projecting. She's stunning. A strand of hair hangs partially over her eye. Instinctively, my hand moves to adjust her hair, but I lower it and turn to leave. Fueled by my concern for her, I turn back to June.

"I'll see you in the morning—no more stunts. If you need to leave, notify me or a team member. Someone will be on guard in the lobby in case you forget." I turn and leave, closing the door behind me but not dousing my desire. I don't turn around to check in on her when I hear the crash of an object hitting the door.

Fuck. Fuck. Fuck. I return to my suite and do something I rarely do on duty—pour myself a whiskey. I pull out my phone and tap the screen.

"Boss," Ben says on the other end.

"No one enters or leaves this building without my knowledge. Put two people downstairs."

"Already done," he says. I end the call.

The audacity of that woman to sneak out of here. But why did she do it? What was she looking for? Aaron's words play on repeat in my head. *"I heard you lost someone precious. I'm here to return her. Don't make the same mistake."* Why did she go to *him*? What mistake? Messing up with Rose? Letting June out of my sight? Is this the life I'm destined to live without a woman by my side except in duty to her? I take another sip and then check my email.

There is an email with an update about June's former co-worker, James. It seems he's looking for employment outside of Saola. I need to keep an eye on that. I continue scanning my email and laugh when I see my brother's email telling me my presence is required at his girl's year-end company bash in San Francisco. Rose and Niall truly are soulmates. *Is June my soulmate?* I try not to allow thoughts of her to consume me as I power through the last of my work.

God damn it. I don't know if I'm falling or flying. Fuck.

I down the last of my drink, walk across the room, and out the door. I don't bother knocking when I arrive at June's suite. I expect she's either in bed or lounging around by now; instead, loud music blares through the walls—Lauren Hill is singing "Can't Take My Eyes Off of You." I open the door. June's back is to me, facing the counter, wine glass in hand, barefoot, wearing a tank top dress that barely covers her thighs. She moves with elegant ease in time to the music like she doesn't have a care in the world. Like I never sent a fucking team of men looking for her. Like I'm not five seconds from taking her against the wall. The lyrics roll off her tongue as she sings along with the artist, and it's all I can do not take her and make love to her. Mesmerized, I watch her. The hips that I want beneath me sway to the music. Arms I want wrapping around me are in the air, celebrating the song.

I walk up behind June and snake my arms around her waist. As I expect, she doesn't pull away from me. She knew I'd come for her. I always will.

"I'm sorry," I whisper in her ear. She continues swaying to the music as I bury my face in her neck and absorb her warmth, her scent, extracting every ounce of the love emanating from her. She tosses her head back, and I trail kisses along her cheek, neck, and shoulder. "What is this?" I touch a spot on her shoulder, bearing a peace sign tattoo. I kiss her there. She doesn't respond. The song ends.

She calls out to the audio system, "Lenni, play 'One Less Bell to Answer.'" She extracts herself from my arms and puts her glass on the counter. I stand there stunned as the song begins to play. She turns around and faces me as the singer croons about one less man. June holds my gaze, smiling like she's harboring a secret. I go to her. She takes one step backward for every step I take forward until her back is against the counter.

I put my hands on the counter, one on either side of her, and lower my face to hers. "We can change the song. I'm not leaving. Lenni, play 'Baby I'm Back,'" I say, smirking. She narrows her eyes at me, but I don't care. I dust my lips across hers. Every cell in my body buzzes, wanting to be buried deep inside her.

She presses her fingers against my lips, putting space between us. "Lenni, play 'Back Stabbers,'" she calls out.

I lick her fingers, and she pulls them away. "Lenni, stop." I slide my hands down her body, then up her dress, slowly removing it as I inch my hands up her body over her hips, brushing her nipples with my thumbs along the way. I pull the dress over her head and toss it behind me. Then, I pull her naked body toward me, arching her back as I press my lips to her breast. Her breath hitches as I suck one and then the other. I lick my way up her body, her chest, neck, chin—until my lips are hovering over hers. "Is that really what you want playing when I make love to you?"

"Lenni, play 'Do Me Baby,'" she says around a wry grin.

I whisper, "That's more like it." Pressing my lips to hers, I open her mouth with my tongue and lick into her. My desire rises thick between us. The need to be deep within her takes over. I lower my hand to her hips and lift her until she straddles me. I carry her to bed and lay her down. Breaking the kiss, I hover over her, staring into the eyes of the woman who will soon be mine. "I'm going to make love to you, sunshine. Afterward, you're going to tell me why you ran."

CHAPTER 20

Moan

"Don't ever think I fell for you or fell over you. I didn't fall in love; I rose in it."

– Toni Morrison

June

ON THE DRIVE BACK to the suite from London's office, after I practically threw myself at him, he told me to be patient with his friend. *"King is short on words and big on action. Give him the space to get himself together. Read his eyes, beautiful. They will reveal exactly what he wants...you."*

Initially, I was terrified walking into Aedan's suite with London. I was afraid of leaving the comfort of a man I've loved most of my life, but I was even more afraid of admitting I was *in love* with the man sworn to protect me...Aedan. Then I heard him shout at someone, *"I want to know the second she gets back to her suite."*

I didn't hesitate to make my presence known. *"Is this fast enough?"* Aedan turned and looked at me. When I saw the storm brewing in his eyes—I knew. Just as London said, they revealed everything.

I was furious when Aedan fast-walked me to my suite. My mom once told me that music soothes the soul. She was right. I cranked the music and got lost in the song. It wasn't long before he came back. I knew he would.

When he kissed down my neck and shoulder—it took all my energy not to beg him to take me on the counter. I never told him the story behind the tattoo—that my mom used to wear a gold necklace with a peace sign pendant. I must have searched for that thing for a month after she died. I never found it. No, I didn't tell Aedan because I didn't want to detract from the moment.

I got my moment. And right now, my man is hovering over me, looking like he's about to devour me after giving me two earth-shattering orgasms, first with his fingers and one with his mouth. I'm here for it all...all of him.

"Aedan," I pant his name. My breaths come out rushed and unsteady. "Please." I reach between us and stroke his length, wanting him in me. He groans, pushing my hand away, and when I reach for him again, he places my hand above my head.

Looking down at me, he says, "June, are you ready to be my woman? Will you let me claim, protect, and give you everything you need? Will you allow only me to fill you?"

"Yes."

"Brace yourself," he warns, sliding hot steel between my folds, coating it with my release. "God, I've never wanted any woman more than you," Aedan groans right before he pushes into me thick and raw until he bottoms out.

"Ah, it's so good," I moan. He covers my mouth with his as he pumps in and out of me with long, steady strokes. I feel every vein and ridge in his shaft as my walls squeeze around him. Our kisses are urgent, wet, and messy. I close my eyes and take it all in. The cacophony of our cries and moans as our bodies clash in a desperate rhythm, chasing the need to be with each other in a way only sex can satisfy. My walls clench around him.

"I'm coming," I call out as I dig my fingers into his hips, pushing him deeper.

"Come for me. I'm here." He pumps in hard, steady rhythms, and I sense by his guttural groan that he's chasing his release. "Now," he grunts. He pushes in, and my body convulses around him. In response, he pours pieces of himself into me in waves, one after the other. "Oh, god." I ride the waves until I come again around his length, and his seed spills out of me. Until my walls stop pulsing. Until he pulls me on top of him, and I bury my face in his sweat-drenched neck. Until our breaths and hearts are in sync.

"I'm in love with you, Aedan."

"I'm in love with you, too, sunshine."

***

When Aedan returns from his suite wearing black cotton lounge pants and a white T-shirt, he finds me sitting on the couch, knees bent, legs tucked under me, mid-bite of his mushroom flatbread while listening to neo-soul. He sits beside me and takes a swig of the fizzy lime water drink I made for him. When I realized he refused to drink alcohol around me, I stocked my fridge with his favorite drink—something he picked up while in the military.

"Eat your pizza," he says, taking the flatbread from my hand and biting into it.

"I wanted to see what the hype was about."

"And?"

"I'll stick to my heavily meat-laden pizza."

Aedan returns his food to the plate and pulls me on his lap until I sit astride. Sliding his hand along my legs under my t-shirt, he grabs my bare hips and pulls me toward the bulge in his pants. "I have all the meat you need."

My breath hitches, and my sex clenches, thinking about the four orgasms he gave me earlier. I want this man. I lower my lips to his and whisper, "Yeah, you happen to be my new addiction." I lower my hand between us, grab his length, and squeeze.

He's the first man I've let claim me. The first man I've fallen in love with. The first and only one I can see forever with.

"Sunshine," Aedan growls at me. I press my lips to his. He takes over the kiss, parting my lips with his tongue and mingling it with mine. He swallows my groan. I'm so consumed with him that it's hard to breathe. Aedan cups my cheeks and pulls away from the kiss. "God, woman. I want you so bad. But we need to talk."

"After." My words come out in a pant.

He dusts his lips across mine. "This is the after. I need to know why you went to Aaron. If you wanted to talk, you could have come to me."

I pull at the waistband of Aedan's pants. He grabs my wrists and holds them to his sides. The flex in his muscles as he holds me is proof that I won't get what I want until he gets what he wants. "You're not going to like what I have to say," I tell him.

"I'm listening."

"I promised London I would come to him first when I was ready for something more with a man."

"My god, woman. What are you saying? You slept with him?" He moves to push me off him, but I resist, leaning into him, putting pressure on my writs in the process. He immediately releases me because that's who he is; he'd never hurt me. His sudden release causes me to fall forward into him. I wrap my arms around his neck. I need to calm the storm brewing in his eyes.

I dust my lips across his cheek and suck his earlobe, grinding my body against his still-hardened shaft. "I want you so bad; I can come right now, thinking about how good you feel inside me."

Aedan untangles me from him. His ice-blue eyes pierce my soul. "I'm waiting for an answer. Did you sleep with him?" his words come out pronounced.

"No. I've never slept with him. You don't know London as well as I thought you did."

"He's a man. If you give yourself to him, he will take you."

"He's not like that. He would never take anything that wasn't his."

"Then what?"

"When I went to his office, he knew immediately why I was there. He read it in my eyes. He assessed that I wasn't there to be with him. He questioned why I wasn't with *you*."

"I still don't understand why you went."

I blow out a breath. Tears well in my eyes and spill down my cheek. How do I help him understand the magnitude of what he is asking? Everyone who knows London and me has witnessed our unbreakable bond. How do I make Aedan understand how far it extends? "Because I love him."

"You love him, but you're here with me. What is this, some game?" His expression changes and there is a fire in his eyes.

"Let me finish. You've been around us long enough to know I'm not in love with him. I've said as much."

"Still, you went."

"I consider him my safe place to land. Because I'm certain that he would never break my heart even though we're not in love. I know that if I gave myself to him, he'd protect my heart and that whatever we built would last forever. Because that's who he is. I went to him because I didn't want to face the alternative."

"You think I would break your heart? That something could cause me to leave you after I finally found you?"

"You walked away from Rose to side with a family member who was in the wrong. Then you moved on like she didn't matter. Like how fast my dad moved on when my mom died. Like Leon did while I was still with him. Aedan, I've never felt for anyone like I do for you. I told you I'm in love with you. But you walked around acting like you didn't feel anything for me. I couldn't handle it. So, I went to where I was certain I was wanted. Because if I gave myself to you and you walked away, it would break me. And being broken once in my lifetime is already too much."

I attempt to stand. Aedan's strong hands grip my thighs, securing me in place.

"Rose and I were never meant to be together. We both knew that from the beginning. Even after I realized there was a connection between her and Niall, I didn't want to let her go. But she was born to be with Niall, just like you and I were destined to be together. I didn't move on, June. As Aaron did with you, I was forced to let go of Rose so she could be with the person she was meant to be with. I didn't believe finding someone like that was possible until I met you. I'm in love with you. Don't you understand now that I've found you, I will never let you go?"

I rub his arms. "You believe you found what you're looking for in me?"

"Every fiber within me tells me you are everything I've been searching for and more. I promise to protect your life, your heart, everything."

I touch his face and comb my fingers through his hair. He pulls my hips toward him. He presses his lips to mine and kisses me hard. I come up for air panting.

"You're not upset with me?"

"Furious. You sought out a man who wasn't me."

"A friend who brought me to the man who claimed me as his."

He stands and makes a swift move. I find myself lying on my back on the couch with Aedan hovering over me, hands on either side of my head. "Are you mine?" He dips his head and licks my lips. "Are you done running?" He searches my eyes, waiting for my response. I nod. "June," he growls my name.

"Yes, Aedan. I'm yours. I can't promise that I won't run again because sometimes fear takes over, and it's all I know."

"I'll never give you a reason to run. But if you happen to, I will always find you. I am your safe space. I am the man who loves you." He reaches between my legs and strokes my sweet spot. "I am the one who soothes the ache between your thighs." He continues stroking. "God, woman, you're so ready for me." He removes his hand, frees his raging shaft, and runs it along my folds, coating himself with my juices. Slowly, he pushes in. "I am the only one who can fill you."

"Ah."

"Show me what you want." He pushes in hard. My body clenches around him, craving all the pleasure he's offering as he thrusts in and out of me. I squeeze him like he's giving me life.

I lift my hips to meet each thrust—in and out. "Ahh, Aedan. I'm coming."

"Who am I to you?" He pushes in and holds it. I'm on the cusp of giving him everything he wants: my body, soul, and everything, because that's what he is to me.

"You're my everything." He pumps into me, and my body contracts around him, giving into the feeling of having the weight of his body on me, surrounding me with his essence, consuming me.

"Aedan," I cry out.

"I got you, sunshine." He continues pumping through my release, chasing his own. His rhythm is relentless, and I come again, this time with him pouring all of himself into me as we climax together. "June," he grunts. "Fuck," he says, collapsing. Our sweat mingles as our hearts race. My walls still throb, craving his thickness in me. I need more. I squeeze my walls, milking him.

"Aedan, I'm about to come again." He smiles against my lips, lowers his hands, cups my hips, and pushes them up and into his still-thickened shaft.

"Squeeze me, sunshine. Take what you need." He lifts me so that his length is deep within me. I squeeze his shaft, grinding my hips, taking what I need—chasing the feeling. My movements reactivate him, and he takes over, pumping in and out of me with strong, powerful thrusts. "My god, woman," he grunts, and together we come again, and his love spills out of me.

CHAPTER 21

When I'm in Your Arms

"Love is composed of a single soul inhabiting two bodies."
– Aristotle

Aedan

EVERYTHING IS STILL WHEN I open my eyes to a sliver of light peering through the curtains, casting a soft hue on her silky brown skin. The warmth of her body pressed against mine, and her arm molded around my chest, assures me she's mine. Traces of amberwood and honey mix with my scent, and the smell of sex surrounds me. No words can adequately express the incredible lightness of being I feel with her in my arms.

The body I spent the evening worshiping is now lovingly draped over mine. My hand molds to the contours of her hip, and the other caresses her arm across my chest. Her wild hair spills in waves over my shoulder and tickles my chin. I'm tempted to stroke it, but I don't dare wake my woman. Instead, I count the rise and fall of her chest against mine: One. Two. Three.

She stirs suddenly, pushing against my chest. A faint whimper escapes, followed by mumbling against my skin. Whatever she's dreaming is causing distress. I prop myself up, bringing her with me.

"It's okay, sunshine. I'm here." She continues squirming. "June, honey, I'm here. You're safe."

"What?" Her voice is barely audible.

"It's a dream. You're safe. It's Aedan." I brush the hair off her face. She's burning up. "Sunshine. Open your eyes. I got you."

She opens her eyes. "He was there."

"It was a dream. It's only me here. You're okay. Look at me." She reaches for my face. I kiss her fingers, then pull her astride me. "Hey. It's me, hon." I cup her face and press my lips to hers. It's brief, so she knows I'm here. I got her.

"I saw him."

"Tell me. Who did you see?"

"The one from the restaurant. He had a knife at my throat."

I pull June into me and hold her, stroking down her back. Her heart is racing against my skin. I hold her tight with her chest pressed to mine and her head buried in my neck until her heartbeat syncs with mine.

When she dusts her nose against my ear, I ask her, "Are you ready to talk?"

She lifts her head. "Maybe."

"All right. When you're ready, I'm going to ask you some questions, okay?" She nods. I give her a few moments to pull herself together. I stroke her arms. "You said he held a knife to your throat."

"It was sharp. He touched my neck."

"Did he have a knife that day? Or only in your dreams? I ask because there's no mention of a knife in the police reports."

"He had a gun."

"Reports describe him wearing a dark hoodie with a cloth covering his nose and mouth. How does that show up in your dream?"

"Like a faceless, dark-cloaked person."

"Were you using a knife the day you were at the restaurant?"

"No. They only provide regular utensils upon request. I've only ever used chopsticks when eating Asian food."

"Could the knife have been a symbol on his clothing?"

"I don't think so. There were no labels, no markings, no pictures. He was prepared."

"How did you know he was a man?"

"His eyes. I remember his eyes. His voice was deep and raspy. And his hands...." She looks down at her hand, palm up, flips it, and repeats the gesture several times as if trying to figure something out.

"What about his hands?"

"I remember he held the gun sideways. Like this." June simulates holding a gun and then turning it to the side.

"It would be difficult for a good marksman to shoot using that stance. He was emulating something he saw. What did his hands look like?"

"Big. There was something there, but I don't know."

"Like rings, jewelry?"

"No. I don't know."

"Sunshine, do you recall whether he had any tattoos?"

"That's it. Right here." She points to the skin between her thumb and index finger. "There was something here."

I close my eyes briefly and reopen them. This is the clue: a tattoo of a sword or blade. Her subconscious is trying to help her recall the repressed memory of the markings—the missing piece. Now I know where to start my search for the monster who haunts her dreams. I won't stop until I find and eliminate him.

I stroke her sides. "Okay, sunshine. No more questions. You did good. During breakfast, I'll teach you some techniques to help you recover faster from these sleep terrors. Your heart rate was high when you woke."

"I'm usually alone when this happens."

"When you're with me, we'll get through it together."

June wraps her arms around my neck and holds my gaze. "I never felt safer than in your arms."

"I recall you telling me Aaron was your safe place," I say, narrowing my eyes at her.

"Don't be jealous. That's different. Anyway, I never slept with him."

"Because you're my woman, and I love you."

June's smile fades, and she looks contemplative when she says, "I need you to believe me when I tell you I'm completely in love with you. I'm not in love with London. You're the man I want. The one I'm with."

I hold June's chin, bring her mouth to mine, and kiss her. She opens her mouth to receive my love as I lick hungrily into her. I love everything about this woman: her beauty, her strength, her vulnerability, her wild streak—all of it.

I break the kiss. "We have to leave soon. Are you ready for me?" She nods, lifts her body, positions herself over my shaft, and sinks onto me. She feels so good, so right, and she's all mine.

Belfast

Chapter 22

The Business at Hand

"You may not control all the events that happen to you, but you can decide not to be reduced by them."
– Maya Angelou

Aedan

"Send me the article as soon as possible," I say, exiting the elevator on my way to June's office. I nod to a member of my security team sitting in a chair close to her office door. I walk in and close the door behind me. June is standing in front of the wall of windows on a video call with her cousin.

"Rose, I need to talk with Aaron and see where this is coming from. I promise this won't get in the way of our deal with Knight Development Corporation."

"You have company. Aedan, good to see you," Rose greets me. I put my hand up in a salute. June turns around.

"I'll let you know what I hear from Aaron. In the interim, I'll have our attorney review the agreements. We'll get this resolved. Goodbye," she says, ending the call.

I slip an arm around June's waist, dip my head, and kiss her. It's loving but brief because if I do anything more, I'll have to take her home and make love to her. The past week, we've been inseparable, enjoying the newness of what we have. Falling into our routine feels so natural. I never knew it could be like this—loving June is so easy.

"You're early. I need to call London before I leave for the day."

"If this is about James, I need to be here."

"You heard the news?"

"Get him on the phone."

June calls Aaron on video. He picks up immediately, making my jaw tick. "June. You heard about James."

"Do you have any idea what this is about? Why is my name being blasted in the news associated with your employee?"

"He alleges you tried to recruit him. Do you have any idea why he would say that?"

"Are you questioning my ethics, London?"

"No. This is business. You know how this works. I need confirmation that what he's saying is false."

"No. He never applied to any role with me. Nor have I attempted to poach him. I haven't seen him since your keynote speech."

I stand beside June so I'm on the screen. "What does this man want?" I press.

"Aedan. I doubt this is a security threat."

"But you don't know for certain, do you?"

"I want this cleared up, London. Make him retract the statement," June demands.

"He's been terminated. It's in the hands of our attorneys."

"When was he terminated?" I ask.

"You're not privy to that information, King."

"I am," June interjects. "When was he terminated? Was it a clean break?"

"Two weeks ago. We followed all the procedures required for dismissal. He doesn't have a retort."

"He wants something," I say.

"What?" June asks.

"We need to find out. Whatever it is—he's using Ross Enterprises and Saola Technology to get it." My phone buzzes. It's a text from my research team. I pull up the article and read it.

"Double Trouble. It appears American titan Ross Enterprises can't stay out of the news. Once again, they're on the wrong side of it. Known for its groundbreaking AI technology, Ross Enterprises is led by the mega genius Rose Ross. Ross Enterprises and Saola Technology appear to be in a legal conundrum here in the UK. Former Saola employee James Drummond alleges he was wrongfully terminated after applying for an open role vacated by their former COO, June Ross. He further states that Ross Enterprises' European operation discriminated against him after he applied and was rejected for a position there, subsequent to being terminated from Saola. He asserts, 'I believe Mr. Adler, President of the European offices, and Ms. Ross, Ross Enterprises' new COO, are in cahoots on recruiting and hiring practices in the UK.' He further cites seeing them together recently at a technology event wherein Mr. Addler was the keynote. As of the date of this article, we have not spoken with either Saola Technology or Ross Enterprises."

"That article is bullshit," June says. "And so what if people see London and I together? There's no law against it. Neither of us is violating any agreement between our companies. He doesn't have a leg to stand on."

"You're saying we're just pawns in some scheme of his?" Aaron asks.

"James is likely not behind it. I've seen this MO before," I say.

It is not unusual for criminals higher up to use someone close to the subject to get what they want. It happened last year with Rose's kidnapping attempt. I've seen this numerous times. The key is to get ahead of it now that it's beginning to unfold.

June pinches the bridge of her nose. I want to pull her into my arms to alleviate her stress. But I also need to respect her boundaries at work. "I have a multi-million-dollar contract hanging on this. If this deal falls through—"

"It won't fall through," Aaron assures her. "We'll solve this. King, if you get any indication that this man is trying to hurt June—"

"He'll die first."

"That's all I need to hear. June, I promise I'll do whatever I can to clear this up," he tells her. Although I sense he's masking his concern for her, I can't help but feel protective of June, even around the man who brought me to her.

"Thank you," June says.

"Adler."

"Yeah, mate."

"Thank you for everything."

"Same. Don't make me regret it," he says, then ends the call.

Whether I like it or not, we will always have an unspoken understanding similar to what I have with Niall. Even though I don't want to, I respect the love they share. It's the love that facilitated their discussion and led her to me.

I take June in my arms. I'm learning she's more like herself when she feels safe. Despite being a couple, I still have a job to protect her at all costs. After our first night together, I explained why I couldn't hold her hand in public until we entered the building and established ground rules for our conduct. My ability to protect her hinges on how fast I can act in an emergency, which at times may require me to access my weapon.

Much to her disliking, there will be no public displays of affection. We have a routine. In public, I kiss her before we leave the vehicle. I tell her how much I love her. In those moments, we take the time to express whatever emotion we're feeling. Before I walked her into the restaurant for dinner last night, I sat in the car and stared at her. She's so beautiful. I smile, thinking about it. Then, after we exit the vehicle, I always have a hand on her—either her back, shoulder, or waist—somewhere so she feels my love yet knows she's protected. Those simple gestures cause the rigidity and defensive posturing I used to see in her to dissipate. I first noticed my effect on her that night at the restaurant when there was a disturbance. I went to her. I reassured her that the disturbance would be over shortly. It immediately alleviated her trauma response.

I dust my lips against hers. "I promise we'll get to the bottom of this."

"We will. I just don't know why James would do this. How does he benefit from spreading lies that can easily be disproven?" June steps away from me, gathers her belongings, and drops them into her tote: lipstick, which I will kiss off in the car, cell phone, mini spray bottle, and mail.

"Money would be the only motivator behind something like this. What's that?" I point at the letters she dropped in her tote.

"We're starting to get mail here. So far, just congratulatory cards or charity invites—things like that. Anyway, James is not suing anyone. Neither company has received a request for settlement."

"That's the answer."

"What?"

"Someone else is providing the money. The only question is, how do they benefit from this mess? There has to be an endgame."

"I'll call Raven Nichols when we get upstairs; if anyone can put this to rest—she can. Let's go. I've had a tough day."

"Do you still want to eat out?"

"No. Take me home."

***

When we return to June's suite, dinner is the last thing on her mind. She drops her purse and phone on the credenza near the door, reaches beneath my suit coat, and wraps her arms around me.

"Hey, King."

"Hey, sunshine. I didn't mean to walk in on you and Rose."

"Eventually, we need to tell her and Niall about us. Do you think they'll be mad? She was pissed at you for a minute when you two were together."

"Honestly, she's focused on work and my brother. There's no getting past the fact that she and I aren't meant for each other. She said several times that she wanted me to settle down, find a woman, and be happy. I think she'd be ecstatic we're together."

"I'm not so sure."

"Why wouldn't she be? I love you. That's everything."

June rises on her toes, seeking a kiss. I dip my head, meet her lips with mine, and give her a baby-making kiss.

Conscious of her idiosyncrasy to be on the same level as me, I raise her pencil skirt to her waist so I can pick her up—when I do, she wraps her legs around me, deepening the kiss. This is the part I love. The nearness.

The warmth of her body in my arms. Her scent surrounding me. The tiny groan that escapes her, revealing her desire for me. I love how our bodies are designed to fit together like threads in a woven fabric, seamlessly connecting with every touch. I hold her hips and stand with her in my arms, reveling in everything about her until she comes up for air.

"God, Aedan. Is it supposed to be this good?"

I smile against her lips. "I sure hope so. I've been waiting so long for you to come into my life."

"Forty years," she deadpans.

"Are you making jokes about my age? Have I not shown you the benefits in bed?"

She dusts her lips against mine. "You'll get no complaints from me. You've been waiting a while because I was born to be with you. It took me some time to get here, but I made it. And you were designed especially for me. I love you so much, Aedan."

I respond with a brief kiss because my woman is getting distracted.

"You should start on those calls you need to make, sunshine, and I need to arrange for our dinner since Stella is off. Are you okay with that?"

"Yeah. Can I get that with two orgasms on the side?"

"Can you handle four?" I lower her to her feet and groan when she slides across the proof of my desire for her. "It could take all night if you're up for it."

"Yes, I won't be long," she says, heading into the small office. I sit at the kitchen counter and order her favorite meal for dinner. Then I call Ben.

"Boss, how can I help?"

"We'll be in the remainder of the evening. Secure the building after all the staff have left. As usual, no one in or out."

"Did you review the brief I sent?"

"When did you send it?"

"Five minutes ago."

"Give me a sec." I open the brief Ben sent while I was loving on my woman. The report I requested lists anyone documented in the United States with a blade, sword, or dagger tattoo. I scan the report. It begins with a statistic that thirty-two percent of US citizens have at least one tattoo. I read past the statistics and jump to the section of those that have been documented through any business establishment or public, private, or government system in the United States with a blade or dagger tattoo. The one data point I'm interested in is the number of people documented within a thirty-mile radius of the restaurant location over the past twenty years. There are precisely fifteen that meet the minimum criteria. Four meet the skin tone.

"Ben, I want an eyes-only picture of person numbers one, four, seven, and twelve. Have those to me by morning."

When June awoke from her nightmare, I knew it held the key to finding her assailant. She may not have realized he had a tattoo at the moment, but her brain imprinted it. All this time, she held the key to finding her mom's murderer, and I'm going to eliminate him once and for all.

San Francisco

Chapter 23

Pretend

"The most beautiful discovery true friends make is that they can grow separately without growing apart."
– Elisabeth Foley

June

It feels good to be back in San Francisco after weeks of traveling between London and Belfast. I should be excited about my first trip to the city with Aedan, but I have mixed feelings. Not about us or our love, but this will be the first time we're with family, and no one knows we're dating. To add another layer of complication, London is also here. Since I originally RSVP'd with him as my plus one, and he's my brother's best friend, it would be unusual for him not to show. Besides, everyone knows how close London and I are—they expect us. Then there's Aedan—no one expects us as a couple.

When Aedan learned about the plus one thing, he didn't hesitate to remind me who he was to me. *"Whenever you see him, I want you to remember whose body you crave,"* Aedan said right before he gave me a set of mind-blowing orgasms. He didn't lie—I'm addicted to him. I was sore the whole week. My sex clenches thinking about it...thinking about him. That's what he does to me.

228

Together, Aedan and I are insatiable. Not a day has passed that he hasn't made love to me. Sometimes, during that time of the month, it gets messy. That's one of the benefits of being with an older man who understands that life is going to happen. He doesn't care—he wants me, and I want him right back. I never knew it could be this way with a man.

Aedan sits at the kitchen counter, reading something on his phone while seventies music blares over the sound system. I snap my fingers to the beat. He looks at me and winks, then takes a sip of his favorite lime fizzy drink, which, luckily, they have here in the States. My man and I both need to stay hydrated. We haven't left my house since we arrived last night. We've been too busy loving each other. And if I thought I was sore the week he learned about the plus one, I'll likely be walking funny well into next month. I can't be with him as part of a couple at the party tonight, but I will certainly feel him. My man is so possessive. And I'm here for it.

The song changes, and *Foxy Lady* by Jimi Hendrix comes on. It's wild and funky, just the way I like it. I walk over to my man, throw my arms around his neck and suck his earlobe. "Dance with me, honey?" He puts down his phone and gives me a look that's all sex and sin wrapped in a smile. He's so fine.

He stands, slides his hands under my shirt, and grips my waist, pulling me to him. I move to the rhythm of the music against his body. His need for me rises thick between us and presses against my body as we sway to the beat.

"Are you seducing me, sunshine?" He dips his head, nibbles, and kisses my neck, cheek, and ear.

I tip my head, giving him better access. "Always. I love the way you love me. It's so complete. So intense."

Aedan kisses me slowly like he's savoring every bit of me. I'm so consumed by him, but I want more. I break the kiss, panting. "Pick me up." He lifts me, and I crush my lips to his, deepening the kiss and taking from him what I need. He holds me, kissing me as the music plays out. When it stops and another song cues, he pulls back.

"Lennie, stop the music," he calls out, then sits me on the counter.

"What are you doing?"

"Don't worry, sunshine. I promise to finish. I want to talk about the event," he says, sliding his hand beneath my shirt and brushing his thumbs against my nipples, making it hard to focus.

"What about it?"

"Do you want to tell Rose and Niall about our relationship? At some point, they have to know."

"I'm not sure. I don't want it to impact my job, and we have this thing with the BDC that is still outstanding."

"You mentioned your attorney has a solution."

"It'll likely be resolved by week's end."

"Maybe we shouldn't put this off. We'll see them tomorrow. It may be best to talk to them then."

"Is this a deal breaker for you? This feels like you're pulling away from me."

"Why would you say that?" Aedan takes off my shirt and wraps his mouth around my breast, licking and sucking it, making my body wet for him. He lifts his head. "Does this feel like a man pulling away from you?" He dips his head and sucks the other breast. My back instinctively arches, needing him in me. Knowing my body, he slides his fingers between my folds, moving them in and out in a slow, steady motion. My body, still sore from before, throbs for him. I groan.

"Ah, god, Aedan." My walls grip his fingers and I move in time with the rhythm of his hand.

"Let it go," he says, increasing the pressure, his pace pulling my climax from me.

"Aedan," he swallows my groan with a kiss, curling his fingers in me until the pulsing subsides. Until my breathing slows. Until he's satisfied with his handiwork. Then he removes them.

"I'm right here, sunshine. I'm not going anywhere." He dips his head again and sucks one breast and then the other. When he's done, he pulls me to him and holds me. "Now, talk to me. Tell me what *you* want to do."

Still, in my Aedan haze, I say, "God, give a girl a minute to recover." He kisses the corner of my lip and then smiles against my cheek. He's so sure of himself—that alone is sexy. "I need to tell Jake. He'll figure it out the second he sees us. He always knows everything."

"What does he know about Aaron?'

"Same as you. That we're close. That he loves me." His jaw ticks when I say London loves me. I touch his jaw, then kiss him there. His muscles relax slightly.

"Does he know you're not in love?"

"I believe so. I told you he sees everything. Aedan, you're going to have to control yourself around London."

"You mean to suppress the urge to punch him whenever he touches you?"

"He's our friend. He would do anything for me. Anything for you. He brought me to you. Promise you'll be your normal self around him."

"I haven't seen him since I've been inside you. Since my seed has run down your thighs. Since I've savored *you*. My need to protect what's mine is in overdrive. I can't make promises like that." Aedan cups my face and licks across my lips. There's a fire in his eyes. I push him away and slide to the end of the counter. He helps me down. I take his hand and lead him out of the kitchen and down the hall to the first room I come across. I scoot to the top of the bed. He sheds his clothes, gets on the bed, and hovers over me. I widen my legs, stroke his length, and guide it to where I want him.

"Take me," I tell him. I don't have to wait. He pushes in, giving me everything I need and more.

***

Our drive across town is no different than any other. We get all our loving glances and kisses in. Aedan's a breast man, so there's that. Even now, we're locked in a kiss, his hand in my dress, pinching my nipple. I press my hand to his chest. He lifts his face. "Aedan, I'm...," I call out.

"Sunshine, are you seriously coming?'

I nod. "Oh, G—." I groan, unable to speak.

It's a good thing I made him give me two orgasms with his hands, one before I got in the shower and one during, to eliminate the excess evidence of our love dripping from me. Because my man came in me four times today. Otherwise, it would be running out of me right this moment.

Aedan kisses me, then smiles smugly against my lips. He knows what he does to me. "Put your lipstick on, sunshine. We're almost there."

"I know what you're doing."

"Besides making you feel good?"

"This is about London," I blurt out. His eyes pierce mine.

"This is about me and you. Should we stop the car so I can demonstrate?"

I touch his cheek, then dust my lips against his. "I shouldn't have said that. I feel your love. I see it in your eyes. You've seen how your touch alone makes my body pulse. You're the only man I want. Tonight will be difficult, but I promise I'll make it up to you."

The car slows as we approach the vast double-lot, two-story home in Saint Francis Wood. Even now, with my adult lens, the house seems large. Growing up, I never knew my dad had bought the neighbor's house, expanding our home to its current size. I thought everyone had a courtyard at their house. My mom used to throw the best birthday parties for Jake and me in the courtyard. That all ended when she passed.

It wasn't until high school that I learned our home was originally a two-story, nearly four-thousand-square-foot home. That was before my parents had children. That all changed when Jake came along. With the addition of the home on the left, the house is now over eight thousand square feet.

The car stops and Aedan puts on his game face. "Ready?"

"Yes."

Aedan exits the vehicle and then helps me out. He stands beside me, his hand barely touching my back, as we walk to the front door, which is flanked on either side by men in black suits. Classical jazz comes from inside. The gentleman on the right taps something on his lapel, and the door opens, held by a woman in a black suit. Her hair is slicked back in a ponytail like in the military. Aedan acknowledges the security team members with a nod.

Inside, I follow the hall to the left, which leads to my dad's ballroom that opens onto the courtyard. At least sixty people are milling around, drink in hand, chatting it up. I take a deep breath and walk through the crowd with Aedan.

"There she is," I hear Jake before I see him. The crowd parts, and he walks up to me. He hesitates for a second. His eyes shift between me and Aedan. *I can't do this. I have to tell him now,* I say to myself. He already suspects something. He's that intuitive when it comes to me. Has been since the day our mother died. Without saying a word, I grab his hand and lead him back down the hallway and into the library with Aedan in tow. I shut the door.

"What are we doing? What have you done? And why is Aedan here and not Mack? You do know Aaron's looking for you, right?"

"Slow down."

"Start talking, sis."

"Mack is outside with the other security people. I just arrived."

"And Aedan?"

I hold my hand out to him. He places his hand in mine. "Aedan and I are a couple. But no one knows but you. Oh, and London. Actually, he had something to do with it."

"What do you mean Aaron had something to do with it?" My brother pulls out his phone and types a message.

I reach to grab his phone, but he moves his hand away. "Don't do that."

"Don't say another word. I want to hear it from him directly."

I bite the side of my lip. Within seconds, the door opens. I can't help but smile when London appears. He closes the door behind him, walks over to me, holds my gaze, and doesn't hesitate to kiss my cheek.

"Hey, beautiful." I sense the fire consuming Aedan beside me. "Hey, mate," he greets Aedan, then turns to my brother. "You summoned me."

Jake gestures between Aedan and me. "You knew about this?"

"Yes. They're in love."

"I thought you and June were in love."

London smiles. It's so cute; it makes me smile. Then he turns to me, cups my cheek, and stares into my eyes. I know he's doing it to goad my brother because that's how they are. Even so, I'm lost in his stare because it's him. "June and I love each other. We both agree on that. But we also both agree that we're not in love. She's in love with my mate here. Right, beautiful?" I nod in his hand. "And if he doesn't do right by her, I will crush him and take her back." Still holding my face, his eyes shift between me and Aedan.

"The show is over, mate." Aedan's deep accent cuts through the tension like a knife. London removes his hand from my face and smiles at me.

Jake looks at me. "Is this true? Do you love him, June?"

"Yes, I'm in love with Aedan."

My brother's face is unreadable as he extends a hand to Aedan. He takes it, and they shake. "You know Troy." It's not a question. And he doesn't expect an answer. My brother is making a point. "If I hear so much as that a tear fell from her face, I will send Troy to find you and kill you."

"Don't worry, mate. I got this one," London assures Jake.

"Okay, can you two stop? Nobody needs to do anything to Aedan...except me."

"Oh, god, sis, did you have to go there?"

"He's right, beautiful. You could have spared me that one," London adds.

"Get over it, mate," Aedan pipes in, and he has a slight smirk for the first time since our arrival.

"Who else knows?" London asks.

"Those in this room. We're not telling anyone else for now."

"Good luck. There's a tough crowd out there. Aedan, I suggest you ease up on my sister if you're trying to keep a low profile. I saw something between you two the second I laid eyes on you. People expect Aaron to do the hovering thing—that's been his MO for a while." London narrows his eyes at my brother. "No offense, man. You've had a thing for my sister since you met her. Everybody knows that."

"I'm not offended. We love each other. There's nothing wrong with that," he quips. "Listen, Aedan—JR's right. Let us do our normal thing. I promise not to haul our woman off into a room alone." He turns to me and smiles. "Unless you specifically request that, beautiful."

"Play nice, handsome."

"See. Just like normal," London chides.

"Aedan, it'll be fine, but first, I need something only a King can provide." I put my finger under his chin and bring his face down to meet mine. I tip my head, and he presses his lips to mine and pulls me into him.

"Spare me," my brother says.

"Good one, beautiful," London adds.

I lick evidence of Aedan from my lips, then say, "Ready, you guys."

London opens the door and gestures for me to exit the room. "Ready," he says.

CHAPTER 24

The Great Equalizer

"Each friend represents a world in us, a world not born until they arrive, and it is only by this meeting that a new world is born."
– Anais Nin

Aedan

WHEN I LEARNED JUNE was attending her father's birthday party with Aaron, it became apparent I had to rely on my tactical training to rein in my temper. However, standing in the presence of June, Jake, and Aaron, I've come to understand that love is the great equalizer. The teasing, veiled threats, and death stares are all in service to the woman we all love in one form or another—brother, friend, lover.

Still, it'll be a while before the urge to punch Aaron in the nose for the way he looks at June dissipates. I wonder if Niall feels the same when I look at Rose. The difference is that I wasn't with Rose long enough to fall in love. Of course, I love her now as a sister, but our connection was nothing like what June and Aaron share.

When June tips my head to kiss me, I revel in the moment we alone share. She's mine. When all the pomp and circumstance is over, and the last person says goodbye, we'll go home together as a couple.

As Aaron leads June from the library, I hang back to avoid the appearance of the doting boyfriend, but I don't let June out of my sight.

I need to find my brother, so I pull out my phone and text him.

Me: Where ye?

Niall: Making the rounds. Far side of the courtyard.

Trailing June and Aaron, I spot my brother beyond where June's father is talking to his brother, Rick. June heads straight to them while I bypass them on the way to Niall and Rose.

"You decided to come after all," Rose says when I lean in and kiss her cheek. The lavender and vanilla surrounding her reminds me of our time together. It preceded her entering a room.

"Someone, I won't say who…your fiancé…told me I would be remiss not to accompany June to her father's event."

"He was right. It's good to see you. My cousin is lovely, but she can be a handful."

"I'm learning her ways."

I clasp hands with my brother. "How long are you in town?"

"A few days. We return to Belfast, then my lady wants to take a brief holiday before returning to San Francisco for her art exhibition."

"I heard this is another big show for you, Rose. Congratulations."

"Thank you."

"Our mate, Parker, and his girl will be there. We plan to meet up," Niall says

"Sorry I'll miss it. June's schedule is tight."

Rose purses her lips. "With so much demand for executive presence at various events, she and I will split them up through the remainder of the year. I'm just glad she's on board."

"She seems happy about it."

"Now I just need to get her settled with the right man." She tips her chin in the direction where the Ross clan is standing. "She and Aaron look cute together, but she needs someone who can handle her wild antics, not enable them."

"They have a close bond."

"They share something rare that's developed over the years. But I know June well enough to say that if she wanted him, she would have had him the year they met. I need you to keep a close eye on her, Aedan. She's attracting the wrong attention with her high-profile political stance on crime. I already unwittingly handed her to the wolves when she joined RE. But this other element—they're a lot more dangerous. She's already been through the trenches. I need her healthy, happy, and safe."

"Don't worry. I do have eyes on her."

The lovely sound of June's laughter tickles my ear, and I turn to see her head tossed back, having fun with her family.

I smile and say to myself. *I do.*

Chapter 25

Conversation

"Time is a brisk wind, for each hour it brings something new."
– Paracelsus

June

I spent so much time stressing over attending Dad's party, but it didn't live up to the hype. Mainly because I haven't broached our usual topic and partly because I'm enjoying listening to my uncle regale us with stories of how his child prodigy, my cousin Rose, corrected him in a business meeting during take your kid to work day. It feels good to be amongst family and enjoy life. It wasn't always like this, especially in the years following Mom's death. I miss her. Watching Dad with Jeannett, I get why he chose her. Some of her mannerisms, the way she flips her hair back with her hand, and the crinkle in her nose when she's focusing on someone's conversation remind me of Mom. That was what he was looking for—a version of Mom. *Did I get it wrong?* He never forgot her.

"Dad, do you have time before we cut the cake?"

"Of course, princess."

I touch London on the shoulder. "Can you keep the bodyguards at bay? I need to chat with Dad. I'll come find you when I'm done."

London caresses my cheek. "I got you covered, beautiful. Signal me if you need me."

My dad shakes his head. "The way you and Jake spoil this girl is too much."

"Just looking out for her, sir."

Before I turn to leave with my dad, I look across the courtyard and catch Aedan's gaze. He winks, I smile in return, and then I leave with my dad. We head down the hall to his office, which I haven't been in for a few years. I'm surprised when I walk in and find he has pictures of us all at various stages of our lives lining his credenza.

"You want a drink, princess?"

"Sure." I stand by the credenza and lift a picture frame. It shows me and my siblings with Mom. Jasmine, Mom, and I are in identical dresses. Jake's pants match our color scheme. We look happy. Dad hands me a drink.

"There's one of me with you all like this. Your mom was behind the camera. I keep it in my desk drawer. I want to remember this idealized version of us. Not the version of me without her. Princess, I heard what you said the other day. I never moved on. I didn't know how to live without her."

"Oh, Dad. I'm sorry for what I said. I've been such a mess since that day."

"You said you felt like you've been floundering alone. You haven't been alone. I know I wasn't there. But I always made sure you were safe. I watched as your brother helped guide you. I cleared every obstacle for him to do so."

"You spent so much more time with Jasmine."

"She was too young to process what was happening. You had already developed a sense of independence long before your mom passed. All this time, you thought it was because you were forced to fend for yourself following her death. In actuality, you were perfecting the learned behavior you got from her. We used to talk about you all the time. How one day you would do great things and fight a good fight. And you're doing just that. I'm proud of you."

"I didn't know you were paying attention."

"I'm always paying attention. Watching, listing, guessing your next move."

"You wouldn't even look at me."

"Because of all our children, you are your mother's mirror image. I couldn't look at you and not hate myself for not being there that day. It was a privilege to look upon your face. One I didn't deserve."

"Oh my god, Dad." I go to him and hug him. My eyes fill with tears that fall down my cheek and soak his shirt. He holds me and strokes my hair.

"I'm sorry, princess. I'm so sorry."

We stand like this and hug while I cry. I cry for me. I cry for Mom. I cry for Dad. I cry for all the children whose parents were stolen from them. I cry until my head hurts. Finally, when I'm all cried out, Dad pours me a glass of whiskey, and we stand across from each other, staring, in a moment of silence for Mom and in celebration of him.

"Princess, we have to get back or they'll send the search party for us." He laughs and I do, too.

"I wish you would have told me these things long ago."

"I'm telling you now because you need to hear it to move on to the next stage in your life. Move forward without fear. Move forward in love."

"I'm trying."

"I know. I see a certain gentleman is in love with you?"

"London and I are friends."

"The Irishman."

"You know?"

"Yes."

How could he not know? The moment I was standing around talking with family, I sensed it—his stare was like being touched by love from afar. I couldn't resist its pull. And when my eyes shift to his, they smile back at me. Anyone who sees him look at me knows.

Dad rejoins the party, and I text Aedan to meet me upstairs in the restroom so I can wash my face and pull myself together. He has a worried look on his face when he joins me.

"Are you okay?"

"I'll be fine. As you can see, I need to freshen up."

"I'll wait outside the door."

"Join me." He steps inside the restroom and leans against the door, one hand in his pocket while I wash my face. *So much for makeup.* The little I had is all but gone—likely on Dad's shirt. "I need a drink."

"That bad?"

"Just...the conversation with Dad was deep, but I'm glad we had it. He knows about you."

"You told him."

"No. Your eyes did." Aedan pushes off the wall and, in one step, clears the distance between us. I stare at our reflection in the mirror. He turns me around and kisses me deeply, giving me exactly what I need to pull myself together so I can return to the crowd.

He breaks the kiss and looks at me. "I'm so in love with you."

Aedan and I make our way back to the crowd, which has moved from the courtyard and is now gathered in the ballroom. My Uncle Rick gets everyone's attention.

"Everyone. Champagne is being passed around. Make sure you get a glass." The server walks by with a tray of champagne-filled glasses. Aedan hands me one. He takes one for himself, although he won't drink it. "Reed, we're here today not just as a milestone in your life. We celebrate a man who reached that milestone with grace and determination. Despite experiencing despair, you pushed through and paved the way for three brilliant children to thrive, whose contributions to our society are unmatched. Your resilience is something to celebrate. Our family legacy is secure because of you. Tonight, we celebrate you. Salud."

Everyone raises their glass and says, "Salud" in unison.

CHAPTER 26

The Look of Love

"The events in our lives happen in a sequence in time, but in their significance to ourselves they find their own order, a timetable not necessarily--perhaps not possibly--chronological. The time as we know it subjectively is often the chronology that stories and novels follow: it is the continuous thread of reve-lation."
– Eudora Welty

Aedan

THIS IS EASILY BECOMING my favorite hour of the day: the moment before daybreak, when the sun says farewell to the moon as it peers over the horizon, when it casts a soft hue over the earth, when, for a moment, life stands still, and when my woman lies perfectly molded to my side.

It was past midnight when we arrived home from Reed's birthday bash. June sat on my lap in the car, her head buried in my neck, exhausted. She remained that way as I carried her into the house, shoes dangling from her hands. We shed our clothes in the walk-in closet before getting in the shower. That's where I had her. The sound she made when she came around my shaft as I took her against the wall while water poured over us was music to my ears. I love being inside her. I love making her come more.

Lying beside her, breathing her in, my chest rises and falls with the weight of her pressed to my body. Caressing her bare hips, I think about last night. She was so tired following an evening of partying with friends and family that she immediately fell asleep in my arms after our shower. I slip her bonnet off her head and stroke her hair. I love everything about her. She stirs slightly as sleep escapes her. Her hand slides up my chest to my face. She curls her fingers in my beard and crawls up my side.

"Good morning," I whisper.

She lifts her head, smiles lovingly at me, and steals a kiss. Holding her in place, I pull her leg across me, then reach over her hip and slide my fingers between her folds. A tiny groan escapes her as my fingers glide easily in and out. She's so slick and wet. I circle her sweet spot with my index finger. Sucking her tongue, I swallow her moans as she grinds against me, chasing the feeling of my fingers—chasing the high of having a part of me in her. Her hip lifts, and her walls cling to my fingers as I increase the pressure. Her breath is erratic, and her moans increase as my woman comes on my hand, falling apart on me.

Body still pulsing around my hand, she breaks the kiss. Breathless, she says, "God. Where'd you learn that?"

In a swift move, I roll her on her back and position my rod at her entrance. I hold her gaze as I slowly enter her. Her mouth falls open, and her eyes shut. "Open your eyes, sunshine. I want to see what I do to you," I say before filling her.

Yes, mornings are my favorite time. Watching my woman fall apart beneath me, filling her with my love, it all feels so right.

June is exhausted from our morning activities. I take my shower while she sleeps and then go to the kitchen. Breakfast consists of oatmeal loaded with berries drizzled with honey, ricotta sliced apple-topped toast, and coffee.

Sitting at the counter enjoying my meal, I receive a text from my brother.

Niall: Rose's calendar is tight today. Not sure I'll see you before we head out.

Me: If anything changes, text me.

The news has me conflicted. As much as I love hanging out with my brother and Rose, I don't want June to be stressed about them discovering we're dating until she's ready to tell them. Since she came into my life, my priority has been protecting her at all costs, including her feelings, heart, and life.

Using the quiet time, I scroll through my email. One in particular from the researcher piques my interest. My inquiry into the four tattooed individuals has caught the attention of someone from the DOJ. They want to speak with me because one of the individuals is also on their target list. *Fuck.*

I dial my researcher. "Read your email. Talk to me."

"Good morning, Mr. King. I suppose you have questions about the DOJ inquiry."

"I do. How did they get involved in this?"

"As part of gathering the information you requested, our accessing state records on the subjects triggered the DOJ."

"Which of the four files were they tracking?"

"That's the issue. They won't disclose."

"What do they know about my inquiry?"

"Only what we requested. However, they asked what our interest was in collecting data. I told them they'd need to speak with you. Their contact information is in the email."

"Got it. I'll reach out to them," I say, then end the call. Now that the Justice Department is involved, I need to talk to June.

I'm in the process of plating an omelet by the time June comes down for breakfast.

"The lovely scent of amberwood and honey has my body buzzing," I say.

"How do you do that? I wasn't even in the kitchen yet," she says, coming up behind me and wrapping her arms around me. I add bacon to her plate, then turn around in her arms.

"It's all part of those special skills I have. Are you ready to eat?" I dip my head and kiss her.

When I break the kiss, the look of lust on her face reveals my effect on her. "Ready for more of what you were offering this morning."

"We'll get to that. But first, have a seat, sunshine." Untangling myself from her, I finish dressing her plate with fruit and then place it on the counter.

She sits, takes a berry from the plate, and pops it into her mouth. Before I can walk away, she grabs the waist of my pants, pulls me toward her, and tips up her chin. I dip my head, covering her mouth with mine. Her natural sweetness, mixed with a hint of blueberry, seduces me, and I suck her tongue, giving her another toe-curling kiss. Pacing myself, I break the kiss.

"Thank you. I can't get enough of you."

I brush the pad of my thumb across her lips. "I'm not complaining. Now eat." I say, turning her around in her chair.

She eats a piece of bacon. "It never dawned on me that you could cook. Just another odd thing to add to the list."

I pour myself more coffee and then sit next to her. "Care to elaborate on other oddities you discovered about me?"

"Besides your hyper ability to compartmentalize?"

"Can you be more specific?"

"The way you are with me...like a moment ago when you look down at me like I'm all you ever need."

"Because you are."

"But then the moment we step outside, you're different."

"Different, how?"

"There's a coolness about you that's hard to reconcile with the man I'm looking at now. But it doesn't last long, just long enough to—"

"Get you away from the crowd. The public. Whatever it is I'm shielding you from. I'm protecting you, sunshine. I won't disregard your safety."

"I'm not asking you to."

"Do you feel I don't love you in those moments?"

"It's different, but I feel it. Although the look you give me in those moments isn't like the one you're giving me now, like you're about to devour me." I smirk at her words. I want to show her how much she means to me. But I also need to listen to her express how the things I do when I'm protecting her make her feel. "I'm just saying it takes getting used to. I didn't mean to put a damper on breakfast."

"Expressing what's on your mind isn't an issue. It's exactly what I need. It's validation. Early on, even before you were my woman, I realized you needed a little more of the human side of me when we were in public. It seemed to calm you."

"It does. You were right. I saw glimpses. A touch on the back. How you looked at me when you put the coat on me that day. And that time I came running out of the stairwell."

I smiled, thinking about how nervous she was. "When you jumped into my arms."

"Yeah. You didn't seem surprised. You didn't push me off or chastise me. Well...not about the jumping part, but you were slightly annoyed I didn't tell you I was on my way."

"You were exactly where I wanted you."

"I wasn't sure then. I am now."

"Speaking of talking, we didn't get to last night."

"Because you sexed me up."

"Giving my woman what she wants. How do you feel about last night?"

"The sex was off the chart."

"Sunshine."

"Besides exhausted? I'm happy I went." June eats from her plate.

"Did you want to talk about it?"

"Not particularly. My dad and I had some unresolved issues. We got through it."

I go to June and turn her chair toward me. She snakes her arm around me, and we hold each other, sharing a moment. I pull back and hold her chin in my hand. "The night was difficult for me—being unable to be with you openly. Also, do you know how hard it was for me to watch you with Aaron?"

"We talked about this. You realize he's intentionally goading you, yet you always fall for it. He does the same thing to Jake."

"Goading or getting what he wants—more time with you?" I pick a strawberry from her plate and hold it to her mouth. She takes a bite, and then I finish the rest. I don't want to argue with June, but this topic is unavoidable. My mate is a good friend of hers. But I won't hesitate to destroy anyone who tries to take her from me.

"How will you resolve the fact that he's always going to be in my life?"

"Besides my need to bury myself deep inside you to remind you that you're mine?"

She laughs. I give her a chaste kiss, then take my cup to the coffee station and refill it. I turn to face June, lean against the counter, and purse my lips.

"Listen, sunshine. While we're sharing, I need to update you on something I've been researching."

"You look serious. Is this about James?"

"No. I've been looking into the man that's haunting your dreams."

"There's nothing else to discover. The police have been at a standstill for years."

"You mentioned that he had a knife and a tattoo in your dream. I searched for individuals with knife or sword tattoos and found four people who could have been near the restaurant that day." The fork in June's hand drops to her plate. "I'm sorry to surprise you like this, but it's my job to protect you. I'm determined to find this person."

"It's okay. I want to know. Who is he? Do the police know about this?"

"Only you can tell me if we have the right person. I received pictures of the individuals, including one of their tattoos. There are four of them. If you want, I can show you the pictures, and you can identify the person."

"I can try. All I've ever wanted was to find this person and bring them to justice."

"There's something else. My investigation triggered an alert at the Department of Justice. It appears one of the individuals is on their wanted list. They haven't shared which one. They asked to talk to me, but I doubt it's me they want to speak with."

"They want me."

"Yes, they won't disclose which of the four is on their list."

"To build a solid case, they need me to ID their person. I know how this works. We're both searching for the same person. If I identify him and they find him, he can't escape charges for the murder he committed."

"That's right. They'll indict him. It gives them more time to build their case against him."

"Part of their case hinges on me. I bet they think if I discover his identity, I'd likely flush him out of the woodwork first. Consequently, if one of the people is the man that murdered my mom, and we find him, they won't be able to make their case stick unless it follows the chain of custody."

"That's right."

"Then I'll do it. Do I have to go to their facility?"

"No. I want this to take place away from government facilities. My friend established a mile blackout perimeter around his offices several months ago."

"What does that mean?"

"If anyone new comes into the area, a satellite surveillance system tracks them until they leave."

"I don't understand. Are you saying if some random person from out of town went to get coffee nearby, he'd know it?"

"His security team would. It has both electronic signature and facial recognition."

"What about me?"

"Both Rose and I are close friends of his. You're already cleared. You may already know him...Josh Blumberg."

June looks at me with fierce determination and says, "Set it up."

Chapter 27

Find Him

"Things don't turn up in this world until somebody turns them up."
– James A. Garfield

June

THIS IS IT. THIS is my chance to uncover the real monster behind my nightmares. To once and for all expose the man who executed my mom. And if given the chance...to slay the dragon.

After our discussion over breakfast, Aedan contacts Josh. I've been to his building many times. Taking up two-thirds of a block, it houses my favorite coffee shop. Within two hours, everything is set up. That's the type of power a man like Josh has. He's an elite—one of the few descendants of elites in California. I met him a while back at an event. He's stunning, dark, mysterious, broody. Looking at him, like other elites, you know something is different. An air of power surrounds him. Like others across the globe within his society, his wealth extends well beyond my family's. I work for a trillion-dollar company, and my father is worth billions. However, for members of the elite society, personal wealth is estimated in the trillions. No one knows their true worth.

"Are you ready?" Aedan asks, leading me to the conference room on the executive floor of the Blumberg building.

"Let's do this."

Josh Blumberg meets us outside the conference room. He watches as I walk toward him. His face is expressionless, but his eyes are soft and welcoming.

"May I?" he asks, arms open. I step closer and briefly hug him. I remember that's his thing. Kind, cordial, beautiful to look at, and one of the most brilliant men in the city.

"It's good to see you again. Thank you for facilitating this. As you can imagine, this is hard for me."

"I understand. Aedan, good to see you again, too."

"Mate."

"June, I won't be joining you in the conference room, but if you need anything, please don't hesitate to let me know." I nod. "There are several members of the force in the room. They'll take you through their process, including signing documents and reviewing evidence. I've already contacted your legal team to have them review any documents you must sign. Your attorney is in the room should you have questions."

"Thank you. I received a message stating the same."

"I'm not privy to the evidence, but if it gets too heavy, I have a professional on standby if needed."

"I understand."

Josh places his hand on Aedan's shoulder. "Let me know if you need *anything*."

"Thank you, mate."

"Good luck, June," he says, then walks down the hall.

Aedan opens the door, and I step into a large modern conference room bordered on two sides by walls of windows overlooking San Francisco. A wooden conference table in the center of the room seats twenty-two. Scattered around the room are various clumps of people—men and women—all wearing suits in grey, blue, or black. Some are watching us, and some are preoccupied with whatever device or document they possess.

One official-looking gentleman with overly gelled black hair stands and extends a hand.

"Hi, Ms. Ross. Mr. King. I'm Dean Wilson. I'll be leading the review of evidence today. These are my colleagues." Dean proceeds to introduce the people around the room. They've already met my attorney, but I still acknowledge him.

Aedan and I sit. Adean watches intently as Dean flips a large digital tablet the size of a laptop. Dean hands me a stylus, flips through a few screens, and then explains a document for me to sign. I review the documents and confer with my attorney before signing. When that's finished, he asks me a few questions.

"For the record," he says before we begin reviewing the evidence.

"Ms. Ross, in partnership with Mr. King's team, we've come to understand that in the case of your mother's murder, four persons of interest have come to light that weren't previously identified. I want to show you pictures of these individuals one by one and see if you recognize any of them."

"I understand. Did Mr. King tell you I never saw his face? Only his eyes."

"Yes."

"Then you understand I won't recognize the face, and the most effective means of identifying him would be seeing him the way I did twenty years ago."

"I understand."

Dean flags a member of his team to his side. The person points at the screen and then returns to his seat. I twist my ring, waiting for the steps in the process.

"Okay, I will show you a picture of the first person from their eyebrows to their cheekbone. Please tell me if you recognize them."

He pulls the first person up. The eyes are brown, the pupil is wider than normal, and the person looks angry. "I've never seen this person," I say. Dean makes a note on the screen and then taps a few places on the screen.

"What about this person?"

The person's eyes are washed out greyish green. Creases are descending diagonally past their eyebrows, reminding me of sexual offenders I've seen recently on the news. "I don't know this person. This is not him."

"Are you sure?"

"I'm sure."

"Please move on, Mr. Wilson," Aedan insists.

Dean goes through the same process as before. "Do you recognize this person?" he slides the large tablet before me. I look down into eyes that are dark as midnight and feel as if they're piecing my soul. He's looking at me. He knows me.

"That's him."

"You know this man?"

"This is the man that killed my mom. I'm sure of it." I grab Aedan's hand. "My god, this is him."

"It's okay, June, we'll get him. Mr. Wilson, do you have a picture of his tattoo?"

"I do. Would you like to see the tattoo, Ms. Ross?"

"Yes."

Dean pulls up a picture of the man's hand. It has a sword exactly like the one in my dream, but it's tattooed on his hand instead of him holding it.

"This is exactly what I see every night in my dream."

Dean nods to a member of his team across the table. The person makes a note on their tablet.

"What about the fourth person? Is that person or any of the first two the one you were looking for?" Aedan asks Dean.

"No. The person who Ms. Ross identified as having allegedly killed the elder Ms. Ross is also the person we are investigating for an unrelated crime."

"I want to know what other crimes he's committed," I press. Dean and his team seem hesitant to respond.

"Mr. Wilson, as you know, Ms. Ross is a high-profile executive with security around the clock. As head of her security, I need to know who this man is and what he's done."

Dean purses his lips, then says, "I understand, per Mr. Blumberg, that despite my process, I need to disclose that information to you." Dean pulls up a full picture of the person in question. "This man is Darrien Goodman, a career criminal. He's wanted for several racketeering-related offenses, but he's most wanted for arms dealing."

Aedan stands up. The look on his face as he directs his question around the room scares even me. "Tell me you know where this man is."

"We are unsure of Mr. Goodman's whereabouts at this time. That's why when a member of your team inquired into his background, it flagged us. We've been following up on all leads. He's a dangerous man. We want to find him as much as you do."

"Is this man looking for me?" I ask.

"That's unclear at this moment. We've been tracking people trying to get close to Rick or Rose Ross, hoping it will lead us back to him."

"Because Ms. Ross developed technology that foreign governments would pay millions to gain access to," Aedan adds.

"That's right. If they get a hold of the technology Ms. Ross developed, there's no telling how they'd use it—they can weaponize it. Until recently, we didn't know your backstory of witnessing your mother's death. Your father and uncle did an incredible job hiding your identity regarding the incident at the restaurant. We came across your profile when we saw the press conference, and you stated your intent to lead the program to remove assault weapons from the street. As he's moved on from directly involving himself in that level of crime, we assumed Mr. Goodman might send a gopher to intercede once your program begins."

He's right. Darrien has unfinished business. Even though it's been a long time, he might have his hands in the small stuff for nostalgic reasons, namely his unfinished business...with me.

My eyes shift to Dean. "Does this man Darrien know you're after him?"

"Anyone in his position should assume the government is looking for them. I believe the question you meant to ask is, does he know we're here?" I steeple my fingers, waiting for his response. "You have powerful friends, Ms. Ross. As it stands, no one other than those in this room, Mr. Blumberg, and a select member of his staff know we're here."

"No one can know she is part of your investigation, Mr. Wilson. And we need to find this man ASAP. Are we clear?"

"We're working on that."

"Where is the last place you tracked him?"

"We suspect he's somewhere in California."

I stand next to Aedan and look down at Dean. "Mr. Wilson, one thing I've learned over the past twenty years is that the best place to hide is in plain sight. Consider me an expert. I assure you that Derrien Goodman is here in San Francisco. You have forty-seven square miles. Find him." My voice booms, bouncing off the walls. I turn to Aedan. "We're done here."

Belfast

CHAPTER 28

Rain

"Your present circumstances don't determine where you can go; they merely determine where you start."
– Nido Qubein

June

LIKE THEY SAY, "WHEN it rains, it pours." Ever since I left San Francisco, I have been in crisis mode. Between the media storm with James, Saola, and Ross Enterprises, trying to conceal my relationship with Aedan, and now the revelation of Darrien Goodman, it's a lot to take in. On top of it all, I'm trying to keep this deal with Knight Development Corporation from falling through.

My assistant rushes into the room. I've been fielding calls back-to-back since we left San Francisco, and she's doing her best to weed out the most important.

"I have Ms. Nichols holding for you. Your lunch is on the way, and Mr. King insists he join you." I look at her and smile.

"Thank you. Oh, and give Mr. King the task of bringing my lunch in if he's so inclined to join me." The strained look on her face tells me that's the last thing she wants to do. "Don't worry. He won't give you any flak."

"Understood," she says, then leaves.

I pick up the call from Raven. "Raven, please tell me you have good news."

"The British Daily Corporation retracted their story."

I breathe a sigh of relief. If we can ink this deal with Knight Development, Ross Enterprises can begin expansion, and I will have set us on a path to making billions.

"This is good news. Talk to me. How did you get James to back off?"

"You were right, he lied. The BDC didn't research the facts. It turns out they took a payout to print the story. Parker interceded and got the retraction." This confirms Aedan's suspicion that someone else is behind this. *But who?* Who would be motivated enough to take me down and spend that kind of money for a reputable media company to jeopardize its name by printing a lie?

"He's a power player in this space. I suspect he has something on them for them to fold so fast."

"I suspect you're right. I'll update Knight Development. The deal is still set for Monday."

"Then I'll see you Monday in Seattle. Good work, Raven." I say, ending the call. I stand, go to the window, and look over the cloud-covered city.

It's raining. Black domes pass on the street below, protecting holders from the rain. It's ironic. We spend nine months in our mother's protective womb before being born into a world where she spends another eighteen years shielding us from it, getting us ready to do the same—where we protect ourselves from everything from the weather to war. Because, at the end of the day, we live in a world that's full of beautiful and bad things simultaneously. Where at a moment's notice, someone on the street may hand you a flower, while another won't hesitate to take your life.

A sudden tap on the wall, followed by my man's voice, snaps me out of my sentiments of the past.

"I'm here with your lunch." I turn to find Aedan with a sexy smile, holding a bag in one hand with the other hand in his pocket. I walk over to him, take the bag, and set it on the table near the window beside a vase of lavender carnations he brought me. Since my first day in Belfast, I haven't gone a week without fresh flowers from Aedan. And since we became a couple, I haven't gone a day without feeling loved by him or making love to him. It's hard to believe he wasn't always this way. I turn around and smile at him.

"I feel special. Billionaire bodyguard, lunch-bringing boyfriend. I think I hit the jackpot."

Aedan walks over to me, snakes his arms around me, and says, "I feel the same about you. I'd bring you lunch daily just to see this hungry look in your eyes." He dips his head and delivers a kiss that promises more to come. He's right. I am hungry...for him.

I break the kiss and smile against his face. "Can you handle that I'm addicted to you? I'm ready to skip lunch and head upstairs."

He barks out a laugh. "Music to my ears. I promise you'll get your fill later." He gives me a chaste kiss. "Let's get you fed." He steps back and holds a chair out for me. I sit, and he joins me.

I open the bag and remove its contents: a chicken Caesar salad for me and pasta salad for him.

"I heard back from Raven. The BDC retracted the story." I hand Aedan his meal and a fork.

"That's good news. Any more potential issues looming related to the contract?"

"Not unless something comes up between tonight and Monday."

"Congratulations."

"There's one problem with the scenario. The BDC never validated James' story."

"They didn't care because they were paid to print the story. Who do you think their intended target was? You or Aaron?"

"The Adlers aren't people I can see anyone coming after. Their clients and ours are very different."

"So, you're saying you're the target?"

"I'm saying nothing is gained by destroying the Adlers."

"Let's play this out. What would happen if the public bought James' story, and somehow you couldn't close the deal with Knight? Would you have to resign?"

"No. They couldn't fire me either, because I could always partner with a different developer. Getting to the final contract stage would take time, but it's doable. Besides, my employment is not solely based on closing this deal. There are several ways for me to help Ross generate revenue—some of them already in the works."

"But whoever orchestrated this media storm doesn't know that." It's not a question. He knows they wouldn't.

I stick my fork in his pasta. He gives me the same look he always does—seductively annoyed.

"Not enjoying your salad?"

"It's good. Not as good as your pasta, but it'll do." He dishes some of his pasta into my salad. "Listen, whoever is behind this wasn't smart enough to know that someone like Parker Page could pull the rug from under a multibillion-dollar media company's leg. They certainly would have no idea about the inner workings of a trillion-dollar company."

"What other benefit could come out of this?"

"Heightened media attention could cause other news outlets to dig into my background looking for their next big story."

"Then whoever is doing this wants something from you. This is personal."

Seattle

CHAPTER 29

Happy Birthday

"If I know what love is, it is because of you."
– Hermann Hesse

June

IT's JUNE IN SEATTLE. My namesake, because what else would a hip mom name her first daughter? Sitting in a lounge chair, sun streaming through the windows, I look out over the blue waters of Elliot Bay and reflect on yesterday's meeting with Knight Development Corporation. Roman and his brothers, Noah and Mark, did a great job briefing me on their plans to help develop properties across the globe for Ross Enterprises. They're rising stars in this space, and rightfully so. We successfully closed the deal within my desired parameters thanks to Raven Nichols's brilliant work. Later, I celebrated the win with Aedan and Jake, who also shared a pre-birthday toast with me before he had to fly out.

That was yesterday. Today, Aedan and I have a mini reprieve and get to be together without hiding the fact that we are in a relationship from others. It feels good. I reach across the table and sort through the cards and gifts I received when I arrived at the Four Seasons residence yesterday. Aedan didn't seem to be surprised by the onslaught of gifts. I should have known he had my assistant arrange for all my gifts to be overnighted here, so I had them on my birthday.

I pick up a black envelope with gold writing on it. It's from the Knight brothers. I open it to find a card with a picture of a yacht. It lists a phone number on it. *"You have carte blanche whenever you're in town. The Knights."* Free access to their super yacht. I'm impressed.

"Happy birthday, sunshine," Aedan says, walking up to me fresh from his shower, wearing a black t-shirt and matching sweats.

"How was the workout?"

"I sweat better with you beneath me." He sits beside me and pulls me onto his lap so I'm facing him. "What's this you're looking at?" He slides his hand under my t-shirt, caressing my skin. His warm hands make my body buzz as he palms my breast.

"It seems Roman has given us full access to his family yacht whenever we're here," I say, holding the card between us.

"That's generous. Are you opening your gifts now?"

"I wasn't planning to. I was waiting for you so we could have breakfast."

He pinches my nipple and growls. "I should have ordered it for later," he says, lifting my shirt and sucking my breast. I look down, watching as he takes his time to worship my body. Heat radiates through me. I comb my fingers through his hair, and my body throbs where I want him most.

"We don't have time to finish this," I pant. "Let me open one more. I've been dying to see what my dad sent," I say, arching my back and reaching backward to the table. Aedan grips my sides, steadying me.

"I should lift you and have you for breakfast."

I grab the gift and sit up. "You're insatiable." I examine the brown, orange, and yellow retro-designed wrapping paper. "Look, how cool is this?"

"Just your style."

I tear off the paper to reveal a black leather box and open it. "Oh my god, Aedan, check this out." I try not to cry as I turn the black and silver Olympus OM-1 camera over in my hand.

"It's in perfect condition."

"It was my mom's camera. She loved photography and had several cameras. He bought this vintage one for her as a birthday gift one year. It was made the year she was born. This was one of the smallest to come out at the time."

"It's a lovely gift. Will you be taking pictures with it?"

"Maybe. Do they still develop film?"

"I believe so. I'll have Lorn order some for you."

"When we went to Dad's party, I noticed the credenza in his office was lined with photos taken with this camera."

"Then we'll do the same—make new memories with her camera."

"That would be nice." I lean in and kiss Aedan. He reaches under my shirt and cups my breasts, massaging them. Deepening the kiss, I groan into his mouth. My body craves him. I break the kiss, panting. "Breakfast is on the way. We don't have time."

"It's your birthday. We have time." He takes out his phone, taps the screen, and then tosses it aside. Afterward, he reaches between us and between my folds, testing me. "Lift for me." I follow his command, lifting as he frees his thick shaft. I lower myself onto him and begin rocking into him. I'm so wet for him that he glides in and out of me with ease.

"Take me, sunshine." He holds my hips tight against him, guiding my rhythm and giving me exactly what I need. He's so thick that I'm completely full of him, consumed inside and out. My pace quickens, and my walls clamp down on him as I chase the feeling. "That's it. Come with me." He pumps up in me with hard, short, fast thrusts. "Give it all to me."

And I do; I come hard and fast around his shaft, rocking into him, calling out his name. "Aedan."

He grunts, giving into his release, and my body continues pulsing around him. But he knows I'm not finished because although his love is pouring into me, I need more.

"Squeeze baby, come again for me," he says, and I do. It's so intense that the only sound coming from me is whimpers and heavy breathing.

"I love you, baby. Happy birthday." I lower my face to his and kiss him until my body stops pulsing around him. He stands, bringing me with him, carries me to the bathroom, and sits me on the counter. "I told you we had time."

After breakfast, I inform Aedan that I don't need a car to get around the areas of Seattle I want to see. Unfortunately, we can't leave immediately because his security team needs to change out of their suits to blend in with the crowd. I don't mind. I crank the music and groove to the beat while Aedan scrolls through whatever is on his screen. He has another thing coming.

I walk over to him, sit astride him, and take the phone out of his hand. "Hey, sunshine. What do you need?" I love this man. Anyone else would be annoyed by my antics.

"To be near you." He cups my chin in his hand and dusts his lips across mine.

"I'm here."

"It doesn't bother you?"

"What should I be bothered by?"

"Me."

He has this look I can't quite make out. I smooth my finger across his eyebrow, waiting for his response. "You're stunning, June. When I assigned myself to watch over you, I suppose I was being selfish. I get to see your beautiful face every day. Watch over you as you navigate your day. However, it's not all fun and games. I took the assignment because I believe I'm the best person to protect you. I'm also aware of your situation and the potential dangers that could arise when we're in public. I can't bask in your beauty or enjoy precious moments with you during that time. But behind closed doors, holding you like this…is my favorite part. You're safe in my arms. You're exactly where I want you. And I don't have to worry about people, threats, or whatever comes next. I'm at peace because you're here with me."

I press my lips to his and kiss him. It's pure, loving, and all I need. I break the kiss. "I like that I can be this way with you. This is the real me when I'm not putting on a brave front for the public."

"It doesn't matter which side you show. I love everything about you, from the way your scent lingers on my skin, hauntingly sweet, to the way your laughter echoes in my dreams. I love the banter, the retro wild child, the woman who dances barefoot in the kitchen—all of it." He cups my cheek in his hand, then scoops his hand over my curly afro. "I love all the hairstyles you wear." He twists a lock of hair around his fingers. "Do you want kids?"

"Someday. With the right man. What about you? You've been a bachelor a very, very long time."

"Not the old man jokes again."

"You're not *that* old."

"Gee, thanks. You used to be afraid of me. Are you still?"

"No. Those things you used to do—"

"My defensive posturing, as you call it."

"You're not that way with me anymore. And like now, how I'm sitting, I'm on par with you."

"Until I toss you on your back and make love to you. In all seriousness, I wasn't trying to intimidate you previously." He touches his nose to mine. "June, do you think I'm the right man for you?"

I nod. "I told you I was born to be with you. What about you? You didn't answer my question. Do you want children?"

"With you." In a swift motion, he flips me on my back and hovers over me. He lowers his face and whispers, "We can start now." His smile tickles my ear, but his phone buzzing beside us breaks the mood. "Ugh." He lifts, bringing me with him, then grabs his phone. "The team is in place," he says, helping me up and out of my King Aedan haze.

We pull ourselves together and head out. It's a five-minute walk down First Street to the pier. Before we get to the corner, we stop in front of a store. "This is where I want to go." Aedan opens the door. "This is the Purple store."

"I got that part," he says, looking around where everything from underwear to umbrellas is purple.

"Can I help you with something?" the clerk asks, appropriately dressed in a purple shirt and matching slacks.

I walk toward her. Aedan follows. I point in the direction he came from. "Stay over there," I tell him, attempting to conceal my true purpose for being at the store.

"That's not how this works, sunshine."

I roll my eyes. "Fine." I shake my head at the clerk, then search the store while Aedan monitors my every move. I pick up a purple tie. "Found it." I hold it up to Aedan. "This will suit you perfectly."

"I don't need a purple tie."

"It's a royal color. A king needs a purple tie."

"When will I ever wear this?" He smooths his fingers across the fabric.

"We'll wear it when we come out as an official couple. I'll wear a matching silk dress. Can you handle that?"

He grabs me around my waist and pulls me to him. The look in his eyes is filled with so much love that it makes me weak in the knees. "Anything for you."

I take the tie to the counter. Aedan picks up a butterfly hair clip and sets it next to the tie at the register. "We'll take these two items," he says, placing his centurion on the counter. The sales clerk rings our items and places the tie in a bag. Aedan slides the hair clip into my hair before we leave the store.

"Where to next?"

"This way." I point across the street toward the Pike's Place market sign in the distance.

It's summer and the pier is shoulder-to-shoulder full of tourists and fair-weather friends patronizing the shops and restaurants. Although he has a team trailing us, Aedan is noticeably focused on our surroundings, which makes me feel a little guilty about dragging him out for a walk.

This part sucks: how the constant drama in my life impacts the man I want to be with. The person he has to be to keep me safe is not something I'd wish on anyone. When I was with London, we were free to be ourselves regardless of where we were or how many security members were watching. I want that with Aedan.

When we reach the flower market, I stop.

"Would you like more flowers?" Aedan asks. His hand is on my lower back. He guides me toward the table and then stands behind me.

"Yes...no. This is hard for me." I turn to face him. He's standing so close I have to look up. This is the stance I hate. This is the man I'm afraid of. I blow out a breath. "This is not what I planned. I'm with you, but we're not together."

He cups my cheek. "I have to protect you."

"I just want to buy some flowers, but I want you present."

He purses his lips and then smiles down at me. "I get it." He taps his earphone and says, "Protect the queen." Within seconds, his team, previously following at a distance in stealth mode, encircles us and intersperses amongst the crowd. There's a noticeable bubble around Aedan and me. In a rare public display of affection, he dips his head and kisses me, and I kiss him right back. "Let's get your flowers, sunshine."

"Thank you," I whisper against his lips.

The flower stall attendant, who has been watching the entire scene, asks, "Is there any specific varietal you're looking for?"

Aedan turns me around in his arms to face her. "Would you like more carnations, or did you have something else in mind?"

I point to the roses. "I'll have a dozen each of the orange, the white, and the pink."

Aedan tightens his arms around my waist and addresses the clerk, "Please add yellow thistle, some solidago, and green leaves. You've clipped the thorns, correct?"

"Yes."

While the clerk prepares our order, I tip my head sideways and look up at Aedan. "You know a lot about flowers, don't you?"

"I know what's beautiful. I know beautiful things need protecting. Nature provided roses and thistles with built-in protection."

"You're mine. I didn't mean to break protocol," I say, smoothing my hands along his arms.

"Your flowers," the clerk announces. Aedan hands her his card, and a team member collects my flowers.

For the rest of the afternoon, we pop in and out of shops before we grab lunch at a local restaurant. My haul for the day outside the flowers is modest: chocolate, a graphic T-shirt, and gold sandals. Aedan's haul is a purple tie. In addition, I agree to share the chocolate; he fully intends to be handsy when I wear my t-shirt.

Spending the day openly with Aedan as a couple gives me a sense of what I could have with him had he not been sworn to protect me. I love the ease of our conversation, how in sync our movements are, and how attentive he is. I love that I never have to long for his touch. Now that I have a taste of what could be, the question is, how do I go back?

Chapter 30

To Have and to Hold

"There is darkness in light, there is pain in joy, and there are thorns on the rose."

– Cate Tiernan

Aedan

Over the years, diverting an incident by taking down a bad guy has given me a natural high. But nothing compares to the high of being with June. Her curves perfectly conform to my body when I hold her in my arms. Breathing in the sweetness that's all hers...is everything. She is wild and witty, wrapped in the perfect package—an addiction I never want to get over.

Earlier, the distress on her face, indicating she needed me as her boyfriend, not her bodyguard, nearly broke me. The solution was simple—trust my team and give her what she wanted. I made the right choice. Sitting at the counter surrounded by hints of her scent mixed with those of fresh-cut roses is intoxicating. I look up from my phone and observe her delicate fingers working, selecting flowers from a pile and strategically placing them in one of the four vases lining the counter. She looks happy. She wouldn't allow me to have a member of the staff arrange them.

I put my phone down. "I should recheck those for thorns. You might hurt yourself."

"It's fine. I already checked. See?" She waves her hand across the flowers neatly lining the counter.

"I'll have the team pick up a crate to secure them for tomorrow's flight."

"Tell them to use floral foam between the vases. It's easy to cut and sturdier than other materials. They won't need to empty the water. They shouldn't move if packed correctly. What do you think?" She holds up one of the completed vases.

"It's lovely. You're a woman of many talents. Although, I should have expected it from a professed flower child."

June washes and dries her hands, then rounds the counter toward me. I swivel my chair to meet her gaze. She stands between my legs and wraps her arms around my waist.

"Thank you for today. It was the perfect way to wind down from a successful win and a great start to my birthday."

"Your birthday is not over yet. We have dinner and I have a gift for you."

"And I get to have you."

"There's that. Although, you can have me whenever you want."

She rubs her hands on my thighs. "That's the best part." She returns to the opposite side of the counter and continues filling her vases. Her smile dissipates. Something's on her mind.

I stand and go to her. I turn her to face me, cup her chin, and kiss her. "Hey," I say when I break the kiss.

"Hey."

"Come with me." I take her hand and lead her into the living room, which overlooks the bay. I sit, and she takes her usual position on my lap. "What's going on?"

"You have a big dinner planned for us, don't you?"

"I do."

"Would you be upset if we have it here? I mean, whoever is catering, can they bring it to the penthouse?"

"You don't want the fanfare."

"It's not that."

"Then what is it? We have the entire Sky View Observatory reserved just for us."

"But we still have to get there. I don't want to experience that part of you that has to be on high alert the second we walk out of the building. I want to stay in this moment, where being with you feels natural...easy, and you're not worried about who's watching or looking for me. Just for tonight. I understand it can't always be like this."

How do we get past this? How do I protect my woman and still give her what she wants while there's a monster out there potentially looking for her? How do I tell her tonight is more than just her birthday celebration? How do I converge our worlds without changing who we are? I slide my hand beneath her shirt and hold her waist, stroking her stomach with my thumbs, needing to feel her skin against mine. Needing to be one.

"All right, sunshine."

"We'll stay in?"

"I'll have the caters bring everything here. But we're still dressing up."

"Absolutely." Excitedly, she presses her lips to mine. I part her lips with my tongue, deepening the kiss. She combs her fingers through my hair, gripping and pulling. The heat between her legs radiates through her lounge pants, and I can feel her body throbbing. I slide my hand beneath her pants, gripping her hips and guiding her rhythm as she grinds against my shaft. "Don't," she pants.

"You want me to stop?"

"I don't want to come yet. Not like this. You know I'll want more."

"I'll give you whatever you want whenever you want it. Tell me what you want."

"I want you, but after…" Her breath still heavy comes out rushed.

"After dinner?

"I want to open my gifts."

"You have me so hard, honey, but let's open your gifts," I concede, putting my desire to be in her on hold. She gives me a chaste kiss and a teasing squeeze where she shouldn't. "Sunshine," I warn before she hops off my lap.

June gathers her gifts and places them on the coffee table. Then, she returns to my lap, this time facing the table. "This one is from Nicole. I have an idea what it is by the shape of the box." She opens the card and reads it. *"You almost worn mine out. I figure you'd need this since you're hanging out more in the UK."* She tears the paper and opens the box. "Wow, this is beautiful," she says, removing a semiprecious jewel-handled paisley color umbrella from its sleeve.

"It's fit for a queen."

She puts the sleeve on and returns it to the box. "She's so practical—like my brother." Next, she picks up a small, flat, square gift box, and like the others, she tears through the paper and opens the box. "See. Practical." She holds up a black silk-lined bonnet large enough to cover her hair when she wears twists. "Oh my god. Jake is crazy. Look at this." She places the bonnet in my hand.

I take my time turning the hat and reading the phrases embroidered across it: "Copacetic. Freaky deaky. Fly. Peace out. I can hear you saying that one." She nudges my arm. I continue: "Brick house. Groovy."

"I can't believe he had this made for me."

"I guess you could say it's fly." June pushes her back into my chest. I bark out a laugh. "Well, it is." She takes the hat from me and tries it on, shoving her curly afro beneath it. I slide my hand back under her shirt and cup her breast. I want my woman so bad—bonnet or no bonnet. She quickly pulls the hat off, tosses it on the table, then picks up another item.

"What's this?" she asks, holding a steely grey envelope.

"That looks like one of the pieces of mail I saw on your desk in Belfast."

"Most of it was welcome to Ireland notes or people congratulating me on my new job. The rest, believe it or not, were paper resumes—which I haven't seen in years."

"But I saw a grey one like this. It stood out because of the quality. It's linen."

"I remember. It said congratulations on your new job, but it didn't have a name," she says, opening the card. She reads it. "Happy birthday. May you have many more." She hands it to me.

I examine the card. "This is odd. There's no signature or return address. I'll have Ben look into this. Have you received anything else like this?"

"Just the two." She picks up a gold-wrapped gift with no visible card. "This is from London." She says, ripping the paper off.

"How do you know?"

"Every gift I've ever received from him has been wrapped in gold," she admits, and my jaw ticks. But I don't let on to how I feel about it. Instead, I brush my thumbs over her nipples. She arches her back, leans into me, and I kiss her neck.

"Let's see your gift," I encourage her to continue, although my hands roam her body.

She peels back the paper, revealing a red box with gold embossed lettering. She slides the lid off. An envelope matching the box lies on top of the tissue paper. She opens it and reads the card. *"Happy birthday, beautiful. I hope you're having a wonderful day. Here is something so you never go without your favorite snacks."* The box contains several food packages in various sizes and colors. "It's a Japanese snack box. It says here that it's a monthly subscription. I can't believe he got this. I'll have to call him."

"Not tonight." I squeeze her nipple with one hand and slide the other down her pants and between her fold and stroke her there. "Tonight is about how I make you feel." I slide my fingers into her, and her breath hitches.

"Oh god, Aedan." Her head falls back onto my shoulder as I slide my fingers in and out. She's so slick and wet they move with ease.

"That's it," I say as her breath comes rushed, as her walls throb around my hand, as she succumbs to the feeling. I increase the pressure and circle her clit as she grinds against my hand. "Come for me." Her walls clamp down on my fingers, and my woman comes on my hand, calling my name.

I stand, bringing June with me, then carry her quickly down the hall to the bedroom. I want her to come again, hard and fast. I lay her on the bed and pull off her pants. I remove my clothes while she takes off her shirt.

"This is going to get rough, honey." Hovering over her, I nudge her leg open with my knee, then I position myself at her entrance and fill her. I dip my head and wrap my mouth around her breast and suck her hard in time with each thrust. She screams in pleasure at the top of her lungs as my body slams into hers. Her walls are tight. "Come for me." I slam into her several more times, and she comes violently around my shaft. I continue moving in and out as her core squeezes me. "Fuck, June. You're going to make me come. Squeeze, baby." She milks my shaft, and I find my release and spill my seed in waves into her. "God," I grunt. I continue pumping, and my girl comes again as we fill the room with cries and groans.

When it's over, when her walls stop pulsing, when she stops chasing the feeling of having me in her, I roll over and pull her with me.

"I love you, June. Happy Birthday."

CHAPTER 31

Kiss of Life

"Love is the whole thing. We are only pieces."
– Rumi

June

WHILE AEDAN WAS SEXING me up, the staff was setting up the dining room for my birthday dinner. I never thought I'd fall so fast and hard for a man. But now, I can't envision my life without Aedan.

I stand in front of the mirror, smoothing my hands down my orange and yellow silk ombre dress. Aedan walks up behind me, wearing a black suit and a gold tie that matches the color of my dress. He wraps his arms around me. "You look beautiful. And this feels amazing," he says, caressing my body through the silk.

"Don't be handsy. You know where that leads."

He pulls my hair back and kisses my neck. "Everything is ready for us."

He takes my hand and leads me down the hall toward the dining room. A bright hue from fairy lights strategically hung around the room illuminates a perfectly set table complete with white linen, fine china, candles, and a floral arrangement of white flowers, roses, carnations, and babies' breath. Soft jazz plays in the background. Aedan helps me to my seat and then sits beside me.

"This is so lovely, Aedan."

"I'm glad you like it." He nods to a staff member standing nearby.

They begin by serving Louis Roederer Cristal Brut champagne and a variety of starters consisting of blinis with sour cream, golden caviar, and dill, crostini with grilled sweet onions, and a blue cheese Provençal vegetable tart.

Looking at the spread, I'm grateful that Aedan asked me whether I wanted to have my favorite meal or have him plan something different. Until he came along, I wasn't sure how much of my habits were actually me or me trying to recapture the woman my mom was. I lost myself, wallowing in memories of her.

Now I'm discovering that I like champagne and fancy foods. That I'm addicted to sex but only with him. That I'm still wild, but in times when I need to control it—he settles me. That the way he looks at me sets my soul on fire, and I can't see living without him. That in making new memories with him, I'm finding myself.

"Are you having a drink with me tonight?"

"Of course." He gestures to the server and they pour him champagne. He holds up his glass. "To the most beautiful woman in the world, who breathed life into me. Happy birthday, honey." He leans in for a kiss and taps his glass to mine.

"Thank you for making tonight special. This..." I gesture around the room. "...is so lovely."

"Anything for you."

These are the moments I enjoy most with Aedan: when it's just us, enjoying each other's company and being lost in love. During dinner, I learn more about him and the training he's gone through to prepare himself for the type of work he does. He talks about Rose sparring with Niall and how well she holds her own against him.

"You mentioned previously that your little sister, Jasmine, trained in self-defense."

"My brother convinced my dad to put her in classes when she entered first grade."

"Because of what happened with your mom?"

"Yeah. She's really good at it."

"What made you decide against it?"

"Jake tried to convince me to go, but I refused. In my eyes, the worst-case scenario already happened."

"You were going to accept whatever hand fate dealt you."

"That's right. I still am."

Aedan takes my hand and pulls me toward him, and I sit on his lap. "I promise it will never be like that again. You'll never have to fear for your life or think about how to navigate situations like that. You don't need to fend for yourself. I will be there to protect you."

I stroke his arms. "I believe you. But you have to know that day still haunts me. But let's not talk about that tonight." I give him a chaste kiss. "So, are we going to have cake?"

"Yes, but first, you have to open your gift." He reaches past me and picks up a large square gift wrapped in white paper and bound by a silver ribbon. He places it on the table in front of us.

I lift it. "Oh my god, what's in here, a brick?" I examine the box that I guestimate to be one foot squared. I sit it back on the table.

"Open it."

I slide off the ribbon and rip off the paper, revealing a dark-stained wooden box with a gold-filled peace sign carved into the center. "What is this? If it's one of those trick boxes where something pops out—"

"Open it, sunshine."

I lift the top off the box. Inside is a small square hole holding a solitary diamond ring. "Oh my god, Aedan. Tell me this is not what I think it is. What is this? What are you doing?"

He reaches in and removes the ring. He holds my finger and slides it on. Then he cups my cheek and says, "June, these past six months with you have been the best days of my life, and I never want it to end. When I met you, I felt an immediate connection I've never felt with any other woman. I fell in love with you long before you jumped into my arms, running out of the stairwell. That day was my wake-up call. When I looked into your eyes, I saw the woman I'd been waiting my whole life to find. Now that I've found you, I can't see living another day without you by my side. You are the woman I want to wake up to. You're the woman I want to build a family with. I've sworn to protect your life and I swear to protect your heart. Will you marry me?"

I look at my hand resting in his and the ring he placed there, then at Aedan. I hold his gaze. Tears well in my eyes, blurring my vision until they're so full the tears fall down my cheeks. I see our future with him beside me. I see us building a family. I see all the things I'd been searching for in London but could not find. I see forever in his eyes. "Yes," I say, crashing my lips to his.

Aedan breaks the kiss and stares into my eyes. "My girl is going to marry me?"

"Yeah, without hesitation. But we need to talk to our families."

"We will. No one will question the love between us. But I agree we need to talk to them because June, from this day forward, I don't intend to live separately from you. Can you handle that?"

"Does this mean we'll have a short engagement?"

"Yes. I'd like us to begin planning our future."

"Can we have cake now?"

He barks out a laugh and then kisses me. "Of course. Wife-to-be, we can have cake."

After the cake is served, Aedan dismisses the staff, and he and I retreat to the lounge overlooking the bay. He puts the cake and champagne on the occasional table near the lounger. "Kiss of Life" by Sade plays over the sound system.

"Dance with me, honey," he whispers into my ear. He kisses down my neck. We hold each other locked in a tight embrace, swaying to the music while only the stars witness a moment of love between us.

Everything is perfect because I'm in love.

I'm happy.

I'm safe.

I'm his.

Belfast

CHAPTER 32

The Reveal

"Love takes off the masks we fear we cannot live without and know we cannot live within."
– James Baldwin

Aedan

THE BUILDING'S REPAIRS ARE finally complete, and the lobby entrance looks even more spectacular than when it opened fifteen years ago. After returning from Seattle, I had all June's belongings moved from the corporate suites in the Falcon building into our penthouse. Our next step is to share the good news with our families.

"How's this supposed to work, mate?" Aaron asks. "The second they see me with June, as usual, Niall and Rose will assume we're a couple. However, it's been a while since I've been out with June. I can take her out for drinks, then return here after they arrive." He says it to be funny, but I'm seconds away from punching him. He thinks he's here to throw my brother off my trail. He'll be just as surprised about the engagement news.

"Don't get any ideas," I tell him.

"What ideas is London getting?" June asks, entering the room wearing a purple silk slip dress matching my purple tie. She wraps an arm around my waist. I palm her hip and pull her into me.

"Our mate here is talking about stealing you away."

Aaron holds out a hand. She walks over to him and takes it, and he embraces her. "Hey, beautiful, it's been a while," he says, kissing her cheek.

"Yeah."

He looks at me. "This is how it's done."

June untangles herself from Aaron and returns to me. "Be nice. I don't want my man here to ban you from ever seeing me again."

"Like he could."

"Okay, enough of that. London, I was going to wait until we were with the others, but since you and Aedan insist on duking it out…" She holds up her hand with the ring. "Your mate proposed. God, I have to stop using that word. It sounds like we're a threesome."

"I assure you there will be none of that," I tell her.

Aaron opens his arms to her again and I bite back the urge to tighten my grip when she pulls away. She goes to him and her feet leave the ground when he hugs her. "Congratulations, beautiful." His voice is low yet earnest. When he sets her on the ground again, he uses his thumbs to wipe her tears. "What are these for? Go to your man before I have to kiss these away." He smiles, and I have mixed emotions watching their unconditional love.

When she returns to me, she stands directly before me with a look of love. I cup her chin. "Are you okay, sunshine?" She nods and I dust my lips across hers.

For so long, Aaron has been such a big a part of her life that everyone assumes they'll be married. This is the moment that changes all that. In the future, when people see us, it'll be as man and wife, not as bodyguard and client.

"Congratulations, mate." Aaron pats me on the shoulder. "Treat my girl right because I won't hesitate to take her back. We have years of matching outfits."

"London," June presses.

"So, what's the plan?"

"Niall, Rose, and Jake will be here shortly. I'll serve drinks and then we'll tell them."

"Do you anticipate any issues? If I saw this coming, others would too."

June sighs. "Jake will expect it. I honestly have no idea what Rose will think."

"Niall wants me to settle down," I say.

"Then the only question is...will Rose be in favor?"

June takes my hand and leads me, with Aaron in tow, to the kitchen, which opens into our family room, overlooking the city.

"I could use a drink right now," she says.

I go to the refrigerator and take out a bottle of champagne. "Will this work?" I hold up the bottle.

"Works for me."

"Whatever our girl wants," Aaron says, walking over to the wall of windows.

As I open the bottle, I take in the moment. June joins Aaron, looking out over the city. He puts his arm around her shoulders, and she wraps her arm around his waist. It's tough, but I'm beginning to understand they can't help who they are.

"Are you going to the Pages' wedding?" she asks.

"I'll be there," he responds.

"Thank you for the birthday gift. That was totally insane. I ate five packages already in addition to my birthday cake."

"Anything for you. Don't make yourself sick, though."

The alarm sounds, alerting me that someone arrived in the elevator. "How is it that I'm not surprised to see you two locked in an embrace?" Rose's voice carries across the penthouse as she walks into the room with Niall and Jake. "Hey, Aedan." Rose rounds the counter and hugs me. My brother pats me on the shoulder while Jake's eyes shift between me and June, who's now facing the group along with Aaron.

"You have the good stuff out. What are we celebrating?" Niall asks.

This is the defining moment for us—the point of no return. I inhale and extend my hand. June joins me, lacing her fingers with mine. "Us," I say, lifting June's fingers to my lips. I kiss them, then dip my head and kiss her.

"Wait. What's happening here? Aaron? And why are *they* dressed alike?" Rose questions him.

"This is not my story to tell."

"Rose, Niall, Jake," June addresses them. "There's only one way to say this. Aedan and I have been secretly seeing each other. He proposed to me, and I accepted."

Rose's mouth hangs open but is quickly replaced with a smile. "Finally. Christ, I thought I'd have to chain you two together."

"What are you talking about?" I ask.

"I've been dying for you two to get together. No offense to you, Aaron."

"Why does everyone think I'm offended? Watch this." He walks over and holds his hand out to June. This time, she doesn't leave my side when she takes it. He kisses her fingers and looks at me with a raised eyebrow. "Trust me, he won't kill me." He smiles smugly, then releases her.

I pull June tight to my side. "Only because I made a promise to my woman."

"I've seen everything I need," Jake adds. "Congratulations, you two. So, are we celebrating?"

"You seem at ease with this. Did you know about this?" Rose asks Jake.

"There's not much I don't know about my sister. And I've never seen a man look at her like Aedan does."

"Like he's about to murder anyone that comes near her," Aaron teases. "Trust me, I know the look."

Niall hugs June and then me. "This is great news. I'm happy for you both." My brother takes over pouring the champagne. "This is certainly worthy of a celebration." He hands out glasses. When everyone has one, he raises his glass. "A toast to June and Aedan. May their lives be filled with love and laughter, and may the divine bless them with a home filled with mini kings and queens. Sláinte."

We all raise our glasses and repeat. "Sláinte." I dip my head, kiss June, and then sip my drink. "I love you."

"I love you, too."

San Francisco

CHAPTER 33

Peace

"Absence of evidence is not evidence of absence."
– Carl Sagan

June

I DIDN'T FULLY UNDERSTAND the stress I was harboring about people discovering my relationship with Aedan until it was out in the open. It's as if a cloud lifted and everything is bright and airy. All along, I thought Rose was warning me about Aedan when the reality was that she had always planned to get us together. My father was ecstatic when we told him via video call. He offered to pay for the wedding and our honeymoon.

Aedan and I have been adjusting to our new normal for the past week. He protects me while I navigate my life as a top executive, philanthropist, and social activist. We're back in San Francisco this week as I begin executing the program with the mayor. The mayor exits the front of the building, where there's always a crowd ready to talk with her, and today is no different.

"Mayor, can you tell us how you plan to solve the tech companies' exit from the city?" someone calls out to her as we descend the steps.

I'm surprised when someone calls out my name. "Ms. Ross, I heard they re-opened the investigation into your mother's murder. Has there been any progress?" I stop in my tracks, stunned by the question.

"Keep walking," Aedan directs me. His hand on the small of my back prompts me to move forward. "Look ahead."

I continue walking. "Ms. Ross, I hear you're next on the target list." The deep timbre of a man's voice calls out above the noise. I scan the crowd, searching for its origin, but only find a sea of faces watching.

When we near the car, Mack holds the door open. Aedan helps me in and slides in beside me. He doesn't speak until we are several blocks away from City Hall.

"I'll have a conversation with Dean about what just happened."

"I thought everything was confidential."

"There could be a leak. Don't worry, you're safe with me."

"You shouldn't have to put yourself in the line of fire for me," I blurt out. I'm pissed. He doesn't reply. He laces his fingers with mine.

When we return to the house, I drop my things in the foyer, collect the mail, and go to the kitchen to get water. I sit at the counter and call my dad. He answers immediately.

"Hey, Dad."

"Princess. I saw a clip on the news. Are you all right?"

"I am, but what does this mean? Did they reopen the investigation?"

"It was never closed."

"I never knew."

"There's nothing to know. There hasn't been any new information."

"Then whoever said that must have insider knowledge. Why would they suddenly single me out? Why today?"

"I don't have an answer for you, Princess, but I have requested your security be increased."

"You spoke to Aedan."

"Seconds before you called. Wheels are in motion."

Aedan walks into the kitchen. He puts his phone in his pocket and walks up behind me, positioning himself so my dad can see him. "Hello, Mr. Ross. We're home now."

"You two should plan to return to Ireland before this becomes a media storm."

"I'm not running from this."

"I'll take care of her, Mr. Ross."

My dad purses his lips. "Princess, I'm going to trust you on this."

"I assure you, Dad, if anyone gets close to me this time, it's because I allowed it." My response appears to satisfy Dad momentarily, and we end the call.

Aedan swivels my chair so I'm facing him. He dusts the pad of his thumb down my cheek. "I've got you covered. You don't have to worry about this. But I agree with your father. We should return to Ireland."

I slide out of the chair, pushing past him. I round the counter and pour myself a glass of wine. This should be the happiest time of my life. In my short time at Ross Enterprises, I'm on target to meet our growth projections. The city crime prevention program is gaining traction. I'm in love with the man of my dreams. But that's not enough. The monster that haunts my dreams is still out there. This time, he's looking for me.

Resignedly, I sip my drink and then look at Aedan. "I want to see the police files."

"I have printouts in the office." He extends his hand. I pick up my glass, place my hand in his, and follow him to the home office.

"Have a seat." He gestures for me to sit in the chair. I put my wine on the desk. "They're here." Standing beside me, he opens a thin brown, saddle-leather folder. One by one, he removes pages from the holder. "This is the original unredacted police report," he says, placing a thick pile on the desk in front of me. "This...," he lays an aged newspaper on the desk, "is the original newsprint that chronicles the story."

I pick up the paper. It's still in good condition. Several stories cover the murder from different angles. The last one ends with a plea to turn over the killer. *"Mrs. Ross's family is seeking justice. Anyone with information should contact the local police immediately."*

"This envelope contains photos of the evidence they collected at the scene, including your mother's belongings. This one contains pictures of your mother. I don't suggest you open this."

I pick up the envelope containing evidence photos, take a deep breath, open it, and spread the photos across the desk. Laying out the picture is like stepping back in time. All the emotions of that day overtake me, but I push through, forcing myself to look at the photos.

"I remember this place like it was yesterday," I say, touching a color photo of the front of the Japanese restaurant we visited that fateful day. "This is her purse. She never took it to the counter. I still have it. And this..." I touch another picture. "I wore this silk scarf to my interview with Saola."

"It's a beautiful scarf."

There are so many photos that I quickly sift through them. One catches my eye. "Where is this? Aedan, tell me they still have this. Tell me they have this at the station," I press, pointing to a picture of my mom's gold peace sign necklace. She had it on that day; she never took it off. They would have had to remove it from her body to take the photo. I pick up the picture and hold it to Aedan's face. "Tell me where this is," I scream.

Aedan takes the photo from my hand and places it on the desk. He sits on the desk and pulls me from the chair so I'm standing between his legs. "Sunshine. Stop it. I can't tell you where that necklace is because it's not in the evidence file."

"Where is it? I haven't seen it since that day. They never gave it to us. Had they, London would not have had to get this one made for me." I tug at the platinum diamond peace sign hanging from my neck. "The tattoo you asked me about. I got it when I was sixteen to honor my mom when I graduated. I was so determined to make it on my own."

"You were one of the youngest graduates in your school. Your mom would have been proud." He pulls me into him and hugs me.

Tears stream down my cheeks as memories of the day my mom died assault me. "What happened to her necklace? The documents all show it was logged in as evidence."

Aedan grabs a tissue from the box on my desk and dries my tears. "The only answer is...someone took it."

Chapter 34

Talk to Me

"There is always some madness in love. But there is also always some reason in madness."
– Friedrich Nietzsche

Aedan

To say I didn't take the decision lightly when I decided to settle down with June is a vast understatement. I put myself in deadly situations for a living. I protect those who can't protect themselves from soulless people who'd cut your heart out and eat it for breakfast. People like Darrien Goodman, whom I won't hesitate to exterminate.

As much joy as having June in my life brings, I knew there would be tougher days than most. Getting her on a plane to return to Belfast is one of those days. She won't lift a finger to pack her things, so I contact her assistant to come over to do the job for her.

After the assistant leaves, I go to June, who is on the living room couch, seething. I sit beside her, pull her onto my lap, and hold her until her breathing comes under control.

"Sunshine, you have to snap out of this," I tell her when she refuses to speak. "I love you, but I promise you one thing. I don't care how mad you are at me. I will not tolerate the silent treatment. You have a choice: you can talk to me or come on me, calling my name. We'll communicate with words or love or both. Either way. You will speak to me."

June gets up and retreats to the bedroom, slamming the door behind her. When she agreed to be my wife, she became my family, my everything. I promised to love and protect her. Holding fast to those values, I follow her. Had the door been locked, I would have kicked it down to get to her, but it isn't. She sits on the edge of the bed, crying. I pick her up and sit her on my lap.

"Talk to me, honey," I coax her, sliding my hand up her shirt, caressing her skin and absorbing her warmth. She stares at me—defiance in her eyes. I kiss the side of her lips. "Sunshine, you can be mad all you want, but you have to talk to me."

Leaning back, I take my shirt off, then pull her shirt over her head, tossing them both aside. Holding her close, I kiss down her cheek, her neck, and then I palm one breast while sucking the other. Her hand instinctively reaches for my head, massaging my scalp as I suck her breast because this is what she loves. Her breath hitches, but still, she doesn't speak. I keep sucking and licking until her mouth falls open, groaning. Then, in another defiant move, she gets up and attempts to leave, but I grab her waistband. "If you like this skirt, stand still; otherwise, I'll have to rip it off." She doesn't move. She stands right there holding her breath, trying to be unaffected when I slide her skirt and underwear to the floor. I stand, strip my remaining clothes, pick her up, and lay her on the bed.

Hovering over her, I dip my head and kiss her, opening her mouth with my tongue. She turns her head, and my stomach turns at how fast she can disregard what we have between us. I brush my nose across her cheek and behind her ear, inhaling her essence.

I whisper, "Look at me, sunshine." She looks at me. "Remember who I am to you." I move off her and sit up beside her, then pull her astride me.

I hold her gaze as I touch her cheek, then smooth my hand down her neck, caress her breast, and then grip her hips. Her eyes soften and she buries her head in my neck. I love her so much. All I can do is hold her and give her time to settle her mind. It takes a while, but I hold her like that until she raises her head and dusts her lips against my ear. Then I untangle her from me and lick down her body, paying close attention to her breasts.

"I'm going to make love to you." I suck one breast and pinch the other. "You are going to come on me calling my name." I kiss and suck her neck. "When we're done, you'll get ready to get on the plane." I hold her gaze. "I love you." I cover her mouth with mine, and this time she returns the kiss, sucking my tongue while I swallow her moans. I break the kiss. "Now, tell me what you want."

"You."

That's all I need to hear. I give her two orgasms before we leave and three on the plane. She's still pissed at me, but that's all right. We love each other. That's all that matters.

Belfast

Chapter 35

I Would Die For You

"Love doesn't just sit there, like a stone; it has to be made, like bread; remade all the time, made new."
– Ursula K. Le Guin

Aedan

There are many things I can do in a matter of seconds: assemble a weapon, unarm an assailant, eliminate a target—the list goes on. However, nothing in my training prepared me for loving someone. I'm learning that love takes time. It requires compromise. It means I can't always have what I want when I want it. It requires patience, understanding, and care. I'm getting there.

I take a deep breath and savor a moment of quiet following the storm. I finally got my woman home to Belfast. The effort was worth it, and now we're in bed, and she's molded around my body where she belongs. I stroke her hair. She shifts slightly. Her finger curls against my skin. I lower my hand, cup her hip, and slide her body over mine. The feel of her has me so hard.

"Hey, sunshine." I lift her chin to meet my gaze.

"Hi."

"You still love me?" She nods. "But you don't want to talk to me." She puts her fingers on my lips. Whether it is to silence me or a signal for something else, I can't interpret. "Despite what you think, I'm trying to protect you. Protect our future. You agreed to marry me. You said you want to have *our* children. How can those things happen if you're not around?"

"I get it," she says.

I sit up, bringing June with me. "Do you? Do you know that I would die for you?"

"That's the issue—you shouldn't have to. This is my mess. I need to solve it. When you say things like that, you scare me."

"We're in this together. Soon, you'll be my wife. I love you, too." I roll her on her back and stroke between her folds. She's so ready for me. I remove my finger and position myself at her entrance. "I'll always love you." I push in and watch as her mouth falls open with desire. Even in her defiance, she can't resist her love for me. I kiss her, swallowing her groans as I pump harder and faster. Her body receives me like I'm her life force.

"Oh, god," she cries, chasing the high of having me in her.

"I'm here," I pant, enjoying her tightness as I move in and out. I increase the pace to match the rhythm of her body pushing against me. "Come for me." She squeezes, her walls milking my shaft and pulling my release. "Fuck." I continue pumping, pouring my love into her as we both find our release together in love. "June."

June is so full of my thickness that my seed overflows as she grins against me. I know what she wants. I reach beneath us and palm her hips, holding them in place until she comes against my shaft again. "That's it, honey. Take everything you need." And she does. When her body stops pulsing...when I know she is spent and too sensitive for more, I roll on my back, pulling her with me, allowing evidence of our love to coat us. Proof that we are one.

I pull a sheet over her back. "I love how you make love to me," I tell her, gripping her hips and shaking them.

"Are you calling me greedy?" she whispers. Her essence surrounds me...her hair tickles my face, and her warm breath caresses my neck. The scent of sex and sweat and her sweetness mixed with notes of me fuel my desire.

"Not at all. It's my favorite thing."

"I can't help it. You're so thick and hard."

"Because of you. Being in you does that to me. Thinking about you. Smelling you. Touching you. Tasting you. Even now, the weight of your body...knowing you're mine.... I'm hard for you."

"Speaking of hard. I gave you a hard time in San Francisco."

"You were furious with me. You still are. But like I told you, we will communicate our thoughts and feelings. I am listening to you. You're afraid of what could happen to me in the process of protecting you from Darrien. He doesn't stand a chance against a man like me. He's a trained criminal. I'm a trained professional who spent a lifetime taking people like him down. You asked me in London if you should be afraid of me. I told you no. It's men like Darrien who should be afraid of me. You asked me at the museum if I ever killed someone."

"You didn't answer me."

"It wasn't the right time. But the answer is yes. In my line of work, sometimes people end up dead. I've never lost a client. I *won't* lose the love of my life."

"There's something you're not saying. What are you not telling me?"

"Like you, I lost my father to senseless violence when I was eight. When I was old enough, I found the man who placed a bomb under my father's car. I found him, looked him in the eye, and reminded him of who I was right before I killed him. I gave him a chance to try and stop me. I even handed him a gun. So, when I tell you that Darrien Goodman will go down by my hands, you can take that to the bank. You have absolutely nothing to fear. I guarantee anyone who thinks they can get to you has a date with a bullet to the head and a body bag."

"Aedan."

"Those are the facts—I don't miss."

"I get that you have to be a certain way to perform your job. It scares me. Something changes in you when you talk like that. It's difficult for me to reconcile. I'm trying, but I can't change who I am."

"But you can accept who I am."

CHAPTER 36

The Note

"The past is never where you think you left it."
– Katherine Anne Porter

June

THE CONTRACT WITH KNIGHT Development is moving along smoothly. I've assigned Raven to lead council overseeing the execution and she's doing a stellar job. Although Aedan temporarily limited my travel to the States, my program to eliminate guns from the streets has been well received. Several other state officials have contacted me, wanting to adopt and roll out the program in their states. There is over a sixty percent chance that the gun Darrien used to kill my mother was illegally obtained. Knowing that the illegal gun trade has become his primary source of income, I'm even more committed to removing illegally gained guns from the streets and destroying crime lords like him.

I stack the mail on my tablet, slide it into my tote, and stand multitasking as I talk with Jake via video.

"Can you sync with Raven? She mentioned a few items that may impact the budget for the KDC contract. I'll approve up to ten percent over."

"She and I are scheduled to meet in an hour. Isn't it time for you to head out?"

"Don't worry about my schedule."

"Your man has you on military time. It's almost nine here. You have five minutes before he makes an appearance." Jake laughs, basking in the knowledge that someone is finally reining in my crazy. I laugh, too, because Aedan is the only one who can handle me.

"Two minutes now." Aedan's voice cuts through the laughter. My heart races as he rounds my desk and stands beside me. I love this man. "Hi, Jake."

"King," he greets. "Can you ensure my sis gets a break from work? I've been getting messages since three this morning."

"I got something for her."

"Spare me the details."

"Okay, you guys. Time to go," I tell Jake and end the call.

Aedan snakes an arm around me and gives me a chaste kiss. "Do you have everything?" He steps back and grabs my tote.

"Ready."

We leave the building and walk one block to the steely grey building that's become my new home away from San Francisco. Aedan dragged me back to Belfast kicking and screaming, not because I didn't want to come, because I absolutely wanted to come—around his shaft, that is, but because I didn't want to return to Belfast to hide from Darrien.

Aedan agreed to a compromise: We could walk back and forth between home and the office like normal people. That meant his entourage was banned from stealth mode. That's the deal.

At the penthouse, I drop my tote in our home office and go to the bedroom, where I exchange work clothes for leisure wear. Not one for casual clothes, Aedan removes his coat and tie. He wraps his arms around my hips and lifts me, and I wrap my legs and arms around him.

"I imagine you have a few things to wrap up before dinner." I never thought another man could know me better than London until Aedan came along. The things London learned about me over the years Aedan has absorbed in a matter of months. He knows my routine. He kisses me, giving me everything I need from him. Without breaking the kiss, he carries me out of the bedroom, down the hall, and into the office, where he lowers my feet to the floor. He breaks the kiss, leaving me in a king-sized haze. "I'll bring you a snack and glass of wine while Stella sets up dinner," he says, then smacks me on the butt and leaves.

I sit behind the desk, open my tablet, and respond to several emails before tackling the physical mail. There are several belated birthday cards, four charity event invites, and... *another grey envelope. What the hell?* I reach for the other notes and compare them. It's the same person.

Opening it, my heart races. I read the card: *"Hi, June. You're a hard woman to reach. I wanted to drop you a note to let you know I'm thinking about you and to ask you to reconsider your affiliation with the mayor's office. I'll give you a few days to think about it. Oh, and don't worry, I'm not offended by the tall Irishman who looks so lovingly at you. I won't hesitate to take him from you, too."*

I drop the note on the table, slide my chair back, and stand. The incidents leading up to this moment spin like storm clouds in my head, making me dizzy. The media fiasco, my mom's death, and the sudden public interest in her case are all huge particles swept up by the wind slamming against me. I need to do something. I return the newest note to my purse to conceal it from Aedan.

"Sunshine, I brought you some wine and those snacks Aaron got you." I turn to him, trying to mask the dread running through my veins. He rushes over to me and puts the snacks and wine on the desk. "Honey, what's wrong? You look like you're about to pass out." He helps me back to my chair and then picks up the two cards. "Why do you have these out? Did something happen?" He examines the cards, rubbing his finger along the back. "I didn't notice this before."

"What?" I say, finally coming out of my stupor.

"This." He holds the card out, smoothing the pad of his thumb across the bottom right corner. "This symbol is raised. I didn't notice it before."

"It looks like a peace sign."

He takes out his phone and presses the flashlight symbol, illuminating the card. "It's a sword in a circle—his sword."

For the next thirty minutes, the office transforms into a war room. Aedan and Ben meet with the security teams to strategize how they'll handle the fact that Darrien knows who I am. They hold a conference call with the DOJ, who confirm Darrien hasn't left the city. My staff provides me with the mail logs. It turns out that the cards were originally sent to my San Francisco office and forwarded to me in Belfast by my team. *Good, he doesn't know I'm here.* I file that information away in my head. I don't tell them about the third letter. I can't; this is my fight, and I need to protect my man. But how do I protect him if he's always with me?

After everyone leaves, Aedan and I eat dinner. He's noticeably irritated by the turn of events, which is understandable given that a wanted criminal is after his fiancé. So am I. My heart is pounding, thinking about the note in my tote.

Aedan won't stop going after Darrien as long as I'm with him, and Darrien will kill Aedan to get to me. I'm in a catch twenty-two. I can't go through with this. No one else needs to lose their life.

CHAPTER 37

We Are One

"In all the world, there is no heart for me like yours. In all the world, there is no love for you like mine."
– Maya Angelou

Aedan

THE LOOK OF WORRY on my woman's face during dinner was enough to break me. I pulled her onto my lap, and that's how we sat during the rest of dinner, which seemed to calm her. In a way, it also soothed me, knowing she was safe in my arms. But it didn't silence the beast that wants to see Darrien dead.

After dinner, while June has her shower, I contact Niall and update him on everything. In the past, we navigated getting private clients in and out of countries working to rebuild their infrastructure following wars. Together, there's nothing we can't handle. However, the situation with June is personal, and I need to get my emotions in check. And I do that the only way I know how. When I'm with her, I allow her to consume me, but she becomes my most important client the second we step outside.

Following my call, I find June waiting in bed for me. Usually, she listens to music and dances around the house, coaxing me to dance with her.

Not this time. I get in bed, lift her hips, and eat her for dessert. When I'm done...after she comes on my face...I fill her.

June is sleeping when my phone buzzes. It's Dean. I lower my voice to answer so I don't wake my woman.

"Talk to me."

"There's a buyer in town scheduled to pick up a shipment of weapons."

"And you think Goodman's the seller."

"Based on the size of the demand, it can only be him."

"Then he's there...somewhere. Find him."

"I'll keep you posted."

This is it. We're so close to finding him. The man June has spent her life fearing. The person who fueled her passion for justice. The one who haunts her dreams. The one I will set her free from. Because there isn't a world where I exist without her by my side. The things we do for love often define us. I swore to protect her, and I will with my life.

Looking down at her sleeping, my body grows hard thinking about her. I caress her body, slowly working my way down, cupping her sex. Her heat reverberates through me. I slide my fingers between her folds and stroke, exploring the hot, wet skin between her legs. Her response comes in a subtle pulse of her walls against my fingertips. She turns slightly toward me, and I cover her mouth with mine and suck her tongue while my finger moves in sync with her body, grinding against my hand. When her walls contract against my fingers, I remove them.

She whimpers and sucks my tongue, wanting more. I lift her leg over me and bury my shaft in her. She tries to cry out, but wet, sloppy kisses prevent her. I need her. I push her on her back and pump fast and hard, in and out, with deliberate thrusts. Her body pulses violently around my shafts, quickly finding her release, but I don't ease up. I need her like I need air. My movement becomes more erratic as I chase my release. I break our kiss. "Oh god, June," I grunt into the side of her neck. I continue pumping, pouring myself into her in waves. She comes again, eyes closed, tears streaming down her face, wetting my cheek.

I kiss her as we come together.

As our hearts race.

As we become one.

London

Running

"Some people come into our lives and leave footprints on our hearts and we are never ever the same."
– Flavia Weedn

June

SITTING ON THE TARMAC as the plane taxis toward the terminal, I recall London's words. *"Don't run again, beautiful, but if you do, I'll be there when you need me."*

I tried not to drink on the plane; a glass and a half in, I stopped only because, between the tears streaming down my face and the snot, I was disgusted with myself. If I had kept drinking, it was only going to get worse. Exiting the plane, I put on a professional façade and half smile at the crew members assisting me. When I reach the bottom of the metal stairs and head toward the car, no vehicles are flanking the front or rear of my vehicle. There's no security team monitoring my every move. The driver is standing at attention, wearing the standard black suit, white shirt, black tie, and polished shoes.

"Ms. Ross, traffic is heavy, and your ETA is forty minutes." I nod to the driver, slide into the back seat, put in earphones, and crank my seventies playlist. During the ride, I desperately try to forget the past few months. I allow the music to free me of my father, friends, work, and anything that'll bring me back to reality. Most of all, I try not to think about my king.

My body still aches for him. Following dinner, he made love to me with such a passion that I wanted to pass out. When we were done, I fell asleep with his mouth latched onto my breast. Later, when I woke up, he filled me again, twice. And finally, when my man was so exhausted from filling me with his seed...I left. And now, I'm headed to the only man that can save me from myself. Aaron Adler.

The worst part of all this is that I can't even turn on my phone to call London and let him know I'm here. God, I pray I'm not intruding. It's been a while since I've thought of him with another woman. He's not like most men with a long list of lovers. I can't recall when he looked at another woman when I was around. *What do I do if he's not available?* I'll soon find out.

Before the driver turns onto his street, hot tears break free and stream down my face. I hate this; feeling lost, consumed by the fear of falling in love with a man who wants to protect me with his life while seeking comfort in his friend, is all too much. The car slows as we reach the quiet street lined with three-story luxury homes. My driver rounds the car and opens the door. I look up, and London's silhouette frames his doorway. A sigh of relief I didn't realize I was holding escapes. Quickly, I exit the car and sprint toward him. I swear I've never run so fast. When I reach him, I jump in his arms, and he doesn't hesitate to catch me. Holding me, he carries me in and kicks the door behind him.

I'm lightheaded. Exhausted, I close my eyes.

"Beautiful," he whispers, and I bury my face in his neck. For what feels like forever, he stands in his foyer holding me. My arms wrapped like a winter scarf around his neck. My legs locked at the ankles behind him. "Look at me," he commands. I shake my head. "I need to see your face, June. Look. At. Me." I lift my head. London closes his eyes, lets out a breath, and reopens them. "You're not hurt." I shake my head.

He carries me into the living room and sits with me, still wrapped around him. He shakes his head. "What are you doing? You do realize he knows you're here." He swipes a thumb across my wet cheek.

"I couldn't help it."

"What's happening between you two?"

"I can't do it. It's too hard, I'm afraid." I lean into London, bury my face in his neck, and kiss him there. I know these feelings are not for him, but I can't help myself. I need him to make me forget what I left behind. He grabs my arms and pulls me away from him.

"Stop. What are you doing? You're not mine to take."

"I am if I give myself to you."

"Why would you do that?"

"Because loving you is easy. I'm not afraid of you."

"You should be."

"There's nothing you can do to make me fear you."

"You need to leave. Go back to Aedan. Fix whatever is happening be-tween you."

"I'm not going back. I'm giving myself to you. I'm not afraid of you."

"You need to leave now."

"I'm not afraid of you. I'm not leaving. I'm offering myself to you."

"Are you sure?"

"Yes."

"So, if I kissed you like I did the last time you were here, would you be afraid of me then? Would you be afraid of the repercussions?"

"No."

"And if I were to stretch you out on this couch and make love to you. You wouldn't be afraid of me then?"

"No."

"I'm going to ask you again. Are you sure about that?"

"There's nothing you can do."

"God, June. Don't do this. You're a beautiful wild child, and I love you, but you need to leave right now. I don't understand why you're here. But you belong to someone else."

"No. You said I could come to you when I needed you. I need you."

"You need him."

I reach between us and stroke his shaft. "I need this."

London lifts me off him, lays me on my back, dips his head, and kisses me like he did that day in his office. He sucks my tongue, and I lick into him like he's giving me life. I reach between us and stroke his length, which is pressed thick and tight against his jeans. He breaks the kiss and removes my hand.

"You have no idea what you're doing. I told you—you should be afraid of me."

"I'm not afraid of you. Give me this moment." I take his hand and press it between my legs. "I want this." He pulls his hand away, but I return it to where I want it. Stroking it along my pants. Pressing his fingers into me. I grind on his hand, groaning. "Aaron, please." Saying his name seems to unleash something in him.

He unfastens my slacks. "You can't undo this, beautiful. And I won't apologize."

"Make me come," I press.

He slides his hand down my underwear and between my folds. I know already what he finds. His fingers easily glide between my slick folds. "Fuck, you're so wet. You don't want this."

My heart races. "I do."

"No, you don't." He inserts his fingers in me and moves them in and out as I grind against his hand. He circles my clit with his thumb as he strokes in and out of me. My mouth falls open, and he covers it with his. His tongue licks into me in time with his hand stroking me, and I'm seconds from coming. He continues the pace with steady, strong strokes. I want to cry out, but he swallows my groans. As my walls contract around his hand, he kisses me on the neck and then whispers in my ear. "Come for me, beautiful. Take what I'm offering you. Because I can't give you anything more than this."

"Oh god, Aaron, I'm coming."

"Let it go. Come for *me*." He kisses me as he pulls my climax from me, and I come calling the name of the man who means the world to me, and it feels good. But it's not enough. I want *my man* in me.

"Take me, London, please."

"No." Instead, he kisses me while his hand stays in place and pulls the last of my orgasm from me until my body stops pulsing around his hand. Until I stop chasing the feeling of his fingers in me. Until my heart stops racing. Then he raises, fastens my pants, goes to the restroom, and washes his hands. When he returns, he brings me water, helps me sit up, and then half sits on the credenza, palms down, bracing himself as he leans forward, watching me with fire in his eyes. Proof of his desire for me is evident in his pants.

I lay there and close my eyes, thinking about how I ran away from Aedan. I think about what he might be feeling. How many men must be looking for me?

I feel like I'm free-falling.

"Aedan," I call out.

"He'll be here in the morning."

My eyes fly open. London is half sitting, half leaning on his credenza, watching me, concern clouding his eyes.

"London?"

"I'm here, beautiful."

"Where am I?"

"You're on my couch. You passed out in my arms at the door."

"It was all a dream?"

"Must have been a good dream. You've been sleeping for the past four hours."

"What? I've been sleeping?" I rub my eyes.

"Given the hour, I don't imagine you slept much yesterday."

"I didn't sleep at all."

"Why are you here? What happened? Do you want any water?"

"I don't want water. I came here to give myself to you."

His eyebrows rise, and he has a curious look on his face. "I know you well enough to know that's not why you're here. Now tell me what happened."

"I'm serious. I dreamed you took me."

"That's not going to happen." He rubs the back of his neck. "What happened between you and Aedan?" His words come out pronounced.

"I left. There's a side of him that scares me. But with you..."

"You think I'd be different."

"You're nothing like him. It's easy with you. I don't have the same fears. I'm here for you. I'm offering myself *to you*."

London taps his fingers against the credenza. "Aedan will be here in the morning. I'll order us something to eat. We can discuss your situation, but nothing is happening between you and me. You'll need to trust my mate to do the right thing."

"I'm offering myself. Why won't you make love to me?"

"You know why. You're not mine. Because you're in love with someone else who is also in love with you. Because for the longest time, you're all I ever wanted. Because if I take you, I can't give you up. And you have to give that ring on your finger back. Because if we do it, your forever begins with me."

"I do love you."

"I've known that for a long time, June. But you're not in love with me. Are you willing to risk it all? Are you willing to lose the love of your life? Because if you are, I will call Aedan and tell him not to come for you. However, you have to be willing to deal with the repercussions. Because despite me telling him not to come...he will. Needless to say, it won't end in his favor. Is that what you want?"

"You'd hurt him?"

"You already hurt him in the worst way by leaving him. What do you think a man like him would do if I were to take his woman? What do you think *I* would do if you gave yourself to me, and he came looking for you?"

"Nothing good." I rise, go to London, and stand between his legs. He doesn't attempt to touch me.

"June, I've loved you for longer than I should have. I don't share. Unlike Aedan, I won't tolerate you running scared. If you want me to make love to you, we're doing this together. Ring. Marriage. Everything. I don't play games. I play for keeps. The choice is yours. Get in my bed or go home."

I touch London's cheek. He kisses the inside of my wrist. "London. I can't go back. Not tonight."

"And you can't have me. You need to tell me what you are afraid of. What led you to me?"

"I'm afraid of loving Aedan. I'm afraid of losing him."

"For Christ's sake, woman. The man would die for you. Anyone who witnesses the way he looks at you knows that."

"That's the problem. He intentionally puts himself in harm's way. I'm afraid of the lengths he'd go to protect me. I'm afraid of the side that can disassociate from the one I've come to love—the one who can take a life. I can't be with him—not like that."

"Can't you see? You can't get past that. I would do the same. I told you—if you were mine, I'd kill for you. That's why you need to go back to your man. He was designed for you. Let him do what he was trained to do. Let him love you the only way he knows how. Did you ever think that you provided the balance he needed? That you alone possess the power to tame him? He's different when he's with you. He has a sense of purpose. He's more human. I've known him long enough to have witnessed the difference. And when you're with him, you can't take your eyes off him. The two of you instinctively seek each other out."

"Like us?"

"No. You and I have a connection I don't yet understand. We're traveling in the same orbit but on different paths. We're two of a kind, and whether or not we want to admit it, we love each other, but we weren't designed for each other." He cups my face and dusts his lips across mine. "Because if we were, I would have never taken you to be with him. I would have taken you home, made love to you, then made you my wife."

"I would have said yes." I close the distance and kiss London because it's him...because I can and because if I don't, I feel like I might die. Even though we both know this won't go any further, he gives me exactly what I need, and I love him even more for it. He pulls me into him and then breaks the kiss.

He brushes his nose against mine, then whispers against my lips, "Open up to King. Show him the side of you you've shown me. Trust that he'll protect you, your heart, soul...your secrets. He loves you. If it's any fraction of what you and I have—I promise you'll be more than fine. You'll be safe because you are loved."

I bite my lip and nod. "You're right."

"But beautiful, you can't come seeking this type of comfort from me again. It's not right." He presses my hips into him until my body molds to his hardened shaft. "Because as you can feel, I am all man, and I won't hesitate to take you and make you mine next time. I'm not afraid of King."

I smile. "I got my kiss."

He barks out a laugh. "Yeah, according to your dream, you got much more than that."

Belfast

Chapter 39

Love Will Lead You Back

"Ever has it been that love knows not its own depth until the hour of separation."

– Joan Crawford

Aedan

TO SAY I WAS five seconds away from strangling my friend Aaron with my bare hands when he opened his door this morning was an understatement. I called him first when June left because I knew their connection would lead her straight to him.

During the call, I told him, "Put her in your car, take her to the airport, and send her back to Belfast the second she shows up at your door." He laughed in response and all I could see was red.

"What is it with you, mate? You can't seem to keep your house in order. I hand-delivered the love of your life to you, and she's on her way back to me. What the hell are you doing?"

"We had a misunderstanding. She's under a lot of pressure," I say, unsure exactly why she left other than her demeanor changed when I told her about my intent with Darrien.

"Misunderstanding, or were you just being your usual overly controlling self?"

"We're working through it."

"Not if she's heading here. If you love her, help her solve whatever it is or provide her relief until you can figure it out. Don't make it so complicated. June will tell you everything she needs from you. All you have to do is listen for once. You're supposed to be her safe place to land."

"She said that's about you. That's how I know she's on the way there. I need you to send her back."

"No. Let her be. She's coming here for something you're not providing her. I'll talk to her."

"Put her on a fucking plane," I say, punctuating each word.

"Why? Because you're afraid she'll get what she needs from me? Get over yourself, mate. Let me help her, or be prepared to lose her forever. You decide."

"If anything happens to her—"

"Like I'll hurt her—you've done that. She's not in love with me if that's what has your knickers in a bunch. But if you've done something to cause her to break it off, I'm not sending her back. My role as her friend is to listen, assess what's happening, and give her what she needs to move forward. Whether that's with you or me has yet to be determined."

As pissed as I was, he was right. If anyone could get her to talk—he could. "Talk to her, but send her back tonight."

"You've confused me with someone who works for you. If this is how you're handling June, it won't work between you two. Trust me—your woman does. I suppose that's a given since she's heading straight to me."

"Aaron," my tone issues the warning my fist can't.

"Listen, mate, I'm yanking your chain because you're out of fucking control. Give her the night."

"Then you'll send her back."

"No. Once again, you're confused. If you want your woman, get on your damn plane and come get her in the morning. Show her you want her. I brought her to you once. I won't make the same mistake twice. I warned you about that," he said and ended the call.

Fuck.

***

Two hours and fifty minutes. Almost three hours since I walked into Aaron's home to pick up June, and she still hasn't said a word to me. The last word I heard her say was "thank you" to Aaron after she extracted herself from their embrace. Thinking about it, the heat emanating from me could propel a rocket to the moon.

When we arrive home in Belfast, June furrows her brows when I pull her into me and stare down at her.

"I love you. You can head to the kitchen or straight to bed. Either way, you will talk to me. I told you I don't do silent treatments. I had something prepared in case you're hungry," I tell her, removing her sweater. She lays her purse on a small table near the door and heads into the kitchen. I follow her and watch as she pours two glasses of water. She rounds the counter and hands me a glass. I take a sip and then set the glass on the counter. I grab June by the waist, pull her into me, and mold her hips around the proof that we will eventually make it to the bedroom. "Sunshine, talk to me. Tell me what I'm doing wrong because I don't want to live without you. And I don't want to kill my friend for touching my woman."

A tentative smile escapes her when I say the last bit, and I feel a few pockets of flames being extinguished, knowing we'll be okay. "What we have is too intense. I don't want to change you, but I also don't know how to be with you. I want to openly love you and not have to worry that someone will try to kill you for being with me."

"Openly loving you is all I want. But June, my job is to protect you in my work and as your man. I can assure you that if anyone tries to get near you, it won't be me but them who dies trying."

"Sometimes I'm afraid of you."

"What?" I'm stunned by her words. My beautiful woman, the queen of banter, the one woman who can bring me to my knees, is afraid of...*me*.

"The part of you that won't hesitate to take a life. You're different when you talk about it. Your eyes change. I remember his eyes," she says, getting lost in her thoughts.

The look she's referring to is all too familiar. It's the last look my intended target usually sees right before I pull the trigger. A look I perfected the day my mother called me into the sitting room. The memories flood like water breaking through a dam.

That day she asked me to come sit down in the downstairs sitting room. When I'm back at our family home, I rarely go into that room now unless I have to. The kitchen was always my favorite room. She knew that. If she had something serious to talk to me about, like my grades or something I did that she didn't particularly like, she would usually sit me down in the kitchen. My favorite snack or meal would be waiting for me. Regardless of the discussion, I knew she loved me. But on this day, we met in the sitting room.

"I need to talk to you about something, son," she started. A mix of duty and pain clouded her normally cheerful face. She proceeded to tell me that Dad was dead. That a bomb had exploded beneath his car, killing him instantly. I didn't cry that day. I made a promise to her and myself that whoever killed my father would die by my hand.

It was obvious then why we didn't talk in the kitchen.

I look at June. She's so small compared to me. I can't help feeling the need to protect her. I release her, sit on a stool at the counter, and hold my hand out to her. When she comes to me, I pick her up and sit her against me. "This is not about me." She shakes her head. "I missed you, sunshine. I understand you have a special connection with Aaron. Have I lost you?" Tears well in her eyes and spill down her cheeks.

"No. I'm in love with you."

I caress her cheek with my thumb, but I don't move to kiss her. Something I'm doing frightens her, and I need to allow her to take the lead in whatever way she wants.

"I'm madly in love with you, June." She dips her head to kiss me but hesitates, pulls back, and wipes a tear from her face with her finger. "Does that frighten you?"

"The possibility of losing you because someone is after me does. I've never been in love before you. Of course, I love—"

"Aaron," I say, finishing her sentence.

"Yeah, but this is not about him."

"Then I need to know what it is about. What have I done to make you run from me? Before dinner, we were talking about Darrien. My need to protect you—to protect what's mine—is overwhelming. I'm sorry about how I made you feel," I tell her. Then she says three words that send me into a silent rage.

"He contacted me."

"When?"

June's eyes go wide, and I take a deep breath. This is what she's talking about when I become that man who will destroy the world to protect her.

She touches my face, trying to tame the beast inside. "There was another card. It was a threat."

"When you were in the office. That's what you were looking at?"

"Yes. He knew about you. He said he wouldn't hesitate to take you from me. That's why I left. That's why I'm afraid of loving you. If anything were to ever happen to you...I—"

"Nothing bad is going to happen to me. I'm going to marry you. We are going to fill our house with kids. We'll love each other forever, and when that's over...we'll love each other some more." My words seem to calm her angst, but there's still the undercurrent of sadness.

"I want to believe you."

"Believe me."

She kisses me, and I enjoy the moment, allowing her to take what she needs to help her. When she breaks the kiss, I cup her face, pushing back her afro. "Honey, can you show me the card?"

She slides off my lap, takes my hand, and leads me back to the office. She retrieves the card from her tote and hands it to me. I read, memorizing the words, feeling the tone, embodying its essence, getting into the head of the man who wrote it. Imprinting the threat of a man I will soon silence.

June looks at me with questioning eyes. "I don't know what he wants."

"This is a setup. He intends to contact you again. When he does, I want to know immediately."

"I can't promise that. See, this is why I ran. I need to handle this my way." She grabs her purse and walks out the door and down the hall.

"June. Stop."

"I gotta go."

"God damn it, woman, why won't you let me protect you?"

"I told you a long time ago, there's only me in the end."

"It doesn't have to be that way. How do you know I wasn't bred to be with you—that I wasn't put on this earth to protect you from men like Darrien? How do you know I wasn't designed to protect your heart? That I'm the one who will love you and keep you safe forever."

"I don't."

"When you look in my eyes. When I take your hand, you know. You can't deny I'm the one who was designed specifically for you. You left a man you've loved half your life to be with me. June, I love you. You asked me that day in London why I'm still single. All along, I was waiting for the woman who could capture my heart. That's you."

"I need to do this."

"Do what? Run back to Adler? That won't solve this. If a man like Darrien will come after me, he'll certainly come after him."

June sets her purse down and turns to me.

"What do you propose?"

Chapter 40

We'll Be All Right

"Love is a fire. But whether it is going to warm your hearth or burn down your house, you can never tell."
– Kahlil Gibran

Aedan

It's been almost twenty-four hours since I've been buried deep in my woman, and I'm hard as a rock. I've chased, talked, and strategized with June all before we finished dinner. However, I've yet to discuss what happened at Adler's. Although it hurts like hell, I'm learning how to love her.

The mood in the house, like the music, is somber. June is stretched out on a blanket on the sofa, with one arm leaning against the back, watching me. Standing at the wall of windows overlooking the city's lights, I stare at her reflection.

Unable to resist, I walk over to her, dip my head, and kiss her, then sit, pulling her onto my lap. "God, woman, when you look at me like that, all I want to do is strip you naked and make love to you."

She takes my hand and guides it to my favorite spot under her shirt. Her nipple hardens under my touch. She repositions herself so she's straddling me and takes off her shirt, giving me the access I want—my dick twitches.

335

"Take me," she commands. I suck one of her breasts briefly, just enough to get her wet. But despite my desire to flip her on her back and dive in, I don't.

"We need to talk about you running from me."

"I shouldn't have left. I made a mistake."

"You're back. That's the important thing. But I want to know what happened." She attempts to leave my lap. I hold her hips against my raging hard-on. "What are you doing?"

"You may not want me after what I tell you."

Softening my expression, I stroke her arms. She bites her lips and brushes invisible lint from the blanket.

"June, I love you. You have to stop running. Whatever happened, we'll get through it." I say the words that will hopefully alleviate her fears and coax whatever truth she's hiding.

She blows out a breath. "I told London I was afraid of navigating this relationship with you and offered myself to him."

When she says the last part, my fingers automatically curl into a ball, and I regret not bashing in Adler's face. I attempt to control my anger when I say, "What are you saying, woman? You slept with him?"

"No. He wouldn't take me. But I did my best to tempt him."

"Damn it, June. Why would you do that?"

"I was mad at myself for being afraid, mad at you for making me afraid when all I wanted was you." When she says that, I close my eyes, attempting to douse the flames that burn within at the thought of her with him. I slide her off my lap, stand, and cross the room, keeping her from getting burned.

"That's no excuse for running. If you wanted sex, you could have come to me. I'll give you whatever you want whenever you want it. If you want to ride my dick in anger—god damn it, woman, ride it."

"It's not just that. You were so busy being King Aedan, seeking out danger, that I didn't think I could ever get through to the real you. With London, I knew that if I...if he... I'd never have to worry about him chasing monsters. I don't know what I was thinking. I was just scared. I shouldn't have run."

"I told you, if they come after me, they'll come after him. The change you see in me when I'm protecting you, you'd see in him, too. There is no softness in keeping you safe. We have to transform into something else to do that. But you already knew that. Still, you were willing to risk everything?"

"He wouldn't let me because he knew I loved you. He tried to help me understand you better. He told me that I should return and tell you what I needed. Even then, I pressed him. He told me that if he took me, it would only be as his wife and that I needed to decide to get in his bed or go home. I love you."

How do I do this? How do I douse the flames?

"She will tell you what she wants," Aaron told me.

"Then, June, sunshine. Tell me what you want. Tell me what I can do to get you to stop fighting me. To stop running from me and to run to me." She stands bare-chested in blue silk panties and joins me across the room. "Tell me," I yell. "Is this what you want?" I cup her face and run my nose along her neck, biting and licking as I work my way to her ear. "Is this what you want?" I pull her lip down with my thumb and lick into her. She's lost in the kiss as I walk her backward toward the couch. I break the kiss. "Or this?" I take her hand and press it to my shaft, straining to be free. I lower her to the sofa, grab her silk underwear, and rip them from her body. "I need to know." I hover over her, reach between her legs, and stroke her. "Fuck," I growl. "Talk to me. Do you want this?" She nods. "Damn it, woman, say the words. Tell me what you want." I continue stroking, fingers sliding in and out of her wetness.

She groans and her walls clench my fingers. "Stop, stop," she screams. I lift off her, then get off the couch. Tears stream down the side of her face and onto the sofa.

"You don't want me?"

"I want you...*in* me," she pants. She doesn't have to say another word. I strip off my clothes, kneel over her, dip my head, and kiss her. She reaches between us and positions my shaft at her entrance. I break the kiss, lift her leg over my shoulder, and look where my body meets hers. Slowly, I move in and out. My body grows hard as steel as I increase the pressure, creating a rhythm for us.

"Deeper," she calls out. She lifts her hips and I sink into her—my thrusts faster, more aggressive. Her walls begin to pulse, and I increase the pace, bringing her to climax as her body convulses against me, threatening to pull my own climax from me. Her walls tighten, and I continue pumping through her climax, coating my shaft in her release. Soothed by the rhythm of our bodies clashing.

"Oh, god, I'm going to come again."

"I got you," I say, timing my rhythm to her chasing the feeling of love between us, chasing her fears away. "Come for me," I tell her. I push in, and her body sucks me in, squeezes my shaft, milking my release. "June," I grunt, spilling waves of my seed in her. I kiss her as we fall fast and hard in love together.

"Aedan."

I collapse on her, then roll her until I'm on my back, pulling her onto me, still connected, evidence of our love spilling between us. I hold her hips in place as her walls continue pulsing against my shaft. "Don't let go," she begs. I move her hips in a slow rocking motion, gliding her clit along my shaft, which is still thick inside her.

"Take what you need from me. Squeeze baby. Count it down." She squeezes, once, twice, until her climax begins, and my body hardens. In one motion, I flip her on her back and pump in fast, powerful thrusts. "Feel me. Let me take you over the edge." I continue pumping. "God, woman. I'm coming." I tell her, and our bodies smash together until we both come again, calling to one another. She's so full of my seed that I have to hold her hips to keep from slipping out. "That's it," I tell her, allowing her to experience the last of her release. At that moment, clinging to each other, kissing her, coated in our love, I realize that despite everything, we'll be all right.

San Francisco

CHAPTER 41

An Act of Congress

"There's no use talking about the problem unless you talk about the solution."
– Betty Williams

June

AN ACT OF CONGRESS would have been easier to accomplish than convincing Aedan I needed to return to San Francisco. Nevertheless, being called to testify as an expert witness at a hearing did the trick. Until then, he was dead set on me residing in Belfast until Darrien was located. The good news is I'm back in my local office and can catch up with friends and family while here.

"With our growth plans, I'd like to add a chief of staff under me. They can be based in California since I'll spread my time across Europe," I tell Jake, secretly hoping he'll overlook the fact that I added staff to each location under me.

"So which headcount are you giving up to pay for this chief of staff?"

"You can give me a few of your finance heads."

"That's not how this works. You need to figure out where you're going to pull the money from. I'll leave it to you to figure it out. But remember, it's coming out of your budget," he says, emphasizing the last part.

I pinch my forehead, thinking through my options while my penny-pinching CFO brother types something into his device. These monthly budget meetings with him stress me out. Not because they're hard, but because we have to set an example, and sometimes unexpected expenses arise, and he's the perfect person to keep us on track—rather—keep me on track.

"Give me a day to reevaluate my headcount and get back to you."

"Take two."

"Oh, you are so generous. Are we done?"

"We're done. Where are you rushing off to?"

"Nowhere. Home. I spent most of the day in court and the rest with you and Raven. I'm sure Aedan is beside himself."

My brother laughs. He's been trying to rein me in for years, so he's thoroughly enjoying that Aedan has come the closest to succeeding. Even I have to admit that I can get completely out of control. "He's just across the hall. Nothing's going to happen to you. What's going on with this situation with Darrien?"

"Haven't heard a peep since the last note I received. But I'm worried about Aedan."

"He's worried about you. Let him do his job."

"He says if he finds him, he'll kill him."

"What's the issue? This has been plaguing us our whole lives. It's impacted the trajectory of your life the most. If it's not him—it'll be Troy."

"Troy?"

"I told him that if this man surfaces, remove him from the face of this planet."

"Jake."

"June. Be honest. What do you want to see happen to this man?"

"I want him found and disposed of."

CHAPTER 42

Loose Ends

"Be sure you positively identify your target before you pull the trigger."
– Tom Flynn

Aedan

"THIS MUST BE IMPORTANT," I tell Ben, who arranged a video call with Niall and me at five-thirty in the morning Pacific time. I stare past my phone screen to the closed study door. June will be up soon.

"What do you have for us?" Niall asks. I can tell by his background and the modern aesthetic design of his study at his and Rose's San Francisco home that he is doing the same as me. Neither of us wants to wake our women.

"These...," he holds up two grey envelopes that mirror the ones sent to June, "...are the two cards sent to Rose's office."

"She never received those. She would have mentioned it to me," Niall says.

"No. They were unmarked. She only reviews mail from known donors or other foundations. Her assistant takes care of the rest," Ben announces.

"That's right," Niall confirms. "She responds to donors via phone."

"I sent you pictures," Ben says.

I swipe the screen on my phone to review the photos. The color, size, and everything else match, including the emblem on the back. I swipe back to the video call.

"The first card is a congratulatory card similar to the one June received. The second one is a Happy Independence Day card," Ben says.

Interesting. June's second card was a birthday card. This person is reaching to establish their target.

"Like the first two June received, these are benign. The person sending these is trying to rattle the cage," I say.

"Ben, have either Jake or Jasmine received one of these?" Niall asks.

"No."

"I want to know who's sending these cards," I say.

"We're on it," Ben assures me.

The sound of the shower down the hall signals my woman is awake.

"I gotta go. Great work, Ben. Keep me posted on anything else you find," I say and end the call.

***

It took time, but my team uncovered a money trail linking James Drummond and the British Daily Corporation. The only problem is locating the person or entity behind the money trail. James is the weak link in all this. He was just in it for the money. I won't have information on why the BDC took the risk until I find out who's holding the money bag. I have my suspicions about who it is. When I discovered the same person had also sent Rose vague cards—I knew. They never happened to make it to her. Since they had no contact information, her assistant never passed them along. But I don't dare share that with June. She has enough to worry about.

The past few days have been hard on her. Yet, she's handling everything gracefully, demonstrating how great a leader she is in both the private and public arena. All the while, the constant reminder of her grief is splayed like an open book before her. I blame one person: Darrien Goodman.

Sitting across the hall from her, I multitask on a video call with Dean and my security team.

"Our sources provided information that an exchange will occur in two days," Dean reveals.

"You're certain?"

"Yes."

"You need to be on top of it. I can guarantee you he won't hang around after it's done. He's only here to get it through and wrap up any loose ends. You have one shot to get him. If you don't take it—I will," I say, looking at the manifest on my screen.

This is the missing piece. This proves Dean is behind the BDC debacle. Kill two birds with one stone. Get your money, get the girl, wash your hands, and leave. He needed to flush June out, so he took a chance with the media. Generating a huge scandal with the Ross family meant people would start digging into their family secrets. He didn't know it was June who could identify him until a reporter asked her about her mother. I saw the news clip—the look on her face spoke volumes. After twenty years, he had found his target.

"Don't worry. Well, get him."

Glancing up, I glimpse my woman in deep conversation with her brother. Knowingly, her eyes shift from him to me, and I wink. She can't help but detect my gaze. That's how it's been since the day we met. Like magnets—always needing to be near one another even when apart. Her half smile lets me know I've almost broken her concentration. I know what that's like. But thankfully, I'm trained to handle it.

I have to. I need to remain focused...for her.

CHAPTER 43

The Final Straw

"If you're going through hell, keep going."
– Winston Churchill

June

I ALREADY KNOW WHAT this is. Sitting in my study, I slide my gold metal letter opener through the top seam of the envelope. Carefully, I slide the grey linen card from it. I open it. It takes a few seconds to get my breathing under control, but I process the words in my head. Hearing them the way he meant them to be delivered, in the deep, raspy voice I recall from years ago.

"June, it's time we meet. Or should I say meet again? It's been a while. Dare I say I've missed you? I'll jump straight to the point. We have some business to conduct. I've included my number. It's good until the end of today. Text me the location you want to meet, or I'll be by your house at seven tomorrow morning. You don't want that. D."

Darrien. I close my eyes and see his.

Dark.

Diabolical.

Deadly.

Heat crawls up my neck. I twist the ring on my finger as fear grips me. This man has had more control over my life than the IRS. I don't know how, but I need to end this. I open my eyes, take out my phone, and text the number on the card.

Me: 7 a.m. tomorrow JB Garden's Coffee

Unknown: Good girl

There. It's done. I put the card in my purse. Aedan will never know it was mailed to our home today. He'll never know I'm living my worst nightmare. When he finishes his workout, I'll give him all my love, and he'll be none the wiser. This is on me.

My fight.

My fate.

My life.

CHAPTER 44

Fate

"One is never afraid of the unknown; one is afraid of the known coming to an end."
– Jiddu Krishnamurti

June

LOOKING BACK ON THE sum of my life, I wonder if I could have done anything differently. Could I have implemented more programs to save lives? Could I have reached more children through my philanthropic efforts? Did I do the right thing, following my instincts and not acting on the crush I had on London ten years ago? Because I could have. The look of lust in his eyes when I put on that sweatshirt is seared in my memory. That was our moment—the point of no return. And neither of us took it, yet that moment left us connected. A string sends signals between us even now, five thousand miles away.

That's why, before I left the house this morning, I sent him a snapshot of the recent card I received from Darrien. My caption: *"Just in case. You know what to do."* Then, once again, I left, leaving behind my phone, tracker, and the love of my life. I don't know if I'll ever see Aedan again or whether he'd ever want to. I could have told him Darrien wanted to meet me, but I didn't. This is not his battle to fight. It's mine. I built a life surviving purely out of spite—it's all I know.

That was several hours ago. I imagine Aedan's beside himself by now. Wandering city streets that I'd come to know like the back of my hand, I thought about him. Sitting on a bench overlooking the bay, I thought about our plans to have children. That'll likely never happen now. I never told him I went off birth control the day after he disclosed he wanted to have children with me. God, I'm so addicted to him. I woke him up at three this morning, stroking his shaft, needing him inside me—wanting to feel his hot, heavy breath on my ear when he found his release. I'll never forget how he looked at me with a smile full of lust and love. *"I suppose I won't get any sleep tonight,"* he said right before rolling onto me and filling me...full. I feel him still. The soreness between my thighs reminds me for a brief time that he was mine.

I'm outside in the brick-clad courtyard of my favorite coffee shop in the Blumberg building. Fairy lights strung across the pergola, high-top tables and chairs, and lush green plants and flowers create a magical atmosphere. It's the perfect time of day when everyone is doing their thing, getting ready for the end-of-summer weekend. It's clear that coffee is the last thing on their minds, as I'm the only one in line.

Holding my coffee, I walk to my favorite spot, one of the high tables near the brick arch that divides the patios from the garden area. I look around. Birds are chirping. A slight breeze rustles the leaves on the trees and causes the fairy lights to sway. The sound of water running in the garden fountain makes this the perfect setting. Sitting here, taking it all in, I think about my mother. *She would like it here.* But she's not here. She never will be. He made sure of that.

I sip my drink, take a deep breath, and prepare myself for whatever hand life deals me. I look around, scanning the scarce patio where a few people have taken up residence. *Where is this bastard?*

"Looking for me?" the deep, raspy voice shatters the silence.

I turn to find my worst nightmare staring back at me with the same dark, haunting eyes from years ago. But these eyes are set in a face marred with lines that speak of the weathered years like the rings on a tree. Gone is the dark hoodie and face mask, replaced with black dress slacks and a white shirt rolled up at the sleeves, revealing his ink.

He sits on the high chair across from me, places a newspaper on the table, and rests his hand on top. Unsurprisingly, the weight of his hand doesn't cause the paper to flatten. It's then that I notice on his wrist, next to his Patek Philippe Grand, a gold double-strand chain, and at the end of the chain is my mother's gold peace sign pendant.

"For someone named Goodman, you sure make a strong case for false advertising. Why did you summon me?"

He smirks, and I want to slap it off him. "Beautiful. Smart. Witty. I did you a favor, letting you live. I want a favor in return."

"No."

"To which of my statements are you dissenting?"

"Both. You didn't do me any favor, Mr. Goodman. You took my mother's life and, in doing so, destroyed mine. And I don't owe anyone anything because I don't do favors. So, whatever you need from me, you'll get from the bullet waiting for me in your gun." I tip my head toward his hand.

"I should add 'badass' to your list of monikers. I pegged you wrong, thinking you'd give me what I wanted in exchange for letting your man live. Instead, here you are, all alone, ready to face your maker, looking like you did that day in the restaurant. Defiant."

"I'm no longer that innocent girl who used to believe in fairytales, Mr. Goodman. I left that person in the restaurant that day."

His jaw ticks, and I imagine he's irritated that he has to kill me in public to end this charade. "Seems I've created a woman with a heart of stone that wants for nothing. It's a damn shame it has to end this way. You really are beautiful."

"You have something I want." I tip my head in the direction of his arm.

He flexes his wrist. "I believe I earned this," he says, and the burn of bile in my throat begs to be free. I take a deep breath. He tips his head toward the necklace London gave me. "I see another trophy awaits me."

I need to end this, but I want him to see her before I do. "Do you ever think about her? Do your victims haunt your dreams?"

"I don't have time to reminisce on collateral damage."

"You should." I reach for my purse.

He pats the newspaper. "I'd be careful if I were you."

"Don't worry, Mr. Goodman. The extent of my protection is lipstick and cash. Certainly, a man like you isn't afraid of that." I take out an envelope, open it, take a photo, and slide it across the table. "Look. This was her the week before."

His eyes penetrate mine, and then he says, "I'm not interested in a trip down memory lane."

"I never pegged you for a coward. Look at her," I press, mustering the courage to push his buttons. To dare a man who's about to take my life to reexamine the one he took from me. I watch as the same tattooed hand I see in my dreams slides the picture toward him. His hands are thicker than I remember. His skin is darker and weathered with age. I wonder how many times he lifted that hand to pull a trigger. I wonder how many will follow me.

He pushes the picture away. I lock eyes with him while I retrieve another picture from the envelope. He looks down but not at the picture I lay on the table.

"I don't have time for this. Goodbye, Ms. Ross." He reaches for his gun, and I feel myself being pulled away, followed by a bang.

"Goodbye, Mr. Goodman," Aedan says, shoving me behind him into someone else's arms.

I try to turn to see what's happening but can't.

"We need to leave," Niall commands, ushering me out of the courtyard and through black scene shields, leading me to an SUV. He opens the door, helps me in, and slides beside me. The other door opens, and Aedan enters. The car is eerily quiet as it pulls away. Aedan turns to me and pulls me onto his lap, cups my face, and stares at me.

"You have to stop crashing through life like you're out here alone."

"That's all I know."

"Now you know differently."

CHAPTER 45

Tell Me

"Love recognizes no barriers. It jumps hurdles, leaps fences, penetrates
walls to arrive at its destination full of hope."
– Maya Angelou

Aedan

*Think about the good things, think about how beautiful she is, think
about your love.* This is the mantra I say over and over in my head in the
car as I hold her tight against me, in the foyer when I help her out of her
sweater, and when I leave her to come upstairs.

I take my gun and holster off and store it. I strip my clothes, and in
the process, I symbolically remove the parts of me that can put a bullet in
a man's head, then walk away. Because that man I have to be to do that
frightens her, and I don't want my woman afraid of me. Stepping into the
shower, I allow the hot water to wash it all away. The anger I felt awaking
to an empty house. The fury I felt getting a call from Adler, followed by
Blumberg alerting me June was on his property. It didn't take long to
assemble the SWAT team. Placing my hands against the wall, I close my
eyes, push them out of my head, and let the water flow over me. I love her.

I stand like that for a while, letting it all go. Then I feel her body pressed to my back. Her hands wrap around me and snake up my chest. I turn in her arms, dip my head in her neck, and let the tears fall.

Following our shower, we put on loungewear, and I help her dry her hair. We don't talk. I allow the silence between us to speak volumes. This is my life—I can process the day's events quickly, but I need to allow her time to digest what happened in her way. When we finish her hair, I take her hand and go to the kitchen. I plate the late lunch I had delivered. But she doesn't want anything, so I pour two glasses of whiskey.

"You're drinking?" she asks.

"We're drinking," I say, leading her to the family room.

I sit on the couch, and she sits on my lap facing me, resting her head on my shoulder while I sip my drink.

"I thought I'd never live to see you again."

"I told you I'd find you. Lift your head, honey. Have some of this." She lifts her head, and I tip my glass to her lips but she doesn't drink. "It's over."

"There will be others."

"Not likely. Not like him. And not coming after you."

"How can you be sure?"

"He was one of the most dangerous criminals out there. He came face to face with you and didn't survive. Coming after you is a death wish no criminal would want to risk." I drink my whiskey.

"It'll be on the news?"

"It's in your best interest that your family doesn't suppress the story this time."

"Based on what you're saying, they won't."

I set my drink down and cup her face. "Honey, after all you've been through, I didn't want you to see me like that. Are you okay?"

"Because of you, I am."

"Are you afraid of me?" I slide my hand up her shirt and caress her breast.

"No. I'm afraid of losing you."

"Then you have nothing to fear." June holds my gaze and traces her fingers along my face and beard. "Sunshine, you may experience some effect from what happened today. I prefer you take something to help you sleep for a bit."

"I've experienced worse. I don't want to sleep. You might run away." I pinch her nipple. "Ouch." She laughs.

"I'd never run from you. But we need to talk about that. This need of yours to—"

"Don't say it. I'm done running."

I tickle her. "Are you? Are you done? Because you see, like I told you, I'll find you."

"I'm done. I promise I'm done."

"You sure?" I raise her shirt and wrap my mouth around her breast.

"Ahh, yes, I'm sure."

"I love you, June." I remove her shirt and suck one breast while pinching the other. She arches her back, and I watch her experiencing my touch. She closes her eyes, enjoying the moment, but there is a look on her face I can't quite place. I pinch her breast. *There. What's that look?* I palm them with my hands, pinch them, and observe her.

"God, that feels so good."

"Sunshine, look at me." Her eyes fly open, surprised by my command. "Am I hurting you?"

"No. God, if anything, I need you right now."

I hold her gaze and squeeze her breast. Her eyes close again. "Baby. Look at me, June." She looks at me. "Are you pregnant?"

"I don't know. Maybe."

"Are you off protection?" She nods and looks at me, searching my eyes. I know exactly what she finds: tears. "Tell me you're having my child. Tell me we're having a baby."

Her voice is tentative when she says, "It's possible."

I flip her on her back, position myself between her legs, and bury myself deep within my woman. "I want to make sure," I growl into her ear and then make love to my woman.

Belfast

Epilogue

I Love You

"The love of the family, the love of one person can heal. It heals the scars left by a larger society."
– Maya Angelou

June

Two months later

Neo-soul music blasts through the home speakers as I groove to the beat while finishing a floral arrangement—the timer dings, alerting me that my cake is done cooling. I go to the sink, wash and dry my hands, and then take my wire racks with baked goods to the island counter. I could have let Stella make a cake for Aedan's birthday, but I decided to make one instead and let her focus on the family dinner, which she'll come by later to make.

I stick my finger in the icing to sample it. *God, that's good.* I could eat a bowl of it, but I don't. Since finding out I was pregnant, I learned I have two cravings: sweets and Aedan. I thought I was addicted to him before, but I didn't realize how bad I had it for him until one night after my fifth orgasm, and I asked him for another. He said, *"Sunshine, I'm going to sleep; you can have me when I wake up."* I blush thinking about it.

I grab a pack of retro candy from the basket on the counter, open it, and pour some into my mouth. Then, I pick up a knife and begin icing the cake. Seconds later, my man enters the room, sets something on the counter, and wraps his arms around me.

"Hey, Mrs. King. You got a lot going on here," he says, kissing my neck. I smile whenever he calls me Mrs. King. He was adamant that we should get married immediately after he learned I was pregnant. As head of his family, it's important to him, and I'm okay with that.

It rains a lot in Belfast. It didn't rain that day—it was lovely. We held our ceremony on the grounds of his family's property, with the three-story, ornate, grey stone castle-like house in the backdrop—the same place Rose hosted her famous art exhibition. Aedan and I stood beneath a lavender hypnosis carnation flower-filled arch in front of our friends and family. I wore a crown of baby's breath flowers in my hair. My seventies-inspired white silk mini dress complemented his black tuxedo. I smile, thinking about it—thinking about his words.

"There will never be another time in this universe where we aren't together. When I found you, I found my friend, my lover, my life force. I exist for you. I love you, June," Aedan said, eyes filled with tears, right before he kissed me. Neither of us could keep it together. We cried, we laughed, we celebrated. When it was over—we made love. Yeah, it was a lovely day.

While he's loving on me, I pour more candy into my mouth. He turns me in his arms, lifts my shirt, and kisses my belly. "Hey, little one," he says.

Then he gives me a little treat, or maybe it's more for him when he sucks my breast. Either way, my sex clenches. While he's doing his thing, I eat more candy. He straightens, covers my mouth with his, and licks into me, sucking my tongue. He pulls away quickly, "What in the world are you eating?"

I reach beside us and pick up the package. "This."

"Pop Rocks. Where in the world did you get that from? And why did you let me kiss you with candy popping in your mouth?"

I laugh. "Honey, you were sucking my breasts. I was enjoying that, but I'm also craving sweets. Oh, and these are the candies London stocked for me when I first came to Belfast. He brought by another box last week."

"Aaron? I swear that man is always around."

"Actually, he's not. That's your perception. You have to get over your feelings about him, honey. I'm married to you. I'm pregnant with your child. I'm standing here dripping wet, wanting you. Can you think of one night you haven't had me since we've been together?"

"You're right. I never imagined I could have what we have. I never thought I could hold someone and never want to let them go. I knew I wanted a family with you the second I looked into your eyes. Then you looked at me in San Francisco, and I asked if you were pregnant. I already knew the answer. I felt it in my heart and couldn't be happier."

"I felt it, too. So, does that mean you're going to leave London alone?"

Aedan rolls his eyes. "You had to mention him again. There's something about him that gets me going."

"To be honest, I did it on purpose. I want sex. I'm thinking of mentioning him more often. I get the best pounding from you afterward. Maybe the next time I want that sixth orgasm—."

"You are pushing your luck, Mrs. King." He pinches my breast. "God, I love these." He licks one and then the other. "Can we have another kid after this one?" he asks between sucking and licking.

"Yes. As long as I get as much sex as I want."

"Sounds like you're ready for me." He sucks my breast.

"Always. I love you, Aedan. I love everything about you. I love how you make me feel. I love that you proved you would give your life for me. I love how you support my work. I love your strength, integrity, and sense of family. I love that you're the father of my child. I especially love that you're a breast man because, oh, my god, that is my kink." I pull his hair and lift his head so he's looking at me. Then I say, "I think I'm a sex addict when it comes to you. Is that even a real thing? I might need therapy," I deadpan.

He barks out a laugh at my confession. And his laughter and love fill the room, and I feel truly happy, safe, and wanted. "I love you too, sunshine. How are your boobs feeling anyways?"

"Needy." He dips his head again and wraps his mouth on my breast. I comb my fingers through his hair, and he picks me up and carries me to the bedroom, his mouth still on me.

He lowers me to the bed and says, "I'm going to enjoy my birthday gift."

"Happy birthday, babe."

***

Aedan

One week later

I never knew life could be this wonderful. My wife and I have our routine down. I still take point on her security. We still head down the street to our penthouse after five. Sometimes, she has to work before dinner, and so do I, but we enjoy our free time together. Whether that's taking in a play, show, or dinner out together or with friends and family. We live a normal life. Just like she wanted, open and free. When I walk down the streets, I pull her to my side. Sometimes, she steals a kiss. I'm still protective of her. My guys are still in stealth mode, but she has my attention when I'm with her.

Because of her courage to fight her fears, we were able to slay the dragon together. We toppled the monster from her nightmares and, in doing so, made her untouchable. I was right. A news report detailed how a notorious criminal sought to kill the person who could identify him for a murder twenty years ago, naming June as his intended target. Subsequently, a story recounted how his death led to the takedown of his gun cartel and shined a light on her work to clean up the streets. "The untouchable" is how they hail her in subsequent stories.

Later, we learned his goal was to convince her to hand over AI technology to help build weapons of mass destruction and put an end to gun legislation she was working on to put forward to Congress. The barter...her life or mine. He didn't anticipate she'd give her life to save mine.

He didn't anticipate me.

"Sunshine, this came in the mail today," I say, plopping beside her on the couch. "What are you looking at?" I pull her onto my lap as she shares her screen.

"Baby stuff."

"We hired people for that."

"We still have to make choices."

"Then let's see what we have." I take her phone and scroll. "I love these colors. This bluish green reminds me of a top you wore when I first met you. The buttons were open down to your stomach." I cup her cheek and dust my lips across hers. "I swear if you were mine then, I would have palmed your breast that day."

"You might have gotten slapped."

"Yeah. I was convinced you hated me. You had me so hard. Just like now." My woman reaches between us, grabs proof of my desire for her, and then kisses me. I give in to the kiss, but only briefly. "Honey, hold on a minute. Let's open this." I pick up the box then she takes it from me.

"This better be worth at least three orgasms."

I bark out a laugh. My girl is insatiable, and I love every bit of it. "Oh, I got that and more for you. I promise. Now, let's see what we have. I'll open it." I take the box and press the nail of my thumb across the tape cutting it open. I open it and take out a small black velvet pouch. June takes it from me and pours the content into her hand.

Tears stream down her cheeks as she examines the gold peace sign necklace. "They sent it back."

"I see that. It's beautiful."

She touches the one on her neck. "I already have this."

"You don't want to wear your mother's necklace?"

"No. I don't want to think about his last words when he wore it. I think I'll give it to Jasmine on her birthday."

"I'm sure she'd love it."

I brush her tears away with my thumb. "Are you okay?"

"Yeah. It caught me off guard, is all," she says, still touching the diamonds on her neck. "You know London gave me this one."

"Sunshine," I growl.

She smiles wryly at me because she knows she's caught. "What?"

"You only mention his name because you want something from me." I laugh because my woman is so wild, wonderful, and zany. I wouldn't change a thing.

"Well. What you got?"

"You. I love you."

"I love you, too.

I pick up my woman, haul her off to bed, and give her all the love she wants and more.

THE END

Enjoyed **Taming a King**? Please take a moment to leave an online review. Thank you!

What to read Aedan's backstory? See where it all began in "30 Days in Belfast," available in ebook, paperback, and hardcopy.

If you're interested in whether the other characters from the series make love connections, subscribe to my newsletter at https://www.ritaagordo n.com/subscribe-page to stay updated on upcoming releases.

Blurb

Taming a King

She was born to rule his heart. He was sworn to protect hers.

IN A WORLD WHERE fairy tales are nothing but broken promises, June Ross has learned to trust no one but herself. Scarred by a traumatic childhood event, she's built her life on the ironclad belief that love is a dangerous illusion and guards her heart with walls so high that even she can't see over them. But when a deadly threat from the past resurfaces, she finds herself under the protection of Aedan King, a hardened bodyguard with his own battle-worn past. Trained to take a bullet without flinching, Aedan never expected to be blindsided by the one mission he can't walk away from: breaking through June's defenses and convincing her that true love isn't a fairy tale—it's the most perilous adventure of all. With danger closing in, June must decide whether she's willing to trust someone else to protect her for the first time in her life, or if she'll let fear keep her from the only man willing to risk everything—even his life—for her.

Excerpts

Praise for "30 Days in Belfast"

***Publishers Weekly* Indie Spotlight February 2023 (Romance & Relationships)**

"An addictive, rollicking tale of friendship, love, and lust."

— Kirkus Reviews

"Gordon's debut offers readers a winning combination of intrigue and romance, revealed slowly through the lens of opulent travel and luxurious living."

— BookLife Reviews

"I loved the relationships between the characters, the storyline was heartwarming and after a while, I couldn't put it down. Would definitely recommend!"

— LoveReading, Indie Books We Love (starred review)

"...It's the best book I've read, period."

— Sana Aubuliel, Author of Letters to The Person I Was

"A[n] easy, beautiful, knowledgeable read!"

— Brianna, Goodreads Reviewer (five star review)

Blurb — 30 Days In Belfast

Just one distraction could lead to failure—several may spell ruin.

As the daughter of the wealthiest Black man in the country, Rose Ross struggles to make a name for herself as the COO of her father's tech company. She's even forced to let go of a promising relationship to focus on her career, but still cannot seem to escape her father's legacy. Rose fears that if she remains at Rick Ross Enterprises, she will never rise above the vast shadow his name casts.

When her ailing friend reaches out to her for help, Rose doesn't hesitate. She has just thirty days to curate the most important charity art exhibition in Europe and break into a field she is truly passionate about. However, just before she leaves for her flight to Belfast, her father informs her that she has only three weeks to decide whether she will succeed him as CEO.

With her concentration already split between one life-altering decision, Rose is stunned when she meets her friend's handsome and overprotective brothers. Right away, she recognizes an undeniable, yet different, attraction to both.

Her mind in turmoil, Rose's focus is now fractured among love and business. If she cannot make a decision—or if she makes the wrong one—she will lose everything she has worked for and, perhaps, more.

30 Days In Belfast *is a standalone contemporary romance.*

Excerpt — 30 Days In Belfast

PROLOGUE

We Have Time

"If you love somebody, let them go, for if they return, they were always yours.
If they don't, they never were."
– Kahlil Gibran, *A Tear and a Smile*

"I'll race ya," Shannon called as she ran past Rose toward the foam remnants of a forgotten wave on the shoreline.

Rose stopped scribing her initials in the sand heart drawing, a covert confession of love to her celebrity crush. She jumped up and headed toward the water. "Wait for me," she shouted to Shannon, who didn't see her. The glare from the sun dancing on the waves mimicking a million miniature mirrors distorted her view. Rose chased a wave and jumped in the water, pushing through the powerful current. When it subsided slightly, she popped up. "Shannon!" she called over the waves, but didn't see her friend. Rose continued to push through the currents, shoving the waves back with her arms, which were growing sore by the minute. With each breath she took, she became more panicked, still unable to spot her friend.

Rose looked toward the shore to see if Shannon had made it back. "Shannon, where—" Rose called out before being sucked under by the current. Before it all became a faded memory.

Fifteen years later, the aftermath was fuzzy in her head. She remembered eventually getting herself to shore. The shock and overwhelming sense of loss she felt when she realized Shannon was not by her side finally came into focus as people crowded around her in the sand. An endless stream of questions rushed through her. The sudden end of a forever friendship stolen by sun, sand, and sneaker waves. Rose felt her face grow warm as memories of Shannon flooded her mind. Her heart started to race. Panic washed over her as she relived the day her friend died. All she wanted to do now was run.

"Rose, talk to me. I know it feels like it came out of left field. Tell me what you're thinking." The sound of Alejandro's voice sitting across the table pulled her out of her head. He was staring at her with a mix of concern and longing in his eyes. Shelved was the swoon-worthy smile that usually greeted her. The smile that made her melt after spending weeks away from her man. He reached his hand across the table.

Rose averted Alejandro's gaze and looked around his London flat, where they had just spent the last three evenings wrapped in each other's arms. Where they had made love for hours until they were both sore, satiated, and spent. Where they had shared rare stolen moments between their busy schedules. She was the one who convinced him to get the flat since he spent so much time traveling between New York and London. He was busy building his career as an international attorney, and Rose was recently promoted to COO. A reward for endless hours helping her father build his business and developing new technologies to innovate the company. Living on the West Coast, paired with the busy travel schedule that came with her new position, meant they spent more time on video calls than in person.

Rose focused her attention on the modern, muted earth tones of the room. Her eyes were drawn to a painting she commissioned: A Black woman with a crown of flowers blooming from her head and partially covering her face. Rose remembered posing for the portrait with her chin turned toward her bare shoulder. "Think about your man," the artist had instructed her.

Now, she was sitting across the table from the man she thought she could build a life with. His words washed across her, pulling her down like the sneaker wave that snatched her childhood friend from her life forever. Stirring within her was the same sense of shock and sudden loss.

Rose sucked in a breath. "You sure about this?" she said, sounding as if negotiating a business deal—placing a wall around her heart and tamping the need to reach across the table to take his hand.

"No. But I do know we're both committed to our work. The time in between when we finally get together keeps growing. I'm torn between you and the job, and I don't want to ask you to bend for me. I respect that you're building your career, too. I want to make it work, but I can't see a way. You just got promoted and want to make a name for yourself away from your father's shadow. That's a tall order, and I'll use all my resources to support you in that effort. But trying to build something more between us is no small feat. Think about it. How many things did you and I have to shift to get these three nights together?"

"Quite a bit," she answered, hesitant to strengthen his argument.

"That's exactly the point. You and I know that you had to rearrange twice as much as me. I won't continue asking you to do that. Your father is my largest client. I know the demand he puts on me. I can only imagine how exponentially higher that is on you. I care about you, but I won't be the one to stifle your success. Let's take a step back and focus. Let's give ourselves a year." Alejandro leaned back in his chair and ran his hands through his hair.

Rose knew he was rethinking his words. But they were out, weighing heavy between them.

Was he right? Should they take a break, allowing time to establish themselves? Could they walk away and get back when the time was right? Would it ever be right?

The idea of them not being a couple made Rose feel like she did when she lost her best friend. The same emotions flowed through her all over again. She paused to think, unaware of what was keeping her from ending the conversation, putting her foot down, and refusing his suggestion.

Rose closed her eyes, inhaled, and opened them. Alejandro's gaze was still locked on her. "This isn't about something else. Or is it? You—" she started.

Alejandro stood, rounded the table, and pulled Rose to her feet and into a tight embrace. He planted kisses all over her face before touching his forehead to hers.

"Oh, Rose. Don't ever think that. I...I'd be hard-pressed to believe I could be with anyone other than you. You are the center of my universe, but I know I'm not yours. This is me setting you free—giving you time to do what you need to do. To be you without me interfering."

Rose listened intently, her breath becoming synchronized with his.

"I'm not saying it's just about you," he continued. "I also need to figure out why I haven't moved heaven and earth to be by your side. And for that, I'm at fault." Alejandro swallowed, then turned to look out the window.

Rose held onto his hand, walked up behind him, and pressed her chin to his back.

"Okay." Rose paused. "We'll give it some time."

30 Days In Belfast

Copyright © 2023 Rita A. Gordon

Acknowledgments

I PUT OFF WRITING this book for a while but decided to buckle down and finish it. Once again, thank you, Cassandra, for editing this book. You continue to support me and help me grow on my writing journey. To my besties at The Smut Peddler Collective, thank you for your friendship, support, and online check-ins. Janil and Natasha, I'm forever grateful to you. You are the best! Thanks to my family and friends who've encouraged me along the way. Lastly, thanks to everyone who hung in there waiting for this story to be told.

Love you all,

Rita

About The Author

Photo by Abigail Huller

Rita Gordon is an indie author and former corporate baddie who writes black and interracial romance stories where love always wins. As an emerging voice in the contemporary romance genre, she brings a fresh perspective to storytelling. Inspired by the power of love and the beauty of cultural exploration, her writing captures the essence of human emotions, leaving readers spellbound with each page turn. When she's not busy working through her TBRs and writing, she travels, draws flower designs for her coloring books, and volunteers in her community.

To learn more about the author, visit **ritaagordon.com**.

Connect With Rita

Let's stay in touch! You can find me here:

Subscribe to her newsletter:

https://www.ritaagordon.com/subscribe-page

Follow Rita on:

X | Instagram | Pinterest:

@rgordonshaw

TikTok:

@authorritagordon (ritagordonwrites)

Facebook:

https://www.facebook.com/authorritagordon

Goodreads:

https://www.goodreads.com/author/show/21524163.Rita_A_Go rdon

Also by Rita A. Gordon

Standalone Novels

30 Days in Belfast

Taming a King

Let It Rain Series

To be read in order

Seven Days in Seattle (Book 1)

The Days with Rain (Book 2)

The Fall of Us (Book 3)

Inspirational Books & Journals

The Book of Love

On a Positive Note

Grateful

Coloring Books

Little Flower Garden

The Big Flower

www.ritaagordon.com